Born in Sussex, Alice Marlow attended the University of Sussex and worked in Hertfordshire as a primary school teacher for many years before giving up teaching to concentrate on her writing. She includes among her interests reading, drawing, pottery and clay sculpture and animals, with four Burmese cats of her own and two donkeys who visit on holiday from Weston-super-Mare. Alice Marlow lives in Wiltshire with her husband and two children.

Alice Marlow is the pseudonym of an author who has, under the name Pamela Belle, written many acclaimed historical novels, including WINTERCOMBE and TREASON'S GIFT, and a series of fantasy novels including THE SILVER CITY.

For Barbara Tollinton –
a friend who is quick to listen, slow to judge,
and *always* ready for coffee and cake!

Chapter One

'Kate, darlin'? Got a proposition for you.'

If it had been anyone other than Charlie speaking, Kate Williams would have been tempted to punch him on the nose, or at the very least say something extremely cutting. But he was her employer, his money paid the bills, and besides, she actually liked the old chauvinist, even if some of his attitudes would have made Mrs Pankhurst weep.

She put down her fork and stood up, trying not to wince – she'd been bending down for much too long, and the twinges in her back were an ominous sign of advancing age. 'What sort of proposition?' she enquired, rather warily.

'Ha, got you going there, didn't I?' said Charlie gleefully. 'Don't worry, girl, it ain't your lucky day.'

Since Charlie was a small man with the air of a disreputable garden gnome, and well into his fifties, luck hardly came into it. Kate decided to humour him. 'Never is,' she said, in mock despair.

'Bollocks, you got that Justin, ain't you? Tarn thinks he's a bit of all right, you done well for yourself there. Wedding bells soon, I bet.'

To her annoyance, Kate felt herself blushing. 'You must be joking. We like things just as they are.'

'You mean, he does,' said Charlie, who could be infuriatingly sharp at inconvenient moments. 'Nice little bachelor life and you just down the road whenever he wants – suits him down to the ground, I reckon. But not you, eh? Women like a bit of commitment.'

'Not this woman,' said Kate, untruthfully. 'I've got used to life without a man under my feet, and so have the kids. I want a bit of freedom too, you know.'

'But you missed your husband when he died, didn't you?'

'Of course I did, but that was five years ago. I've grown up a bit since then, learned to cope on my own. I'm rather proud of

1

it, actually.' Kate gave him her brave smile, hating the disloyalty of the lie. *Col, I do still miss you. But I've had to be strong, for my own sake as much as the children's – I couldn't let us all be overwhelmed by my grief.* 'I can change light bulbs now, you know, and I've even been known to put up a shelf or two.'

'No need to be sarky with me, darlin',' said Charlie, with a grin. He was wearing an Oasis T-shirt today, rather strained over his prominent paunch, and Calvin Klein jeans that had probably cost more than Kate had spent on clothes in the past two years. His grizzled, straggly hair was scraped back from his balding forehead and tied in a ponytail more appropriate for a man thirty years younger. *But if you've made all those millions managing rock groups,* Kate thought wryly, *it doesn't matter if your hair looks like a dead animal slowly slithering down the back of your head.*

'So what's this proposition, then?' she asked, adopting his tone of teasing banter. 'And is it to my advantage?'

Charlie took a quick, furtive glance around them. They were standing in the front garden of Moxham Court, and apart from Darren, one of the under-gardeners, who was mowing the lawn thirty yards away, there wasn't another soul to be seen. 'You know my Project?'

The whole village, not to mention the whole of Wiltshire, knew about Charlie's Project. Moxham had been talking about nothing else for months with, as usual, opinions radically divided, just as they had been when the identity of the new owner of the Court had emerged. After old Lady Blount, gradually sinking into senile decay along with her beautiful home, the prospect of a famous media personality moving into the village had come as a delight to some, a curse to others. People like Charlie brought stars, glamour, excitement: those who were unimpressed by such things muttered darkly about drugs, wild parties, sinister goings-on and, worst of all, the likely effect on property values.

It was to Charlie Dobson's credit that most of these fears had proved unfounded. He was using local craftsmen and builders to refurbish and restore the Court to its former glory, with, obviously, no expense spared. Several villagers, including Kate, had been employed to help run the house and garden. He had made no complaints about the stench from the pig farm, which periodically wafted across the village and which tended to get up the noses of the more fastidious residents. He'd made an extremely generous donation to the church roof appeal, and offered the use of the gardens for next year's spring fête. He and

2

his wife, 'gorgeous busty blond ex-page-three model Tanya' as she was regularly described in the *Sun*, drank in the village pub, patronised the village shop and the village milkman, and bought their petrol from the local garage. They didn't send their daughter to the village school, but that was because, as Charlie had explained to Kate, it wouldn't be fair to his Angel to move her. As Jayde Dobson attended an exclusive and frighteningly expensive girls' boarding school near London, this was probably just as well: Moxham St Peter's, with two-and-a-half teachers, fifty children and dilapidated premises, would undeniably be something of a come-down.

After several months, even the snootier villagers had been forced to admit, grudgingly, that Mr Dobson wasn't as bad as they'd feared. And then, with perfect timing, he'd submitted his planning application. Moxham Court was Elizabethan, with a medieval core, and its beautiful Georgian stables, set on the north side beyond the walled garden, had once been almost as palatial as the house. Now, however, they were redundant, and rapidly deteriorating: and Charlie had decided to transform them into state-of-the-art music studios.

All hell broke loose. Rumours batted from house to house like mishit tennis balls. The Mothers' Union feared for the moral fabric of the villagers. The Moxham Heritage Society, dedicated to preserving the picturesque appearance and tranquil atmosphere of their home, visualised streams of cars clogging the narrow lanes, and got up a petition. But every inhabitant under twenty (and quite a few who were older) looked forward with excited anticipation to catching a glimpse of the rich, the talented and the famous, and hoped that the killjoys wouldn't have their way.

Kate, by now employed as the Court's head gardener, had gained considerable amusement from the antics of the Anteyes, as her daughter Tamsin had called them. Some of their objections were based on prejudices so wild and inconsistent that even the vicar, firmly nailed to the fence, had made an appeal from the pulpit for reason and common sense to prevail. And last week, in return for sworn assurances about noise levels and promises to retain every precious architectural detail of the grade one listed buildings, planning permission for Charlie's Project had been granted.

Nobody had seriously believed that he would succeed, and there had already been malicious rumours about backhanders and knowing the right people. But Charlie was a cockney who had barely set foot in Wiltshire before buying Moxham Court, and Kate suspected that the planning committee had examined the case on its merits and decided accordingly.

'What Project?' she enquired innocently.

'The Court studios, of course. Tarn thought of calling 'em Court in the Act, ha ha, good one, eh? Work's going to start next week – it'll take most of the summer at least. I've got a bloke coming down from London to sort it all out; he designed it for me, and he's going to see it through, and maybe manage the day-to-day running of the place when it's finished – if I can make him a good enough offer, persuade him out to the sticks. And he'll need somewhere to stay while he's here. So I thought of you.'

'*Me?*' Kate stared at him in astonishment. 'Why me? You've got twelve bedrooms in there,' she added, gesturing at the house behind them. 'Can't you squeeze him in? There must be *some* space in amongst Tanya's clothes.'

'They're starting on the top floor next week, there ain't no room,' Charlie said. 'And you've got that en-suite downstairs, haven't you, doing nothing?'

'Except when my mother or my in-laws come to stay.'

'Then tell 'em they can't stay for a while, you've said you see 'em too often. And I know you could do with the money. A hundred quid a week, cash in hand, no questions asked. What d'you say, darlin'? You can't tell me it wouldn't come in handy – after all, I don't pay you a fortune, do I?'

Kate stared at him, a variety of thoughts and emotions churning inside her head. Of course she was tempted. At Col's death, so unexpected and at such a young age, she and the children had immediately ceased to be comfortably off, and had wobbled for a while on the brink of real poverty. The mortgage on their home, Mermaid's Cottage, had been paid off, but not the other debts, and Col's pension had turned out to be woefully inadequate. The bleak early years of her widowhood had been a long struggle to make ends meet, to keep her two children clothed and fed and shod, and above all to shield them from the worst of the worries that had kept her awake through the long, lonely, bitter hours of the night. Until Charlie had, amazingly, offered her the job as head gardener at the Court, she and Luke and Tamsin had survived on state benefits, irregular gifts from Col's parents and from her own mother, and gardening work around the village. She ran a battered old Astra estate car, grew most of their own vegetables, bought clothes at secondhand shops and car boot sales, and kept the elderly household appliances going by sheer will-power.

A new washing machine, Kate thought, with delight. *Three weeks and we'd have enough for a new washing machine – no more leaks or funny noises or flashing blue lights. Hooray!*

But there were questions that she must ask first: although the money would be marvellous, she had the serious responsibilities of single parenthood. 'What's he like, this bloke?'

'Jem? Known him for years. He was the sound engineer at Moonrock studios, did all Serious Money's hits, remember them?' Charlie began to hum, tunelessly. How someone apparently tone deaf had become such a big name in the rock business was a mystery, although Kate suspected that it wasn't as much of a handicap as you might think. 'Then he moved on, did a bit of A&R, then one of the big Indie labels got hold of him and he was their top bloke for a while, before I asked him to do this place. He's been around a bit, has Jem, but he's settled down now. Married this fabulous bird a couple of years back, real class act she is, fashion editor on one of those glossy magazines, you know? Reminds me a bit of my Tarn, to look at, but right out of the top drawer, know what I mean?'

'I don't have to put her up too, do I?' Kate enquired dubiously. Living in close proximity to such an icon of good taste and impeccable breeding was bound to induce an acute inferiority complex.

'Nah, course not! She's just got herself a plum job in New York, so don't worry, darlin', she won't be around.' Charlie winked.

'It's O.K.,' Kate said firmly. 'I wouldn't dream of trespassing on someone else's territory. But I want to know a lot more about this Jem guy before I let him into my house. I've got two kids, remember?'

'He ain't into drugs, if that's what you mean – clean as a whistle. He don't smoke neither. He likes a pint down the pub, no harm in that, so do we all.'

'He's not a vegetarian?'

Charlie looked quite shocked. 'You must be joking!'

'Not into funny diets, either? He'll keep the room clean and tidy? He won't wander about in the nude or play loud music after Tamsin's bedtime?'

'No, no, no and no,' Charlie said. 'Look, he's coming down tomorrow, you can meet him then.'

'It's Saturday, remember?'

'Then I'll send him round and you can give him the once over. If you like the look of him, have him on a week's trial. And if you ain't happy at the end of it, I'll find him somewhere else and no hard feelings. What could be fairer than that, eh?'

'Not a lot,' said Kate, smiling. 'Look, Charlie, could you make sure he comes over in the morning, when the kids aren't there? I don't want to get their hopes up prematurely. If they think they're going to have a bloke with a hotline to every star they've ever loved actually living in the same house, it won't matter if he's a raving pervert, they'll still blame me for turning him away.'

''S all right, darlin'. I understand. I've got a daughter myself, ain't I? But you ain't got no worries about Jem. He's a good bloke, one of the best.'

'Which is probably what everyone said about Ronnie Kray.' Kate grinned. 'It's O.K., Charlie, I trust you. I really do believe he isn't an axe murderer or a child molester or a rapist or a drug dealer. But that still doesn't mean I'll like him, or that he'll like me.'

'Bollocks, darlin', everyone likes you!'

'My mother doesn't. If it wasn't for the sake of seeing her grandson, she'd happily cut me out of her life for ever. My mother-in-law isn't exactly a ray of sunshine, either – it took me years to convince her that I hadn't trapped Col into marrying me.'

'Some women,' said Charlie shrewdly, 'think no one can possibly be good enough for their precious son. You'll be some poor bird's mother-in-law yourself, one of these days.'

'I can hardly wait. Anyway, Luke's only fifteen, and as far as I know he hasn't even got a girlfriend, let alone a wife. All he's interested in are Justin's bloody cars.'

'Give him time,' Charlie said, with yet another wink. 'The quiet ones are always the worst. All right, darlin', I hear what you're saying. I'll send Jem round before dinner tomorrow, O.K.?'

'O.K.,' Kate said, remembering that Charlie's dinners took place at midday. 'Tamsin will be at the riding stables all morning, and Luke will be at Justin's, so that should be fine. I'll look out for him. I might even give him lunch, if he seems sufficiently housetrained. And thanks a lot, Charlie – it's very kind of you to think of me.'

'Cobblers. Kindness don't enter into it. You scratched my back a few times, having Jayde in the holidays and all that. Now it's my turn to scratch yours. And if you don't reckon you can

6

rub along together, then no offence, O.K.? Right, then, ta-ra, see yer.'

'See you,' said Kate. 'And thank you very much!'

She watched him bounce away towards the front of the house. All his movements and mannerisms were quick and jaunty: in twenty years' time he'd be described as a 'sprightly pensioner'. He was an old rogue – no one made that amount of money in that business without being at least slightly shady – but a kind one. And if this Jem turned out to be a reasonably tolerable lodger, then Charlie would have done her a real favour.

And himself, of course. Because his new studio manager was probably an attractive man, and if Charlie had any sense he wouldn't let someone tasty anywhere near his wife. Kate suspected that one of the reasons he'd bought Moxham Court was to protect the rampantly lovely Tanya (whom he invariably referred to as 'my Tarn') from city sins and city temptations. It hadn't worked, of course: he couldn't lock her up for twenty-four hours a day, and besides, he was often away on business, or playing golf with his old mate Ken in the Algarve. In his absence, Tanya was down the pub most nights, the centre of an adoring crowd, knocking back the gins and entertaining her admirers with saucy stories about her colourful past. To Kate's certain knowledge, she'd already had flings with one of the barmen, the under-gardener before Darren, the plumber who'd installed Moxham Court's central heating, and the muscular young man who maintained the new swimming pool. Tanya liked a bit of rough and a bit of fun, and it seemed incredible to Kate that Charlie didn't know – or, if he did know, didn't mind that his wife's extra-curricular love life had entranced all the Moxham gossips.

Still, it was their marriage, and their business. Kate looked at her watch. Nearly five. Time to go home, have a shower – it was exceptionally hot for May – and a quick tidy up, then cook the supper. Tamsin had gone to a friend's house after school, and Luke was staying late for athletics training. He would be cycling back afterwards, and invariably arrived ravenously hungry.

Kate bent to pull a last handful of weeds, and dumped them in her barrow. The noise from the mower had diminished into the distance as Darren drove it round to the Folly, where all the gardening equipment was kept. Cautiously stretching her back – she'd have to be careful, she couldn't afford even a few days laid up – she glanced around at the front garden of Moxham Court.

A year ago, when the house had been up for sale ('highly

desirable Elizabethan gentleman's residence, twelve bedrooms, Victorian orangery, staff cottage, Georgian stable block ripe for conversion, formal gardens, walled kitchen garden, hothouse, thirty acres of parkland including trout lake, set on the fringes of one of Wiltshire's most picturesque and unspoilt villages but within easy reach of the M4'), the area where she was standing had been waist-deep in brambles, nettles, docks and other undesirable weeds. Old Lady Blount had kept just one elderly man to look after all the grounds, and out of necessity he had restricted himself to the beautiful walled garden at the back of the house, where he had managed, just, to keep nature at bay and produce excellent vegetables and fruit. Charlie, realising that old Bob was the only person who knew how the hothouse boiler worked, had persuaded him to stay on, though he was well past retirement age and suffered from a variety of well-publicised ailments. But the splendour of Moxham Court required an appropriate setting, and once the small army of labourers had cleared away the worst of the undergrowth and revealed the bones of an elaborate series of formal gardens (designed, had he known it, by the great Gertrude Jekyll herself), Charlie had begun the search for a head gardener who could restore them to their former glory.

Mention of his quest to the landlord of the Unicorn had led him to Kate. At first reluctant to believe that a woman was capable of doing the job (in Charlie's experience, they didn't like getting their hands dirty and were always worrying about the state of their nails), he had approved of her brisk, no-nonsense manner. She was tall, and looked strong and fit, and although she had the voice and confidence of the well educated middle classes, her nails were cut brutally short and she obviously didn't give a toss for her appearance – which, in Charlie's connoisseur opinion, was a crying shame. Wearing decent clothes and with her butter-coloured hair allowed to hang loose around her pale, slender face, she'd be a real stunner. Those big blue eyes were sensational, and yet she was obviously quite unaware of her beauty.

He was even more impressed by the delightful garden which she had created singlehanded from the wilderness around her cottage. This, albeit on a very much larger scale, was exactly what he felt Moxham Court needed. And she had a ten-year-old daughter, the same age as his, who could play with Jayde in the holidays.

So to Kate's delight and astonishment, he had offered her the job. The pay was adequate – unlike most very wealthy men, Charlie was comparatively generous – and this was the challenge she had always craved. Better still, it was here in Moxham, where she could cycle or walk to work, and where she could keep an eye on Tamsin in the holidays. And he had promised her a free hand and an almost unlimited budget, so that at last she could give her imagination and her skills free rein on a grandiose scale. It seemed almost too good to be true, and in the first few months she had to keep reminding herself that it wasn't a dream.

It wasn't a doddle, either. Admittedly she had Pete and Darren, and their amorous predecessor, to do the mundane jobs. Old Bob still ruled the walled garden, and nurtured the vines and the fig tree in the hothouse and the pears and apricots, nectarines and peaches, trained against the ancient stone walls. It had helped, too, that she was more or less starting from scratch, although she'd kept some lovely old roses and some of those larger shrubs that hadn't been choked by brambles or died of neglect. And the removal of the undergrowth had revealed balustrades and steps in lichened stone, several glorious eighteenth-century statues, and a pond with a cast-iron fountain in the form of fat, exuberant dolphins and fatter cherubs. But she preferred to do the planting and weeding herself. The young man before Darren had been very beautiful (hence Tanya's interest), but absolutely ignorant. When she'd found him throwing on the bonfire the philadelphus she'd just put in ('I *thought* it come up a bit easy!'), she had decided to restrict her minions to mowing, digging and watering.

But she was happy. Really happy, for the first time since Col's death. She had a job that she loved, a place, a purpose. Her children were doing well at school, and after five years seemed to have accepted the loss of their father. And she had a lover.

As she put her tools away and heaved her bike out of the Gothic folly that some whimsical eighteenth-century Blount had built at the end of the sunken garden, Kate thought about Justin. As Tanya had apparently commented, he was indeed a 'bit of all right'. Six-foot-two, eyes of blue, with golden hair and an abundance of easy charm, he was everything most women dreamed about. His family had owned Silver Street Farm, just down the lane from her cottage, for generations, but neither Justin nor his sister had shown the slightest interest in country life: after Oxford, he had worked in a big City bank, and Camilla had married an American businessman and now lived in Los Angeles. After his father's death, his mother had sold all the land except the three fields closest to the farmhouse, using the money to finance an extremely comfortable old age. Kate had encountered her son occasionally, but hardly noticed him. Since meeting Col, at university, she had never had eyes for any other man.

But Col had died, so suddenly of a brain haemorrhage that she hadn't even had the opportunity to say goodbye to him, to draw a line under eleven years of happy marriage, to tell him so that he could be in no doubt that she loved him. For the children's sake, she had grown a strong capable carapace so that she could cope, alone, with all the worries and problems and responsibilities that she and Col had once shared. But it had been a long time before she could lift her head from the banal bustle of everyday life that had kept her sane, and look around her once more. By then, old Mrs Spencer had died. Everyone in the village had expected Silver Street Farm to be sold, but it had stood empty for months. Then, suddenly, Justin had moved in.

She could remember, as if it had happened this morning, the circumstances of their meeting, almost a year ago. She had been mowing the lawn in front of the cottage, and had glanced up to see a convincing imitation of a Greek god standing by the gate. The weather had been hot and sunny, and she was wearing a skimpy T-shirt and cut-off jeans. It had been a very long time since Kate had been the object of such overt masculine admiration, and she realised that she was blushing like a teenager.

Justin had strolled over, smiling, and she had stopped the mower. 'Hi, I'm your new neighbour.' He held out a hand. 'Justin Spencer.'

'I know.' Kate took it, aware that her nails were filthy and her fingers heavily stained with grass and dandelion juice.

'News travels fast in Moxham.' His grip was warm and firm. 'You haven't been here long, have you?'

'Only nine years,' Kate said, grinning. She had lost over two stones in the months following Col's death, when she had been too miserable to eat, and a couple of years back she'd lost patience with her long fair hair and had it cut back to a much more manageable bob, so it wasn't surprising that he had failed to realise who she was.

'Good grief! You're Kate Williams! I didn't recognise you!' Justin gazed at her in frank and extremely flattering appreciation. 'You're looking very well, I must say.'

'So are you,' she had said, wondering why they were chatting like old friends when they'd hardly exchanged a dozen words in all their past acquaintance. 'Would you like a drink?'

'I don't want to interrupt you when you're busy—'

'Not at all, I could do with a break.' She led the way to the front door. 'Something long and cold? I've got some Pimms.' She had managed to make that bottle last for nearly a year, but this was hardly an occasion for scrimping.

'That would be wonderful,' said Justin, with enthusiasm.

They had sat on the patio in the shade of the walnut tree, and talked. She learned, to her surprise, that he had decided to move back to Moxham permanently. 'I'm bored with City life, bored with my job. I've made plenty of money out of it, bonuses and so on, and I thought I'd branch out into something quite different.'

'Which is?'

'Buying and selling British classic cars. Aston Martins, Jaguars, MGs, that sort of thing. It's been a hobby of mine for years.'

'I've seen your car,' said Kate. 'Aston Martin DB5, isn't it? It's beautiful.'

'You know about cars?' he said, looking so excited that Kate hated to disappoint him.

'Enough to know it's like James Bond's, but not a great deal else. My son Luke does, though. He's fourteen, and if you could do a GCSE in classic British sports cars he'd get top marks.'

'Fourteen, eh? Is he willing to get his hands dirty? Not afraid of using a bit of elbow grease?'

'He'd wash a car like yours with his best shirt if he thought it would get a good shine.'

'Then I may have a job for him,' Justin said, with satisfaction. 'I'm sure he'd like to earn some pocket money, and I could do with a reliable extra pair of hands. I've got some tame mechanics who come out from Chippenham to do the major work, but I'm on my own most of the time. Could you mention it to him?'

'Of course I will. He's at school now, but he'll be back by four.' Kate smiled at him, rather shyly. 'Thank you very much indeed.'

'Not at all,' said Justin, and smiled dazzlingly back.

And that was how it started. Luke, of course, had leapt at this wonderful opportunity, and would have spent every leisure hour round at the farm if she hadn't insisted on tedious necessities like food, homework and bedtime. He talked cars at every meal until Tamsin, at breakfast one Saturday, took off her jumper to reveal a T-shirt announcing that 'This Conversation is Unbearably Boring', and Kate threatened to make Luke one with the 'this' changed to 'my'. She had expected the initial enthusiasm to wear off eventually, but Luke had continued to work for Justin three evenings a week, and most Saturdays, washing and polishing and even, to his great delight, helping to strip down an engine.

Luke thought Justin was wonderful, which had made it easier when the inevitable happened. After all, Col had been dead for nearly four years now, and he wouldn't have expected his widow to live like a nun for the rest of her days. They had enjoyed a good sex life, and once the initial period of grief and mourning was past, Kate had begun to miss the presence of a man in her bed. She found Justin very attractive, and it was obvious that he fancied her, but it was still three weeks before he even asked her out, and several dates after that before they made love.

She had put it off, trying to explain to Justin that it was her, not him; that she didn't feel quite ready, that this irrevocable step would be, in a way, a symbol of her final parting from Col. He had listened to her confused explanations with understanding and sympathy, and he had given her as much time as she wanted. After that, of course, it hadn't been very long before she was in his bed at the farm, astonished that the very tasty Justin found her gorgeous and sexy, and even more amazed at the fervour of her response to him.

He was a good lover, handsome and charming and considerate. Her friend Megan was sharp with envy, although she and Simon had been happily married for six years. Luke thought his mother's new boyfriend was brilliant, and, obviously, began to measure Justin for his dead father's shoes. The only dissenting voice belonged to Tamsin. She had been only five when Col died, but she had worshipped him, and regarded Kate's relationship with Justin as an almost adulterous betrayal.

It had saddened Kate, but she refused to give up something so marvellous to please her temperamental daughter. In any case, she knew that Tamsin would have resented almost any lover, however wonderful. She was a child of fervent moods, of passionate loves and desperate hatreds. Unlike Luke, so laidback that adolescence had had no obvious effect on his behaviour, Tamsin had always been difficult, and Kate dreaded to think about the approaching teenage years, tossed by rampaging hormones.

All last summer and autumn, her life had been idyllic. She had basked in the warmth of a man's adoration, and had returned his feelings. But during the long dark days and nights of winter, a little of that initial euphoria had begun to trickle away. He said he loved her. He *proved* that he did, every time they made love.

He called her darling, he gave her flowers, he took her to expensive restaurants, he brought her a beautiful silver and turquoise necklace back from Los Angeles at Christmas. But he had never proposed a weekend away, never talked about the future, never suggested that their two households, separated only by the field called Mermaid's Ground, should unite. He just seemed to assume that their lives would continue exactly as they were, for all time to come. And if Kate ever hinted of her growing dissatisfaction with this state of affairs, he ignored her.

She wanted him to make some concrete demonstration of commitment. She knew that if he really did love her as much as he claimed, it would be the next step in their relationship. Without it, they were as loosely bound as a pair of carefree, irresponsible teenagers.

And what's the point of that? Kate asked herself, as she cycled down the Court's freshly gravelled drive. *I'm thirty-seven, and I've grown out of being happy as someone's bit on the side. That sort of arrangement might suit a lot of people – it obviously suits Justin. But not me. I like my life, and I want to share it properly, not just a night here, a meal there.*

But it seemed increasingly possible that he was the kind of man who shied away from real involvement, however sincere his protestations of love seemed to be. Perhaps, to be charitable, the experience of his first marriage, to a woman who by his account was an idle, grasping bitch, had put him off commitment for life. *But he can* see *I'm not like Helen*, Kate thought in exasperation. *I'm beginning to wonder if he really does love me.*

And if she loved him. Surely, if she could ponder the problem with such wry detachment, she wasn't truly involved either?

I need him to make some effort too, she told herself, pedalling along Chippenham Lane towards the village. *But I'm not going to make an idiot of myself by grovelling at his feet – no man's worth that, however gorgeous. The trouble is, even if he is just stringing me along as Charlie implied, I don't want to give up what we have got, for the sake of an ideal future. After all, we've only been together for less than a year. And it isn't really surprising that he's holding back, after that messy divorce. I'm a gardener – I can be patient, surely, for a little while longer.*

The estate agent hadn't lied: Moxham was indeed one of Wiltshire's most beautiful villages. It was not quite as perfect or as popular as Lacock or Castle Combe, familiar settings for many TV costume dramas. But visitors came in droves every summer weekend, to feed the ducks on the pond, sample the excellent food and beer at the Unicorn, and stroll around the Green, admiring the picturesque stone houses and the stunning Perpendicular church of St Peter, with its spire and flying buttresses and the famous Blount chapel, adorned with crockets and gargoyles outside and an assortment of more or less tasteless and ostentatious tombs inside. Kate had lived here for ten years, and still she never tired of the vista opening up before her as she swept round the bend. The weathered stones of the Old Vicarage, the last of the red and yellow tulips she had planted for Colonel Sims the previous autumn still smouldering in the front garden. The even more venerable masonry of Three Gables, beyond it, where Mr and Mrs Enright, founders of the Moxham Heritage Society, lived with their five yappy King Charles spaniels. The comical notice, painted by Tom Ross, the village's resident artist, warning drivers to Beware of Ducks Crossing. The sign of the Unicorn, also painted by Tom, prancing joyfully above the pub door. The row of cottages facing the Green, thatched and gabled and featured in every county guidebook. And the huge copper beech in front of the church, just come into leaf, its deep crimson foliage the perfect foil for the deep viridian serenity of the yews on either side of the lych gate.

She swung left, down the road which led to Corsham, where Luke went to school. Twenty yards along, it bent round to the left, and Silver Street ran straight on, down a gentle hill to the ford at the bottom. After that, it dwindled into a little-used green lane, meandering across the fields for a couple of miles before dropping down into the steep-sided valley of the By Brook. Kate sometimes walked the dog that way, in winter when it wasn't overgrown.

Mermaid's Cottage was the fourth on the right: number seven Silver Street. Even before they had set eyes on the place, she and Col had been entranced by the sheer poetry of the address. And the house itself had fulfilled all their expectations, even though it had been in a terrible state, the damp rising inexorably up to meet the rain soaking down through the roof. There was woodworm, dry rot and deathwatch beetle. The garden was a jungle, with a dozen straggling fruit trees trying to keep their heads above the nettles, and the previous occupant, an eccentric old lady, had obtained all her water from the well by the back door.

Their friends had said they must be mad. They had a five-year-old son, and Tamsin had only just been born. The easy, ordinary, conventional solution would be a nice new house on an estate in Chippenham or Bath. But Kate and Col had fallen in love with the place, and with their devoted skill, their hard work and determination, Mermaid's Cottage was restored.

It had taken years. For the first few months, while the major work was being done, they had lived in a caravan in the garden. Col, a surveyor, had friends and contacts, but even so it had cost them a small fortune.

But worth every penny, Kate thought, smiling, as she opened the gate. It would, with hindsight, have been easier to have sold the place after Col's death, for every stone, every beam, every corner was such a sharp and poignant reminder of how much he had loved Mermaid's Cottage. But by the same token, she knew that she could not move out, however much it hurt, however much she missed him. She could never have borne to see someone else living in the house that they had, essentially, created and made their own.

There was a cow looking over the hedge which separated her garden from the field beyond. It was eyeing up her herbaceous borders with considerable interest. Kate went to shoo it away, and with a roll of its eyes and a swish of its tail, it lumbered off to join the rest. Ignoring the scrabbling of Smith, the dog, on the other side of the front door, Kate stood for a moment, gazing wistfully at the expanse of rough grass between her house and Justin's farm. It was called Mermaid's Ground, so it had presumably once belonged to this cottage, but Justin had told her that it had been part of Silver Street Farm for at least a hundred years. If ever she could afford to buy it, Kate had plans for that field. She had even mentioned them to Justin, once, and he had brought her down to earth with a severe jolt. 'A *plant* nursery? Whatever for, darling?'

'To grow plants, of course,' Kate had said patiently. 'Cottage garden plants, to be precise. Rare pinks, primroses, auriculas, that sort of thing.'

'Well, there can't be much money in that,' said Justin, who had the banker's tendency to judge everything by its potential profit-ability.

'You'd be surprised. There are millions of gardeners in this country, and a large number of them want something different, something unusual. I'd like to sell them by mail order, perhaps even one day exhibit at Chelsea. Don't look like that! Can't a woman dream?'

'As long as she realises that it *is* all just a dream,' Justin had said, rather dismissively.

'Well, you had a dream, didn't you? And realised it, in the end. So have I. Mermaid Nurseries, gold medal winner, thriving business. You see, Justin Spencer. One of these days I'll show you!'

But he hadn't taken her seriously. He didn't seem to be taking their relationship seriously, either, and in the dark moments of the night, when he was not speaking to her or touching her or close to her, she could not help wondering if he really meant all the wonderful things he said.

She had a new weapon ready, though, fortuitously placed in her grasp by Charlie Dobson. If she suddenly acquired a handsome male lodger, that might well force Justin's hand. She knew him well enough to suspect that he wouldn't like the idea at all. He might even be jealous, and although he wouldn't have cause to be, it would do no harm to let him know that he wasn't the only pebble on the beach.

'So let's hope this Jem bloke turns out to be a tasty morsel, eh, Smithy?' she said to the dog, liberated at last. 'Whatever else, that'll certainly give Justin something to think about.'

Chapter Two

Kate was still in the throes of tidying up when the front doorbell rang. Tamsin's horsey books and magazines were piled up in the sitting room, and Luke had washed his filthy hands in the kitchen sink and left smears of black oil everywhere. Still, she reflected, as she threw the ruined hand towels into the washing basket and shoved it hastily into the glory-hole cupboard under the stairs, if this Jem was going to share their household for three months, there was no point in giving him an inaccurate picture. After all, he was inspecting them, just as much as she would be assessing him. And if he was a tidiness freak, then he'd be much better off somewhere else.

Smith was going mad at the front door, hurling himself at it so that the glass panel rattled. A burglary a few months after Col's death had made Kate feel very vulnerable. Her parents had always kept dogs, and she'd missed a canine presence: Col had been allergic to anything with fur, so they hadn't even had a gerbil. With the children, she'd gone to the RSPCA kennels in Bath and chosen an apparently quiet and docile black mongrel, taken in because his elderly owner had died, and pining for a normal life. After a few hours at Mermaid's Cottage, it had become obvious that this was only half the story. The well behaved dog had changed into a wild, joyous creature who raced round the garden as if pursued by demons, dug up her herbaceous borders, chewed Tamsin's toys, ate several library books, and found gaps in the hedge that she'd assumed, erroneously, to be too small for him to squeeze through. Fortunately, the cows in Mermaid's Ground had not taken kindly to the intruder, and the dog had been chased back to safety with his tail between his legs. But he still tried to escape at every opportunity, until Kate hauled him off to the vet for an operation. After that, he had quietened down a little, but every visitor was greeted with an overwhelming exuberance that could be terrifying if you didn't notice his wagging tail.

She dragged him away and shut him in the kitchen, wondering whether Jem would still be there when she opened the door. She wouldn't have blamed him in the least if he'd turned tail and fled: to the uninitiated, Smith's assault on the door sounded as if the Hound of the Baskervilles was inside.

But he was standing in the porch, smiling a little warily. 'Hallo. Kate Williams? I'm Jem Forrester.'

And he definitely was attractive. Tall, lithe, muscular, he was wearing a baggy blue T-shirt and grey shorts. In Kate's considered opinion, not many men could wear shorts successfully, but Jem was certainly one of them. His face was friendly and rather mischievous, with wide-set dark eyes and beautiful cheekbones, all fringed and enhanced by neat short dreadlocks.

Charlie hadn't told her that Jem was black. Kate grinned at him, and held the door open. 'Come on in. Don't worry about the dog, I've shut him away.'

'I like dogs,' Jem said. 'My dad has retired greyhounds. They've hardly got two brain cells to rub together, but they're good company on a run.'

'Smith is very sweet, but far too enthusiastic for most people's comfort. Once the novelty has worn off, he's as quiet as a lamb.' She led the way through the door on the right. 'This is the sitting room. Would you like a drink? The sun's just about over the yardarm, as my father always used to say.'

'I'd love one. Have you got a beer? I ran round from the Court, and it's given me a thirst.'

'It's not very cold, I'm afraid,' Kate said, pouring it out carefully into a pint tankard. 'There is some in the fridge, but that means braving Smith.' She handed it to him. 'And before you ask, he's called that because when we got him, every time anyone opened a door, he made a bolt for it.'

'Better than having to call him Handyman, I suppose,' said Jem, with a commendably straight face.

'Handyman?'

'A dog who does odd jobs all round the house.'

'The oldest ones are always the best,' Kate said, trying not to laugh. 'I'm glad we seem to have a similar sense of humour. You certainly need it, in this household. How much has Charlie told you about us?'

Jem was looking round. At least it was comparatively clean, but there was a heap of magazines – cars, horses, gardens, food – on the coffee table, one of the pictures was crooked, and she'd forgotten to sweep out the hearth, which was pock-marked with specks of fallen soot. He said, with apparently genuine appreciation, 'This is a beautiful room. Is this house very old?'

'Sixteenth century, I think, but with later additions.'

'Yes, Charlie told me you and your husband had done a lot of work on it. And the garden. I can see why he wanted you in charge at the Court – if you can make that garden look like this one, it'll be wonderful.'

Kate shrugged, trying not to look too pleased. 'It's a lot of hard work. One day I might be happy with it, but not for years, I think. Gardeners have to have a lot of patience.' She poured herself a lemonade, and added, 'So what else did Charlie say? Was my left ear burning?'

'I doubt it. He said your husband had died a few years ago, and you were bringing up two children on your own.'

'Well, I could hardly hand them over to social services,' Kate said drily. 'Hundreds of thousands of women are single parents, in far worse circumstances than mine. On the whole, I think I've been very lucky. And Charlie's been a great help. He didn't have to give me that job, after all.'

'And he also told me that you were far too modest,' Jem said, with a grin.

'I'll have a word with him on Monday. He's got a lot to answer for, one way and another.'

'Including suggesting that you take in a lodger?'

Kate studied him. She had a tendency, which she strongly deplored, to take people at face value. It made her many friends, but it also meant that occasionally she was badly let down. Instinct, however, told her that Jem was indeed 'a good bloke'. Even on five minutes' acquaintance, she liked him.

'Including that,' she said at last. 'But I thought, why not? And we could do with the money. Don't tell me, Charlie said that too.'

'I'm afraid so. Charlie always calls a spade a bleeding great shovel, as I expect you've noticed. It's all part of his Lovable Cockney Geezer character. Don't get me wrong, he *is* a good bloke. But if you ever do business with him, be careful. You don't make that much dosh without being fairly ruthless.'

'I don't intend to do business with him. He employs me.' Kate indicated the bulging, shabby sofa, its deficiencies only partly concealed by a beautiful Indian cotton throw in shades of peach and russet and terracotta. 'Go on, be brave, sit down.'

'Thanks.' Jem sank with feline grace into the dubious depths. 'Of course, he employs me as well. He likes to think he's a good

19

judge of potential talent, and not just musical. He gave me chances I thought would never come my way, and I took them. I owe him a lot. This studio, if it comes off, will put my name up in lights. It's what I've always wanted to do.'

'So you've never been tempted to make music rather than produce it?'

'Oh, yeah. Trouble is, I have a small problem – lack of talent. I play sax, but at about the same level of skill as the average busker. I was in a band for a while, when I was at school, until they found someone who could actually play. I didn't want to leave it all behind, though. My parents had plans for me, thought I'd make a doctor, but I faced them out and got a job as a gofer at Moonrock Studios.'

'Charlie's place.'

'Yeah. That was my first break. I still can't believe he hired me – I nearly plugged his top act into the national grid, my first week. But he kept me on, amazingly, and I learn fast. A few years later another studio enticed me away, but we stayed in touch. It's a small world, everyone knows everyone else – you keep bumping into the same people at gigs and parties. Back in February, he called me up and told me about his Project, and I knew the bunch I was with were going nowhere, so I thought I'd take him up on it. Three months building the place, and then managing it if I want to.'

'And do you?'

'I'll see.' Jem grinned. 'Depends how much money he puts on the table. I know how much I'm worth, and so does Charlie. Depends if I like the country life, too. I'm a city boy, Greenwich born and bred. All these green fields and wide open spaces hurt my eyes.'

'If you've only lived in London, Moxham will be a bit of a culture shock,' said Kate. *And Jem will be to them,* she thought, with a certain amount of relish. *Some of them have probably never met a black guy before.* She pictured Colonel Sims's face, and his likely reaction, and added, 'You might have to put up with some pretty old-fashioned attitudes, too.'

'That's their problem, not mine,' Jem said. 'If you let racists get to you, then they've won.' He grinned mischievously. 'Some of my best friends are white. Including my wife. Ex-wife.'

'*Ex*-wife? Charlie just said she'd got a job in New York.'

'She has, but we already knew we'd come to the end of the line, and we agreed to split before she went.' He smiled ruefully. 'Don't worry, it was all quite friendly. We were both so busy, we hardly ever saw each other, even at weekends. No kids, and both of us earning good money, so we can afford to be reasonable. I'm not crying myself to sleep. This is just what I needed, a break from the city rat-race, for a few months at least. And if I like it here, I might stay.'

'It'll cost you an arm and a leg if you do. People pay a fortune to live in Moxham.'

'Well, I'm not exactly poor,' Jem said. 'And I'd love a place like this, something old, a bit of history behind it. Our flat in London is in a new block, and for me it's got about as much style and character as a plastic cup. Caroline liked it – she's into the modern look, all bare walls and floorboards and furniture you can't sit on for more than five minutes. It was like living inside a magazine – I never felt comfortable there.'

'I prefer old houses too. This one took years of hard work, it was all but derelict when we bought it. There was even death-watch beetle – the man from Rentokil was very impressed. And so damp we found a newt living behind the skirting board. Would you like a guided tour?'

'Too right I would.' Jem swallowed the last of his beer and hauled himself out of the sofa's embrace. 'Lead on, Mrs Williams.'

'Kate, *please*! You make me feel like some old seaside landlady with carpet slippers and a fag hanging out of her mouth.'

'Sorry, Kate.' He looked so comically apologetic that she had to laugh. *I like this man*, she thought, as she went out of the door. *I could certainly have him as a lodger.*

'The hall,' she said, rather unnecessarily. 'Downstairs toilet. Stairs up. Coats. Telephone.'

'We'll have to come to an arrangement about bills.'

'As long as you're not phoning New York every five minutes, I'm not bothered. A hundred quid a week covers everything pretty generously.'

'Cheap at the price,' Jem said, looking at the kitchen door, which was shivering under the onslaught of Smith on the other side. 'Come on, let's get it over with. I can take it.'

'Do you really mean that?'

'Yes. Go on, open the door.'

A torrent of ecstatic black mongrel hurled itself at Jem, jumping and barking with excitement. Kate realised that she hadn't warned him that Smith invariably went straight for the groin, but fortunately he moved fast. Then, having warded off the initial assault, he stood still while the animal frisked round him, letting him sniff and investigate. 'What a nice friendly dog.'

'I can't believe you're saying that. He's a real pain in the butt.'

'Good to have him around, though, if you're on your own.' Jem looked up at her, his hands busy fondling Smith's lopsided ears. 'You're a bit quiet here, a bit isolated.'

'Hardly. There are the Hamiltons next door, and the Pagets and the Taylors opposite. And Justin at the farm down the road. We did get burgled once, a few years back, which is why I decided to get a dog. But not since.'

'Hardly surprising. Anyone who comes to the door must think they're going to be eaten alive.'

'Poor Smithy,' said Kate. 'Everyone gets the wrong impression. He's quite harmless, unless you're a rabbit. And even when he's caught one, all he wants to do is lick it. Go on, Smith, *basket*!'

The dog looked at her beseechingly. Sternly, Kate repeated her order, and he slunk off to his bed, in the warm corner of the kitchen next to the Aga.

'Good God,' said Jem. 'What's that he's eating?'

'A giant marrowbone,' Kate told him. 'The butcher I get it from calls it a Postman's Leg. I don't know what you want to do about food—'

'I hope I'm not expected to share that with the dog,' said Jem, straightfaced.

Kate laughed. 'Only at weekends. You're welcome to eat with us, but of course you may be working late.'

'I could cook for you sometimes,' said Jem, glancing round at the pale wood units, now rather shabby, which Col had fitted ten years previously. 'If you don't mind, that is.'

'You *cook*! Brilliant,' said Kate. It was another mark in his favour. Justin usually ate at the pub or at frighteningly expensive restaurants in Bath, and she doubted if he even knew how to boil an egg. 'I'm trying to teach Luke – that's my son, he's fifteen and more than old enough to learn. But he's not really interested.'

'Tell him it's a good way to attract girls. That's why I started.'

'Unfortunately, Luke's not interested in girls either. The objects of his adoration have four wheels and three-litre engines. That's where he is now – worshipping at the shrine of Justin's cars.'

'Charlie said you had a daughter, too, the same age as his.'

'Yes, Tamsin. She's ten, and heavily into horses. She helps at the riding stables at Minty's Farm, mucking out and grooming in exchange for lessons.' Kate hesitated. 'I haven't told them about you yet. I didn't want to raise their hopes. Like all the other village kids, they think there's going to be an endless stream of pop stars coming to Moxham, and the possibility that they might actually have the studio manager staying in this house would be so wonderful that if it didn't come off, they'd never forgive me.'

'O.K., understood.'

'Anyway, this is the kitchen. The usual conveniences, of course, cunningly hidden away – fridge, washing machine, dishwasher. All rather elderly, and in need of TLC, or they'll refuse to work. The Aga, which was here when we bought the place. It took me years to get the hang of it, I'll have to give you lessons in all its little foibles if you want to use it. The cats sleep in the bottom oven in the winter, which is why the door is always left open. Patio outside, we often eat out there if the weather's nice, or in the conservatory if it isn't. There's a barbecue too, of course.'

'Don't worry,' said Jem. 'I'm not one of those guys who regress to cavemen every time they stand over an open flame with a pair of tongs in their hands, offering no choice between cremated and raw.'

'I'm glad to hear it,' Kate told him, with sincerity. 'This is the dining room. We don't often use it except for breakfast – somehow we always seem to end up having supper in front of the telly. And this is the annexe, through here.'

It was as spotless as any bed and breakfast bedroom. This part of the house had been built on to Mermaid's Cottage in Victorian times, so it lacked the beams and character of the other rooms, but it was well proportioned and light, with three windows, one looking onto the patio and the others onto the garden. There was a bedroom suite in walnut, which had belonged to Kate's grandmother, and an elderly armchair which had succumbed to Smith's teeth, the holes concealed by another of her Indian throws, this time in shades of blue and turquoise. The walls were painted a rich dark cream, and hung with an assortment of pictures, chosen for no better reason than that Kate liked them. She had picked a bunch of lilac and put it in a tall blue vase on the chest of drawers, and the scent filled the room.

'Do you like it?' Kate asked, as Jem stared round. 'I mean, this is the room you'd have. That door there leads to the bathroom, we had that built on. My mother and my in-laws sleep here when they come to stay.'

'Together?' Jem enquired quizzically.

'Hardly – they're barely on speaking terms. My mother thinks

23

they're beneath her, and they think she's stuck up. Anyway, if any of them do descend on us, there's another spare room upstairs, so don't worry about that. Do you like it?'

'Like it?' Jem's face curved into his flashing smile, 'I'll say I like it. It's exactly what I need. The question is, are you happy to have me here?'

'Of course I am. I think we'd get on, don't you? We're a very easy-going sort of household, not many rules, people tend to come and go as they please really – even Tamsin. But let's give it a week's trial, shall we, just to make sure?'

'Fine,' said Jem, and held out his hand. 'Great doing business with you, Kate. Do you want the first week's money now? I've got it with me.'

'Gosh.' She stared at him, laughing. 'You must have been very confident.'

'After what Charlie told me, I was pretty sure I'd like it. Here you are. Don't spend it all at once.'

With a slight sense of disbelief, Kate took the notes and tucked them into the back pocket of her jeans. 'Thank you. Thank you very much. When would you like to move in? It's ready, as you can see.'

'I was hoping for Wednesday. I've got a few things to sort out with the Camden flat. It'll have to be put on the market now I've split with Caroline, so I'll bring my personal stuff down with me. Don't worry, I don't have much, and what won't fit in here can be stored at the Court.'

'It seems odd that Charlie won't have you to stay there.'

'Oh, it's not *Charlie* who didn't want it – *I* didn't.' He gave her a speculative glance. 'Don't get me wrong – I like the old scoundrel, and I like Tanya too. Which is why I didn't want to be under the same roof. She's easily tempted, is Charlie's Tarn, and a refusal might spoil a beautiful friendship.'

'Has anyone *ever* refused?'

'More than you'd think. Charlie knows all about it, but he prefers to turn a blind eye. He really loves her, you know, and he adores Jayde. He'd rather Tanya spread herself all round London than risk breaking up his little family.'

'And she's not complaining,' Kate said, thinking of Charlie's beautiful wife, spending her husband's money so freely on the clothes and make-up and manicures and hairdos without which she would be just another fading ex-model. 'I like her too. Underneath all that glamour, she can be surprisingly down-to-earth.'

Jem laughed. 'I know exactly what you mean. Do I get a look upstairs, as well?'

'Of course,' Kate said, and led the way back to the hall. Smith, fortunately minus bone, was now lying in his favourite place, right at the top of the stairs, and she called him down so that they wouldn't have to step over him and risk a broken neck.

'Don't take any notice of what your lady says about you,' Jem advised him as he bounced past. 'You're a good dog really.'

'If you're still saying that after the first week, I'll buy you a pint at the Unicorn,' Kate told him. 'This is the landing – very big, but it was two bedrooms originally, with all the others leading off it. Obviously that wasn't a particularly practical arrangement, so we decided to reorganise it and put the children's bathroom in there. I really wouldn't advise you to go in unless you're desperate, or keen on toxic waste or horror movies like *The Blob*. Those doors on the right belong to Luke's bedroom and the spare room, over the sitting room. Tamsin's room is next to mine, which is there, above the annexe. And this is the airing cupboard – sheets, pillowcases, extra blankets, et cetera in there if you need them.'

'It's very well planned,' Jem said, looking round in obvious admiration.

'Col – my husband – was a surveyor, and he knew an awful lot about old houses. And he knew a lot of useful people, too. Those beams in the bathroom wall came from a barn at Minty's Farm that was being demolished. Nearly all the windows needed replacing, and he found someone to make new ones at very low rates. It's listed, you see, so we couldn't just put plastic ones in.'

'No way,' Jem said. He walked over to the window which looked out across the patio and the garden beyond. 'What's that big tree nearest to the house?'

'It's a walnut. It blocks off the view and the roots don't do the patio any good, but it's too nice to chop down.'

'I agree. Trees like that don't grow on trees.'

'You'd make someone a good straight man.'

'So I've been told,' said Jem, poker-faced. 'So how far does your garden go?'

'As far as the hedge which you can just see there, and the orchard beyond it is ours as well. The trees are all old varieties of cider apple – one day, I'd like to buy a press and make my own. It's all very overgrown, and Tamsin and her friends still use it as a giant playground. Sometimes I borrow the Court's big mower and try to make some sort of impact on all that grass, but it's like

25

painting the Forth Bridge. We used to have some chickens in there, but bloody Brer Fox had the lot last summer, seventeen of them, including a bantam cockerel Tamsin had reared from the egg. I decided it just wasn't worth the tears.'

'It's a perfect place for kids,' Jem said, smiling. 'You're very lucky. And Mermaid's Cottage is a wonderful name. Was it a pub once?'

'Not as far as I know. I looked it up in the library, and it was probably originally Mere-mead, which means a meadow with a pond in it. The field over there, to the left, used to belong to this cottage too – it's called Mermaid's Ground. But it was sold to Silver Street Farm a long time ago. A real shame – I could have done a lot with that land.'

'Such as?'

Kate hesitated. After Justin's disparaging comments about her ambitions, she wasn't sure that she wanted to expose her plans to Jem's critical gaze. But this was a very different man, and the disparity surely ran deeper than the skin. She said at last, 'I'd like to start up a plant nursery. I love the old historic cottage garden flowers, and they're very fashionable at the moment. I'm sure I could make a go of it, and there isn't a lot of competition, certainly not in this area. I'd breed scented plants like pinks, and rare old favourites like auriculas and double primroses, and perhaps have display areas planted up to look like mediaeval or Tudor or Victorian gardens. There are some beautiful old trees in the field, and part of it has probably never been ploughed, so there are cowslips in summer and wild mushrooms in autumn, and a patch at the far end by the brook where there are some quite rare wildflowers – I wouldn't touch that part. I'd make it all the focus of a wildlife garden as well—' She broke off and glanced at him ruefully. 'Sorry. I tend to get carried away. Anyway, it hasn't a snowball's chance in hell of ever coming off. For a start, it'll take a lot of money for greenhouses and equipment and getting the land into good heart. And buying the field itself would take a lot more.' She knew that she would have to buy it; her earliest dreams, of going into some kind of partnership with Justin, had withered under the impact of his scorn without ever being voiced.

'It sounds a great idea,' said Jem, confirming her instinctive judgement. 'Surely you could find a friendly investor?'

'They don't grow on trees either. The only millionaire I know is Charlie, and he's hardly likely to throw his money away on a plant nursery. I have enough trouble persuading him and Tanya that beds full of scarlet salvias and orange marigolds don't really set the Court off to best advantage.'

Jem laughed. 'He said he liked what you were doing very much, but Tanya thought it could do with a bit more colour around the place.'

'Like a council bedding scheme, regimented in rows and replaced three times a year. If she really wants that, he'll have to pay me quadruple. That sort of gardening is hard work and labour-intensive. Aside from which, I swore years ago never to touch another begonia in my life.'

'What's a begonia?'

'There are lots of different species, but the one I particularly loathe is an inoffensive little plant with pink or red flowers, very popular in pots and front gardens. Irrational, I know, but I just can't stand them.' Kate grinned at him apologetically. 'Sorry. If you become part of this menagerie, you'll have to put up with a certain amount of garden-speak. But I do have other topics of conversation, honestly. And if you have an overwhelming desire to talk cars or horses, try Luke and Tamsin. He knows every variation on every model of every British sports car since the Second World War, and she can recite the pedigrees of all the Derby winners since nineteen hundred. This is a household of obsessions, so you'd better be warned.'

'I'll contribute the life histories of Tamla greats, if you like, and Famous Rock Artists who have Pissed Me Off. Is that your son back?'

A male voice was calling from downstairs. Kate felt a sudden twinge of apprehension. 'No,' she said. 'It's Justin. Come and meet him.'

Her lover was standing in the kitchen, glass in hand. He had already helped himself to the rather nice bottle of Frascati which she'd put in the fridge in case Jem stayed for lunch. To Kate, seeing him with new eyes, he seemed very big and leonine compared to the lithe, dark Jem. As her new lodger walked in behind her, she saw his thick yellow eyebrows rise questioningly. 'Hallo, darling – who's this?'

'Jem Forrester, Charlie's project manager. He's going to be staying in our annexe while the building work's in progress. Jem, this is Justin Spencer – he owns Silver Street Farm, down the road.'

'Hi,' said Jem, with his friendly smile, and held out his hand. 'Great to meet you.'

'Hallo,' said Justin again, and shook hands affably. 'So, you're

27

going to be staying here. Wasn't there enough room up at the Court, then?'

'They're having the roof done, so the top floor's out of action,' Jem explained. 'I needed somewhere to stay, and Charlie thought of Kate.'

'I see,' said Justin cheerfully. Kate looked hard at him, searching for signs of covert hostility, and found none at all. It was difficult to decide whether his apparently genuine friendliness made her feel relieved, or somehow disappointed.

'After all, it's not as if we're short of room,' she added. 'The kids will love having Jem, it'll do wonders for their street cred, and the extra money will come in handy.' She was, perversely, coming to the conclusion that she would have preferred him to show some signs of jealousy.

'It's just for three months,' said Jem. 'When the studios are finished, I'll probably go back to London.' He glanced at Kate. 'I'd better be off. Tanya's assumed I'm one of her lunch guests.'

'Shame,' she said, smiling. 'I was going to ask you if you'd like to eat here. But how about having a meal down at the pub this evening? It's nice enough to sit out in the garden, and you can meet the kids and we can thrash out a few ground rules.'

'Does this invitation include me?' Justin enquired.

'Of course it does,' said Kate, giving him a breathtakingly joyful smile that, had she known it, captivated both men. 'Half past seven? Great. See you then. Bye.'

'I didn't know you'd decided to acquire a lodger,' Justin said, as Jem jogged out of the gate. 'Do you really need one?'

'Yes, I'm afraid I do. He's paying me a hundred pounds a week, cash in hand. It's a very significant improvement in my income. And if he stays all summer, that'll be a grand and a half, nearly. It may not seem much to you, but to us it's a lot of money. A new washing machine, a week away, Tamsin's grown out of her shoes again—'

'I'm not especially keen on the idea,' said Justin, moving closer. 'It might cramp our style, darling.' He slipped his arms around her. 'If you know what I mean.'

'I'm not sure I do,' said Kate, feigning innocence. 'Can you be more specific?'

His kiss left her in absolutely no doubt of his feelings, or hers. A while later, she said softly, 'Lunch? Or an aperitif?'

'I'd love to say yes to both, gorgeous, but I can't.' Justin smiled down at her regretfully. 'I'm meeting a potential customer at the Unicorn in half an hour. I came over to say that Luke's still busy

– he's valeting the TVR before this chap takes a look at it. I told him he could have a bonus if he finished it in time.'

'And he will.' She smiled back at him, basking like a cat in the warmth of his charm. He was so very good-looking, even if all those pub lunches and fancy restaurants were beginning to have an effect on his waistline. But the only exercise he took was on the golf course: he was a member of a very exclusive and expensive local club, as was Charlie. Needless to say, the two of them had never played together: Justin, whose grandmother had been a Blount, found it difficult to adjust to the fact that an accredited member of the lower orders now occupied the Court, which he still seemed to regard as his ancestral home.

'Tonight, then?' Justin was nibbling her ear, and it was having a gloriously unsettling effect on her breathing. 'I haven't made love to you for two whole days, and I'm ravenous.'

'After the pub. We can finish off that Frascati when the kids are in bed.' She kissed him, exulting in the effect he had on her feelings.

'I can hardly wait,' said Justin, his hands caressing her and his mouth against hers. 'Beautiful, adorable Kate.'

But once bereft of his compelling, exhilarating presence, that little tendril of doubt woke again at the back of her mind. Her bones melted and her skin glowing, Kate ignored it. As long as he could make her feel like this, she didn't really care. Why spoil something so delightful, when there was no need?

Chapter Three

Kate was ordering the drinks at the bar when Jem walked in. She could tell it was him, without turning round, because the whole pub went suddenly and absolutely quiet. Then the buzz of conversation began again, several notes higher and several decibels louder.

'Blimey,' said Marcia, the landlady, in a hoarse whisper. 'Who's that?'

Kate glanced round and waved. 'Jem Forrester,' she said, with a mischievous grin. 'Charlie's studio manager. And my new lodger. Hi, Jem. My shout – what are you having?'

'Pint of best, please,' Jem said. He was wearing a baggy white collarless shirt over dark trousers, and a very flash embroidered waistcoat that Kate thought might be a genuine antique. In the smoky, typically English bar of the Unicorn, he looked entrancingly alien and exotic. 'But I'll get the food. No, I insist. What's on offer?'

Marcia, her eyes on stalks, silently handed him the menu and then busied herself with pulling the pint. Kate, gleefully aware that she and her companion had riveted every eye in the pub, pointed out the specials blackboard above the bar. 'The fish is always good, it comes straight from Brixham. Or the pork and sweet pepper hotpot.'

'Forget about me for the moment – what are you going to have?'

Kate hesitated, torn between the hotpot – familiar, cheap and cheerful – and the Thai-style red mullet, which sounded delicious but was almost twice the price.

'I'm having the mullet,' said Jem, solving her dilemma. 'Join me?'

'Yes,' Kate said with relief. 'And the kids always have ham, egg and chips.' At least that wasn't expensive, and she didn't like the feeling that she was sponging off his generosity and obviously superior income.

'What about Justin?' Jem enquired, as Marcia wrote it all down. 'Is he still coming?'

'As far as I know. I haven't heard any different. But I can order for him – he always has steak au poivre when it's on, he says it's better here than anywhere else.'

'One of our best customers, Mr Spencer,' said Marcia. 'I'm glad to hear we're appreciated. That'll be forty-three pounds fifty for the food, sir, and two Cokes, a St Clements and a pint of best is four-forty. Where are you sitting, Kate? In the garden?'

'Yes, by the well. If Tamsin misbehaves, I'll drop her down it. Can you take one of the Cokes, Jem?'

'Here, have a tray,' said Marcia, producing one from beneath the counter. With care, Jem balanced the four glasses on its uneven surface, and carried it outside.

A couple of years previously, Marcia and her husband Mick had asked Kate to redesign the Unicorn's tatty and uninspiring beer garden. They had wanted a rich, cottagey effect that would enhance and harmonise with the ancient pub, but which would require minimal maintenance. Accordingly, she had planted the back border with tall perennials to flower all summer, scattered a host of self-seeding honesty and foxgloves and Canterbury bells amongst them, and persuaded her clients to pave the rest with a pattern of weathered stones, putting sweet-scented thyme and chamomile in the gaps. Every spring, a golden lake of daffodils announced the arrival of warmer weather, and she filled up the stone pots and tubs with colourful bedding plants which would only require regular watering to give a splendid display. The garden was now one of the Unicorn's chief attractions, and had won several brewery awards. Even better, Mick's glowing recommendation of her work had led to Charlie's offer of the job at Moxham Court.

Luke and Tamsin were sitting at one of the wooden tables, their eyes fixed on the back door. Even Luke, who sometimes seemed so laid back that he was almost asleep, had greeted the news about their prospective lodger with eager interest. And Tamsin, as wholehearted in her passions as in her hatreds, was overwhelmingly delighted by the idea. She had examined her wardrobe with cries of horror ('*Everything* I've got comes from Oxfam!') and had completely failed to be impressed by the information that all the coolest people went to charity shops these days. 'Jayde doesn't.'

'Jayde isn't interested in clothes. Her mother buys her wardrobes full of fancy gear, and she usually just wears jeans and

T-shirts,' Kate had pointed out calmly. After ten years of dealing with Tamsin's paddies, she could judge her turbulent daughter's moods with the exactitude of science. 'And so do you.'

'But I *can't* meet this guy wearing my school *uniform*! He'll think I'm a *baby*!'

'He certainly will if you carry on like that,' observed Luke, sticking his head round his sister's bedroom door. 'Want to borrow my new Bath rugby shirt?'

Sometimes, Kate acknowledged ruefully, her son was better at handling Tamsin than she was. Clad in leggings and the rugby shirt – which almost came down to her knees, but which was apparently the ultimate in cool as understood in the top class of Moxham St Peter's – and with her dark wild hair looking as if it had been styled by the nearest hedge, her daughter wouldn't earn Granny's approval, but if it kept her happy then Kate didn't mind. Luke had been unable to get the oil out from under his fingernails, but at least his hair was tidy, and he'd managed to find the only pair of jeans that didn't have a hole in the knee or a split crotch seam.

Surveying her children, Kate thought it was fortunate that current fashion suited their limited income perfectly. She had long since given up trying to dictate what they wore: unpleasant memories of her own mother's strictures always came back to haunt her. 'But you can't dress in *rags*, Katherine! And what *does* your hair look like! Why don't you wear that nice tweed skirt I bought for you last week?'

Once university had put her safely beyond her mother's attempts at control, Kate had evolved her own style, casual but fashionable. Col had liked her to wear expensive clothes, and she had accumulated a very good wardrobe. But after his death, she'd lost so much weight that everything was far too big. Severely practical, she had done a deal with a local dress agency, and had exchanged four suitcases full of oversize jackets, dresses and skirts for a few very good, classically dateless garments that actually fitted her. She was wearing one of them now, a silk blouse in a beautiful shade of cornflower blue, over a pair of navy tailored trousers. She liked dressing up, it was a welcome change from the earth-stained shorts and jeans and worn-out shirts she wore for work. And Justin was the kind of man who invariably noticed her clothes, and commented on them.

'This is Jem,' she said, as he set the tray carefully down on the table. 'Jem, meet Luke and Tamsin.'

At least Luke wouldn't embarrass her. He got to his feet, a tall, self-contained boy with his mother's fair hair and strong bones, and his father's warm hazel eyes. 'Hi,' he said, holding out a hand with a smear of ground-in oil across the knuckle.

'Hi.' Jem took it without appearing to notice. 'You're the car freak, right?'

Luke grinned, rather self-consciously. 'That's right. Are you into cars?' he added hopefully.

'Not really. I've got a bike.'

'A *bike*? A push-bike?'

'I don't think Triumph make them any more,' Jem said. 'A Daytona, to be precise.'

'You've got a Triumph Daytona? Wick*ed*!'

'Look,' said Tamsin, thrusting herself into the conversation with her usual lack of grace, 'if you're going to be boring and talk about engines and stupid things like that all evening—'

'Don't worry, we won't,' Jem said, sitting down beside her. 'Here's your Coke. What would you rather we talked about, then?'

Tamsin went bright red. 'You,' she blurted out. 'What you do. The studio. All that sort of thing.'

'It's like Smith,' Kate explained, taking the space opposite Tamsin, with Luke on her right. 'Best get it over with now, and then you won't be bothered again. Anyway, we're all interested. How *do* you turn a quadrangle of dilapidated Georgian stables into a world-beating music studio?'

'By throwing vast quantities of money at it,' Jem said. 'This is Charlie's dream, and he wants it done properly. And fast – he's already got a couple of bands booked in for the beginning of September. The idea is that they stay in one wing of the quadrangle – luxury suites, a sort of private hotel, the coach-house will be the rehearsal room, and the actual recording studios on the other two sides. Everything they could possibly need on site and available at all times.'

Except buckets of drugs and gallons of booze, Kate thought wryly. *Not to mention the groupies – although perhaps Tanya might oblige . . .*

'No distractions,' Jem was saying. 'Some bands come in with everything pretty much worked out already. Then it's just a case of sorting out the details with the producer, and laying down the tracks. Others like to spend months experimenting, writing, doing it as they go along. Those tend to be the ones with unlimited funds and indulgent record companies. They usually

34

go to the US or the Caribbean – Charlie wants to bring them here instead.'

'Nice though Moxham is,' Kate commented, 'I don't think its weather can compete with Jamaica's.'

'That's probably an advantage,' Jem told her. 'They can't lie on the beach all day drinking rum cocktails.'

'Well, they can always go to Weston-super-Mare – mud, kids, donkeys, and a tide that goes out so far you can't see it. Not quite the same atmosphere, somehow.'

'Oh, I don't know,' said Jem. 'Didn't Morrissey do a song about the charms of a typical British seaside resort?'

'He was probably being seriously ironic,' said Kate drily. 'So, who have you worked with? Would we know them?'

'*I* would,' said Tamsin. 'I like Hunkydory best, and Kaden George is *gorgeous*. Gorgeous Georgious, that's what Charlotte calls him.'

Kate was fairly sure that these were little more than names to Tamsin, whose idols up until now had been exclusively four-legged, with exalted pedigrees and supercilious expressions.

'Haven't worked with any of them, I'm afraid,' said Jem. 'Sorry.'

Tamsin looked relieved rather than devastated. She could have held a knowledgeable conversation with any jockey in the land, but in the field of sub-teen pop stars, she was decidedly out of her depth.

'Oasis?' Luke was saying. 'Blur? U2?' He was much more interested in music than his sister, and every evening he did his homework to a deafening background of more or less tuneful rock, varying widely in quality and vintage. Kate, whose own tastes veered towards the melodic, but who had also clung to a nostalgic fondness for the Punk bands of her youth, chipped in with her own contributions. 'The Clash? The Stranglers?'

'Before my time, I'm afraid,' Jem said. 'Serious Money, remember them? Charlie's biggest act, around the end of the eighties. Then I went to Whip Will Records and worked with a lot of people there. Captain Haddock was one of mine, I did both their albums.'

'I've got them!' said Luke, looking almost excited. 'They're wicked. Mum says they're a band that really exploits atonality.'

'It wasn't meant as a compliment,' Kate said, trying not to catch Jem's eye. 'But do you have any choice in who you work with? What if you're asked to do a group you really can't stand?'

'Captain Haddock wasn't easy, I will admit.' Jem gave her his flashing smile. 'But the bottom line is, I'm just the sound engineer, the minion, the guy who pushes the buttons and disguises the singer's sore throat and fills in the drummer's missing beats. My own likes and dislikes don't come into it. As I've got a fondness for old Tamla records, that's probably just as well.'

'What's Tamla?' Tamsin demanded.

'A record label, started in Detroit in the sixties by a guy called Berry Gordy. Most black artists – the Supremes, the Temptations, the Four Tops, and the king of them all, Smokey Robinson. You'd know them if you heard them – half the ads on the box use Tamla songs as a soundtrack.' And he sang a couple of lines from 'Tracks of My Tears'.

He had a surprisingly good singing voice, dark and tuneful. As Kate smiled in appreciation, he added, 'I also like rock, soul – and ska and reggae, too, in moderation. Going back to ma roots, man!'

'Does your family come from Jamaica?'

'No, my dad's from Barbados. He arrived in the fifties, did well, started his own mini-cab firm. He sold the business and retired a few years ago. Mum's English, from Greenwich – that's where I grew up. I've got a younger sister, Maia, she's a teacher, got two kids, and my little brother Chris is at London University, doing law.' He grinned. 'Our parents were very ambitious for us. Mum still thinks I let them down. She can't see what I do as a "proper job" at all.'

'Doing what makes you happy, I think that's the most important thing.' Kate glanced at her son. 'But that doesn't mean I want a certain person to spend his entire life lying under a sump.'

'I don't intend to,' Luke said. 'I'm going to get my GCSEs and A levels, do a mechanical engineering course and get a job designing cars.' He grinned at her. 'Don't worry, Mum, I've got it all sorted out.'

'Glad to hear it.' Kate, her back to the pub, saw Tamsin's face stiffen suddenly, and her eyes narrow. Justin must have arrived. She turned, hoping that his potential customer had agreed to buy the TVR. Luke had said that he had seemed very interested.

With relief, she saw that Justin was carrying a bottle unmistakeably topped with gold foil. The Unicorn carried a small but select stock of champagne, and Mick had told her that Justin was almost the only person in the village who drank it – at their prices, anyway. So he must have sold the TVR, and that meant that he would be in a good mood.

'Hallo,' she said as he approached. 'Celebration?'

'Double celebration,' said Justin, with the charming, expansive smile she loved. 'My good fortune, and yours.'

'Mine?' Kate stared at him in bewilderment as he set the bottle, and three glasses, down on the table, and pulled up another chair.

'Yes, yours, darling,' said Justin. He was wearing one of his best shirts, made by a firm in Jermyn Street, and a pair of immaculate chinos, their creases unnaturally sharp. All his laundry went to a local company, of course, at considerable expense.

'Your lodger,' he went on, untwisting the wire, while Tamsin placed both hands over her ears and screwed up her face in anticipation. 'That's good luck, isn't it?'

There was something about the brittle expansiveness of his mood that didn't quite ring true, but Kate ignored it. 'Of course it is,' she said, with a glance at Jem. 'And don't tell me – yours is that you sold the TVR.'

'Correct. Well, he hasn't actually signed on the dotted line yet, but the fish is well and truly hooked, if not landed.' Justin brought out his wallet, removed a twenty-pound note, and set it down in front of Luke. 'And that's your bonus. He said he'd never seen a car in better condition.'

'Thanks,' Luke said, flushing with pride and pleasure. 'Thanks a lot, Justin.'

'You worked hard, and you deserve it.' Justin bestowed the benefit of his smile all round the table, not excluding Jem. Kate caught a whiff of whisky on his breath, and realised that he'd been celebrating already. That explained the exuberance: a good malt, from the assortment that Marcia kept on a high shelf behind the bar, always made him cheerful. The cork shot out of the bottle with a bang that clearly startled the elderly couple at the next table, and a torrent of bubbles cascaded wastefully down the gold foil. With a flourish, Justin poured champagne into the three glasses. 'Here's to Kate,' he said, raising his high. 'Well done.'

'I didn't do anything. I've just got a spare room, that's all.'

'You're too modest,' said Justin, and the way he looked at her made her knees tremble. 'Darling Kate . . .' He took a generous slurp of champagne, and added, 'So what are you going to do with all Jem's loot?'

'Spend it wisely,' Kate said, wishing that he wouldn't talk quite so loudly.

'Here's Mrs Stevens with the food,' said Tamsin. 'God, I'm ravenous!'

The red mullet, cooked to perfection, lay on a bed of glistening, steaming vegetables, with a circle of aromatic jasmine rice around it. It smelt so wonderful that Kate ignored the pleading fishy eye looking up at her from the plate. Her squeamishness annoyed her, but she had never managed to conquer it, despite the efforts of her two cats.

For a while there was silence as the three adults and two children consumed the food. Kate ate slowly, savouring the delicate taste. Tamsin and Luke devoured theirs with healthy appreciation, but Justin, unintimidated by the large, almost raw steak in front of him, was the first to finish. He poured out more champagne, lit a cigarette without asking, and addressed Jem with slightly condescending civility. 'So what exactly do you do down at Charlie's stables?'

'I don't think you'd really want to know all the tedious details,' Jem told him cheerfully. 'I warn you, I'm quite capable of boring the pants off everyone until midnight, if you let me. Basically, I'm making sure that the builders and the electricians and all the other workers carry out my ideas. And, most important of all, ensuring that the soundproofing works – the council will be down on us like a ton of bricks if it doesn't.'

'The studios are a quarter of a mile from the nearest house,' Kate pointed out.

'Charlie promised the planners that none of the villagers would hear a thing,' said Jem. 'And if I get it wrong, there'll be hell to pay.'

'Let's hope that you don't,' Justin told him. 'A lot of people in the village are still deeply unhappy about this business. And they'll be watching like hawks, ready to pounce on anything that proves their point.'

'Which is?' enquired Jem, with that look of guileless interest that Kate was already beginning to recognise.

'That this studio development is completely out of place in a village like Moxham, doesn't belong here, and will bring no benefit to any of the inhabitants.'

Kate thought of pointing out that three local firms would be able to guarantee several months of employment to more than thirty people because of Charlie's project, but she didn't feel like antagonising Justin, when he was apparently in such high spirits. Even his words to Jem seemed to be just a friendly warning. 'So you'd better watch out for hostile natives,' she added, grinning.

'Or they'll put me in a pot?' Her new lodger smiled back at

her, gently teasing. 'Diplomacy is my middle name. It has to be – some of the bands I've worked with would make the most unreasonable prima donna look like a UN negotiator. I admit I'm not used to village life, but it can't be that different from Greenwich or Camden.'

'Oh, dear,' said Kate. 'You are in for a shock. Emmerdale and the Archers have nothing on Moxham. All human life is here, and then some. For a start, there's the feud between us and Brimley – that's the next village – over the time Bob Wiltshire's onions were marked down at the flower show, all of thirty years back.'

'And the arguments over who's going to be in the cricket team,' Luke put in.

'The car vandal who's never been caught but *everyone* knows who it is,' said Tamsin.

'The dispute over the millennium celebrations.'

'The smell from the pig farm.'

'The upkeep of the village pond and what to do about the rapidly increasing duck population.'

'And don't forget the wife-swapping ring.' Kate grinned at Jem's surprise. 'Yes, honestly. My friend Megan is on the playgroup committee and she hears all the gossip. You wouldn't believe how vicious some people can be, over what seems like absolutely nothing. We call the village shop the Cauldron, because all kinds of unpleasant things go in and get stirred around and turned poisonous. Don't whatever you do let *anything* slip to Sal, who runs it – she knows my business better than I do.'

'All villages are a hotbed of gossip,' Justin pointed out. 'Moxham isn't exceptional. But I was born here, so perhaps I can accept it as typical of community life, in a way that others can't.'

Kate felt a little irritated by her lover's assumption that, even after ten years, she was still an outsider. In her opinion, the divisions in Moxham were still, despite the pontifications of various Tory politicians, firmly based on class. Like most of her friends, who had all sent their children to the village playgroup and the village school, who had helped to run Brownies and Cubs and coffee mornings and the Wives Group, she fell somewhere into the middle, between the inhabitants of the council estate and the wealthy, patrician residents of the imposing houses round the Green. And if Old Moxham resented her, she had never felt it. Indeed, she suspected that the tragedy that had shattered her life had made her, in the eyes of Sal and her cronies, almost 'one of us'. To the village, Justin would always be Mr Spencer; she was Kate.

'It's like everything else,' she said mildly. 'You get out what you've put in. Charlie's cottoned on to that, and it's worked. I think a lot of people here are actually rather proud of him and what he's doing. He's put Moxham on the map.'

Justin was looking extremely sceptical. She didn't want to embark on an argument, and besides, the bottle in front of him was only half empty. 'How about another round of champagne?' she suggested.

Tamsin demanded a sip and recoiled in disgust: Luke professed himself quite happy with another Coke. Marcia and Kelly, the eldest daughter of a large family whose youngest and least civilised member terrorised Megan's twins at playgroup, cleared away their plates and brought the next menu. Justin, as predictable as the clock, ordered bread-and-butter pudding, and Luke followed his example. Equally reliable, Tamsin went for the chocolate fudge cake and cream.

'What are you having?' Jem asked Kate. 'The home-made ice-cream looks good.'

'Mum makes her own,' Tamsin informed him. 'It's the best ice-cream in the world.'

'If I had to take just one food to a desert island,' Kate said, 'it would be coffee ice-cream. But for now I'll settle for the raspberry crême brulée.'

'And I'll have brown bread ice-cream,' Jem said to Kelly, who was waiting with poised pencil and a hopeful look. Ever since she'd been discovered with a boy from Brimley in a very compromising situation (and in full public view in the phone box in Weaving Lane) at the tender age of thirteen, she had done nothing to diminish her reputation, which was only now being threatened by Tanya's. Kate didn't know whether to be relieved or worried that Luke's lack of interest had kept him safe, so far. But Jem was obviously new, and different, and exciting. To judge from his expression, however, teenage girls with pelmet skirts and panda eyes were not to his taste.

Kelly sashayed off to the kitchen door with a flick of her flared black skirt. Kate heard Tamsin say to Luke in an undertone, 'You fancy her, don't you?'

'Nah,' said Luke comfortably, sipping his Coke. 'I'd have more chance with Sharon Stone.'

'In your dreams,' said Tamsin, who was constantly trying to

get a rise out of her big brother and just as constantly failing.

'Children, children,' Kate warned them mildly. She turned to Jem. 'So are you still planning to move in next week? Or have these two delinquents succeeded in frightening you off?'

'I don't think they could. Apart from anything else, the thought of home-made ice-cream is irresistible.'

'My bargain of the year,' said Kate. 'I found a machine for a couple of quid at a car boot sale, and it had never even had a plug on it. Fresh fruit ones are the best, but the rum and raisin is pretty good.' She grinned at him ruefully. 'Sorry. Why does the conversation always end up turning to food?'

'Or cars,' said Tamsin.

'Or gardening.' Jem was smiling. 'Is this one of yours?'

Kate glanced round at the burgeoning flowerbeds with modest pride. 'Yes, it is – the first one I did. It's O.K., but I think I'd design it differently now, perhaps go for a bolder, more individual look. Oh, thank you, Kelly.'

The waitress had brought their puddings, and at a whispered request from Justin went back inside, to reappear a few moments later with a bottle of a very expensive muscat. 'Here you are, sir. Enjoy your food!'

'She'll be saying "Have a nice day!" next,' Justin observed caustically. 'That's one American import I could really do without.' He poured the muscat into the three empty champagne glasses, and then emptied the jug of Jersey cream, from the herd at Home Farm, liberally over his bread-and-butter pudding.

'You mentioned ground rules,' Jem said, when everyone had almost finished, and Justin had refilled their glasses. 'Run some of them up the flagpole.'

'Ah.' Kate, caught off-guard, hesitated. 'Charlie said you didn't smoke.'

'I don't. And I don't do anything else, either, so you needn't worry about that.' Jem gave her a mischievous grin. 'I'm a pretty regular guy, really. No boring vices, unless it's watching old Hammer horror films. I've got a little portable TV, so you needn't worry about finding me curled up on your sofa with Peter Cushing.'

'That doesn't bother me,' said Kate. 'Anyway, the idea is that you're part of the household, not locked away in the annexe like Rochester's mad wife in the attic. Eat with us, walk the dog, watch telly, have civilised conversations – is that O.K.?'

'Of course it's O.K. I don't want to impose, that's all.'

'You won't be. We're looking forward to it.'

41

'So am I. I'll hire a van and bring my gear down on Wednesday, if that's all right with you. Then I'll return it to London and come back on the bike.' He smiled ruefully. 'I may have to give in and get a car. It's probably a lot more practical out here.' He turned to Justin. 'What have you got in stock?'

'What price range? I take it you wouldn't be interested in an Aston? I can do you a very nice Vantage, full history, for eighty grand.'

'Afraid not. Just a little out of my league. Up to about 15K, for the right motor.'

'Ah.' Justin was frowning. 'The TVR would have done nicely, but it's gone. I've got an MGB, or a Frog-eye Sprite – really nice condition for the year—'

Jem was shaking his head. 'Ideally, I'd like four seats and a hard top. Got a Mark 2 Jag? I've always fancied one of those.'

'And the sawn-off and stocking mask to go with it?' Kate queried.

'Bank robbers used to use them as getaway cars,' Luke explained to Tamsin, who had begun to yawn ostentatiously.

'I haven't got one, I'm afraid,' Justin was saying. 'I tend to deal in sports cars rather than saloons. But I can put you in touch with a man who does – and I happen to know he's got a good example at the moment. Original condition, never been tampered with, low mileage – sound your sort of thing?'

'Sounds ideal,' said Jem. 'But has it been pre-cherished, pre-owned, or pre-wrecked?'

'Fresh MOT and full warranty,' Justin told him, with the air of pulling a rather dubious rabbit out of a hat. 'Here's his card. He's in Bath, so it's local. You've got a bike, you say? What is it?'

'Triumph Daytona,' said Jem, and the conversation continued to deal in brake horsepower, top speeds and what Kate and her daughter, when alone, had always laughingly referred to as big boys' toys. She sipped the muscat and let her mind drift away into more natural pastures. Could she persuade Charlie to transform the courtyard garden, immediately behind the house, into a replica of an Elizabethan parterre? Or would he go with Tanya's suggestion of a Mediterranean patio, full of huge antique urns and extravagant palms? It wasn't to her own personal taste, but it might be rather fun to do, and it would match the style of the swimming pool, newly installed in the Victorian orangery, which formed one side of the quadrangle, and which featured a collection of potted trees and shrubs which wouldn't have disgraced the greenhouses at Kew.

Justin was addressing her, asking if she wanted more wine. With surprise, Kate realised that the sun had dropped behind the roof of the pub, and that Tamsin was now yawning in earnest. She shook her head apologetically. 'No, sorry, I'd love to, but it's getting late and someone needs her beauty sleep.'

'I'm *not* tired, I'm just bored to *tears*,' Tamsin hissed. 'Come *on*, Mum.'

Kate said goodbye to Jem and to Justin, who indicated with a significant nod that he would drop in on his way home. As they left the pub garden, she glanced back and saw the two men still deep in mechanical conversation. The sight gave her considerable pleasure. If Jem was going to become part of her household, even for a short time, then it was essential that he and Justin would be able to get on together. At least they seemed to have a common interest, even if it was one that she didn't share.

The children were asleep, and she was watching a comedy show on Channel 4, when Justin came in. Smith was frisking round in his usual exuberant fashion, but she sent the dog off to his basket with a sharp word, and went to embrace her lover.

'Hallo, darling,' Justin murmured against her mouth, his arms pulling her close. 'Sorry I'm late – been talking shop with your lodger. Are you tired? Want to go to bed?'

'But not to sleep,' she said, kissing him back. '*Definitely* not to sleep – yet.'

He'd obviously had a few more drinks in the pub, and his hands were everywhere, very enjoyably. She managed to persuade him upstairs before things got too serious – there was always the chance that Luke or Tamsin might come down and discover them *in flagrante* – and then, with her bedroom door firmly locked, abandoned herself to the delicious sensations which he always aroused in her.

This time was no different. Later, as she lay sated and drowsy, watching him dress, she wished that she could let him stay. But the thought of what would happen if she did – Tamsin's fearsome scowl at the breakfast table, and the atrocious behaviour that would be the inevitable consequence, probably lasting all week – had always prevented her. And Justin had never queried this condition, that she had laid down at the very beginning of their affair. *Although we're sleeping together, we've never actually* slept *together*, Kate thought, smiling.

Her lover bent over her as she lay against the pillows, and kissed her lingeringly on the lips. 'That was wonderful, darling. Good night, and see you tomorrow.'

'Good night,' Kate said sleepily, but he had already gone. She waited until she heard him lock the back door behind him, and then turned out the light.

It's going to be all right after all, she told herself, as she drifted blissfully into sleep. *He* does *care – and he gets on O.K. with Jem. All that worry for nothing.*

And her dreams were all of sunlight, and of gardens.

Chapter Four

'You jammy devil, Kate Williams! Honestly, you have all the luck!'

Kate glanced at her best friend, and shook her head wryly. 'Oh, no, I don't.'

'Well . . .' Belatedly aware of what she'd said, Megan hastily revised her words. 'I suppose not. But you have to admit, it's not every woman who manages to land not one hunk, but two!'

'I haven't *landed* Jem, as you put it – he's only the lodger, for heaven's sake!'

'Nudge, nudge.' Megan grinned at her. 'And we all know what lodgers do, don't we?'

'You've got the filthiest mind in Moxham, and that's saying something.' They were walking across the green towards the school, where already a small group of mothers were waiting for their offspring at the gate. 'Anyway,' Kate added, 'how do you know Jem's a hunk? You haven't even clapped eyes on him yet. He's only supposed to be moving in today.'

'I have my sources.'

'I know. Marcia, for a start.'

'Marcia did say something about him. Chiefly, that even though she was probably old enough to be his mother, she thought he was, and I quote, "absolutely edible". Is he?'

'He's a really nice bloke, that's all.'

Megan snorted. 'And the rest!'

'You're incorrigible, Megs, you really are. Anyone would think you were on the pull, instead of a happily married mother of three.'

'A woman can dream, can't she?' Megan Mortimer was, like Kate, in her late thirties, and, like Kate, had a ten-year-old daughter. There, however, the similarities ceased. Charlotte was the product of her first marriage, which had ended in a messy and acrimonious divorce: her second, to the long-suffering Simon, had produced the twins at present hauling eagerly on her hands, trying to steer her towards the village shop and its racks of brightly coloured, tooth-rotting sweets. And although Megan lacked entirely Kate's stylish blonde good looks, being short and rather plump, with untidy brown hair and a distinctly mumsy appearance, she had a connoisseur's eye for handsome men. Kate suspected that if any one of the hunks she fancied from afar actually came up and propositioned her, she would run away screaming. Certainly, her husband Simon looked exactly like what he was, an executive accountant.

'Please, Mum!' whined the twins, as they came up to the shop. 'Want sweeties, Mum!'

'Oh, all right,' said Megan, who always took the line of least resistance. 'I'll have to get some for Charlotte as well, though.'

Not without some misgivings, Kate followed her into the shop, the domain and fiefdom of the fearsome Sal Perks. No chance of slinking in unobserved: the bell jangled violently on its metal rod nailed to the top of the door, and the postmistress broke off her conversation at the counter. 'Afternoon, ladies!'

Kate muttered a greeting. She hadn't been into the shop for a few days, and the paper bill needed paying. She still had most of Jem's hundred pounds, but it was stashed safely in her secret hidey-hole behind the wardrobe in her bedroom, and there was only loose change in her jeans pocket.

'Come to pay the paper bill, Kate?' Sal waddled along the counter. An enormously fat woman with straggling grey hair and scarlet jowls that wobbled like a hen's wattles, she had inherited Moxham's village shop from her mother, close on forty years ago. As a consequence, she knew more about her customers probably than they did themselves. She had once told Kate, in a hoarse whisper, that the very proper elderly spinster whose excellent fruitcakes were the mainstay of the WI sales, was actually not her alleged father's daughter at all, but the product of a long-ago adulterous liaison between her mother and a commercial traveller. 'And that's why she's so sour, see?' Sal had said, her small dark eyes glittering salaciously. 'She always *knew* she was different, without knowing *why*.' And the only person in Moxham apparently ignorant of this fact was poor Miss Carey herself.

'Er – how much do I owe?' Kate asked, as the twins began demanding chocolate bars in strident tones.

Sal heaved the huge tatty book onto her counter, crowded with lottery scratchcard dispensers and piles of the *Bath Evening Chronicle*, and began flicking through it. 'Seven Silver Street.

Four pounds thirty – delivery's gone up.'

'I don't know where this myth that the inflation rate's so low can possibly come from,' Kate said cheerfully, pulling out the contents of her pockets and sorting out the relevant coins. 'Every time I go shopping something's gone up. Oh, I have got enough. Here you are, Sal.'

'Your Luke doesn't want to do a round, I suppose? One of my lads has stopped – his mum reckons he needs to work for his exams.'

'Sorry, Luke's not one of the world's early risers, I'm afraid. Anyway, he does a few hours for Mr Spencer, and I think at his age one job's enough.'

'You see Mr Spencer around, don't you?' said Sal, as if she didn't know that he and Kate had been lovers for nearly a year. 'Tell him he owes five weeks' paper money, if you'd be so good. Much more, and I'll have to think about cancelling his order.'

'I'll tell him,' said Kate. She stepped aside to make way for the twins, each clutching a small packet of sweets, and nearly bumped into Mrs Graves, the customer to whom Sal had been talking when they came in. Eileen Graves was a small, bird-like old lady with a deceptively fragile appearance, and blue eyes as hard as glass beads. She put out a papery claw to detain Kate. 'I hear you're taking in a *lodger*.'

'That's right,' said Kate, wishing that sometimes she could cast off her inherent desire to be nice to people and tell them straight to mind their own business. 'He moves in today.'

'A *foreigner* of some sort, is he?' Mrs Graves always gave distasteful words special emphasis.

'He's from London,' Kate told her, suppressing her annoyance.

'Oh, is he really, dear? Because I heard—' her voice dropped to a dramatic whisper – 'someone told me he was *black*!'

'So he is.'

'Then he *is* a foreigner,' said Mrs Graves triumphantly.

'No, he isn't,' Kate said patiently. 'He's English. Born and brought up here.'

'No, dear, he can't be.' The old woman's mouth was turned down disapprovingly. 'Not being *black*. Not one of *us*, is he, dear?'

'As far as I'm concerned,' Kate said, unable to disguise her anger, 'he's as English as I am. Come on, Megan, we'll be late for school.'

Outside, in the warm sunlight, she was surprised to find

herself actually shaking with rage. 'Narrow-minded prejudiced old cow!'

'It's that generation,' said Megan placidly. 'They've still got a colonial mind-set. She probably thinks civilisation ends at Dover. No, Holly, *don't* open the packet now or you'll drop—'

'Too late,' Kate said, as the sweets cascaded onto the path. Holly, bereft, began to howl, and after a fractional pause, James came out in sympathy. 'I'll go and get the girls,' she added, and walked briskly down the road to the school.

Charlotte and Tamsin were just emerging from their class-room, a temporary structure that had been part of the school buildings for nearly twenty years now. As ever, the contrast between them was almost painful. Charlotte was a sophisticated young lady with the beginnings of a bust and a precociously teenage taste in fashion and music. Her clothes were still neat, her rucksack was immaculate and her shoes unscuffed. Tamsin, however, was clutching books, lunchbox and bag, and carrying her bottle-green school cardigan in her teeth. There was a smear of something brown across the flat chest of her white blouse, and her dark curly hair had come loose. She looked so like Col that Kate's heart contracted with love and grief.

'Hi, Mum. I thought you were working.'

'I've taken the afternoon off – Jem's supposed to be moving in, remember? And he hasn't got a key yet, so I've got to get back quickly in case he's waiting outside.'

'Mum, can Charlotte come home for tea?' Tamsin demanded, glancing at her friend. '*Please*, Mum.'

'Sorry, no can do,' Megan said, puffing up with a bawling twin clutched in either hand. 'We've all got a dentist's appointment at four.'

'In any case,' Kate pointed out, 'I don't think Jem will want to move all his gear in with two of you underfoot, Tamsin's bad enough. And if you sulk, my lady, I'm sure Megan will take you to the dentist with her.'

As she had intended, that wiped the scowl off her daughter's face. Kate said goodbye to Megan, exchanged greetings with several other mothers while Tamsin was stuffing her belongings into her bulging rucksack, and then set off back to Mermaid's Cottage, with more than a twinge of pleasurable anticipation.

There was a large blue van parked outside the garage, with Self-drive Hire and a London phone number painted on its sides. Music drifted softly from the open windows, and when Kate walked round to the cab she saw Jem sitting sideways in the driver's seat with his feet up, reading *Q*. *Marcia's right*, she thought, studying the width of his shoulders and the lively intelligence in his face. *He's absolutely edible*.

'Hi,' she said. 'Sorry – have you been waiting long?'

He grinned down at her through the fringe of dreadlocks. 'Hi, Kate. No, only about five minutes. It took a lot more time than I thought it would to load everything up. I just hope there's room for it all.'

'Well, there's always the garage,' said Kate. 'Or the Court. Would you like a cup of tea first, or shall we get going?'

'*We*, white woman?'

'Well, you didn't assume I was going to stand idly by and watch you work up a sweat, did you?' Kate demanded. 'Oh, you did. Tough. With three of us to do the carrying, we'll soon get it done.'

'You haven't seen how much there is,' said Jem, unlocking the back doors with a flourish. 'But that's all my worldly goods – the big stuff's been sold.'

Trying, sometimes in vain, to avoid falling over the frisking dog, Kate and Tamsin helped Jem to carry the contents of the van through the house to the annexe. Most of his possessions seemed to be connected with music: hundreds of CDs, albums, tapes and singles; a peculiarly shaped case which must contain the saxophone; volumes of music magazines going back several years; and a bag of books with *The Motown Story* on top. Soon it was impossible to see the carpet for stacked boxes, an expensive hi-fi system stood on top of the chest of drawers, three suitcases, a couple of holdalls and a rucksack cluttered the bed, and the van was empty save for two packing cases.

'Assorted knick-knacks, a couple of rugs, that sort of thing,' Jem told her. 'I'm going to leave them at the Court.'

'You travel light,' Kate said, gazing round at his possessions. 'It *looks* a lot, but it isn't really.'

'Not much to show for thirty-four misspent years. I thought I'd never manage to sort it all, but in the end it was surprisingly easy to throw stuff out. Fresh start, pastures new, a good incentive.'

'Not to mention the prospect of squeezing it all into a rather small room.' Kate glanced at Tamsin, who had flopped into the chair, groaning ostentatiously. 'How about that cuppa?'

They sat on the patio under the welcome shade of the walnut tree, with the tea brewing contentedly inside her biggest pot, the Portmeirion one that Col had bought for her one Christmas, and a pile of home-made flapjacks in front of them. Jem leaned back in his chair and gave an appreciative sigh. 'If this is a sample of country life, I'm all for it.'

Above them, a wood pigeon had begun its monotonous, strangely soothing croon, and Tamsin chimed in. 'It's no *good*, Greyling, can't *catch* me, Greyling!'

'Greyling is one of the cats,' Kate explained, seeing Jem's puzzled look. 'She's a mighty hunter, and particularly fond of pigeons, so we always imagine that they're sitting up there and taunting her.'

'She likes racing pigeon best,' Tamsin said. 'Last summer she had three of them, one after the other – just left the feet and feathers. We had to get the birds' number off the rings and call the owners.'

'Don't worry, she doesn't leave the remains in the house,' Kate added kindly. 'She's learnt not to bring her prey indoors! If she does, for some strange reason there's a lot of shouting and it gets taken away from her. So she generally eats *most* of it outside the back door. If you go out first thing in the morning, be careful.'

'She left a mouse in Mum's wellies, once,' Tamsin added.

'Still all for the country life?' said Kate, grinning at Jem's face, which was a picture of comically exaggerated horror. 'A few days in this madhouse will soon cure you of ideas like that.'

'It sounds like a scene from a video nasty,' said Jem. 'Is that Greyling?'

A bright ginger cat was peering nervously round the wall. At once Smith, who had been lying under the table, bounced up with a joyful bark and launched himself in pursuit. The cat shot across the lawn and leapt into the nearest apple tree. He scrabbled up through the branches until he could go no further, and stood precariously balanced, each large peach-coloured paw on a separate twig, and his tail bristling with outrage while the dog pranced around below.

'No, that's her son, who's a complete bumbling idiot,' said Kate. 'Smith wouldn't dare chase Greyling – she'd turn and give him a quick right and left across the nose. But Sevvy is so thick he keeps forgetting how to get through the cat-flap. He can barely catch his own tail, let alone a mouse. And when he *did* manage to catch a mouse, once, his own mother mugged him for it as he was proudly carrying it up the garden path.'

Jem laughed. 'You're having me on.'

'No, she isn't – I *saw* her do it,' Tamsin assured him. 'And another time, he brought a mouse in and it was absolutely flat – he'd found it in the road and tried to pretend he'd caught it.'

'That doesn't sound as though he's stupid; just a kid with a domineering mother who's in need of encouragement.'

'I know the feeling,' Kate said wryly. 'But Sevvy's definitely a few whiskers short of a set.'

'Sevvy?'

'Nothing to do with Spanish golfers – it's short for Seville.'

'It could have been worse,' Jem remarked. 'You could have called him Navel, or Blood.'

'Don't laugh so much, Tamsin,' said Kate, as her daughter cackled raucously. 'You'll wake the dead. See what I mean about this being a madhouse?'

'So what if it is? I think I'm going to enjoy it here,' said Jem, and gave her the benefit of his heart-stopping smile.

He left soon after that, with a key to the front door because, as Kate pointed out, if he had to unload the packing cases at the Court, take the van back to London, pick up his bike and ride it down, he probably wouldn't arrive until after everyone had gone to bed. She wondered what he looked like in motorbike leathers, and ruthlessly suppressed her curiosity. Much more of this, and she'd be worse than Megan.

In fact, she didn't have to wonder. It was only half past ten when she heard the unmistakeable, throaty roar of what Luke called 'a *real* bike' coming up the lane and snarling to a halt outside. At once, Smith leapt up from his usual place, draped over her feet. Before he could indulge in his unique style of welcome, however, Kate grabbed his collar and dragged him into the kitchen, praying that he wouldn't wake the children, by now hopefully asleep.

She opened the front door just as Jem was about to put the key in the lock. He had his helmet under one arm, and even in the limited light in the porch, he did indeed look superb. The black and red all-in-one leather suit set off his long, lithe body to very considerable advantage, and Kate gave herself a mental rap over the knuckles. *Shameless woman*, she thought. *You're with Justin, remember? Fancying the lodger isn't allowed.*

'You shouldn't have stayed up,' Jem said, extracting himself from the leathers with what looked like considerable difficulty, while Kate firmly resisted the temptation to offer a helping hand.

'I didn't, I was watching something on the box. Do you want anything? Beer, wine, a nightcap?'

'I'd rather have something hot, if it's not too much trouble.

Tea, or chocolate if you have it. Riding along the motorway at eighty-five is perishing cold, even in May. Where shall I put these?' he added, indicating his leathers and the pair of long, black, buckled motorbike boots.

'With the coats, for now,' said Kate. 'Are you ready? Smith's in the kitchen, and I don't want to make too much noise down here in case I wake the kids up.'

Once the dog had been put outside for his late-night wander in the garden, and two steaming mugs of instant chocolate had been poured, they went back to the comfort of the sitting room. Jem flopped down in the armchair with a sigh of relief. 'There's no doubt about it, I'm getting too old for bikes. The discomfort used to be just about balanced by the convenience – it's a whole lot easier to weave through the jams on two wheels. But even so it was no joke last winter. You could have lifted me off still frozen in position, some mornings. So I'm definitely going to buy a car.'

'The one that Justin was talking about?'

'Possibly, though I haven't got round to ringing the number he gave me yet.' He took a sip of chocolate and added, with a quick look at Kate, 'Sorry if I'm being nosy—'

'Don't worry, everyone round here is, and I'm as bad as the rest. It goes with village life.'

'I take it you and Justin are an item?'

Kate felt herself blushing. 'Yes. Yes, we are.'

'He's a nice guy. Very helpful about the cars. Knowledgeable, too, as far as I could tell – I'm no expert, I just like driving them. Most of what goes on under the bonnet is foreign territory.'

'Justin's not very interested in the mechanical side, either. He tunes and tinkers, but he's got a couple of guys who come out from Chippenham to do the serious stuff like engine rebuilds. Luke's dying to help them, but so far he's only been allowed to do the simple things. Which makes sense, when some of the cars are worth thousands and thousands, but I think he's finding it a bit frustrating. He doesn't tell me a lot, though. He's quiet, is Luke, and usually very placid. He gets that from Col. God knows where Tamsin's moods came from. She's just like Col to look at, but nothing like either of us in temperament.'

'I like her, though. I like all of you – even the dog.'

'Just as well, if we're going to be living together for three months,' said Kate lightly. She hesitated, wondering whether to tell him about her encounter with the odious Mrs Graves, and decided against it. She'd already warned him about the prejudice he was likely to meet, and she had no doubt that he would cope with it more than adequately. And this moment was so comfortable, so pleasant, that she didn't want to spoil it.

She added, 'Are you starting work tomorrow? What about unpacking?'

'Oh, that's not urgent. The studios are, though. Charlie's beginning to jump up and down – he's afraid they won't be finished in time. You probably won't see much of me for the next few days, while I get everything sorted and kick ass.'

'I can't imagine you doing that.'

'Believe me, I can. This mild-mannered exterior conceals a ferocious heart. If necessary, ass will be kicked.'

The antique brass clock on the mantelpiece began to announce that it was now eleven o'clock. Jem finished his chocolate. 'If you don't mind, I'm off to bed. What time do you get up in the morning?'

'Tamsin's usually awake by seven, I give Luke a call half an hour later, and we have breakfast around eight. Do you want to be earlier than that?'

'Eight's fine. See you tomorrow. Sleep well!' He paused at the door, smiling. 'Thanks for everything, Kate.'

'All part of the service to our guests, sir,' she said, with mock humility, and had the satisfaction of making him laugh.

Later, she lay in bed, thinking of Justin. He'd mentioned something about having to see someone in London today. She had no idea what the meeting was about: Justin never involved her in his business affairs, and to be honest she hadn't been interested. Her own finances were difficult enough to manage, without becoming concerned in her lover's as well. But a little worm was beginning to niggle away at her mind. Justin had become increasingly moody over the past few weeks, and distracted. She had noticed him staring into space several times, with an expression that on someone less self-assured might be interpreted as anxious. In the end, she'd tried a little gentle probing, the last time she'd seen him, two days ago. When questioned, Justin usually told her not to bother her lovely head about such boring things. That was irritating enough. This time, however, he'd told her, in no uncertain terms, to mind her own business. He'd apologised afterwards, and they had made it up, in time-honoured fashion, in bed, but the memory still disturbed her. She loved him, she trusted him, she *knew* him – or she had thought that she did. It was like feeling quagmire beneath her feet, when she had expected solid ground. And the sense of bewilderment, even of loss, was sharp and hurtful.

Of course he's right really, she told herself. *It* isn't *any of my business. But if he loves me, he ought to share his worries with me, surely? Let me in, just a little? I know I couldn't give him any practical help, but I make a good shoulder to cry on.*

Perhaps she should approach him more subtly, let him know that she was there if he needed her. *But I always* am *here for him*, Kate thought ruefully. *That's half the problem. He probably takes me for granted. He even took Jem in his stride, quite happily – no trace of jealousy at all. And I'm still not sure if that's a bad sign, or a good one.*

She smiled into the dark. It was very strange, to think of her lodger sleeping in the room below hers, amidst the piles of boxes and bags. They'd have to alter their slapdash habits slightly, of course – no more undressed Sunday mornings, no more leaving the bathroom door open, no more knickers festooning the radiators. But that didn't matter. For three months, and a hundred pounds a week, and the interest and excitement and sheer fun that she suspected Jem would bring to their household, it was more than worth it.

Chapter Five

Kate was right, Jem thought, as he left Mermaid's Cottage for his first morning at Charlie's studios. Moxham was not in the least like Camden. For a start, the air was clear, rain-washed by a heavy overnight shower, and entirely free from traffic fumes. True, a distinctly agricultural aroma was wafting past his nose, and he could hear the distant hum of cars on the main road, but close at hand the only sounds were of birdsong, sweet and joyful. Despite the breeze, and the puddles on the road, there were plenty of blue patches in amongst the high white clouds, and as he began to jog up Silver Street towards the centre of the village, the sun came out.

He made a habit of running at least once a day, but the half mile or so through Moxham to the Court would not be enough to maintain his present level of fitness. He'd have to ask Kate if he could borrow a map and work out a longer route for the evenings. And perhaps, come the winter, there'd be a local football or rugger team he could join. He'd always enjoyed sport, and the running was a good way of keeping his body in training trim.

Come the winter . . . Come the winter, he'd be back in London, glad of the warmth and bright lights and familiarity of city life. The country in summer was fine. By November, the cold and rain and long dark nights would probably be doing his head in.

He grinned to himself as he came to the junction with Corsham Lane. It was ridiculous to imagine that he, a city boy, could possibly feel at home in these very different surroundings. And yet he did. He liked the quiet. He liked the fact that there was grass everywhere. He even quite liked the whiff of what Kate called, in a mock Wiltshire accent, 'fer'loizer'. And above all, he liked the Williams family, their air of slightly-out-of-control disorder, their cheerful friendliness, the way he had been welcomed and assimilated into their household without formality or

55

fuss. Even the chaos at breakfast that morning – 'It must be ready,' Tamsin had told him, 'I can hear Mum scraping the toast' – had been a welcome change from the silence in the empty London flat, or the chilly precision with which he and Caroline had conducted their lives together.

How could I ever have thought it would last? Jem asked himself in bewilderment. *We're total opposites, in every way.* And once the initial drama of their mutual passion had inevitably subsided, they had been left with no points of contact at all.

Well, at least they had both realised it in time, and the separation had left them still on friendly terms. He didn't regret their love, brief though it had been, but he did regret marrying her. It had forced the relationship to continue long after it had died a natural death, and made the process of splitting up more complicated and hurtful than it need have been. He suspected, though, that his pride, and hers, had been damaged more than anything else. Even his parents, so eager to see him settled with a nice girl, had not been too disappointed, or surprised, when he'd told them that he was getting divorced. And if he was in Wiltshire for the next few months, he wouldn't have to put up with the endless stream of suitable young women that his mother, and Maia, would certainly want to push in his direction.

He was still smiling, lost in thought, as he came sprinting round the corner by the Green and almost cannoned slap into someone coming the other way.

It was an old lady, with white hair curling out underneath a soft, shapeless bottle-green velour hat, and a little brown terrier on a lead. She staggered back, and Jem instinctively put out a hand to stop her falling over.

The old lady didn't seem to want his assistance. 'Let go of me!' she shrieked, and swung her handbag at him, while the dog rushed forward, yapping frantically, and tried to take a piece out of his trainers.

'Sorry?' said Jem, astonished. He stepped back, trying to avoid the malicious attentions of the terrier, and his assailant advanced, swinging the handbag again. 'Go away, you thieving mugger! You're not having my pension!'

'I don't want your pension,' Jem said, dodging hastily out of her reach. 'I'm sorry I nearly bumped into you – could you call your dog off, please?'

'Go on, Benjy, bite him!' the old lady shouted, as the little dog worked itself into a frothing frenzy, snarling and choking at the end of the lead in an effort to reach its victim.

'Look,' Jem said, loudly and clearly, 'please can you get this straight, lady? I'm *not* a mugger, I'm *not* after your handbag, I was just jogging round to the Court and I nearly bumped into you. O.K.? That's all. I'm sorry if I frightened you, but it wasn't intended. Now if you'll let me past I'll be on my way.'

Two faded but still fierce grey eyes stared up at him in hostile disbelief. 'What do you mean? Of course you're a mugger!'

'No,' said Jem, with what he considered to be commendable patience. 'No, I'm not.'

'Well, what do you expect me to think, when one of *your* sort as good as sends me flying—'

At this point the dog, sensing that its owner's hold on the lead had slackened, wrenched it out of her hand with a sudden jerk and hurled itself at Jem. It was fortunate that it sank its teeth into one of the trainers, rather than the ankle above them: and also fortunate that the postman, who had just pulled up in his van, had the presence of mind to grab the lead and haul the dog off.

There followed a loud and rather confusing session with everyone talking at once. The old lady seemed to have taken refuge in righteous indignation ('Well, how was I to know any different, young man?'), while Jem and the postman made strenuous efforts to restrain the dog, which was exhibiting a snarling ferocity that would have done credit to an animal twenty times its size.

Eventually, the old lady was persuaded to continue on her way, still muttering to herself, and Jem, grinning, held out his hand to his rescuer. 'Thanks. I probably owe my foot to you, if not my life.'

'If I had my way, I'd throttle that little mutt with its own lead,' said the postman, who was young, balding and bearded, with a name-badge that said 'Matt'. 'It's nearly had me for breakfast an' all, more times than I've had hot dinners. You're Charlie Dobson's new bloke, aren't you? Lodging down at Mermaid's Cottage?'

'Blimey,' said Jem, startled. 'How did you know?'

'Word travels quick around here.'

'I wish it'd got round to her,' Jem said, with a rueful glance at the old lady, who was dragging the still snarling Benjy towards the post office, and another down at his trainer, now exhibiting the toothmarks of a considerable mauling.

'Lucky that wasn't your foot, mate. It had a paper boy a couple of months ago, on a bike – grabbed his ankle and wouldn't let go. Sank its teeth in right down to the bone, kid had to go to hospital. But when the police went round, you should have heard her: "My poor little doggie wouldn't do a thing like that," she was going, "not my poor little Benjy, he wouldn't hurt a fly, it's just that he doesn't like trousers, and he must have bitten the boy's leg by mistake!" So they let her off. And she's an old tartar and all, is Mrs Starling – my brother's little girl reckons she's a witch. Well, see you round, Mr Forrester.' He dived back into the van and emerged with two letters in his hand. 'Almost forgot – these are for you. Saves a bit of trouble giving them to you now instead of later, eh? Cheers, mate. Bye!'

Jem thanked him again, and watched in some bemusement as his benefactor marched whistling up the path of the cottage beside them. Then, keeping a good watch out for any more ferocious dogs and homicidal old ladies, he continued his run to Moxham Court.

As he jogged up the drive, a snappy little soft-top sports car, sparkling new, swept towards him. He moved to one side to let it past, and instead it stopped with a jerk, spraying him with gravel. The passenger window slid down with a gentle hum, and a woman's voice said cheerfully, 'Wotcher, Jem! Run all the way from Camden?'

'I'm planning to do it every day,' he said, grinning. Tanya was always good for a laugh, and now she threw her head back and gave a raucous shriek. 'Oh, that's a good one, that is! Must tell Charlie that. This your first day? Bit early, aren't you?'

'I always give good value for money,' said Jem. 'Anyway, I could say the same about you. I thought you never got out of bed until ten.'

'And wouldn't you like to find out!' said Tanya, with a flirtatious glance. She looked stunning, her thick mane of blond hair flowing down her back in careful disorder, her make-up immaculate and her talons painted a fashionable deep red. She was wearing a long narrow skirt, split to the thigh and belted to accentuate her tiny waist, and a very tight cashmere jumper that, he couldn't help noticing, emphasised every generous inch of her figure. 'Well, must be off, got a massage booked at the health club at half nine. See you later, eh? Ta-ra!'

Caroline had looked a little like Tanya, but Caroline's sexiness had been cool and understated. He'd long ago come to the conclusion that he preferred women who weren't too obvious, who didn't push it at him. Tanya was fun, amusing, the life and soul of any gathering, but he didn't fancy her.

And just as well I don't, he thought, as her car turned out of the gate with a squeal of abused tyres. *The complications wouldn't bear thinking about.*

Charlie was standing outside the entrance to the stable court-yard, talking to a big man in the incongruous combination of posh suit and hard hat, whom Jem guessed, correctly, to be the council's building inspector. A look of some relief came over his employer's face as Jem ran up. 'Am I glad to see you! Look, could you explain to Mr Baldwin here about the soundproofing? He's giving me a hard time and I don't know nothing about it.'

Thanks for dropping me in it before I've even started the job, Jem thought. But he'd had years of practice being soothing and diplomatic. 'I'm your man,' he said. 'Jem Forrester, project manager. If you come with me, I'll tell you what we're doing.'

And that was only the start of it. Once Mr Baldwin had gone away, his doubts eased and his questions answered, there were the other guys on the team to meet, the work already done to inspect, the deficiencies in the wood supplies to sort out, and a multitude of other jobs heaped on his plate. The men he would supervise seemed a pleasant enough bunch, as yet indistinguish-able in voice and personality, except for Martin, who was also black, and plainly from Cardiff rather than Wiltshire. The management aspect of the job had worried Jem most: he had never actually been in charge of a team before. But he knew that he was good at handling people, and he relished a challenge.

And challenge, he thought, looking round at the desolate remains of what had once been very grand stables, was certainly the right word. It seemed impossible that in less than four months the sagging ceilings, thickets of cobwebs and precarious plaster would be transformed into the state-of-the-art studios that he, and Charlie, had specified. But it could be done: it *would* be done, and he would ensure that it was, because his reputation and his future career, not to mention his own pride and self-respect, depended on it.

He had planned to bring sandwiches, but Kate had told him that he would be expected to have lunch at the Court. 'Charlie's very hospitable, isn't he? Even if he and Tanya aren't around, there's always a nice little buffet laid out in the breakfast room.'

'I don't suppose it's prepared by Tanya's own fair hands, is it?'

'Of course not, they've got a very good cook-housekeeper, who lives in the staff cottage and comes in every day. Tanya freely admits she's incapable even of boiling an egg.'

'She probably has other talents,' Jem had said, grinning.

He had to walk right round the house to find the side

entrance. It was a big place, and although he'd been here several times now, he was still getting the geography confused. He looked with interest at the gardens, which were showing signs of all Kate's hard work. In a few years, he could imagine it looking fabulous, especially the charming sunken garden at the side of the house. But the grass sloping down to the little ornamental lake in front of the Court was rough and unkempt, despite recent mowing, and all the shrubs had been ruthlessly pruned. The dolphins and cherubs on the fountain in the round pond gazed forlornly down at the absence of water. The stone lion by the steps was covered in moss and lichen, and mourning the loss of an ear. And the plants in the flowerbeds still had all their labels on, fresh and white against the bare, newly turned soil.

He walked in through the side entrance, which was open. The passage in front of him led to the main part of the house, and the new swimming pool was, if he remembered correctly, just through to the left. And the breakfast room, according to Kate, was here on his right.

It was a pleasant, stone-walled room in what was probably the oldest part of the house. There was a long table, laid for five, a sideboard laden with enough bread, cold meats and bowls of salad to fuel a sizeable party, and an array of glasses, bottles and jugs on a tray. The kitchen lay beyond, through an archway, and a small, middle-aged woman who must be the cook was bustling around with an apron on.

'Jem, me old mate! How'd you get on? Sent that Baldwin geezer off with a smile on his face, anyway.' As ever, Charlie was effusive in his welcome, the cockney accent almost stagily overdone. 'You know Kate, of course.' He chuckled.

'We have met,' said Kate, grinning at Jem. 'Over a couple of slices of burnt toast, wasn't it?'

'You want to get your money back, mate,' Charlie said, with mock indignation. 'That hotel's obviously not much cop.'

'Oh, I think it'll do me fine,' Jem told him, with a wink at Kate. 'This is quite a spread, isn't it? Is it like this every day?'

'I always do a good table,' said the cook, carrying in a tray of pickles and chutneys. 'Now don't let's stand there looking at it, get outside it.'

'Jem, this is Mrs Wallis,' Charlie said, belatedly performing the necessary introductions. 'Our miracle-worker, she is. You ain't lived till you've had her steak-and-kidney pie. Forget that foreign muck all the trendies are so keen on – this is *real* food.'

Mrs Wallis, who fortunately seemed to have a sense of

humour, rolled her eyes up to heaven. 'He won't let me even cook a curry,' she said plaintively. 'And I do a lovely korma, too – not too spicy, lots of cream and saffron, but he won't hear of it. Is Mrs Dobson back yet, sir?'

'She always calls me sir,' said Charlie to Jem behind his hand. 'I can't stop her doing it. I keep telling her I ain't some bloody feudal squire, but she don't take a blind bit of notice.' He removed the hand, ignoring Mrs Wallis's look of exasperation, and continued, grinning, 'Yes, she is, but she's gone for a quick dip. She'll be along in a moment, don't bother to wait around, just grab what you want and find yourselves a pew. We don't stand on no ceremony here,' he added unnecessarily to Jem. 'Those what don't ask or don't take, don't get.'

'Here I am!' Tanya cried, breezing in surrounded by a thick cloud of heavy perfume. Her hair was wet and loosely plaited, and she wore a thin, brilliantly-coloured silk sarong, with almost certainly nothing underneath. 'Gawd, Sylv, that looks the business. I'm starving, I could eat a whole horse and then some – it really takes it out of you, this exercise lark.' She turned to Kate. 'But it means I *can* eat a horse, see, and not put any on. If I didn't have me daily swim and me session at the gym twice a week, I'd look like a house.'

'Never, darling,' said Charlie, patting his wife fondly on the bottom. 'And even if you did, I'd still think you was gorgeous.'

'Nah!' Tanya flashed her wonderful smile at him, including Jem almost as an afterthought. 'I know you – you'd be off after some tart young enough to be your granddaughter. I'll have some of that ham, Sylv, and a nice big helping of salami, thanks.'

The long-suffering Mrs Wallis carved and cut to order, and then sat down with them. For a while there was a silence dedicated to Wiltshire ham and lush young green salads picked, as Charlie had proudly informed them, that very morning from the walled garden.

'Seems you've made your mark already,' Tanya said to Jem, who was sitting opposite her. 'Terrorising innocent old ladies, from what I hear. What you bin up to, eh?'

'Innocent old ladies? Do you mean Mrs Starling and her hound from hell?'

'The awful Benjy,' Kate said. 'He nearly had a piece out of me, once, and she had the gall to tell me that he wasn't trying to bite me, he'd just got his teeth caught in my jeans. So what happened?'

In entertaining detail, Jem described his encounter earlier that morning. 'She took one look at me and assumed I was about to nick her handbag. I barely escaped with my life.'

'I'm glad you can laugh about it,' Kate said with feeling. 'If it'd been me, I'd have been livid. Was it because you're black?'

'Well, let's put it this way, I don't suppose a near miss with Luke would have achieved the same reaction. How did you hear about it?' he asked Tanya.

'Sal, of course. I popped in there to get the *Sun* and she beckoned me over – you know how she does.' Tanya's voice changed to a passable imitation of the shopkeeper's salacious whisper. ' "You'll never guess what that Coloured Gentleman's gone and done – not being horrible, but he scared the life out of poor Doris Starling this morning".'

'That's what Sal always says,' Kate added. 'All the juiciest pieces of gossip are announced by "not being horrible, *but . . .*" '

'Trouble is,' Charlie said, 'they're not used to seeing blokes like you round here. Give 'em time and most of 'em will be O.K. In fact, I'll lay you odds on what'll happen next. Colonel What's-his-face will collar you in the pub and ask you to join the cricket team. He's bound to think you're a demon bowler.'

'And are you?' Kate enquired.

Jem shook his head, grinning. 'No, but I do play, when I get the chance. There wasn't much call for it in Camden, so I'm seriously out of practice. I keep wicket, and bat a bit.'

'Oh, well, you'll be in there then,' said Charlie. 'The Colonel's even asked me, shows how desperate he is, I don't know me silly mid-off from me long stop.'

'Keith Parker will be after you for the football team an' all,' Tanya added. 'If you're staying that long, of course.'

'Depends whether I get the job done on time or not,' Jem said. 'After that, it depends on Charlie. And on whether I can convince the good residents of Moxham that I'm not a mugger or a drug dealer.'

'And you'll have a hard time doing that,' said Charlie darkly. 'You should hear what they say about me, though I ain't exactly whiter than white.'

'My point exactly,' said Jem, and laughed.

It had been a pleasant introduction to his new job, he decided later, saying goodbye to the building team as they all finished work at half past five. There was a great deal to do, and he was beginning to think that three months was hardly long enough for half of it, but he always relished a challenge, and he'd had life too easy lately. He liked to work hard and play hard, and being under pressure would shake him up and do him good.

Kate was wheeling her bike down the drive in front of him. He ran faster to catch her up, and she turned, smiling in welcome, at the sound of his feet. 'Hi. What was your first day like?'

'Terrifying! No, it was O.K., but I'm just beginning to realise what I've let myself in for. I think I'll enjoy it, though. Charlie's a good bloke to work for. He's fair, and he's not the type to interfere too much – as long as he thinks I'll come up with the goods at the end of the day, he's quite happy to let me get on with it.'

'I know. I'm really glad he's moved here. Apart from the benefit to me, I think he's done Moxham generally a lot of good. It tends to be much too complacent and cosy and middle-class – someone like Charlie is a breath of fresh air. And you, of course – an emissary from the *real* world.' She grinned at him. 'If you want to run, go ahead. The chain's come off my bike, *again*, so I'll have to wheel it.'

'I think I'll walk round with you, if you don't mind. You can protect me from Mrs Starling's handbag!'

As they walked towards the centre of the village, a black BMW swished past, hooting. Kate raised a hand in reply. 'That's my friend Megan's husband, Simon. They live just up here, in the big new house next to the Old Vicarage. Her daughter Charlotte is friends with Tamsin. When Jayde's home for the holidays, they go round in a threesome, and a more ill-assorted lot you can't imagine. Have you met Jayde?'

'As a little girl, yes, but not recently.'

'It's funny, really, you'd think with Tanya for a mother she'd be very sophisticated and heavily into clothes and all that sort of thing, but not a bit of it. I suspect Tanya's rather disappointed in her.'

'Charlie adores her, though.'

'Yes, and she's very bright, and artistic – and horse-mad. When she hasn't got her nose in a book, she loves messing about in stables and she always seems to wear muddy jeans. She's much more like Tamsin than Charlotte – a real old-fashioned girl.'

'And like you,' said Jem.

Kate laughed ruefully. 'Not to hear my mother! But then she'd make the Queen seem bad-mannered. This is Megan's house – I've got to stop and pick up Tamsin. Do you want to come in and meet them, or go on?'

'I'll come in,' said Jem, and followed her through the gate.

Megan's Simon was an executive with a Bath firm of accountants, and money was not a problem. Little Orchard, recently built in real stone on part of the Old Vicarage's unnecessarily large garden, had five bedrooms, two bathrooms, a sumptuous kitchen and garaging for three cars. Kate knocked on the front door, which was answered by Megan, her eager dark eyes covertly assessing every detail of Jem's rather dusty and dishevelled appearance. 'I thought it must be you – come in, the girls are upstairs, you can hear them.'

Two youthfully tuneless voices were singing along to Hunkydory's latest. Kate chuckled. 'Well, *they'll* never make a fortune in the music business.'

'I wouldn't be so sure,' Jem said darkly.

'So this is your lodger?' Megan beamed at him. 'Hallo, I'm Megan Mortimer. Cup of tea?'

'Now that's an offer I never refuse,' said Jem, and they followed her into the kitchen, where Simon, a tall dark man with glasses and the well-satisfied look of the highly paid, was pouring boiling water into a very large teapot.

'Let's take it out onto the patio,' Megan said, with a wink at Kate. 'The afternoon's too nice to sit indoors.'

As they sat down, the brisk snipping of shears could be heard on the other side of the beech hedge which separated the house from the Old Vicarage next door. Jem saw the two women exchange glances, and waited expectantly. Sure enough, the clipping stopped, and a very English voice said commandingly, 'Is that you, Kate?'

'Hallo, Colonel.' His landlady rose to her feet and moved closer to the hedge. 'How are you?'

'Not so bad, not so bad, though this damn leg's giving me gip.' Jem caught a glimpse of a shiny bald head through the leaves. 'I say, is that Charlie Dobson's new chappie?'

'He's been lifted whole from one of those RAF war films,' Megan whispered. 'Every time I hear him I feel like saluting and keeping a stiff upper lip.'

'Yes, this is Jem Forrester,' Kate said. 'He's lodging with us for the summer.'

'Splendid, splendid. D'you think I could have a word?'

Suppressing a wayward desire to laugh, Jem went over to join Kate. Close to, the Colonel proved to be a tall, rather stooping old man, with a fringe of bristly white hair around his bald and burnished crown, and a nose of truly valiant proportions. 'Delighted to meet you,' he said, through several inches of fresh green hedge. 'I hope you don't mind me asking, but I'm in a bit of a stew, and you may be able to help out. Play cricket, do you?'

Kate's obliquely eloquent glance nearly ruined everything, but Jem kept his cool with an effort. 'Not really.'

'Come on, old chap, none of this false modesty, you people all play bloody well – much better than our lot, eh? Ha ha.' Colonel Sims laughed cheerfully. 'Thing is, you see, we're a bit short and there's a needle match coming up on Saturday – Bank Holiday weekend, Moxham versus Brimley, bit of a local derby, eh? We could do with a good spinner to shake them up a bit.'

'I'm afraid I'm not a bowler,' Jem said apologetically.

'Not a bowler? Dear me, dear me, and I thought you chaps could all send the stumps flying, ha ha. But you do play?'

'I do, but not very well. Middle order bat, a spot of wicket-keeping.' To his alarm, Jem heard himself beginning to mimic the Colonel's well-bred tones, and hastily reverted to his normal, London-flavoured accent.

'Wickety, eh? Hmm. Sounds useful, very useful. Could you turn out for us on Saturday?'

'I haven't got any kit – not even a bat.'

'Minor detail, *minor* detail, old chap. We can lend you some whites. In fact, you could have my own – don't play now, of course, with this leg, but the stuff's all still there in a cupboard somewhere, Peggy will know where it is.' He beamed at Jem. 'Well, I must say that's very kind of you. Got us out of a hole, eh? I'll have it sent round before the day. Well, must be getting on. See you on Saturday.'

'I haven't played for at least five years,' said Jem, flopping back onto his chair. 'I hope he's not expecting much.'

'Only Gary Sobers and Viv Richards rolled into one exciting, match-winning package,' said Kate, grinning at him. 'Well, I did warn you. Do you actually *want* to play?'

'I'll make a total fool of myself, but I've had plenty of practice at that,' Jem said, taking a generous swig of reviving tea. 'No, I don't mind, as long as they don't. How many feathers am I going to ruffle, do you think? Is there going to be some gallant old-timer who'll take umbrage because I've ousted him from the team?'

'I shouldn't think so,' said Simon. 'He always has trouble making up the numbers. I used to be the opening bat, before someone sent a bumper down too fast.'

'Christ,' Jem said. 'Serious damage?'

'Broke his finger,' Megan informed him. 'It's a dangerous

game, cricket, and round here you're a wimp if you wear a box, let alone a proper helmet.'

'And apparently Brimley have a bloke playing for them who used to bowl for Gloucestershire,' Kate added. 'If I were you, I'd get a diplomatic bout of the 'flu on Friday evening.'

'No, I won't,' Jem said, smiling. 'I told you, I like a challenge. And if I'm out for a duck, well, the Colonel can't say I didn't tell him.'

Chapter Six

Perhaps fortunately, it poured with rain that Saturday, and the cricket match was cancelled. But it did mean that the Williams family, and their lodger, were actually on the premises when a surprise visitor arrived on the doorstep, just before lunch.

Kate was in the kitchen, liquidising carrot and coriander soup. Usually she'd given up cooking what she always thought of as winter food by April, let alone the last week in May, but it was so miserable outside that she had let herself be persuaded by Tamsin, who had an unlikely passion for carrots.

'That must mean you were a donkey in a previous life,' Luke had suggested, and had earned himself a furious rebuke and a thrown cushion for his pains. Not surprisingly, he'd taken himself off to Justin's, and had told his mother that he might not be back for lunch. Kate had resisted the temptation to ask for a report on her lover's behaviour. She'd hardly seen him all week, and she hadn't dared to ask him how the mysterious meeting in London had gone.

If she was truly honest with herself, though, she was almost relieved that he'd kept out of the way during Jem's first few days at Mermaid's Cottage. She was beginning to realise that having an adult male lodger on the premises might indeed cramp their style, just a little. It had been bad enough having to think about the children when entertaining Justin in her bed, without worrying about whether Jem was lying awake in the room below hers, listening to squeaking bedsprings and muffled sounds of passion.

Don't be silly, she told herself sternly, as she poured the scalding orange liquid back into the saucepan, while trying to avoid third-degree burns. *We're all adults, and Jem knows the score. I shouldn't feel embarrassed about it, and neither should he.*

'That smells wonderful,' said her lodger, entering from the dining room. 'Funny how doing nothing makes you ravenous, isn't it?'

'You haven't been doing nothing, you've been unpacking,' Kate pointed out, gingerly lifting a wooden spoon to her lips.

'Believe me, compared to work at the Court, this counts as nothing. Trouble is, I keep stopping to read bits of book, or put on tracks I haven't heard for years.'

'You sound as bad as me. Col used to tease me unmercifully because I was always reading the newspapers on the floor when I was supposed to be decorating. Have a taste? I think it could do with a bit more salt.'

'Hmm.' Jem paused consideringly, and then swallowed. 'Yes, you're right. Just a tad.'

'Luke says that. What *is* a tad?'

'Something very small and to do with computers, I think.'

'I thought you were into computers.'

'Only when they coincide with work. I'm not an anorak Internet surfer. We did have a PC in the flat, but it was Caroline's.'

The doorbell rang, making Kate jump, and at once Smith leapt up from his basket. She grabbed him before he could perform his usual welcome, and Jem said, 'I'll answer it.'

'It's probably someone collecting,' Kate told him, forcing the dog back into the kitchen. 'If it is, I've got some cash in the pot.'

He opened the door and found a tall, elegant, elderly lady on the step, wearing a very tasteful beige cardigan and a tweed skirt. She obviously wasn't expecting to see him, and her astonishment defeated her efforts to conceal it. 'Good afternoon,' she said, in extremely well-bred tones that reminded him immediately of royalty and Christmas broadcasts. 'Is my daughter at home?'

'Yes, she is – come in,' Jem said, stepping back and holding the door open. 'Kate, it's your mother.'

'My *mother*?' There was no disguising the horror in his landlady's voice. 'Christ, what's she doing here?'

'I have come to pay you a visit.' The refined presence glided past Jem as if he wasn't there, and paused in the hall. 'Is that dog safely shut up?'

'He is now.' Kate emerged from the kitchen rather warily. To Jem's outsider's eye, she was very noticeably changed from the confident woman with whom he had just been chatting into an apprehensive adolescent expecting punishment. 'I've put him in the garden.'

'Good. I've brought Humphrey with me in the car, and as you know, the poor little lamb is petrified of Smith.'

'Er . . . have you come to stay?' Kate enquired. 'I mean, you

68

should have said, there's nothing ready, the spare bed's not made up . . .'

'No, I'm going back to Cheltenham this afternoon. I just thought I would drop in and see how you all were. After all, it's been several months since my last visit.' Her grey eyes, sharp and hostile behind the gold-rimmed spectacles, swept round the hall and came to rest on Jem. 'I don't think we've been introduced.'

'Er, this is Jem Forrester, my new lodger. I mentioned him when you rang, didn't I? He moved in on Wednesday. He's working for Charlie Dobson at the Court. Jem, this is my mother, Mrs Bennett.'

Overwhelming Pride, and a great deal of Prejudice, Jem thought. He smiled. 'Hallo.'

'Good afternoon,' said Kate's mother, with a look that would have frozen fire. 'I must say, Katherine, I had no idea – where have you been put, Mr Forrester?'

'He's in the annexe, of course,' Kate said. 'We were just about to have lunch. Would you like a sherry, Mother?'

'I shall be driving home, naturally, but yes, just a small one,' said Mrs Bennett, and stalked ahead of her daughter into the sitting room. Kate glanced back at Jem, her face anguished, and hissed, 'The bread's in the top oven, can you get it out?'

As he was putting the two loaves, one herb and garlic and the other cheese and onion, onto the bread board, Tamsin came in. 'Wow, that smells great! Who was that at the door?'

'Your grandmother,' Jem said.

A look of complete horror suffused her face. '*Granny!* You mean Granny Bennett? Oh, God. She's *awful*. Has she come to stay? Mum didn't say anything about it, and I do like to be *warned*. If I'd known I'd have gone round to Charlotte's.'

'She didn't say anything because she didn't know either,' said Jem sympathetically. 'Mrs Bennett just turned up unannounced.'

'She probably wants to inspect you,' Tamsin said. 'Granny does like to poke her nose in. She's always nagging me about what I wear, and Mum says she used to nag her when she was young too.' She grinned with sudden mischief. 'Did you know, Mum pierced her nose with a safety pin once, when she was sixteen? She said Granny nearly had a heart attack. I can't imagine Mum being a rebellious punk teenager, can you?'

'It happens to us all,' Jem pointed out. 'It'll happen to you too, one day, but you'll almost certainly grow out of it eventually. Some people take longer than others, that's all. I know a couple

69

of rock stars who are still stuck at that stage, and they're in their fifties.'

'Who? Who are they? Have you got any stories about them? *Do* tell me!' Tamsin said eagerly.

'Later,' said Jem, as the door opened. But it was Kate, rather white around the mouth. 'Jesus Christ,' she said, shutting it and leaning against it as if to keep out something malevolent. 'I wish she'd let us know. I haven't hoovered the floor for days, and Luke *still* hasn't cleaned round the basin in the downstairs loo.' She gave them a rueful smile. 'Tamsin, could you be an absolute angel and lay the table in the dining room? Posh cutlery, in the case in the sideboard, and the Denby china.'

Her daughter made a face, but obeyed. As she left the room, Kate said fervently, 'I don't like to slag my mother off too much in front of the kids, but sometimes she's *impossible*! And to make matters worse, she's the exact opposite of Charlie – she stands on ceremony so hard she flattens it.'

'Do you want me to keep out of the way?'

Kate made a rude noise. 'Of course not! You're part of the household, for Christ's sake, and if she thinks I'm going to hide you away as if you're something to be ashamed of, then she can bugger off home. Oh, pardon my French, but Mother always gets me on the raw, somehow.'

'That's the trouble with family – they can twist the knife where it'll hurt the most,' Jem said sympathetically. 'Look, can I do anything?'

'Help Tamsin. She's left-handed and if she's under pressure she gets muddled about which way round the knives and forks go, and Mother is more than capable of pointing out any errors, in a really nasty, snide sort of way, naturally. Soup ready, bread ready, I'll put the cheese and pâté on a plate, and if she doesn't like it all so informal, tough. She should give advance notice if she wants the boat pushed out in her honour. And she's brought her stupid little dog with her, so poor Smith will have to spend the afternoon in the rain because the last time he met Humphrey, he didn't *know* it was a dog and tried to chase it . . . Sorry,' Kate said breathlessly. 'I'd better go back to her, before she starts running her finger along the mantelpiece to see when I last dusted.'

Mrs Bennett was sitting bolt upright in the armchair nearest the fire, nursing her sherry, which Kate had poured into one of her lead crystal glasses in her mother's honour. At her feet crouched Humphrey, her Maltese terrier, trembling in every limb, as if he expected Smith to leap out from behind the

70

furniture. 'Ah, there you are,' she said, as if Kate had been gone for two hours, not two minutes. 'I brought Humphrey in. Poor lamb, he so hates this dreadful weather. You don't mind, do you, Katherine?' she added, as an afterthought, and obviously expecting an answer in the negative.

'Of course not,' said Kate, although she found Humphrey, tiny and timid, a pathetic apology for the canine race. 'Lunch is pretty well ready – Tamsin and Jem are just laying the table.'

'This Jem person . . .' Mrs Bennett paused delicately. 'My dear, do you think his presence here is entirely . . . *suitable*?'

'Why shouldn't it be?' Kate heard the truculent note in her voice and mentally told herself to calm down.

'Well, I'm sure you know . . . I mean, having a *black man* living under the same roof . . . Is it quite *safe*? After all, you never know, do you?'

'Never know what?'

'Well, I mean, what is his *background*? One reads such terrible things in the newspapers. He could be some dreadful criminal, a mugger or a drug dealer.'

'Mother . . .' Kate was pouring out a very stiff gin for herself, glad that Mrs Bennett couldn't see her face. She thought of all the terrible things that she wanted to say, that she couldn't say, and dug her nails into the palm of her hand. *I want to tell her to shut up, to stop being such a prejudiced, bigoted old cow, I want to shake some sense and tolerance into her – but it's no use, her mind's all barred and shuttered.*

Her brother David would probably have said it, but he was their mother's favourite, and she would forgive him anything. Kate, 'only a girl', had always been made to understand that she was somehow an inferior being in every way. Fortunately, her father had more than made up for her mother's unending hostility, but he had died long ago, just after Luke's birth, and she still missed him, especially at times like this.

'Jem is a very nice man,' she said firmly, turning to face her mother with a determined smile on her lips. 'Charlie vouches for him, and anyway I wouldn't let him into the house if I had the slightest doubts about him.'

'I should think not, with the children to consider,' said Diana Bennett. 'But in any case, if I were you I would hesitate to place any reliance on Mr Dobson's word. A man like that is hardly trustworthy.'

'Charlie has been very kind and generous to me,' Kate pointed out.

'So he may have been, but one must ask oneself the question, why? He must surely have some ulterior motive. I mean, why else should he give you that position?'

'It might be because he thinks I'm a bloody good gardener,' said Kate. She had swallowed half the gin in one, and already it was giving her much-needed courage. 'And I am, you know, Mother. The Unicorn won Best Commercial Display in the Moxham Flower Festival last year, and the brewery's Best Beer Garden competition, against pubs all over Wiltshire.'

'Really?' said Diana, in disbelieving tones.

'Really.' Kate finished the rest of the gin, and set down her glass on the mantelpiece with a vigorous thud. 'Shall we go and have lunch?'

The dining room had undergone a miraculous transformation. The table had been cleared of the usual heap of papers, magazines, and morning post. Kate glanced round covertly, but there was no sign of them. Instead, the blue floral tablecloth was complemented by the deep glowing indigo of her best Denby china, and the paler colours of some freshly picked bluebells, drooping elegantly in the fat azure vase she'd bought at a local craft fair last year. The soup, decanted into a tureen, steamed temptingly in the centre, and the bread had been cut into wedges and heaped in a basket beside it. Tamsin was placing the last napkin by the last plate as they came in. At the sight of her grandmother, she jumped back and stood behind the chair, hands behind her back as if she'd done something wrong. There was no sign of Jem.

'That looks lovely – thank you, Tamsin,' Kate said, giving her daughter an appreciative smile. 'Where's Jem?'

'Gone to wash his hands,' Tamsin said. 'I'll go and do mine. Hallo, Granny.'

'Hallo, Tamsin.' Diana offered one deceptively soft, peachy cheek for a dutiful kiss. 'And where is Luke?'

Just as David had always been her favourite child, so Luke was her preferred grandchild, simply because he was the only boy. David had manipulated his mother's love to his own advantage: Kate loved her brother dearly, but had no illusions about him. But Luke seemed to have no idea that he was special. Like Tamsin, his feelings for Diana were a mixture of active dislike and wary respect, in which affection had little place.

'He's over at Justin's, and he said he probably wouldn't be back for lunch,' said Kate. 'I'm sorry he isn't here. If you'd only rung—'

'If he fails to appear, I am sure that Tamsin will not mind fetching him,' said Diana, taking her place, as of assumed right, at the head of the table. 'This looks interesting, Katherine. What is it?'

'Carrot and coriander soup,' said Kate. Fortunately, she'd made plenty, intending it to last all weekend. Her mother was one of those enviable people who could eat large quantities without any discernible effect on her waistline, an asset which she had ungenerously failed to pass on to her daughter.

Jem entered from the annexe, and sat down next to her, opposite Kate. Unseen by Diana, his left eye closed in a wink. Remarkably heartened both by the gin and by his obvious sympathy, she ladled soup into bowls, passed round the bread, and pointed out the virtues of the cheese and pâté.

'Hmm. Very good, Katherine,' said Diana, after sampling the latter. 'Is it home-made?'

'Only by Mr Sainsbury,' Kate told her. 'I'm afraid I haven't got much time to make that sort of thing.'

'I would have thought that with both the children at school, you would have had time to spare.'

'Well, I do work all day,' Kate pointed out. She was wondering, with considerable apprehension, whether her mother would utter one of those malicious, offensive remarks which were her speciality. A dreadful memory of Diana informing her, in front of an Indian college friend, that she thought that her daughter *might* be happy married to a coloured man, if *only* he were intelligent enough, returned to haunt her. If she said something like that to Jem, or used the same, breathtakingly insulting terminology with which she had described Linford Christie . . .

'I cannot understand, Katherine, why you seem so set on this gardening work,' Diana was saying disdainfully. 'Surely you could find some nice little part-time job, in a shop perhaps, or an office. Something not too *demanding*.'

'I do have a degree,' Kate reminded her.

'I thought it was in English, not in horticulture.'

'If I'd known then what I know now, it *would* have been in horticulture. Anyway, I only did English because I couldn't think of anything else.'

'Which rather proves the point I remember making when you were at school, that your university place was a waste of time and effort,' said Diana. 'Yes, I will have a little more soup. And what do you plan to do when you grow up, Tamsin?'

Startled, the child nearly choked on her bread. When she had

73

stopped coughing, she said hoarsely, 'Anything as long as it's to do with horses.'

'You're not *still* obsessed by them, are you? Oh dear. Well, I suppose it is a stage many young girls go through. But it must be a worry for you, Katherine, when *both* your children are so set on manual labour.'

'I thought Luke wanted to be an engineer,' said Jem, entering the conversation for the first time.

Diana turned and looked at him as though surprised he was intelligent enough to talk. 'But is that not the same thing?'

'Not at all.' Jem's voice was relaxed and pleasant. 'One of my cousins is doing an engineering degree at UMIST – University of Manchester – and I doubt he's ever got his hands dirty. Most of his work is done on a computer. Not, of course,' he added, with a quick smile at Kate, 'that there's anything wrong with getting your hands dirty. I don't suppose it worried Brunel.'

'And what exactly *do* you do, Mr Fisher?' Diana enquired.

'The name's Forrester,' said Jem amiably. 'I'm an engineer too, but a sound engineer, which is a bit different. I'm supervising the construction of Charlie's studios.'

'I see. Is it a *temporary* job?'

'Could be permanent. It depends on how I get on – whether I like living here.' He shot a grin at his landlady. 'So far, I'm quite keen.'

'And where do you come from? Originally.'

'London. Greenwich, to be precise.' Anticipating her thought, if not her question, he added, 'Born and bred.'

Kate was reminded of the story about Lenny Henry, who, when told to go back to where he came from, went into his house and shut the door. She said, 'More soup, anyone?'

'Yes, please, Mum.' Tamsin held out her bowl eagerly.

'There seems to be no sign of Luke,' Diana said, glancing with disapproval at her granddaughter, who was sucking the liquid loudly off the spoon. 'Would you very much mind going to tell him that I am here, Tamsin?'

'But it's pi— er, pouring with rain, Granny.'

'Goodness me, what a fuss about a few raindrops! If you run between them, you won't get wet.' She smiled at her own joke.

'Do I *have* to?' Tamsin said, appealing to her mother. 'And can I finish my soup first?'

'Of course you can,' Kate told her. 'And rather than you go out in this, I'll give Justin a ring and ask him to send Luke back.'

'I'm sure the child could do with some fresh air and exercise. She's looking rather peaky.'

'It's quite all right, Mother, I'll phone him.' Decisively, Kate rose to her feet and went out. It was really very strange, she thought, how she could be outwardly so calm and rational, and inside boiling with rage. And the irony was, that probably the identical conversation with a friend would produce an entirely different response. It was Diana who invested her words with such exact and scathing malice, and she, Kate, who overreacted.

She dialled Justin's number. It was answered on the second ring. 'Hallo?'

'It's me. Kate,' she added helpfully. 'Is Luke there?'

'Busy polishing. Shall I fetch him?' His voice sounded rather cool and distant, as though they were acquaintances, not lovers.

'Don't bother – can you just tell him that Granny Bennett's here and can he come over *prontissimo*?'

'There's a client coming in half an hour,' said Justin, and she hoped she had imagined the sharpness of his voice. 'Can't it wait until he's finished, darling?'

'I suppose so.' Kate paused, and then added, 'Is everything O.K.?'

'Of course it is. Why shouldn't it be?'

The snap in his words told her different. Her blood already fizzing because of Diana, Kate said, 'I was just wondering. We haven't had the chance of a talk recently, and you seem very preoccupied, somehow.'

'Business matters. Nothing to concern you,' said Justin, and now there was no mistaking the annoyance. 'I'll send Luke over when it's done. Bye.'

Annoyed and disturbed, she replaced the receiver and went back into the kitchen. Something *was* wrong, she was sure of it. Luke had said that last week's customer hadn't bought the TVR after all, and she knew that Justin had been more than usually pleased at the prospect of a sale. Perhaps he was just irritated at being let down: or perhaps there was more to it.

He might *be in trouble,* Kate thought, removing an apple pie from the freezer and putting it in the microwave to defrost. *But I always assumed he had loads of money – certainly enough to give up his job and move back here. And his lifestyle isn't exactly frugal. All those champagne bottles and posh restaurants must set him back a bit. Maybe something else is bothering him. I wish he'd tell me, I wish he wouldn't shut me out.*

In the dining room, Jem was collecting bowls, and Tamsin was receiving an inquisition from her grandmother. 'Do you mean to say that you are unable to do long division yet? Whatever do they teach you at that school?'

'They *have* taught me long division,' said Tamsin belligerently. 'But it's difficult. And anyway, what's the point when I can use a calculator?'

'That is the lazy way out, my dear. What would you do if you had no calculator with you?'

'I don't think I've had to use long division in anger since I left school,' said Jem. 'Life's too short. And I *always* carry my calculator with me.' He made a performance of hunting in his jeans pockets, and spread his hands in comical despair. '*Nearly* always.'

'Ah, Katherine.' Diana turned to her daughter, while Tamsin made a grimace of disgust at her back. 'I trust Luke is on his way?'

'He'll be back in a bit,' said Kate. 'Would you like some apple pie? Cream? Ice-cream?'

'I'll come and help,' Tamsin offered, eagerly jumping up.

'It was *awful*,' she confided in her mother, as soon as they were safely out of earshot in the kitchen. 'She was *grilling* me. And I did know the answers, most of them, truly I did, but somehow when she looks at me like – like a stoat looks at a rabbit, everything goes right out of my head.'

'I know. Don't worry, sweetheart. Think of it as good practice for job interviews and things.'

'I'm only ten! I mean, what does she *expect*? A child genius?'

'I doubt it. You're a girl, after all,' said Kate. Normally, she tried to encourage her children to respect their grandmother, but she was still furious with Diana, and she didn't see why poor Tamsin should have to put up with such a hostile interrogation. 'Look, try and be nice to her. I know it's difficult, and believe me, I'm finding it difficult too. But she doesn't come very often—'

'Thank God!' Tamsin muttered.

'—And she'll be gone in a couple of hours. Come on, let's make the effort. Jem is, and he isn't even family. Family are people you have to try and be nice to, however much you don't want to.'

'And I *don't* want to,' said Tamsin mutinously.

Kate, prodding the pie to see if it was still frozen solid in the middle, sent her a sympathetic glance. 'Give it a whirl. You might even enjoy it.'

A very rude snort from her daughter put paid to that idea. Kate put the pie on a tray, added bowls and spoons, a half-finished carton of cream and some of her Dutch apple ice-cream, and carried everything into the dining room.

Her mother, of course, immediately found fault. 'Have you no jugs, Katherine?' She gave the cream a delicate, dubious sniff. 'When is the sell-by date?'

'I only bought it a couple of days ago. And yes, I do have plenty of jugs, but this is not exactly the Hilton, and I thought I'd save on the washing up. Pie?'

For a moment, the eyes of mother and daughter locked in mutual antipathy. 'Just a small slice, please,' said Diana, with a loveless smile. 'Since it is not home-made.'

'It is, actually,' said Tamsin gleefully. 'My friend Charlotte's mum made it for the cake stall at the playgroup spring fair.'

Fortunately, the pie was pleasantly warm, and the ice-cream, full of cinnamon and raisins, was excellent. Despite her disdain, Diana had two helpings, while Jem kept up a flow of undemanding, humorous small talk that filled the awkward silences and entertained Tamsin. *God*, thought Kate, with heartfelt gratitude, *he deserves a medal for this. In his shoes, I'd have fled to the pub as soon as she walked through the door.*

'Surely,' said her mother at last, dabbing her thin lips with her napkin and placing her spoon and fork exactly together, 'it cannot be taking Luke all this time just to walk from Justin's house.'

'He may have a couple of things to finish off,' Kate told her.

'It really is too bad, when his grandmother comes to see him, if he cannot make the effort . . . and how is Justin?' Diana enquired, swivelling her glare in Kate's direction. 'Such a very nice young man. So extremely *suitable*.'

No prizes for guessing what he's suitable for, thought Kate wryly. In her mother's eyes, Justin, with his public school education and his landed ancestry, was ideal son-in-law material. Far more satisfactory, in fact, than Col, whose father had been a builder.

'Fine,' she said non-committally.

'And what does he think of – of your house-guest?'

'He's delighted,' said Kate. 'In fact, he bought us all champagne to celebrate, didn't he, Jem?'

'Certainly did,' said Jem, who was folding his napkin into intricate shapes for Tamsin's delight.

'So he is quite happy about this arrangement?'

'Of course he is. Why? Shouldn't he be?' Kate demanded challengingly.

Diana pursed her lips. 'Well – he must be remarkably tolerant, I must say, given the situation.'

Finally, and catastrophically, Kate lost her temper. '*What* situation, Mother? Come on, why don't you come right out and say it, instead of making all these snide, digging little remarks?'

'My dear Katherine, not in front of—' Diana broke off and indicated Jem and Tamsin.

'Not in front of children and guests? Why should that bother you? You've been bloody rude to both of them.'

'Katherine! How dare you!'

'No, Mother – how dare *you* come here unannounced just to poke your nose in and criticise everything. It's absolutely none of your business of course, but that's never stopped you, has it? This is *my* life, *my* house, and if you don't like it, tough. You can jolly well bugger off back to your narrowminded blue-rinsed cronies and leave us in peace!'

There was a coruscating silence. Diana had gone very white, save for a bright red spot under the face-powder on each cheekbone. Tamsin was open-mouthed with shocked and delighted astonishment.

'Well, if that is how you feel . . .' Her mother rose to her feet. 'I must say, unsatisfactory though you have always been, I never thought that I would hear such things said to me by my own daughter. I trust that words said in haste will be repented at leisure. I shall be waiting for your apology, Katherine. Goodbye.'

She turned and marched out, followed by the little dog, its ears back and its tail between its legs. In utter silence, the others heard the front door slam. Her car engine started with a roar of anger, and diminished into the distance.

'Oh, God.' Kate sat shaking, her head in her hands. 'Oh, my God, what have I done?'

'You were *brilliant*, Mum, absolutely *brilliant*!' Tamsin came running to hug her. 'Her *face*, she was just *gobsmacked* – oh, I wish Luke had been here to see it!'

'But she's my mother,' Kate protested. 'She's not some horrible old bat—'

'Yes, she is!' Tamsin said.

'She's my *mother*, for Christ's sake! I shouldn't say things like that to her!'

'Why not? She deserves them. It's about time you told her where to get off.'

'She's my mother. I should at least respect her, even if I don't like her very much.'

'In my book,' said Jem quietly, 'respect has to be earned.'

Kate raised her head and looked at him. He was sitting back in his chair, relaxed and casual and normal, and he smiled at her. Suddenly embarrassed, she felt her eyes fill with tears. 'I'm sorry,' she said. 'Sorry you had to listen to all that. I just lost my rag.'

'Don't worry about it,' Jem told her sympathetically. 'I've had plenty of difficulties with my own parents.'

The door opened and Luke came in. He stopped on the threshold, an expression of bewilderment on his face. 'But – Justin said – I thought Granny was here?'

'She's gone,' Tamsin told him, alight with joy. 'Mum was really, *really* rude to her and she left – and I hope she never comes back ever again!'

And it was a wish that Kate, guiltily, hoped would be granted.

Chapter Seven

Cricket, decided Kate, stifling a yawn, was a very overrated game, and a terrible waste of a lovely afternoon. She couldn't even read a book, because Justin was in, and expected her to watch his every stroke. As he was considered to be Moxham's top batsman, she would probably have to give the appearance of rapt concentration for at least an hour, unless Brimley's infamous demon bowler managed to get him out.

He hit a single, and she clapped dutifully, then took the opportunity to close her eyes. The heat, the smell of newly mown grass, the buzz of bees in the hedgerow behind her, and the crack of leather on willow, were all having a very soporific effect. She let her mind drift, listening to the small sounds around her, soaking up the warmth. A wood pigeon, high in the oak tree behind the pavilion, began its soothing croon. 'It's no *good*, Greyling, can't *catch* me, Greyling . . .'

'You ain't allowed to do that,' said Tanya's voice. Kate jumped, and hastily wriggled into a more upright position in the deck-chair. Charlie's wife was standing in front of her, wearing very brief shorts and a tiny white top. 'Mind if I sit down here?' she added.

'Please do. It'll keep me awake, having someone to talk to,' Kate told her.

Tanya unfolded a director's chair with 'Hers' in white lettering across the red back, and sat down. 'Know what you mean,' she said cheerfully. 'What a game! Like watching paint dry. Still, I thought, why not, bit of a laugh, innit, watching 'em all prancing round in their whites, and soak up a bit of sun into the bargain. That your Justin, is it, in the stripy cap?'

'It is indeed.'

'Moves nicely, don't he,' said Tanya, as Kate's lover executed a graceful sweep to leg. The ball bounced nimbly between two converging Brimley fielders, and skipped over the rumpled grass to the boundary. 'You're a lucky girl, you are, him *and* Jem. All

I've got is old Dobbin, ha ha ha.'

'Dobbin?'

'Oh, that's what I call Charlie, cos he *ain't* hung like a horse, see?' Tanya went off into one of her raucous peals of laughter. 'Nah, he's a good bloke, Charlie. I won't hear a word said against him, but I do like a bit of fun, a bit of a laugh, a bit of excitement. Not much point to it all otherwise, is there? Blimey, that was a fast one!'

Brimley had brought on the dreaded bowler at the start of the previous over. Fortunately, it wasn't Justin who had just faced a fearsome bouncer, but the other Moxham batsman, the father of a boy in Tamsin's class. He was shaking his head at the narrowness of his escape. Kate watched as he prepared to face the next ball with the resignation of a condemned prisoner, and was not in the least surprised when all three stumps flew out of the ground in contemptuous fashion. As he trudged back to the pavilion, his son, in charge of the scoreboard, recorded that Moxham were now 43 for 2.

'Jem's playing, ain't he?' enquired Tanya casually.

Kate looked at her, sprawled elegantly in her chair with acres of slender, lightly-tanned flesh on display, and the rest only skimpily concealed. She grinned. 'Yes, he is, but he said his batting was pretty rusty, so the Colonel's put him in at number seven.'

'So who's in now?'

'Justin's number two, and the bloke who's just come in – Geoff Wilson, I think his name is – he's number four.'

'And just out,' said Tanya, as the unfortunate batsman, swinging wildly at another bouncer, sent an easy catch to second slip. 'That's a duck's egg, innit, when they don't score nothing?'

'A duck, I think,' said Kate. 'I'm not very up in cricket. Col never played anything but squash, and my dad was more into gardening than sport.'

'So that's where you get it from!'

'I doubt it. His idea of a good garden was a couple of beds of regimented roses, and a lawn that looked like Astroturf. He used to go demented because my brother was always kicking a ball around it.'

'I didn't know you had a brother.'

'David. He's a bank manager in Bristol. Married, with two teenage daughters. I see him occasionally. We haven't got a lot in common, though.'

'I got three brothers,' said Tanya. 'All a lot older than what I am. I was always their little princess. They didn't like it much when I started modelling, I can tell you. I don't see much of them now. Course, they all wanted a share when I married Charlie, thought they was well in there, but I soon told 'em where to get off. I'll gladly fork out for nice presents for their kids, but I'm buggered if I'm giving them free hand-outs. Oh, Gawd, he's bowled him!'

Justin was staring in furious disbelief at the scattered bails and stumps. Then, with a bad-tempered swipe at the ground, he turned and stamped back to the pavilion.

'Oh, dear,' Kate said, rising to her feet. Tanya reached up and pulled her down. 'You stay right where you are. He's a big boy, he don't need you to kiss it better.'

'Trouble is,' Kate said, laughing rather ruefully, 'I know what he'll be like if I don't. Bear with a sore head isn't in it. And he's been so . . . so grumpy lately, I don't know what's got into him.'

'Time of life, I expect,' said Tanya cheerfully. 'How old is he? Forty-two? There you are, then. Male menopause and all that. You want to watch it or he'll be running off with some bird half his age.'

'That isn't Justin's style,' said Kate, although in her heart she wasn't so sure.

'Cobblers, it's all blokes' style. They all think with their dicks, pardon my French. Still, he's got you, hasn't he? And you're all right. You look bloody gorgeous in that. Where'd you get it?'

Surprised, Kate looked down at the slender, elegant lines of her favourite summer dress, the deep blue scattered with tiny white daisies. 'The Oxfam shop in Bath, actually.'

'You never! Blimey, you'd never know. Really suits you, it does, and your hair loose and that nice straw hat and all – real class, you are, and he'd be mad to look at anyone else.'

'Thank you,' said Kate, blushing. 'But I wouldn't call myself classy. Secondhand rose, that's me.'

'You got to make the best of yourself,' said Tanya sagely. 'That's my motto – keep 'em interested. Charlie now, we been married ten years – six months gone I was on our wedding day – and he's still crazy about me, cause I keep him fancying me, see?'

'You make it sound awfully easy.'

'No, it ain't, it's bleeding hard work! All them hours in the gym or the pool, and I spend a *fortune* on me make-up and me wardrobe. You ought to come down the health club sometime, I could sign you in. It's a real laugh, it is, and Max – he's my personal training consultant, that's what he calls himself anyway

– he's great, he really sorted me out.'

I bet he did, Kate thought cynically. She glanced up as a shadow fell across them, and said sympathetically, 'Hallo, Justin. That was bad luck.'

'Bad luck be buggered! The ball was so low and fast, I hadn't a hope in hell of hitting it.' He flopped down on the ground beside her.

Kate wondered how many runs he'd made, but didn't like to admit that she hadn't been keeping count. She glanced covertly round at the scoreboard, but it was singularly uninformative.

'That bowler's good, ain't he?' said Tanya innocently. 'Look, he's just got another one out.'

'It's bloody carnage out there,' Justin said, as a fifth disconsolate batsman began the long walk, while the Brimley players gleefully congratulated their not-so-secret weapon. 'That chap was playing professional cricket last season. It shouldn't be allowed.' He got to his feet. 'Well, I'd better go and offer some moral support to the tail-enders. See you later, ladies.'

'Oh, dear,' Kate said gloomily. 'Now he's really miffed.'

'Don't worry about it,' said Tanya. 'Let him have his little sulk, and put on something slinky tonight. Make it up in bed, that's my motto, and it's always worked for me.' She giggled. 'There goes your Jem. Bit of all right, ain't he?'

'He's not *my* Jem,' Kate pointed out, as her lodger strode with apparent confidence onto the pitch. 'He's not anyone's at the moment.'

'I know,' said Tanya, with lingering emphasis. She tossed back her blond hair, and gave him a wave. 'Good luck, Jem!'

He acknowledged her with a smile and a lift of his bat, before taking up his position at the crease. His borrowed whites were too big for him, and his brief dreadlocks stood out all round his cap. The Brimley bowler began his very long run-in, bounding with the confident expectation of yet another easy wicket. The ball bounced high, and Jem leapt back as it shot through the space his head had occupied only an instant before.

'God, it looks so dangerous,' Kate said anxiously. 'Justin's right, that bloke really oughtn't to be allowed in a village league, he's absolutely lethal.'

'Jem'll be O.K.,' Tanya said. 'He had a trial for Middlesex when he was at school, didn't he tell you? That's Jem all over, always hiding his light under a bleeding bushel. He's good, he is.' She giggled again.

The next ball was slightly slower, with a wicked illogical

bounce that caught Jem off-guard. It spun off the edge of his bat, and soared up into the air. 'He'll be caught!' Kate said, her hand to her mouth.

The ball fell straight back to earth, with one of Brimley's outfielders sprinting to intercept. He arrived a nanosecond too late, and it plummeted past his fingers to the ground.

A groan, of disbelief from Brimley supporters, relief from Moxhamites, rose from the spectators. 'Blimey,' Tanya said incredulously. 'Lucky sod.'

With exaggerated thankfulness, Jem took off his borrowed dark blue cap and mopped his brow. Then he returned to the crease, and prepared to face the next ball.

It came straight and true, aimed with devastating speed at the stumps. With a crack that echoed round the pitch, Jem drove it past the boundary.

'Told you, didn't I,' said Tanya, with satisfaction. 'You watch. He'll soon show that bleeding cannon-ball merchant a thing or two.'

Kate stared with a combination of interest and alarm, as her lodger proceeded to dispatch a succession of deliveries all round the ground. By the end of that over, he had added three fours and a two to Moxham's paltry score, and the clapping from the pavilion was loud with gratitude. Inspired, his partner at the other end, a boy not much older than Luke, got his eye in and hit a six.

'This is more like it,' Tanya said, wriggling with excitement. 'This'll show 'em.' She cupped her slender, manicured hands round her mouth and shouted, 'Come on, Moxham! Give 'em what for!'

'I thought you said you didn't like cricket.'

'Yeah, well, it's different when it's someone you know what's playing,' Tanya said. She put two fingers in her mouth and whistled like a banshee. Everyone sitting in the pavilion looked round, and Kate, trying not to laugh, saw the Colonel's expression of outrage beneath his Panama hat.

'I don't think that's quite cricket,' she commented drily.

'Boring old farts,' Tanya muttered. Jem hit another boundary, and she clapped and cheered raucously. Kate couldn't help noticing the huge and brilliant rock on the third finger of her left hand. She glanced round at the scoreboard. Moxham were now 70 for 6. It was not a very robust total, but at least, thanks to Jem and the boy, it was much more respectable than it had been a few minutes ago.

As they changed ends after that over, she noticed Megan, for once minus the twins, making her way round the scattered spectators towards them. 'Kate! I thought you'd be here. Hi, Tanya. How are they doing?'

'A lot better now Jem's batting,' Tanya told her. 'He'll show 'em a thing or two.'

'I thought he said his batting was rusty.' Megan plumped down on the ground between the two other women, and fanned herself. 'God, it's hot. Is that the bowler everyone's been talking about? I'm not surprised the Colonel's had trouble making up a team. Simon's well out of it. I can think of better things to do on a nice Saturday afternoon than sitting for three hours in Casualty while they strap up his hand.'

'Or his head. Oh, no!'

The boy had been given out, lbw, and was now trudging forlornly away from the crease. Moxham's number eight was Mick Stevens, landlord of the Unicorn. In his day, he had been a good player, but the years of beer and inactivity had taken their toll, and he hardly looked an inspiring figure as he waddled onto the pitch, sweating profusely.

'Gawd,' Tanya said anxiously, 'I hope he don't have a heart attack.'

'What have you done with the twins, Megs?' Kate asked, as the match continued. 'Buried them in the garden?'

'Don't give me ideas. No, Simon's taken them off to the adventure playground at Bowood, and Charlotte's down at the stables with Tamsin, of course.'

'They all had a lotta fun over half term, didn't they?' said Tanya. 'It's a shame Jayde ain't still here. She's a good kid, I miss her.'

Like hell you do, thought Kate. *Having an eagle-eyed ten-year-old daughter doesn't half cramp your style*. She glanced up, just in time to see Jem, with an elegant sweep of the bat, send the ball sailing up into the limitless blue sky. At once, a Brimley fielder set off in desperate pursuit, but it landed well over the boundary, in the strip of rough grass at the edge of the ground. Delighted applause from the pavilion announced that Moxham's score had passed the century.

'I hope they have tea soon,' Tanya said. 'I could murder a cuppa – or something stronger.'

'I don't think they'll be getting the champagne out just yet,' said Kate, as Mick Stevens, desperate to make some impression on the scoring, managed to get himself ignominiously run out.

'Shame. I could do with a bit of bubbly. Here, Megan, you have my chair for a bit, I'm going to stretch my legs.' Tanya uncoiled herself languidly from her seat and strolled away, towards the pavilion. Her elegant, swaying walk riveted every male eye, and was probably responsible for the next ball being hopelessly wide.

'God, I wish I had her figure,' Megan said, gazing after her. 'But some people are born fat.'

'Some achieve fatness, and some have fatness thrust upon them. I know, I've been there. If it hadn't been for Col's death, I'd still be twelve stone.'

'And happy,' said Meg, looking round at her. 'I'm a selfish cow, aren't I? All *I* need is willpower. My problems are feeble, compared with yours. Have you heard any more from your mother?'

'Not a word since she stormed out, and that was two weeks ago.' Kate gave her a rueful smile. Despite the undoubted support of her children, her lodger and her best friend, she still felt guilty because of what she had said – and not said – to Diana. And yet, it could not be denied that the dominant emotion was relief, that her mother was, at least temporarily, off her back.

'I hope you're not going to crack,' said Megan, who enjoyed a pleasantly casual relationship with her own parents, but was, as ever, happy to give advice, backed up with the fruits of a lifetime's addiction to agony aunts. 'You're a grown-up, you know, with big responsibilities. She can't treat you as if you're still a little girl and expect you to lie back and lap it up.'

'Try telling her that. It's exactly what she does expect. But don't worry, I won't crack. *She* will, eventually. It's her birthday in a couple of months, and she likes expensive presents and lots of fuss.'

'And what about the kids? Do they miss her?'

'Same as me – like a hole in the head. It's amazing, really, I was never that keen on Col's parents, but compared to Diana they're delightful.'

'The trouble is,' Megan commented thoughtfully, 'one day we'll be grandparents too, desperate to interfere and trying not to.'

'My mother doesn't even *try*. If she had her way she'd choose their clothes, their schools and their careers – even their thoughts, just like she tried to choose mine.'

'What a nightmare. I'm glad my own mum isn't like that.'

Megan gave Kate a sympathetic smile. 'It's a good thing life has never thrown anything tough at me. I'm just not equipped to cope with it. Not like you.'

'I didn't think I'd ever cope, but I did. You find it inside, somewhere, because you've got to or go under. The kids kept me going, otherwise I think I'd just have given up.'

'But you didn't. I do admire you, Kate,' Megan said, with uncharacteristic earnestness. 'And you're happy again now, with Justin and everything.'

'Of course,' said Kate, but even to herself her voice lacked conviction.

'You don't sound very sure.'

'I *should* be sure. But something's up with him, and I don't know what. He's been acting so strange lately, grumpy and secretive and really moody. One minute he's up in the clouds and the next he's biting my head off. I thought I knew him really well and now he seems to have turned into someone else half the time, and I'm finding it very unsettling. He's only come over three times in the last fortnight, and that isn't like him *at all*. But if I tackle him about it, he pats me on the head and tells me there's nothing wrong.'

'Ah.' Her friend looked down at her plump hands, lying in the lap of her blue-checked sundress. 'I think I may know the reason for that. I meant to tell you yesterday, but I just didn't have the chance of a quiet chat and it's not the sort of thing I wanted to say over the phone or with the twins yelling in my ear. Anyway, I only found out because Simon asked me to check that the planning application for our conservatory had gone in O.K., isn't it silly, I mean you shouldn't have to have permission for something like that, it's only because it's in a conservation area.'

'Megs, get on with it.' Kate had a hollow feeling in the pit of her stomach. '*What* have you found out?'

'Give me a chance, I'm coming to it,' said Megan patiently. 'So I went into the council offices yesterday to check our application, and out of curiosity I had a look to see if there was anything else in Moxham, and there was.' She paused, and her face was stricken with distress. 'Kate, Justin's put in a plan for houses on Mermaid's Ground.'

Mermaid's Ground. A lovely name for five acres of grass, ten ancient trees, a patch of purple orchids and a badgers' sett. A field which somehow had come to represent all Kate's past happiness, and her future dreams.

'Oh, no,' she said, in bewilderment. 'He can't have – Megs, are you sure?'

Her friend nodded. 'Absolutely positive. But he probably won't get planning permission,' she added soothingly. 'I mean, thirty houses does sound an awful lot. I looked at the plan and they're really *packed* in. They want to put five-bedroom detached on the farm side and a row of terraced ones and garages next to you. You never know,' she added hopefully. 'You might be able to sell them your orchard. You should be able to get quite a lot for it with planning permission.'

'But I don't want to sell my orchard – and I don't want houses on Mermaid's Ground! What about all those lovely trees?'

'The plans did make a point of saying that they were going to keep most of them. All except that really big one in the middle, it's on its last legs apparently.'

'You mean the one Tamsin used to pretend was Robin Hood's oak? They *can't* cut that down, it must be five or six hundred years old. Col measured it once, it was about thirty feet round. And the bit along the back has never been ploughed, there are wild orchids growing by the stream on the far side, and a badgers' sett under the hedge there too. Aren't those sorts of things supposed to be protected?'

'I suppose so,' said Megan anxiously. 'But maybe Justin's very strapped for cash. Perhaps he's desperate for money, and this is probably the only way he can get it, apart from selling the farm, and he can't do that, it's been in his family for centuries.' She paused, studying Kate's face, and then added, 'So that must be why he's been so grumpy. He's been agonising over it and wondering how to tell you.'

'I don't care about *how*, I just wish he'd told me first, for courtesy's sake, if nothing else. He *knows* how important that field is to me – I've told him, several times. At the very least he should have discussed it!'

'Well, now that you know, perhaps you can tackle him about it,' Megan pointed out. 'Anyway, he must know he can't keep it a secret from you for ever. It'll be in the paper next week, and then the whole village will know about it.'

'Well, many thanks for telling me. I'd much rather learn it from you than have Sal leaning over the counter saying, "I'm not being awful, Kate, but you mean to say he didn't mention it?" '

'That was why I thought I'd better let you know now,' said Megan, with feeling. 'But I mean, do try to look at it from his point of view. If he *is* hard up, then what else can he do? If it came to the crunch, wouldn't you rather sell your orchard than lose the cottage? He's no use for that field, he just rents it out to Derek Wright to put his cows on. And probably the reason he didn't tell you is that he does know how much it means to you, and he didn't want to hurt you.'

Even given Megan's talent for seeing all sides of the question, it did sound plausible. *But it doesn't alter the fact that he ought at least to have told me first,* Kate thought unhappily. *And that's what really hurts – that he didn't feel he could talk to me about it.*

But that was better than another alternative, which had slunk unwanted into her head: that he hadn't mentioned it to her because it simply hadn't occurred to him that she might have any reason to object.

She needed desperately to talk to Justin, to find out what was going on, and to receive reassurance, but she could hardly tackle him there and then, in front of most of the cricket team and other interested spectators. It would have to wait until later, when she could find an opportunity to speak to him alone. And in the meantime, there was the rest of the match to watch: the final collapse of Moxham's batsmen, all out for 152 (of which total, Jem had contributed an undefeated 69): and the tea, when she had to force herself to pretend that nothing was wrong. Fortunately, Justin, as Moxham's captain, was busy discussing tactics with the rest of the team. She took care to occupy herself behind the tea urn, knowing that if he spoke, she would be unable to prevent her distress spilling over.

After tea, the match resumed. Megan had gone home, and Kate was joined again by Tanya. She had spent the previous half hour as the subject of an admiring group of males, from both Moxham and Brimley, and her raucously joyful laughter had echoed round the pavilion. *And good luck to her,* Kate had thought, as she dispensed tea to a succession of hot and perspiring cricketers. She liked Tanya, and she knew that the feeling was mutual. And she didn't see her as a threat to her relationship with Justin. If anything, her pursuit of Jem, saviour of Moxham's cricketing self-respect, was so outrageous as to be highly amusing, and not least, so it appeared, to Jem himself.

Kate watched the second half of the match with an interest that surprised her. It soon became apparent that Brimley's principal strength lay in their demon bowler, not in their batsmen. After three quick wickets, she began to think that Moxham, amazingly, might even win the match.

Tanya was of the same opinion. 'And it's all down to Jem,

innit,' she said, her eyes riveted on the current object of her desires. 'He's gorgeous, ain't he? Ooh, I could eat him for breakfast, dinner and tea, I could.'

'Cannibalism isn't legal in this country,' Kate pointed out, trying not to laugh. She was glad of Tanya's company, a good antidote to the unhappy feelings at present churning inside her head.

'I was speaking metaphysically,' said Charlie's wife. 'Go on, Jem, get the bugger's bails off!'

The Brimley sixth, sprinting desperately for a quick single, only just reached his crease in time. Kate noticed that the looks from the pavilion were now full of amusement, and even the Colonel, still watching under his Panama, had lost the fervour in his glare.

'So you fancy Jem,' she said, rather unnecessarily.

'Course I do. Don't you?'

'I've got Justin,' Kate reminded her.

'Yeah, he's all right, is Justin, but Jem's different, ain't he? Justin's a hunk, but Jem is *fun*, a bit of a laugh. You couldn't say that about Justin.'

You certainly couldn't, the way he's been lately, Kate thought sadly.

'So what's it like, living with Jem? Not in the biblical sense, of course, ha ha!' said Tanya eagerly, moving her chair a little closer. 'Go on, spill the beans.'

'It's . . . normal,' said Kate, aware of how inadequate that description was. 'He gets up, has breakfast, jogs round to the Court, does his work, jogs home, has supper, goes to bed. Hardly very exciting. Last weekend he mowed the lawn, and sometimes he takes Smithy for a walk. He's been down the pub a few times, and he's looking to buy a car and sell his motorbike. He plays music in his room, but not so's you'd notice, and he likes old horror movies. Very boring and domestic, I'm afraid.'

'You're a dead loss,' said Tanya, without rancour. 'Gawd, I'd give an arm and a leg to be in your shoes, and to hear you talk you'd think he was your brother or something!'

'What were you expecting? That he runs in the nude?'

'Now *there's* a thought,' said Charlie's wife, positively salivating at the idea. She glanced round at Kate. 'If I was in your shoes, mate, I'd be flinging myself at him like there was no tomorrow, and never mind Justin. Blokes like Jem don't come along with every bus, do they?'

'Sorry,' Kate said. 'I'm just not interested, that's all. He's a lovely guy, I know, and I like him a lot. But I've got Justin, and that's it. End of story.'

'That's O.K.,' Tanya told her, with a grin. 'I don't mind, cos that leaves the field clear for me, don't it? And if you're thinking, what about poor old Charlie, well, he knows me, he knows it's just a bit of fun. He's the father of my kid, ain't he? I'll always go back to him, no matter what. We got it sorted out long ago. He knows the score, so don't worry about him.'

'I don't,' Kate said drily. 'I'm sure he can look after himself. I'm not disapproving or anything, I just couldn't play the field like you do, that's all.'

'Well, takes all sorts,' said Tanya cheerfully. 'Ooh, there goes another one. Go on, Moxham, get 'em all out and then we can go down the pub!'

Over the next four overs, they did their best to obey her, admittedly with the eager co-operation of the remainder of the Brimley batsmen, who were by now thoroughly demoralised. Their doom was sealed with a superb one-handed catch from Jem, at full and lissom stretch. To happy applause, the teams trooped off the field, and Jem, grinning broadly, was presented with a crate of beer to mark his unanimous selection as man of the match.

Kate joined in the congratulations, with a hollow sensation somewhere beneath her ribs. It had been a lovely day, but Megan's news had swept all her happy certainties away. Justin must have decided to develop Mermaid's Ground months ago. She knew how long these things took to arrange and organise, the amount of paperwork and bureaucracy needed. And yet he had said nothing to her at all. He knew of her long-standing plans to put a nursery on the field – plans which, she knew in her heart, were unrealistic dreams, but cherished all the same. He must surely know about the ancient trees, and the orchids, and the badgers' sett. Perhaps, when measured up against the money he would make, they had counted for little. But she still had a right to know, a right to be told. That would have been true even if they had been no more than neighbours. But they had also been lovers for nearly a year, and he hadn't bothered to inform her of his plans. For whatever reason, that omission really hurt. And now she didn't know where she stood, or what to think. She just hoped that, when she did finally manage to speak to him, his explanation would convince her.

Chapter Eight

The big bar of the Unicorn was crammed with jubilant cricketers, celebrating in time-honoured fashion with pints of Mick and Marcia's cool, well-kept bitter. The atmosphere was thick with heat, sweat and smoke, and Kate could feel her eyes smarting. She hadn't wanted to come here, but Tanya had more or less dragged her along, ignoring her protests. 'Don't be silly, it'll do you good to have a bit of fun, and Tamsin's round at Charlotte's, so you don't need to worry about her.'

'Luke'll be home soon, wanting his tea.'

'Come on, he's a big boy now, surely he can open a tin or something? You wanna let yourself go, Kate Williams, open up, live a little.'

The trouble was that standing wedged in the middle of a mass of jovial masculinity, wreathed in choking cigarette smoke and beer fumes, hadn't been Kate's idea of fun since her student days. A raucous chorus of 'For He's a Jolly Good Fellow' erupted into the rafters, and she noted with amusement that Jem seemed to be the subject of it, and that Tanya was hanging onto his arm. She turned, nursing the Pimms that Charlie's wife had insisted on buying her, and made her way towards the door to the garden.

Outside, it was peaceful, and gently warm. There was no one else at any of the tables, so Kate chose the one nearest her herbaceous border and sat down, giving the thriving plants the benefit of her professional eye. There was a gap halfway along the wall, where a couple of delphiniums had fallen victim to snail damage, and she made a mental note to suggest something more robust to Mick.

'Hallo, darling.'

She hadn't noticed Justin's approach, and his voice, almost in her ear, made her jump. He was carrying another bottle of champagne, and two glasses. He set them down with a flourish on her table, and smiled. 'What a match, eh? A truly memorable victory! Fancy a celebration?'

She indicated her Pimms. 'It's O.K. thanks, Justin, I've got this. But don't let me stop you.'

'Don't worry, you won't,' said her lover. He sat down beside her, removed the cork with explosive efficiency, and poured out a brimming glassful. Watching him, Kate marvelled that he could be so unselfconsciously at ease in her presence. There seemed not a trace of guilt in his manner towards her, and yet surely he must know that his silence about the planning application would hurt her deeply, when she found out.

Before her courage could fail her, she said quietly, 'How long have you been planning to put houses on Mermaid's Ground?'

That penetrated even his jubilant mood. He jerked round to face her, and some of the champagne spilled onto the smooth, varnished wood of the table. 'You weren't supposed to know yet,' he said sharply. 'How on earth did you find that out?'

'Megan told me this afternoon. She'd been to the council offices about their conservatory, and saw the plans. Oh, Justin, why didn't you *tell* me?'

His composure recovered, he smiled reassuringly back at her. 'I'm sorry, darling, but I couldn't.'

'So you were quite happy to let me find out from Sal or the paper?'

'You know I wouldn't do that,' said Justin. He leaned forward and took one of her hands in his. 'Oh, darling, I knew you'd be upset – and I just couldn't find the right time. I was meaning to tell you tonight, really I was, but Megan seems to have got there first.'

Kate stared back at him in bewilderment. 'I don't understand. You're talking as if it was something to do with national security, instead of a housing development. Why all the secrecy?'

'Well, I didn't want the village to know until everything had been settled,' said Justin. 'You know what Moxham's like.'

'But surely you could have told *me*?' Kate said unhappily. 'After all, we do share a bed occasionally, and I thought that couples were supposed to communicate with each other, not spring really nasty surprises just when it's least expected.'

'I did want to tell you,' said Justin, taking her other hand and kissing it. 'I really did, darling. But the developers didn't think it was a good idea; they were very much against it. And after all, there's no legal obligation to inform anyone until the council gives official notification in the paper.'

'What developers?'

'Harker and Briggs. They're a big firm in Bath, not some

bunch of cowboys. They approached me some months ago, made an offer to buy the land at a very good price, conditional on my obtaining planning permission. I didn't think they had much chance of success, but it would be stupid to pass up the prospect of that amount of money, so I agreed. They drew up the plans, and I submitted them a week ago. They didn't want anyone to know about it beforehand because they thought there might be opposition in the village. I tried to persuade them otherwise, darling, but they were adamant. If I told anyone, no deal.'

Kate looked at him. Sincerity shone in his face, his eyes, his voice. He was so close to her, their heads were almost touching. *He believes it*, she thought. *So why don't I believe him? Why do I feel that this is only half the story?*

She said, 'But why accept their offer? Why do you *want* to sell Mermaid's Ground? You're not short of cash, are you?'

Now. Now was the moment, if Megan had guessed right about his reasons, for him to look her in the eye and tell her the truth. Kate gazed at him unflinchingly. He didn't even blink. 'Of course not, darling. Whatever gave you that idea? But would you turn away the offer of one-and-a-half million pounds, however rich you were? That's not the way to make money, darling.'

'*One-and-a-half million pounds?*' Kate heard her voice squeak in astonishment. 'For *Mermaid's Ground*? You're joking!'

'No, I'm not. It's a fair price, for that amount of land with planning permission, within the M4 corridor. And with thirty houses on it, it's well worth the developers' money. Even if six of them are low-cost restricted ownership. I insisted on that, it'll keep the village happy.'

Of course it would. Old Moxham, of whom Justin, by birth and upbringing, was the acknowledged but unofficial leader, had been complaining for years about the lack of affordable housing in the village, the young people forced to find cheaper properties in Corsham or Chippenham or even further afield. And although wealthy incomers like the Colonel or Charlie had snapped up the ancient and beautiful houses that made Moxham so picturesque, their less fortunate neighbours, living in the council houses in the Circus and on the fringes of the village, were far more numerous. Their approval could well make all the difference to the success or failure of Justin's planning application.

You cunning sod, thought Kate, with reluctant admiration. And indeed, Justin did look rather pleased with himself. He added, smiling, 'You can't really object to that, can you, darling? You're always saying how unfair it is, that the village is turning into a haven for the wealthy.'

'Six houses isn't going to make much difference,' Kate pointed out.

'But it will to the planning application. And if the council says it's not enough, we can always add more. The developers reckon we can go up to ten without substantially affecting their profits. And once permission is granted, we can always revise the figure back down and the council won't be able to do anything about it.' He took a swig of champagne and beamed at her. 'Money for old rope, darling. Easier than taking sweets from a baby. You can hardly blame me for doing it, can you?'

'No,' said Kate at last. She thought of the people she knew, trapped in unsuitable accommodation and desperate for houses like these, which would mean that they could stay in their own village. Even six would be better than nothing. But she thought too of the tree that Tamsin loved, and the peace and quiet that would soon be shattered if Justin had his way. Moxham needed something like this, but not in narrow, winding Silver Street. There were other, far more suitable sites in the village. But of course, Justin didn't own them.

And whatever the arguments for and against development, one fact still haunted her. 'But you should have told me,' she added sadly. 'You really, really should.'

'I've already explained why I couldn't.' Justin's tone had become curt and dismissive. 'End of story. It's done now, darling. No good crying over spilt milk. After all, you know now, don't you? Come on, have some champagne. It's not every day I have the chance to make one-and-a-half million just by signing my name, is it?' He filled up the glass and smiled at her persuasively. 'Oh, Kate, darling, don't look so miserable. This is a really great opportunity to get the business going. There's a place in Bath I've had my eye on, a really good location, very central. I could buy and refurbish it, build up my stock, perhaps start a hire business as well, drive an Aston for the weekend and pretend you're James Bond, you know the sort of thing. Believe me, Kate, this was an offer I really couldn't refuse.'

'I believe you,' she said. 'But I don't believe you couldn't have told me. I think all that about the developers was an excuse. You surely must have known how much it would hurt me, but you just went ahead regardless.'

'Well, that's hardly surprising, is it,' Justin said. 'After all, I've explained everything to you now, and you still won't accept it.'

'Look,' said Kate. 'I do understand. I know the village needs cheap houses, though I'd be a little more sympathetic if there were more of them, and if you hadn't just as good as admitted that they've only been put there as bait. And in your position, I'd be sorely tempted to do the same. I admit I don't like the thought of all those houses next door, but I know they've got to go somewhere. But do you honestly think you'll get planning permission? There are rare flowers in that field, and badgers, and what about Robin Hood's oak?'

'Robin Hood's oak? Oh,' said Justin, laughing indulgently, 'you mean that poor old thing in the middle. It's dying anyway. But I think you'll find, darling, that when it comes down to it, what do a few trees and plants count for? The village wants those houses. I want the money. Selling Mermaid's Ground suits everyone, and the planning committee are realists. The developers are pretty confident – they must be, they've gone to a lot of trouble over this.'

'You still don't get it, do you.' Kate finished her Pimms and stood up. 'If I try really hard, I can swallow almost all of this. I do know that there's a crying need for affordable houses in Moxham, and I know they've got to go somewhere. It's the thought that you didn't trust me enough to tell me that hurts. And if you think I'm being awkward, well, I'm sorry, but that's how I feel. I've got to go now – Luke will be wondering what's happened to me. Can we talk about this another time?'

'There's nothing more to talk about,' said Justin. 'You're making a fuss about nothing, Kate. Come on, be reasonable.'

Usually his persuasive voice would work its magic, but tonight her hurt and disappointment were too acute to be soothed by a few sweet words and a glass of champagne. She shook her head. 'Sorry, I can't, not yet. Goodbye, Justin.'

She heard his protests behind her as she walked out of the garden, but she ignored them. She knew him well enough to be certain that he wouldn't abandon the bottle to come after her.

Well enough to know that, she thought, as she struggled through the cheerfully celebrating cricketers in the bar, and out of the front door. *But not well enough to realise what he was up to.*

And that was why she was so upset. It wasn't even the thought of the houses, or the threat to Tamsin's favourite tree. It was the realisation that he had deceived her so successfully, and that he had kept such a large part of his life hidden.

What other unpleasant truths had he concealed from her?

'Kate! Kate, are you all right?'

It was Jem, just emerged from the pub behind her. She stopped and turned, trying to appear normal. 'Hi. You were brilliant this afternoon. If that's your idea of rusty batting, I'd like to see it when it's polished and shiny.'

'Probably much the same,' said her lodger, grinning. 'It was nice of them to give me man of the match, but I think it should have gone to Justin, or that bowler.'

'Tanya said you made a habit of hiding your light under a bushel,' Kate told him. 'I'm beginning to see what she meant.'

'You're not all right, are you?' said Jem. 'What's happened?'

His obvious concern was almost Kate's undoing. She said firmly, 'Nothing. I've just heard something a bit upsetting, that's all. You go back in. I've got to go home and get Luke's tea.'

'They won't miss me,' said Jem, as the chorus of a notorious rugby song burst out behind him. 'Anyway, I don't fancy swilling beer all evening. Come on, let me walk you home.'

'Shouldn't that be the other way round? In case you meet Mrs Starling and Benjy?'

'I was hoping you wouldn't suss me out,' Jem said, grinning. 'But yes, my chivalry is only skin deep.'

He looked so friendly, so unthreatening, so blessedly free of bad moods and dark secrets, that Kate relented. 'O.K.,' she said at last. 'If you're sure.'

'I'm sure. Apart from anything else, I have another ulterior motive. If I stay in there much longer, Tanya will be eating me alive.'

'I had noticed.' They began to walk, side by side, along the edge of the Green towards Silver Street. Kate felt herself beginning to relax. It was such a lovely evening, with the sun sinking in a wash of gold behind the church, and the air still full of languorous warmth, that her distress, so painful a few moments before, was already beginning to seep away. She added, smiling, 'But you'll have to be careful not to resist her too strenuously. You can guess what everyone would think.'

'That'd be too much for Moxham, I reckon,' said Jem, laughing. 'Black *and* gay. The Colonel would never get over it.'

'Nor would Mrs Starling. And speak of the devil, it's a good thing I'm with you – here comes the lady herself.'

Jem's attacker of a fortnight ago was approaching on the other side of the road, taking the unpleasant Benjy for an evening constitutional. Kate sent the old lady her most gracious smile, and Jem waved. 'Hallo. I hope you've recovered from your fright.'

Mrs Starling gave him a hostile glare. 'Quite, thank you. Come away, Benjy, leave the man alone.' She dragged the dog past them, ignoring its hysterical yapping.

'Smith is petrified of that horrible little dog, even though he's quite capable of eating it for breakfast,' said Kate, when the pair were safely out of earshot. 'I wish he would, the animal's a menace.'

They strolled down Silver Street towards Mermaid's Cottage. It was very quiet, but Kate could hear the distant sounds of playing children, and the church clock struck once to mark half past eight. Suddenly she had a terrible vision of peace destroyed, of diggers trundling across Mermaid's Ground and ripping up the ancient turf, of noise and dust and ugliness where once there had only been grass and birdsong and cows.

She walked straight past her gate, and stopped at the entrance to the field next door. The low sun flushed Derek's prize-winning red and white Ayrshires with flattering pink, and impossibly long and slender shadows stretched out from beneath the trees. Beyond the next hedge, the stone walls and roofs of Silver Street Farm waited silently for the invasion. Jem came to stand beside her, leaning his arms on the gate. He said, 'That tree must be a thousand years old.'

'Several hundred, certainly. It looks a bit of a mess, it's going stag-headed – see those bare branches? But it'll stand for a few more hundred, if it's allowed.'

There was a pause. Then Jem said softly, 'Is there any reason why it shouldn't be?'

The urge to confide in him finally overwhelmed Kate. 'Yes, there is,' she said unhappily. 'Justin's put in an application to build thirty houses in there.'

Jem's astonishment was so strong that she could sense it without having to look at him. 'Surely he can't,' he said at last. '*Thirty* houses? He'd never get planning permission.'

'He's pretty confident. He's county, and round here that still matters. And he's added a nice little sweetener. Some of the houses are low-cost, for local people.'

'Will that make a difference?'

'It certainly will with a lot of people. And there really is a desperate need for them. The trouble is that Mermaid's Ground isn't the right place. And I'm *not* just saying that because I don't want them next door. There's a big patch of waste ground up by the Home Farm that would be much better – more central, no wildlife to disturb, and no access problems. Silver Street is barely wide enough for a tractor, let alone diggers and dumper trucks. But the application isn't for that site. It's for Mermaid's Ground.'

'Who owns the other field?'

'I don't really know. I'd always assumed it was part of the Court, in which case Charlie does. But I can hardly go and ask him to put in a rival application, can I?' Kate gave her lodger a rather desperate smile. 'So that lovely old oak will be torn down, not because it's dying, because it isn't, but because it's in the way; and the badgers in the far corner will have to move, and the orchids will be destroyed, and I can't do or say anything about it.'

'You could object.'

'I suppose I could. But people will say I'm a NIMBY – that I just don't want them next door to me. And they're right, I don't. But that's only one small reason.' She grinned wryly. 'The main one is that I don't want to have to live with Tamsin's fury if her favourite tree is chopped down. Knowing her, she'll be lying down in the mud in front of the bulldozers, and I can't afford to keep buying new clothes for her, *or* bailing her out.'

'I can just see Tamsin as a dedicated eco-warrior, chaining herself to the trees,' said Jem, laughing.

'Unfortunately so can I, only too clearly. Come on, let's go in,' said Kate, determinedly cheerful. 'Smithy probably has all four legs crossed by now, and anyway I'm ravenous.'

'Didn't you have any of that tea?'

'Of course not; I was dispensing it, not eating it. In village cricket, the men play and drink and feed, and the women only exist to provide them with the required fuel. Any idea that we might actually get to taste any of those fancy sandwiches or slices of cake ourselves is, of course, completely ridiculous. Didn't you notice Peggy? The Colonel's wife? Megan calls her the Memsahib. Built like the proverbial brick outhouse, and a voice that'd make a foghorn sound feeble. If I so much as looked at a cucumber sandwich, she'd rap me over the knuckles and tell me not to be a naughty girl.'

'What does she think of Tanya, then?'

'Probably much the same as my dear mother would think of Tanya. "No better than she should be", I expect.'

'I've heard my mother say that, and I've never understood what it means. Oh, I know what *she* means by it, but it doesn't exactly make sense. How better should she be?'

'Better than she is, probably,' said Kate, opening the front door.

There was no black hairy missile launching itself at them. The house seemed sepulchrally quiet. Kate opened the kitchen door and found a note on the draining board in Luke's handwriting. 'Walking dog and probably calling in on Mark. Got myself some supper.'

The kitchen smelt of overfried fat, and there was a greasy plate in the sink. She unlocked the back door and turned to Jem. 'There's ham, and some salad, and a bottle of plonk in the fridge, and I can defrost a ciabatta. It's not much, but it's a few levels up from Luke's egg on bread. O.K.?'

'More than O.K.,' said Jem.

They carried everything out to the table on the patio. By now, the sun had disappeared behind the trees in the orchard, but the air was still very warm. Kate poured the wine and cut thick slices of bread, and for a while they ate in a companionable silence.

'I can't believe they'd let it happen,' Jem said at last. 'This place is so quiet, so peaceful – surely a big housing estate would be completely inappropriate.'

'And so, if I'm honest with myself, would the plant nursery.' Kate, spreading mustard on a hunk of ciabatta, smiled at him ruefully. 'This is part of the problem, you see. I'm a real hypocrite, because my own plans for Mermaid's Ground were just as bad. Aren't greenhouses and polytunnels even uglier than houses? And a nursery would probably encourage more traffic.'

'It's a much less intensive use of the land, surely?'

'I suppose so. And I'd never have cut the oak down, and I'd have left the orchids and the badgers alone. But I know what the village will say. They're desperate for cheap houses, and if Justin persuades them that agreeing to his plans is the only way to get them, then they'll agree.'

'You can't be sure of that. You can't be the only one who cares about the trees or the other wildlife.'

'I really hope I'm not. But I have a bad feeling about it. Look at places like Twyford Down, or that stretch of road in Bath. They've done far worse damage, and yet they were still approved. Justin knows all the right people. A lot of villagers will want it, and that counts for something too. So I can't help being pessimistic.' She smiled at him. 'I'm sorry. I didn't mean to offload all this on to you, but I just couldn't help it.'

'I don't mind,' said Jem. 'Don't worry about it. I'm a good listener, and a good shoulder to cry on. Like you, I can see that there are good arguments on both sides, but I'm not going to involve myself in any disputes.'

'I don't blame you.' Kate looked up at him, sitting opposite. 'But thanks, anyway. It's wonderful to have a sympathetic ear. I thought Justin and I were on firm ground, and suddenly everything's gone quaky, I don't know where I am any more and I really, really don't like it.'

'Understandable. But a good relationship can survive almost anything.'

'I hope so.' Kate poured more wine, thinking: *but what if it isn't a good relationship? What if this quarrel isn't something to be overcome, but the first real crack, a sign of some fatal flaw? And if it is, then I don't want it to survive.*

'Anyway,' she added, 'perhaps I can talk him out of it. I'm a good persuader. Better than you, probably.'

'That's what's known as "damning with faint praise", isn't it? More persuasive than Jem Forrester. Better looking than Jimmy Nail.'

Kate choked suddenly on her wine. 'Friendlier than Mrs Starling?'

'You've got the idea. More socialist than Margaret Thatcher.'

'More left-wing than Attila the Hun.'

'More tuneful than Captain Haddock.'

'Tidier than Tamsin.' Kate's sides were aching with laughter. 'This one could run and run. Taller than Danny de Vito. More obedient than Smithy. Slimmer than Sal.'

'It's not that funny,' said Jem, laughing in sympathy.

'I know it isn't, but it's cheered me up no end. That's my trouble, you see, I find it very difficult to be upset for long, especially on a lovely evening like this. Look at the sunset. Isn't it beautiful? And there'll always be sunsets like that, no matter what happens. This is hardly the worst thing I've had to deal with, after all. I'll cope. I'll get through. And in a year or two I'll be wondering why I made so much fuss.' She grinned at him. 'So don't worry about me. You've got enough on your plate, what with the studios and Tanya and everything.'

The glowing light in the sky lit only a part of his face, and the rest was in deep shadow, but she knew suddenly that he was looking at her with disturbing intensity. Then he gave her his wide, flashing smile. 'My mum used to say, when I was a little boy, that no matter how much was on my plate, I'd always want to fit in a little more. But there again, she was talking about food. Is there any ham left?'

And, laughing, Kate gave him the last slice.

Chapter Nine

'All right then, Kate?'

'All right,' she said, acknowledging Bob Wiltshire's typical Moxham greeting with a smile. 'Lovely morning, isn't it?'

'Rain afore sunset,' said old Bob, who had a very pessimistic view of the weather. 'Here, you seen the *Star*?'

'Today's? No, I haven't yet.'

'Ah.' The Court's ancient gardener tilted back the battered old tweed cap he invariably wore, his shrewd blue eyes gleaming with curiosity. 'You knew about they houses Mr Spencer's bin planning, then?'

'The ones on Mermaid's Ground?' said Kate, as if, she thought, Justin had applied to build on every vacant plot in the village. 'Yes, I did, actually.'

'Kept en very dark, did'n he? So did you.'

'He asked me not to tell anyone till it was all sorted,' Kate said diplomatically. 'He didn't want to get everyone excited.'

'Well, you can't tell me you'm excited,' Bob commented. 'All they windows peeping over your hedge, I would'n like it. Going to object, are you?'

'I don't know. I can't really, can I? I know Moxham needs cheap houses.'

'Oh, they'm cheap, eh? Sal d'say they'm posh ones, coupla hundred thousand each she d'reckon.'

'*Some* of them are cheap,' Kate said. 'Six, to be precise.'

'Have you seen en, then?'

'The plans? Yes, I went over Monday lunchtime to have a look.' The thirty houses had been squashed into every corner of the field. She had noted the narrow terrace of low-cost buildings sited immediately beyond her hedge, while the most spacious and expensive properties had been placed on the other side, with a broad swathe of garden between them and Justin's farm. Where Robin Hood's oak now stood, the developers had put a car park.

105

'Don't reckon any of they'll have much land to en,' said Bob. 'Thirty houses on that piddly little piece o' ground!'

'There isn't a lot of room, no.'

'Suppose they got to make their money somehow,' the old man observed sagely. 'And Mr Spencer, I d'reckon he'll take his cut.'

'I expect he will.' Kate resisted the temptation to tell Bob the exact size of Justin's cut. Sooner or later, everyone was bound to know, but she didn't want to cause any more bad feeling between her and her lover. Since their talk in the pub garden five days ago he had maintained complete silence, no visits, no phone calls, nothing, and she was beginning to be worried. She still felt hurt and betrayed, but she did not want this difference to linger on unresolved.

I'll go round this evening and try to patch things up, Kate decided. *It's quite a feat, really – neither my mother nor my lover speaking to me, in just a couple of weeks.*

'It's looking good,' she added, indicating the walled garden, Bob's particular domain. 'Your runners are doing much better than mine, but then I only planted them out a couple of weeks ago.'

'Twas a warm spring, see? Put they in the ground good and early, tis the secret.' Bob grinned at her. 'Don't ee be afraid of a bit of hard work, girl.'

'I'm not. How's the hothouse coming along? Has Charlie decided what he wants in it?'

'Orchids,' said Bob, in tones of deep disgust. 'All they vines have got to come out, and the fig tree, and he's putting orchids in. *Orchids!* They ain't no good to man nor beast. What do he want they for, eh?'

'They're fashionable, I think.'

An extremely derisive noise from Bob indicated his opinion of fashion. 'That woman of his have put he up to it, I d'reckon. Here, what's she and your lodger up to, eh?'

Bob Wiltshire was living proof that women are not necessarily the biggest gossips, and Kate knew that whatever she told him would be freely disseminated in the post office and the Unicorn later. 'Absolutely nothing,' she said firmly. 'He works all day and sleeps all night – alone. He's a friend of Charlie and Tanya, and he wouldn't dream of doing anything to upset either of them.'

'Ooh, ah,' said Bob in disbelief. 'That ain't what I've heard.'

'Well, you've heard wrong,' Kate told him. 'People have a tendency to add two and two and make twenty.'

'And somewhen they be right,' Bob said, with a salacious

chuckle. 'Here, talk of the devil.'

Tanya had entered the walled garden from the courtyard gate. Today she wore a turquoise silk sarong and a crisp white blouse, tied under the bust to reveal an enviably flat, tanned midriff. Her hair was braided into a thick French plait, and a pair of Raybans completed the impression of cool and elegant glamour. 'Hallo, Kate, hallo, Bob.'

'Mornin', Mrs Dobson,' said Bob, with a far from deferential touch of his cap. 'Here, have you seen they plans Mr Spencer be putting in?'

'I've heard about them, yeah,' Tanya said, with a sympathetic glance at Kate. 'So what do you think, then, Bob?'

'I d'reckon he be a greedy bugger,' said the old man unexpectedly. 'All they houses packed in like a can o' sardines, 'tain't right in my book. And he's a clever one, ain't he, saying that some of 'em are meant for we locals. Sorry, Kate, but that be what I d'reckon to en.'

'It's O.K., I feel rather the same. But there's no denying we do need cheap houses. And after all, there's not a lot I can do about it, is there?'

'Parish meeting bin called to talk about en, week arter next,' Bob told her. 'You have your say there, I would if I was you, girl. You bain't afeard to speak your mind, eh? Well, go ahead and speak en. There be other ground to put houses in that's better suited. That old bit of wilderness by the Home Farm, for a start. He've bin sitting there doing nothing for years, and the road be good and wide there. Why don't they build on that, eh?'

'The trouble is, Justin doesn't own it, Charlie does, I think. It's part of the park, isn't it?'

'Don't ask me,' said Tanya. 'I don't know what's his and what isn't. Here, you coming down the pub later, either of you? It's me birthday today, thought we'd have a bit of a knees-up. Charlie wanted to throw me a big party, but he's got to fly over to the States tomorrow, so he needs his beauty sleep.' She giggled. 'And no, I ain't letting on how old I am. Old enough to have fun, that's all that matters.'

'If yer too old to have fun, yer dead and buried,' said Bob, with a glance at Tanya which clearly revealed that he was not immune to her charms. 'Well, better be getting on. Plenty of strawberries, Mrs Dobson, you want some for dinner? I'll pick ee a pound or two.'

'I don't believe him,' said Tanya confidentially to Kate, as they watched the old man stump off towards the strawberry patch at the further end of the garden. 'He's just like something off the telly. You could make a fortune hiring him out for voice-overs and that. "Ooh-aargh, boy moy zoider." '

'That's Somerset.'

'Same difference,' said Tanya. 'It's all West Country, innit? There you are then. Well, you coming down the pub this evening? I'm buying.'

'Of course I will. Happy birthday! I'm afraid I haven't got you anything – I didn't know.'

'Don't bother,' said Tanya. 'Between you and me and the gatepost, when you're past the big three-oh, each one's as bad as the next. I told Dobbin years ago, I told him if he put up any of them signs saying Thirty Today, Tarn, I'd sue him for divorce, bless him. Ta-ra, then, see you later, don't work too hard!'

Kate watched as she sashayed back towards the house, and wondered exactly how old Tanya was. *Younger than Charlie*, she thought, with a smile as she remembered Jem's amusing series of comparisons. *Probably younger than me, too – but not by as much as she'd like everyone to think.*

Out of curiosity, she went over to look at the hothouse, which had always been Bob's pride and joy. It had been built along the western side of the walled garden by a Victorian member of the Blount family, presumably to provide grapes, pineapples, oranges and other exotic fruits and flowers out of season, and its cast-iron frame and black and white tiles were typical of its period. Through the years of decay, Bob had kept its ancient boiler running by a mixture of primitive technology, prayer and, probably, a more elementary magic, and the huge vine, its brown twisted arms providing a living sunshield over most of the roof, was a testament to his devotion. The atmosphere was as hot and suffocatingly humid as a sauna, with a thick, wet, earthy smell that clogged Kate's nostrils. A butterfly, frantic to escape, battered at the glass. Carefully, she trapped it in her fingers and carried it out to freedom. Then, with a wave of farewell to Bob, bent double picking strawberries, she went off to the sunken garden, where Darren was meant to be putting waterlilies in the fountain pond and, knowing him, probably planting them upside down.

In any other circumstances, she would be looking forward to Tanya's birthday bash, but the conversation with Bob had been a warning of what to expect. Everyone in the Unicorn would be seeking her reaction to Justin's plans, and she knew that very few would adopt the old man's view. They'd probably assume that she'd been in on it from the start, and they'd also believe that she would benefit from the scheme. The whole village knew that she and Justin were lovers, and they all probably thought that, sooner or later, they'd get married.

Chance would be a fine thing, Kate thought ruefully. *And anyway, I'm not sure any longer that I actually* want *to marry Justin – if I was ever sure in the first place. Oh, why, why,* why *did he have to go and submit that wretched planning application? It's changed everything, and now I don't know what to think, or what to do.*

Entering the Unicorn that evening, with Charlie, Tanya and Jem, she saw Bob, for once without his cap, propping up the bar and talking to Marcia. As she walked in, the conversation very obviously drew to a close, and the landlady moved along to take Charlie's order.

'A bottle of bubbly, darlin',' said Kate's employer, beaming. 'Nothing but the best for my Tarn, eh? If she's another day older, she don't look it.' He squeezed his wife's minuscule waist fondly. 'Ain't she gorgeous, eh?'

For the occasion, Tanya had put on a wisp of a dress that clung to every curve and barely reached to the thigh. Looking at its smooth lines, Kate suspected that she was wearing absolutely nothing underneath, and to judge from the expressions worn by most of the men present, they thought the same. With a flirtatious glance from underneath her impossibly thick dark lashes, Tanya assessed her admirers and then turned back to Marcia. 'Make that *two* bottles. It ain't every day it's my birthday, eh? And Charlie's off to the States tomorrow for Gawd knows how long, so we'd better give him a good send-off too.'

'I hope you've got two bottles,' Charlie said, smiling indulgently at his wife as he fished for his wallet. 'Here you are, Marcia – and put the change in your charity fund.'

'Thank you very much indeed, Mr Dobson, that's very kind of you.' Marcia took the two large red notes, held them up to the light, and stashed them safely in the till. 'Yes, I got some more in, seeing as Mr Spencer's been getting through it recently. But then he's got something to celebrate, hasn't he?' she continued, with a glance at Kate. 'If those houses get built, he'll be in for a packet.'

'If,' Kate said. 'There's a long way to go yet.'

'Well, there's no denying we could do with some affordable houses. My nephew's been on the council list for donkey's years and still no nearer the top, even though he and his wife and kids are crammed into a damp little place in Chippenham with no room to swing a cat. And although six isn't much, it's better than a poke in the eye with a sharp stick, eh? Thanks, Mick,' she added, as her husband put two bottles of vintage down on the bar counter. 'Here you are, Mr Dobson. Will you be eating here? Only the kitchen hasn't really warmed up yet, you could say, and there might be a long wait.'

'Don't worry about that,' Charlie said, with a wink at Tanya. 'We got lots of patience, ain't we, Tarn? Come on, Kate, what can I get you?'

'Not for me, thanks. I've got the kids to see to. Luke's getting a bit fed up with cooking his own supper.'

'Do him good,' Tanya said. 'Go on, Kate.'

'No, honestly, it's very kind of you, but I've got Tamsin to think about too. She's at Megan's and they're going out later, so I can't leave her there too long.'

'Another time then, eh?' said Charlie. 'Still, you can have some bubbly, can't you? That's the ticket! What about you, Jem? You ain't got nothing to get home for.'

'If it's O.K. with Kate, then I certainly will – thanks.'

'Good on yer!' Charlie rashly gave the first bottle a brisk shake and unfastened the wire. With an ear-splitting bang, the cork buried itself amongst the bottles behind the bar. Tanya shrieked, and covered her ears. As the report died away, Kate saw, out of the corner of her eye, the outside door open. As if lured by the broaching of another bottle of his favourite tipple, Justin had arrived.

Fighting sudden, unexpected panic, she turned back to the bar, in time to take the glass that Charlie was holding out to her. She saw Jem glance round, and knew that he had noticed. She heard the familiar footsteps walk up to the counter, and Charlie's cheerful greeting. 'Wotcher, Justin! It's Tarn's birthday, and we're celebrating. Bet you wouldn't say no to a glass of bubbly, eh?'

'You're right, I wouldn't.'

'He's come *just in* time!' Tanya said to Kate, with a hoot of laughter at her own suspect wit. 'Here, you all right?'

'Fine, thanks.' Kate knew she ought to make herself pleasant. She took a big gulp of champagne and turned round, to find Justin smiling at her. 'Hallo, darling,' he said, as if nothing had happened. 'Didn't see you there. Sorry I haven't been in touch, but I've had a lot of business to attend to.'

Once more, she found her uncertainty melting away under the full force of his charm. Smiling back, she went to join him. 'I hope everything's O.K.'

'Of course it is, darling. Why shouldn't it be? Life's looking pretty sweet at the moment, I can tell you.'

So it should if he's got one-and-a-half million pounds due to come his way, Kate thought wryly.

'All better now?' Justin murmured, his arm encircling her waist. 'There's a good girl. I knew you'd come round.'

'Not *entirely*,' Kate said, nettled despite herself by his smug tone. 'But keep working on it.'

'Don't worry, I shall. Listen, let's slip outside for a moment, darling. I've got something I want to put to you.'

The pub garden was empty, but even so, Justin steered her to the furthest table. Puzzled, Kate sat down. 'What's all this about, then?'

'Since I saw you, I've had a word with Harker and Briggs – you know, darling, the developers. I told them about your orchard, and they're very interested in buying it.' He beamed at her. 'Does that make you feel better? They'll have to survey it, of course, and work out a price, but Ray Harker reckoned he could give you fifty thousand for it.'

Kate stared at him, astonished. 'My *orchard*? Fifty thousand for my *orchard*?'

'Not a bad sum, is it?' said Justin, obviously extremely pleased with himself. 'Nice little nest-egg for you. Invest it wisely, I could give you some advice there, and there'd be enough to send the kids off to decent schools, for a start. Marlborough for Luke, and Tamsin could go to that place Charlie sends his daughter to.'

'But I don't want to,' said Kate, staring at him in astonishment. All sorts of questions were jostling inside her head, as well as a sudden flare of anger. 'They're both doing well, and they're really happy where they are. And I like having them at home, they're good company.'

'You can't surely think that they're getting a good education at *state* schools,' said Justin, raising his eyebrows. 'And just think, darling, with both of them away all term, you won't have to worry about them cramping your style, now will you?'

Kate stared at him in disbelief. 'Is *that* why you've come up with this? To get the kids out of the way so that you've got a free hand with me?'

'Of course not, darling. I'm only thinking of you. That amount of money would be a godsend, now wouldn't it? Though I must admit it would be nice to come round to your house in the evening and not have to worry about upsetting Tamsin. It's not exactly convenient, after all.'

'I'm not going to pack my kids off to boarding school just because they get in the way of my love life,' Kate said furiously. 'I've no idea what else has been going on inside your head, Justin, but I can tell you this straight up. I am *not* sending Luke and Tamsin away. They'd be utterly miserable. I think I'd die first, I really would. Whatever made you think I'd even consider it?'

Justin stared at her in apparently sincere bewilderment. 'But darling, that's what people like us do with our children.'

'Well, in that case, I'm *not* like you, and to be honest I'm glad. Anyway, what on earth gives you the right to go behind my back and virtually sell someone else *my* orchard?'

'I thought I was doing you a favour,' said Justin huffily. 'I know it's your land, darling. Of course you don't have to sell it if you don't want to. But you'd be a fool to turn the offer down, believe me. After all, what do you do with it? Absolutely nothing. It's no use to you.'

'But it is! The kids play there. It's space, freedom. It has cowslips and beautiful blossom in the spring, and the apples in autumn. And I don't want houses all over it as well as in Mermaid's Ground. Besides, Tamsin would never forgive me.'

'It's about time you stopped giving in to her. She's becoming a real spoilt brat.'

'She is *not*!' Kate found she was shouting, and hastily moderated her voice. 'A friendly word of advice, Justin. If you want to win a woman round, don't try to do it by criticising her children. Tamsin has lots of faults, I'd be the first to admit, but at least she's honest and up-front.'

'And what's that supposed to mean?'

'You may think I'm a fool, Justin, but did you really think I wouldn't notice that fifty thousand for half an acre of my orchard doesn't seem very much compared to one-and-a-half million for five acres of Mermaid's Ground? Did you tell them that I was an ignorant female so strapped for cash she'd agree to anything, or did you arrange to take your own cut?'

Justin's face was white and distorted with fury. 'How *dare* you say that? How *dare* you?'

Despite the heat of his denials, there was something in the tone of his voice that did not quite ring true. 'So I'm right,' said Kate, and suddenly found all her anger draining away, to be replaced by a disappointment that was somehow not unexpected. 'I'm your lover, Justin, not someone to be cheated and exploited. Or is that what love means to you? It isn't what it means to me.'

'*Will* you shut up?' he hissed savagely. 'We've got an audience, in case you hadn't noticed.'

In alarm, she looked round. Keith Parker and his wife Sue were standing frozen by the pub door, glasses in their hands, their mouths open with astonishment.

'You see?' said Justin viciously. 'Thanks to you, *darling*, our private affairs will be all round the village by this time tomorrow.'

'I'm sorry,' Kate said. 'But it takes two to make a quarrel.'

'And only one to be reasonable.' Justin fixed the unfortunate manager of the village football team with a glare so threatening that he turned and hastily led his wife back inside the pub. 'I've done my best for you, and if you haven't the good sense to take what's offered, then you don't deserve to be helped.'

'But I don't *want* that kind of help,' Kate cried despairingly. 'And if you can't make the effort to understand something as fundamental as that, then I think we're both wasting our time. Sorry, Justin. Goodbye.'

She didn't want to go back through the bar, and face Tanya's bad jokes and Jem's concern. She went out of the back gate, and all the way round to the front of the pub to collect her bike. And fortunately there was no one to see the few, fierce tears she smeared away as she rode back to Mermaid's Cottage.

Luke's bicycle was propped up against the garage door, and Smith came bounding up to the gate when she opened it. As usual, getting herself and her bike through the gap while the dog frisked joyfully round her took considerable effort, and she was unhappily aware that she was shouting at him more angrily than usual. 'Poor old Smithy,' she said, as he followed her round to the back door. 'It isn't fair, I shouldn't take it out on you.'

There was no sign of her son in the kitchen, although a dead mouse lay stiff and stark on the floor in front of Smith's basket. With a sigh, Kate wrapped it up in newspaper and put it in the bin. Then, alerted by the sounds of the television, she went into the sitting room and found Luke watching the local news.

He didn't seem to notice that anything was amiss, and as she became involved in the usual early evening routine – plans for supper, enquiries about school and homework, making sure that both her children had everything ready for the next day – the pain of the quarrel seemed to diminish. Only Tamsin, brought home by Simon in his sleek BMW, gave her one or two covert glances, as if she realised that her mother wasn't quite as normal. But she didn't say anything, and Kate, reluctant to discuss her private affairs with either of her offspring, decided not to

113

enlighten her. If she split up with Justin, Luke would be devastated and Tamsin ecstatic, and between the two of them she doubted she could stay sane.

And the very fact that she could acknowledge that the affair might end, she knew, was an ominous sign.

Jem, of course, was still at the Unicorn with Charlie and Tanya. With surprise, Kate realised that she missed his lively, entertaining presence. They had fallen into the habit, on these long, warm summer evenings, of sharing a drink or two on the patio as the sun went down, and talking about everything and nothing: the weather, gardening, music, old TV programmes, films, books. She had enjoyed those lighthearted conversations very much: it was a pleasure to have another adult to talk to on a regular basis, especially one who was knowledgeable, humorous and amusing, and who seemed to be entirely free of any hang-ups or darker subtexts. She felt that she had known him for much longer than a few weeks, and in his company she could relax, and be completely herself.

There was nothing on the box that evening, and she didn't want to sit out on the patio alone with her thoughts, so she decided on a bath and an early bed with one of the library books she never usually had much time to read. She locked up, knowing that Jem had a key, and went to put the milk bottles outside.

'Kate?'

As the dark figure stepped out of the gloom beyond the porch light, she gasped, her heart thudding.

'Darling, it's only me.'

'Justin! God, you gave me such a fright.' Kate didn't know whether to be relieved or angry. 'What do you want?'

'I'm sorry. Sorry I startled you – sorry about everything.' He came up into the light, and she saw with a pang that his face was full of sadness. 'I saw you were still up, and I couldn't sleep until I'd seen you. Kate, can you please let me explain?'

Looking at his expression, she knew that in all fairness she would have to oblige. 'O.K.,' she said, but stayed firmly in the doorway, determined not to let him in just yet. 'I'm listening.'

'You were right, of course. About the money. I was a banker, remember, darling? And I let all that side of me take over. It's difficult to remember when you're discussing deals that there are real people involved. I got carried away. I did what I shouldn't have, and I'm sorry, darling, I really am sorry.'

'So how much cut were you going to take?'

'A few thousand, that's all. I thought it wouldn't matter – I thought I was doing you a favour. I admit I should have discussed it with you first, but the opportunity arose and I didn't want to lose the right moment.'

Kate stared at him. She realised with dismay that she wanted to believe him, but that she no longer trusted the truth of what he said, no matter how plausible it sounded. It was a good explanation. It had almost convinced her. But still something stuck in her throat, preventing her from swallowing it whole.

'Listen,' she said. 'I want you to get a few things absolutely clear, or there's no point in going on. I am *not* sending the kids away, O.K.?'

'I thought you'd made that quite obvious,' said Justin.

'No harm in saying it again. Second. I know Tamsin doesn't like you much, but I'm not going to nag her about it – that would be completely counter-productive, she'd probably start putting weedkiller in your tea.'

'I don't drink tea.'

Despite herself, Kate smiled. 'I know. Figure of speech. We'll just have to try and work it through gently. And third, and most important. You can tell your developer friends that I'm not going to sell my orchard. I know the money would be more than useful, but we can manage without it. You probably think it's just a patch of useless land with a few old trees that should have been cut down years ago, but that's not how I see it. I remember the hens we kept in there, and the donkeys we had every winter from Weston-super-Mare when the kids were small, and how wonderful all the blossom looks in April, and the cider I want to make when I get the time, and the treehouse that Col built for Luke, and the mistletoe, and I know that I love that patch of ground just as much as the garden, and to see everything torn up for houses would break my heart.' She stared at Justin fiercely, daring him to disagree. 'Compared to all that, I'm afraid the chance of fifty grand in the bank just doesn't weigh equally in the balance. And besides, Tamsin loves the orchard even more than I do. She still hasn't given up hope of having a pony one day. And what good is enough money to buy one, if we haven't got the field to put it in?'

'Well, it's your decision, of course,' said Justin, and a slightly patronising tone entered his voice. 'But I really would advise you to think again. And if you're concerned about the amount of the offer, then I'm sure I can persuade them to put a little more on the table.'

115

'Oh, Justin!' Kate cried. 'You *still* don't understand, do you? You know the price of everything and the value of nothing. I *don't – want – to – sell – the – orchard*. Get it? No deal. Thirty houses on Mermaid's Ground are quite enough to cope with. And in any case, where else am I going to put my plant nursery?'

Justin laughed. 'You're not still hankering after that little pipedream, are you? Anyway, you're being inconsistent. You can't have a pony *and* a nursery.'

'If I sell the orchard, I won't be able to have either,' Kate pointed out. 'And it's rather more than just a dream.'

'Be realistic, darling, it's not going to happen. Now, what am I going to tell Ray Harker in the morning?'

'That it's not for sale,' Kate said resolutely. 'Not now, not next week, not ever. Good night, Justin.'

Jem, strolling back from the Unicorn full of good food and rather more champagne than he would have liked, saw his landlady shut the door firmly on her lover. He heard Justin's muttered and angry reaction, and waited quiet and unseen in the shadows until the other man had disappeared up the lane towards Silver Street Farm. *It's their affair*, he told himself firmly. *They've got to work it out, or not, and it's absolutely nothing to do with me.*

But he knew that it was. After Caroline, he had thought that a few months of celibacy would do him good, allow him to regain his usual equilibrium, give him space to sort out his life and decide whether he wanted to stay in Wiltshire or move back to London. He hadn't been prepared for Kate, despite Charlie's sly comments and nudges: for her understated yet undeniable beauty, classically blonde and English, but possessing a life and spark in her expression and manner that was uniquely her own: for the strength with which she had rebuilt her life after what must have been the appalling blow of Col's unexpected death: and above all for the open, friendly and informal way in which he had been welcomed into her household, and made a part of it. In the few weeks he had lived at Mermaid's Cottage, he had come to feel that he knew her very well. They laughed at the same things, they had a very similar outlook on life, and the difference in their background and upbringing didn't matter at all. Super-ficially, she looked a little like his ex-wife, who was also blonde and tall, but compared to Kate, Caroline was shallow, material-istic and obsessed with outward appearance.

Caro represented the life he had left behind in London, the life to which he had assumed he would return, once Charlie's studios were completed. But over the past weeks, as Moxham and Kate wove their spell, he had found it increasingly hard to imagine going back to the noise, the pollution, the packed streets and crowded, pointless round of socialising with people he didn't like and didn't trust. And without even realising it, he had begun to think about what would happen if he decided to take up Charlie's offer, still on the table, and stay here. He could buy a cosy cottage in the village, see Kate regularly, ask her out, and gently develop their friendship until it turned into something more, something that he found he wanted very much indeed. But it would all be quite impossible if she was still in love with Justin.

He doesn't deserve her, Jem thought, as he walked up to the front door. *I've seen his sort before. Handsome, charming, they all think they're God's gift and that they can get away with murder because they've only got to crook their little finger and the women will come running. But what can I do about it? Not a lot, if she loves him. It isn't easy sitting on the sidelines watching while he gives her the runaround and treats her like shit, but I'll just have to grin and bear it, because it isn't my business, and because I'm not going to own up to what I'm starting to feel about her. Her life's complicated enough without making her think that she owes me something. It'd spoil our friendship, too, and right now we probably both need that more than anything else.*

The ginger cat, Sevvy, appeared with a hopeful miaow as he put his key in the lock. 'Your lady was right, you are a few whiskers short of a set,' Jem told him, opening the door. 'You and me both, brother. But believe me, it ain't nothing a good book and good music won't cure.'

The light and the kettle were both on in the kitchen, and Kate was standing by the Aga making a fuss of Greyling, who was lying blissfully stretched out on top. She turned with a surprised smile as he came in. 'Hallo. How did Tanya's party go?'

'It was great, a good laugh, right up until closing time. We managed to drink the bar dry – of champagne, at any rate. Then Tanya started on cocktails, and wound up poor Mick something shocking, trying them on him to see if he knew how to make them.'

'I'm glad I came home, then. I'm too old for that mallarkey.'

'If you are, then Tanya certainly is – and me too, come to think of it.' Jem gave her a quick glance from under his dreadlocks. 'Christ, I wouldn't want to have her head in the morning. She can certainly put them away.'

'I know. I'm making some chocolate, would you like some?'

'Yes, please, though it might not go too well with the champagne. I'm not used to drinking like a fish. Why are you laughing?'

Kate, heaping generous spoonfuls of instant chocolate into two mugs, grinned at him. 'What you just said reminded me of something I was supposed to have done when I was about six. I can't remember it at all, but Dad always used to swear it was true.'

'Go on, reveal all.'

'If you insist. Well, my parents were holding a very posh cocktail party, and as a treat my brother and I were allowed to stay up for a bit and hand the nibbles round. And apparently there was one guest who fascinated me. I kept hanging around him and staring at him. So eventually he asked me what I wanted. And I said, "Mummy says you drink like a fish, and I'd really like to see you do it." '

Jem gave a delighted shout of laughter. 'You didn't!'

'Oh, yes, I did. It passed into family folklore – you know, trotted out for the benefit of embarrassed boyfriends, along with nude baby photos and my tap-dancing certificate.'

'Don't tell me. I've got a few skeletons in my own closet that my mother likes to bring out for an airing occasionally.'

'Come on, fair's fair, I told you one of mine, now you return the favour.'

Jem pantomimed reluctance. 'Do I *have* to?'

'Certainly you do, or no chocolate.'

'Well, there was the time I stuck my bare bum out of the front window just as the minister of Mum's church was coming up the path.'

Kate giggled. 'And how old were you?'

'Oh, about eighteen. No, I tell a lie, about eight. Mum was furious. She said she'd never be able to hold up her head in church again.'

'I can imagine. Mooning at the minister – the shame of it! Actually, Luke once took all his clothes off and danced at the wedding of a friend of mine, but he doesn't like to be reminded of it. We have the proof on video, though, and it's a powerful blackmail weapon. Even though he was only four at the time.' Kate grinned at him, marvelling how the pleasure of only a few minutes of his company could banish her troubles to the periphery of her thoughts. 'And as for Tamsin, I think we'll just draw a veil over her transgressions. Anyway, she'd never forgive me for telling you. She thinks you're the bee's knees, or hadn't you noticed?'

'Can't say I had.' Jem smiled.

'Well, I have, and I can tell you it makes life a lot easier. Where Tamsin hates, she hates with a vengeance. No half measures with her.' Kate yawned. 'God, I'm exhausted! I'm off to bed.'

'Good night, Mrs Williams.'

'And don't call me Mrs Williams!'

'Surely not!'

'And don't call me Shirley either.' She grinned at him happily. 'Why do I always feel ridiculously cheerful after these silly conversations?'

'That's Doctor Forrester's Tonic, ma'am – a little goes a long way.' Jem smiled back. 'Glad to be of service.'

'Can you put on some music for a bit?' Kate asked him from the door. 'I like hearing it seeping up through the floorboards.'

'Of course I will. Any requests?'

'Something beautiful,' Kate said. In her grubby work clothes, her hair ruffled and her smooth clear skin devoid of make-up and flushed with tiredness, she was utterly desirable and, even more wonderfully, completely unaware of it. Jem said, smiling, 'I know just the thing. Good night, Kate, and sleep well!'

She had not thought, after all the emotional upsets of the past few hours, that she would. But she lay in bed in the dark and listened to the pure, soaring voice of Annie Lennox singing 'A Whiter Shade of Pale', and slumber claimed her quicker than she knew.

Chapter Ten

Moxham's village hall was, in common with most of its kind, a large, draughty and rather shabby building, with the remains of last year's Christmas tinsel still adhering to the highest corners, and paint scuffed and marked by the rampaging children in the playgroup. Almost everyone in the village visited it at least once a week: toddler group for the smallest inhabitants, Brownies, Cubs and Guides for bigger children, keep fit and American line dancing for their mothers, WI and the Wednesday Club (popularly referred to as Wrinklies Afternoon) for their grandparents. The Moxham Minstrels put on their twice-yearly shows on the uneven, splintery stage, and the PTA held fund-raising bazaars and discos for all ages. Like all village mothers, Kate was cheerfully familiar with every rip in the curtains, every quirk of the elderly cooker, and every obstruction to normal life dreamed up by the caretaker, who seemed to regard it as a personal affront to be asked to perform the duties laid down in his contract.

The parish council held their meetings in the hall on the first Wednesday of every month. As a rule, they were lucky to attract a quorum of their members, let alone any interested spectators: after all, the siting of dog refuse bins, wrangles over footpath maintenance and the allocation of allotments were hardly the stuff of high drama. Luke had attended once, as part of a Democracy in Action project at school, and had remarked afterwards that he'd seen more action in a glass of fizzy water.

But this special meeting, called to discuss the plans for Mermaid's Ground, was packed. Filled with unreasonable optimism, the clerk had set out a dozen chairs (grey plastic, ergonomically designed to be as uncomfortable as possible after two minutes and crippling after twenty), and found them occupied within seconds. By the time Kate and her children arrived, just before the advertised start at seven-thirty, every chair in the place had been pressed into service, and the only places left to sit were on the tables at the back.

She squeezed her way through and found a rather precarious perch. Tamsin sat beside her, and Luke beyond. As Kate had expected, her daughter had greeted the news of the possible housing estate next door with passionate rage and denial. 'They can't! They *can't*! What about the badgers? And Robin Hood's oak?'

'There's not a lot you can do about it,' Luke had told her, with the superior worldliness that his extra five years bestowed on him. 'Unless you want to chain yourself to the bulldozers or something.'

'I'll do that, then! I'll do *anything* if it'll stop them!' And Tamsin had turned to her mother, her face twisted with fury, and had shouted, 'This is all *his* idea, isn't it? *He* wants to do it! Well, I hate him and I wish he was dead!'

It had taken some time for Kate to convince her that although she didn't quite share Tamsin's extremes of emotion, she did in general think that building houses on Mermaid's Ground was not a good thing, and that there were other sites in the village where they would be better put. At this point, Kate had realised that Luke had gone rather quiet, and was looking very serious. He had taken no part in any discussion about the plans, though, and had blocked off any attempt on her part to get him to talk. She'd been very relieved when Jem had offered him the job of preparing the Triumph for sale, and the sight of their two very different heads, one blond and one dreadlocked, bent over the gleaming yellow bike, was oddly reassuring. If Luke confided any of his doubts or concerns to Jem, neither of them passed anything on to Kate, but she was glad that her son no longer seemed so partisan in his support for Justin.

Both of her children had insisted on coming to the meeting. She had no doubts about Luke's behaviour, but had been forced to extract stringent promises from Tamsin about what would be appropriate. Her daughter was quite capable of shouting abuse from the back of the hall, and apart from the embarrassment potential, Kate had pointed out that they didn't want to be thrown out of the meeting before they'd had the chance to make their views plain in a sensible and rational manner. 'Screaming and shouting may be what you *want* to do, and believe me, something in me wants to yell about it too. But this isn't the time or the place. No one will listen to ranting and raving, but they will listen to quiet common sense.'

'So you hope,' Tamsin had muttered, but she had promised, knowing that otherwise she would be sent off to Charlotte's.

Kate knew most of the crowd in the hall, at least by sight. Mothers at the school: people she'd gardened for: friends and neighbours. To her surprise, Tanya was sitting at the end of the second row, wearing a short black leather skirt and long boots. Jem, beside her, turned and gave Kate a friendly wave. She saw another resident of Silver Street, John Hamilton, looking very businesslike with clipboard and pen, drawing a sketch of the plans pinned up on an easel by the chairman's desk, and next to him the Enrights, Alec and Priscilla, founders of the Moxham Heritage Society.

No prizes for guessing which side they're on, thought Kate. She hunted for Justin, and eventually spotted him in the first row, just in front of Sal, who overflowed three chairs and effectively blocked her view.

John Minty looked at his watch, banged his gavel on the table and coughed pointedly. At once the clamour in the hall died away into an expectant hush, save for a hungry baby somewhere to Kate's left, and everyone fixed their eyes to the front.

The chairman looked like a businessman, with his neat grey hair and smart suit, but he sounded, incongruously, exactly like a Wiltshire farmer. 'All right, then? I declare this special meeting of Moxham parish council open. As I expect you all know, we're here to discuss the plans which Mr Spencer has put forward for development of the field known as Mermaid's Ground in Silver Street, and by the look of it there's a lot of people want to have their say, so I'll be brief.'

It was all of five minutes before he had finished describing the details of the houses, the proposal that half a dozen of them should be sold at comparatively low cost to bona fide village residents, and the developers' assurance that the mature trees in the field, with the exception of one which was old and dying, would be left unharmed to become a feature of the new estate. Beside Kate, Tamsin had begun to shuffle her bottom restlessly and muttered, 'It's *not* dying, it's *not*.'

Kate had already told herself that she would listen to all the different points of view in a balanced and mature fashion, and form her own opinion as far as possible uncoloured by her personal feelings. This high-minded idea seemed to be receding towards the horizon with alarming rapidity, to be replaced by the distinctly suspect urge to say exactly what she thought of her lover, and precisely where he could put his plans for Mermaid's

Ground. She clamped her lips tight shut, frowned at her daughter, and hoped that the meeting wasn't going to carry on all night – or end in blows.

The chairman finished his spiel at long last, and invited comments from the floor. At once, several hands shot into the air, including, Kate saw, Alec Enright's. John Minty passed him over in favour of John Hamilton, who expressed his doubts about the number of the houses in the field. 'They look as if they're too many and too close together.'

There was a murmur of agreement, but Justin had his answer ready. 'Thirty houses on five acres is, in fact, nearly half the recommended density. According to the regulations, we could put fifty on that field, if we wanted.'

An elderly woman was next. 'Everyone's saying as how there'll be homes for us villagers, but six don't seem very many, do it? And how cheap is cheap? *My* cheap might not be *their* cheap, see.'

'Mr Spencer?'

Justin rose to his feet, with his most charming smile. 'Of course we can't give precise figures at this early stage, but the idea is to build *affordable* houses for local people. And the number isn't set in stone either. If there seems to be the demand, the developers are willing to increase the quantity. But I'll remind you that they're business people, and of course they have to make money. If they're prevented from building enough houses to ensure a profit, then they'll look elsewhere, and Moxham will lose out.'

There was a lot of muttering as he sat down. Alec Enright had been growing more and more restless: at last, unable to ignore him sitting right in front of the table, the chairman indicated that he could speak.

'I represent the Moxham Heritage Society. We are dedicated to the preservation of this extremely picturesque and attractive village, and utterly opposed to inappropriate development. In my view, these plans are completely wrong for the village. As Mr Hamilton has already pointed out, they are too many and far too close together, whatever the regulations might say. However well built, however many trees are kept, they'll be a blot on the landscape that will be impossible to ignore. And the proposal that some of them be kept for villagers is nothing short of bribery.'

'It's all right for you in your mansion,' someone called out from the back. 'Putting up prices so that families who've lived here for generations are forced out, and then you've got the cheek to say we can't have cheap houses!'

'I'm not saying that at all.' Alec Enright's face was growing red above the thick, bushy grey beard. 'I'm not against cheap houses, far from it. I'm just saying that this particular development is in the wrong place and that there are too many houses.'

'But you heard Mr Spencer,' said Dave Castle, who lived at the Home Farm. 'If there aren't so many of them, they won't make no money. And they could've asked for more.'

'And there's the increased traffic to consider,' Enright continued, ignoring him. 'Thirty houses, and every one of them probably with at least one car, if not two or even three. Do we really want our lovely peaceful village to become little more than a suburb of Chippenham or Bath?'

'Highways'll go into that, Mr Enright,' John Minty said. 'That isn't our brief.'

Mick Stevens put his hand up. 'I reckon we need new blood in the village. Apart from a few houses scattered about, there hasn't been any significant building here since the Circus went up, and that's forty years ago. It's all very well for Mr Enright to have his say, but he's only lived in Moxham for a couple of years, and I'm sorry, sir, but you've no idea what it's like for ordinary folk. If we're not careful we'll become a museum piece full of wealthy incomers who haven't got any interest in preserving the community here, only the buildings. Do we really want to be a film set for coach trippers to gawp at? Or do we want to be a *real* place full of *real* people?'

'The Heritage Society are not against *all* development,' said Enright, growing redder by the minute. 'We just feel that a large development like this is not right for Moxham.'

'Well, what *would* be right for Moxham, then?' shouted one of Minty's farm workers. 'And where is it? I don't see it, do you? Take what's offered, I say. Chance like this don't come along every day, do it?'

The chairman rapped the table. 'We would all be grateful if speakers waited their turn. This is a serious meeting, not a free-for-all. Now, Mr Enright, you've had your go, let someone else get a word in. Yes?'

The Colonel's wife rose to her feet, her voice clearly audible above the buzz of comment. 'Peggy Sims. WI president. I really do feel that those who complain about the lack of community here are the very people who take no part in it. We have many clubs and societies for all ages. There is a waiting list for

125

Brownies. Our post office and shop is thriving. In my opinion, we have the balance just right here in Moxham. Moreover, the people most likely to buy the houses will probably work in Bath or Bristol. As Mr Enright has already argued, I don't think any of us want to live in a dormitory village that's dead in the daytime.'

Usually, not many dared to disagree with Mrs Sims, to her face at any rate, but the mood of the meeting had obviously empowered those whom she considered to be her social inferiors. 'You're talking through your hat!' Sal said, and her words drew a chorus of assent.

'Go on, Mum,' Tamsin hissed, nudging her mother in the ribs. 'You said you were going to say something!'

'I'm not so sure now.' Quite obviously most of the people in the hall approved of the development, and Kate could see their point. Justin's carrot had done its work too well: the thought of those cheap houses had blinded most people to the fact that Mermaid's Ground was not the best place for them. She was certain that Justin had quite cynically manipulated and exploited the feelings in the village for his own ends, and equally sure that pointing this out to them would only lead to condemnation being heaped on her own head. But if she didn't speak now, then it would be too late. Reluctantly, she raised her hand.

John Minty indicated that it was her turn. Her heart thumping suddenly, Kate raised her voice. 'Kate Williams. I live next door to Mermaid's Ground, so I'll be the one who's probably going to be the most affected by it, apart from Mr Spencer of course. I'm certainly not against low-cost housing, but I don't think that particular site is appropriate. There are far too many houses packed in, and Silver Street is a very narrow lane with no footpath; it's hardly wide enough for a tractor, let alone big construction machinery. Then all those extra cars are surely going to cause problems too. And finally, no one seems to have thought of the fact that Mermaid's Ground is not just another field: it's undisturbed grassland, of the sort that is almost extinct now. There are cowslips, and wild mushrooms, and rare orchids. There's a badgers' sett, and of course they're protected by law. And the tree that everyone has assumed is dying is in fact perfectly healthy. It could be six or seven hundred years old, easily. It seems a real shame to tear it all up when there are other fields in Moxham where houses would be better put. There's a place by the Home Farm, for instance, that seems ideal. And I think the developers will find that if local wildlife and conservation groups become involved, getting planning permission won't be as easy as they think.'

She was heartened to see that quite a few people were nodding their heads in approval, but a grumble of indignation filled the hall. John Minty banged on the table. 'Quiet, please! May I remind you all that Mrs Williams is just as entitled to air her thoughts as the rest of you. Now, who else wants to speak?'

'Well *done*, Mum,' Tamsin said, her eyes shining. 'You were *wonderful*!'

'I just thought it needed saying, that's all.' Kate found that she was shaking with nervous reaction. 'But there really should be new houses in the village. I just don't think they ought to go there, that's all.'

The man sitting in front of her, father of the girl who helped in the pub, turned round. 'You're all the same, you incomers,' he said. 'Once you're in the village, you want to pull up the drawbridge and keep yourselves all nice and cosy and middle class. Your sort won't be happy till all the likes of us are shovelled off out of your way so's you can enjoy the view without being offended by them as aren't so well off as you. You make me sick!'

'That's really untrue and unfair – that's not what I think at all!' Kate protested, but he had turned round again, ignoring her, and Minty was calling pointedly for silence at the back. She had to sit, taut with distress at the injustice of his accusations, while others had their turn. At last, the chairman called for a vote. 'My apologies to those we haven't heard, but I don't know about you, I don't want to be here all night. It's fairly obvious what it'll be, but I'll see a show of hands anyway, make everything official. Would you do the counting, Mrs Parkinson? Thank you. All those in favour of the development at Mermaid's Ground, please raise your hands.'

There were so many that the clerk had to spend some time totting them up. 'Forty-eight, Mr Chairman.'

'Thank you. And all those against?'

Considerably fewer. Kate raised her arm, and the Enrights, and Colonel and Mrs Sims. Several others – Tom Ross, the artist, and all the other residents of Silver Street – joined her, and Simon Mortimer. And she was surprised and pleased to see Tanya Dobson raising her arm.

'Twenty-nine, Mr Chairman.'

'Would you record that, Mrs Parkinson? Thank you. And thank you all for coming. This matter has obviously stirred up a great deal of interest in the village, and you've had the chance to air your views.' He banged his gavel on the table. 'I now declare this meeting closed. Good night, everyone.'

Amid the noise of scraping chairs and about a hundred people all talking at once, Kate made her way outside. She'd had her say, and a part of her regretted it, because of the bad feeling her reluctant stand would inevitably cause. And Justin wouldn't like it one bit.

Why, oh why did he ever put in those bloody plans? she thought, as she emerged into the dusk. It had clouded over while the meeting had been in progress, and there was rain in the air. The sunset, a thin angry red line in the west, perfectly matched her mood. She looked round for Luke and Tamsin, and found herself accosted by a smart young woman in a navy-blue suit, carrying a tape recorder. 'Mrs Williams? Julie Sharpe, from the *Wiltshire Star*. You were one of those who objected to the plans, weren't you?'

'Yes, I was,' said Kate, acutely aware of the hostile glances being directed her way by some of those who were filing past.

'And would you like to clarify your objections?'

A photographer stepped forward and there was a brilliant flash. *Oh, God, this'll be all over the front page on Friday.* Kate took a deep breath, trying to keep her words as low-key as possible. 'It's – it's mainly because I feel that there are too many houses, on the wrong site. And the conservation angle seems to have been completely forgotten. I'm not at all against development as such. I really do think Moxham needs it. But I don't feel that Mermaid's Ground is the right place. I'm sure if we looked a bit harder we could find some land that wasn't so rich in wildlife.'

'I see. And you live next door to the proposed development?'

'Yes. But that isn't the reason. If I lived on the other side of the village, I'd still think it was in the wrong place.'

'In there, you predicted that if conservation organisations became involved, the developers would find it hard to get permission. Are you a member of any such body?'

Kate shook her head. 'No, I'm not. But I do think they ought to know about the threat to Mermaid's Ground. Their support could prove vital.'

'Thank you very much, Mrs Williams.' The reporter gave her a bright smile and turned away in search of other prey.

'Kate, my dear.' Alec Enright came up to her. He was a rotund bear of a man who had made his money in computer software, sold up at a vast profit, and chosen Moxham as the location for an early and extremely comfortable retirement. 'I would like to thank you for your support. It's not easy, swimming against the tide of greed and materialism, but people like you can make all the difference. Have you ever considered joining our Society? We're planning to publish a booklet on the historic buildings of the village, and of course your house will be featured.'

'I'll think about it,' said Kate. She wanted most urgently to go home, but there was still no sign of her children, and she could imagine, all too easily, what Tamsin might be saying to Justin. 'Sorry, I've got to find the kids.'

Swimming against the tide, she struggled back inside the hall, and found her way blocked by Sal. 'I'm shocked at you, Kate,' said the postmistress reproachfully. 'I thought you'd be bound to be with us, in your situation and all.'

'I'm really sorry, but I can't,' Kate said. 'So we'll just have to agree to differ.' She wasn't in the mood for arguments: the adrenalin had long since stopped flowing, and all she wanted now was a hot bath and a long cold reviving drink, not necessarily in that order.

'I don't suppose Mr Spencer's very happy either,' Sal pursued, with a significant look.

'That's his business.' Kate finally managed to squeeze past her, and saw Luke and Tamsin in animated conversation with Tanya and Jem. Over by the desk, John Minty was talking to Justin as he rolled up the plan of the development. Her lover's savage glare left her in no doubt of the strength of his feelings. She ignored him and went over to her children. 'Come on, you guys. It's almost dark – long past your bedtime, Tamsin.'

'Hallo, Kate. You did good, it must've taken a lot of guts to speak out.' Tanya grinned at her. 'Specially in your circumstances.'

'I only said what I thought was right,' Kate told her. 'Which was probably a very stupid thing to do.'

'You're in trouble with him,' Tanya went on, with a pointed glance at Justin. 'He's looking daggers at you.'

'I know, and I'm sorry, but I had to speak up for the wildlife, no one else was going to.'

'I think you were great, Mum,' Tamsin said, taking her arm and hugging it. 'Really, really great.'

'And the awful thing is that I can't help agreeing with the other side too,' Kate said sadly. 'I just don't think they should build houses on Mermaid's Ground. And I can understand that some people think I'm objecting just because it's next door.'

'I don't blame you,' Tanya said. 'I'd feel just the same in your shoes, but I couldn't speak out like you just did. Gawd, it'd frighten the life out of me!' She gave an elegant stretch. 'Them chairs – it's like sitting on a bed of nails. I could really do with a drink, want to come down the pub, Kate?'

'No, thanks. I've got to take these two home. But how about coming back to my place?'

'Really? Yeah, thanks, that'd be great. I've nothing much to get back for while Charlie's away. He called today, said he's going to be at least another week.' Tanya winked at her. 'And while the cat's away . . . Want a lift, Jem?'

'We've got our bikes,' said Kate. 'And there certainly isn't room for us all in your little car.'

'It's big enough for what I need,' said Tanya, and giggled suggestively. 'Come on, let's go.'

The reporter was interviewing Justin as they left the hall. Kate saw his vehement gestures and angry face, and knew that he was still furious with her. *But I had to speak out*, she thought stubbornly. *I had to put the record straight about Robin Hood's oak, if nothing else.*

It was not far back to Mermaid's Cottage, along Steep Lane from the village hall, a sharp right-hander into Corsham Lane and then straight on into Silver Street. Several times they were overtaken by cars leaving the meeting, and the driver of one of them shouted something as he passed. The words were fortunately unintelligible, but the tone, and the meaning, were all too obvious. Kate set her jaw and squared her shoulders resolutely. Airing her opinions hadn't made her popular, but she knew that her conscience would never have allowed her to remain silent while Mermaid's Ground was destroyed without a struggle.

Tanya's snappy little sports car had been one of those which had passed them, and it was waiting for them in the drive of Mermaid's Cottage when they turned in through the gate. There was no sign of her or Jem, however. Kate unlocked the garage so that they could put their bikes away, and opened the front door to let Smith out. She sent Tamsin upstairs to get ready for bed, despite her furious protests, and reminded Luke that he had his maths homework to do before school in the morning.

'It's O.K., Mum, I'll do it now,' said her son. 'I've already looked at it and it's really easy, it won't take long.' He paused, staring at her earnestly. With surprise, and some shock, Kate realised that he was taller than she was now. He added, in a very low voice, 'Does – does all this mean that you're going to split up with Justin?'

'Oh, Luke, I honestly don't know. It's all gone to pieces so quickly, and I don't see how we can put everything back together again. Not the way it was, at any rate. You do see that, don't you?'

'I suppose so,' he said at last. 'But it's a real shame. I liked Justin.'

It wasn't until he had disappeared upstairs that she realised that he'd used the past tense.

She was taking a bottle of Australian wine out of the fridge when Jem and Tanya came in. Charlie's wife chuckled. 'Wallaby White, Charlie always calls that stuff.'

'Or Kangarouge,' said Jem, grinning. 'What was the line in *Monty Python*? "A wine for laying down and avoiding".'

'You're a bit out of date,' Kate pointed out. 'This is delicious, have some.'

'I'll stick to a Martini, thanks, Kate,' said Tanya. 'With lots of ice and not too much lemon, ta.'

They carried their drinks into the conservatory, and Jem went to put some music on. Tanya sank into the cushioned hanging chair with a luxurious sigh. 'Ain't this the life, eh? You know, Kate, you're right about them houses. Jem's been showing me the field. All packed in like sardines, I wouldn't want to live in 'em. And I reckon once they get planning permission the price of those so-called cheap ones will go through the roof.'

'Well, I've done my bit and said my piece.' Kate took a long sip of cool wine and felt a lot better. 'Now it's up to the district council.'

'Let's hope they listen to you and that Enright bloke,' said Tanya.

'I don't suppose they will. Probably they'll just reduce the number of houses by enough to make it a bit less crowded, without putting the developers off, and get it through that way. It's ironic really,' said Kate, with a rueful smile. 'I've never had much time for the Moxham Heritage Society, and still less for Alec Enright pontificating about the evils of modern materialism while he drives a top-of-the-range Mercedes, but I'm their flavour of the month, while most of the people I *do* like won't speak to me. Oh, God, I wish Justin had never thought of putting those bloody houses up! Whatever possessed him?'

'The thought of lots of dosh, I expect,' said Tanya. 'It's bleeding hard to resist, innit? I've taken all me clothes off in front of total strangers before now, just for a couple of hundred quid.'

'You never know,' Kate pointed out. 'He might be short of cash.'

'Well, he don't exactly give the impression of being hard up.' Tanya was already halfway through her Martini. 'But Marcia said he hadn't paid his slate at the Unicorn for a while. And he certainly does like the high life. All them posh restaurants and fancy booze cost a packet. What did he do before he started being a secondhand car dealer, then?'

'Don't let him hear you call him that. Classic vehicle broker, please.'

'I don't care. 'S all he is, a secondhand car dealer,' Tanya said stubbornly. 'And I never met one that wasn't crooked as a corkscrew. My uncle Terry sells motors, and he'd flog his own mother if he thought there was a market. So, what did he do before?'

'He was a banker with some big firm in the City. I'd always assumed that's how he made his pile.'

'Insider dealing, I betcha.' Tanya tapped the side of her slim, slightly retroussé nose.

'I think he was pretty successful – big bonuses, share options, that sort of thing,' said Kate, feeling she ought to defend her lover's reputation in his absence, even if at present he wasn't speaking to her. 'And his mother was very well off, too, so he must have inherited her money as well as the farm.'

'Well, whatever, Charlie's a millionaire and he wouldn't say no to a bit more,' said Tanya. 'Justin's a businessman, ain't he, he knows the score. You don't get rich by turning money down. Here, I like that music,' she added, as Jem came in. 'African, innit?'

'Spot on. Ladysmith Black Mambazo. They sang on *Graceland.*'

'The harmonies are wonderful,' Kate said, as the unaccompanied voices wove a rich and complicated tapestry of sound. 'I can't understand a word of it, but it's absolutely stunning.'

'Can't understand a bleeding word of opera either,' said Tanya, setting down her empty glass hopefully. 'And that ain't stunning. Any old cat could do better.'

'I finally stopped taking opera seriously when I watched some big prestige production on the telly,' said Jem. 'All sung in Italian, of course, so they had a narrator. He said something like, "In comes the young and beautiful peasant girl," and on waddled an eighteen-stone forty-five-year-old diva with half an inch of make-up and a voice to shatter glass. I'd rather listen to Captain Haddock.'

'If you're not careful I'll take you up on that,' said Kate, laughing.

It was three Martinis later, and well after eleven, before Tanya at last took her leave. Jem said good night and went off to his room. Kate was loading the dishwasher when suddenly the back door crashed open beside her.

She screamed in shock and dropped the glass she was holding. 'You bitch,' said Justin, his voice shaking with rage. 'You bloody stupid treacherous bitch! How *dare you* say all that rubbish in public?'

He was drunk: even from several feet away, Kate could smell the whisky on his breath. She took a discreet step back, hearing her feet crunch on the broken glass. 'I think you'd better go home,' she said, astonished at how steady her voice sounded. 'We'll talk about it in the morning.'

'We're going to talk about it *now*, you lying bitch!' He advanced on her threateningly. Kate retreated until her back was pressed against the worksurface opposite the sink. *The knife-block's just behind me if I need it,* she thought, and then, in horror, *this is* Justin, *not some masked intruder, it's* Justin!

'No, we're not,' she said, with the same brisk firmness which she used to handle Tamsin in one of her strops. 'Now go home and calm down, before you say something we'll both regret. I'm going to bed.'

'Then I'm coming too.' Justin loomed over her, smelling of drink and cigarette smoke so strongly that she almost gagged. She raised her hands to push him away, and another voice broke in. 'Is everything all right?'

To her utter relief, Jem was standing in the doorway to the dining room, an expression of considerable concern on his face. She stepped adroitly sideways, out of Justin's reach, and indicated the back door. 'It's O.K., Jem. He's just going. Aren't you, Justin?'

Her lover stayed put, glaring at the other man. 'This is none of your business, so keep your nose out of it. Go on, bugger off.'

'I'm not going until I'm sure Kate's all right,' said Jem, with a pleasant but obdurate smile. He leaned against the doorpost and folded his arms. 'I believe she said you were just leaving?'

'Yes, he was,' Kate said. She fixed Justin with a fierce, unwavering stare. His blue eyes were bloodshot, and obviously found it difficult to focus. She added, 'For Christ's sake go home and sleep it off! And then we can have a rational discussion in the morning, when you've sobered up and come down off your high horse.'

For a long, long moment she thought that he was going to defy her. 'All right, I'm going!' he said at last. 'But you're not going to get away with it so easily. By the time you've finished, you'll regret you ever went to that meeting.'

'There are a lot of things I think I might regret,' Kate said. 'But I'm damn sure that won't be one of them.'

For an instant longer their eyes met in wordless hostility. Then, with an exclamation of rage, he turned and went out into the night, slamming the door behind him with a crash that seemed to shake the whole house.

Kate ran to it, turned the key and slammed the bolts. Relief washed over her in a tide, leaving her trembling. She leaned over the sink, wondering if she was going to be sick. Something pushed against her leg, and she realised after a moment that it was Smith, trying to comfort her in the only way he knew.

'It's all right, old boy,' she said, laughing weakly. 'All over now. He's gone.'

'Has he got a key?' Jem was bent down with a dustpan and brush, sweeping up the glass. He stood up and stared at her, his brown eyes very troubled. 'I think if I were you, I'd be planning to change the locks.'

'I wasn't thinking of anything so drastic. I mean, it's *Justin*, for Christ's sake!' Kate gazed at him unhappily. 'Thank you – thank you for what you did.'

'I didn't do much.'

'Maybe not, but you were *there*, in the right place at the right time. And I'm really, really grateful. God knows what would have happened if you hadn't appeared. I actually found myself wondering where the knife-block was.' She gave a desperate squawk of laughter. 'And I really can't afford to take time out in Holloway.'

'Mum?' It was Tamsin, her eyes huge in her sleep-flushed face, barefoot in her nightshirt. 'Mum, I heard shouting, what's happened?'

'It's all right, sweetheart. Justin came round and we had a bit of an argument, that's all.'

'Has he gone now? Will he come back?'

'Yes, he's gone, and no, he won't come back. Not tonight, anyway. We'll have to have a talk tomorrow.'

'Will you tell him to get lost?'

'I don't know.' Suddenly exhausted, Kate contemplated the ruins of her love life. 'But that's up to me, sweetheart.'

'Well, I hope you do. He's got no *right* to come bursting in in the middle of the night and upset you,' said Tamsin furiously. 'Don't you think so too?' she added, appealing to Jem.

'As I've been reminded, it's really none of my business,' he said. 'But whatever happens, I'm sure your mother can handle it. She's undoubtedly a woman of steel.'

'Am I? At this precise moment,' said Kate, with some intensity, 'I feel more like a woman of wet string. Come on, Tamsin, I'll take you back to bed.'

'Are you sure you'll be O.K.?' Jem asked softly, as the child went out of the room.

'Positive.' Kate gave him a determined smile. 'Yes, honestly. I – I don't really know what can have come over him, he's never behaved like that before. Too much whisky, I suppose. I could do with a drop myself, but there's none in the house. I'll have to make do with the dregs of the wine.'

'I'll make you some hot chocolate if you like.'

'No, it's O.K., I'm all right. Thanks for the offer, though. And thanks – lots and lots of thanks – for earlier. You probably saved me from a lengthy prison sentence.'

'All part of the service, ma'am,' said Jem, and made her smile. 'Good night, and sleep well!'

'Of course I will,' Kate said firmly, in an attempt to convince herself as much as him. 'Good night, and see you in the morning.'

But despite her stalwart words, it was a long, long time indeed before her thoughts allowed her to sleep.

Chapter Eleven

It was extraordinarily easy, after the dramas of the previous evening, to behave absolutely as normal. After all, Kate thought as she checked Tamsin's rucksack to make sure that she had everything necessary for school, whatever happened there was still breakfast to be made, teeth to be cleaned, and the dog to be walked. Jem had already taken Smith down the lane: apart from a soft, 'O.K., Kate?' he had made no reference to the events of the night before, and she was grateful. She wondered what he thought of Justin now, and suspected that it would not be pleasant. Her own feelings, however, were still too wildly confused to analyse. She simply found it impossible to reconcile the drunken brute who had abused and threatened her with the charming lover who had captured her heart a year ago.

Luke had already set off for school on his bike, and she had no idea whether he was aware of what had happened. She knew she ought to talk to him, but in the bustle of their everyday lives it was hard to find a calm space to sit down and discuss the situation. He had always been placid and quiet: she knew that he thought a great deal, but he never revealed much of what went on inside his head.

Tamsin, on the other hand, was often as transparent as glass. Fortunately, she had overslept this morning, and in the rush to get ready for school in time, there was no space for talk. Kate saw her whizzing off up the lane, pedalling furiously with her overflowing rucksack on her back and her hair unbrushed. Then she locked the house up and went off to the Court, where they were expecting a delivery of the huge pots and giant plants Charlie had ordered for the courtyard.

It was just before lunch when Mrs Wallis, the housekeeper, came out to find her. 'Call for you, Kate – it's the school.'

Up to her elbows in John Innes No. 3, with sacks of compost, unplanted shrubs and thirty terracotta pots stacked up beside her like a regiment waiting for orders, Kate swore softly under her breath and took the cordless phone. 'Hallo?'

'Ah, Kate.' It was Jane Hale, the head of Moxham School. 'Sorry to bother you, but I think you'd better come down. There's been a bit of trouble.'

'With Tamsin? What's happened?'

'There was a rather unfortunate episode in the playground just now, and she's very upset.'

'I'll be right there,' Kate promised, and handed the receiver back to Sylvia Wallis. 'I've got to pop out for a few minutes, but I should be back for lunch.'

'You'd better be,' said the housekeeper. 'I've done one of my quiches and I don't want it going to waste.'

At the school, the playground was full of shrieking children, enjoying their midday break. Kate leant her bike up against the wall and went inside, wondering what she was going to find. Tamsin had never been an easy child, and she'd often been in trouble in the past, but this time, it seemed, she was the innocent party.

She was sitting in the staffroom, with the welfare assistant bathing her leg. With horror, Kate saw that there was a big graze on the side of her face, and her knees were both bleeding. 'What's happened?' she cried.

Although she had been quite composed, at the sight of her mother Tamsin burst into noisy tears. 'They – they pushed me over!'

'Who did?'

'Shelley Baker and Claire Evans.' Tamsin wiped her dirty, tear-streaked face with a filthy handkerchief. 'They started going on about the meeting last night and how we didn't want anyone to live next door to us because we're posh and stuck-up and think we're too good for them, and I said it was all stupid lies and of *course* we didn't think that and then they called *me* a liar and then they pushed me over and kicked me.' She sniffed loudly. 'But I managed to hit Shelley before Mrs Hale came over.'

'Oh, God.' Kate stared at her in acute distress. 'Oh, Tamsin, I'm so sorry.'

'It's not *your* fault, Mum. It's theirs for being so stupid,' said Tamsin fiercely, and blew her nose.

'Mrs Hale is dealing with the girls now,' said the welfare assistant. 'She'll be along in a minute. I think that's got all the dirt out. You've been very brave, Tamsin, some of those cuts are quite deep. I'll just put some cream on, and a plaster on that knee. I don't think the other one's so bad. I've already done the one on her face.'

'Is it bad, Mum?'

'It looks quite impressive,' said Kate, inspecting the damage, 'but I don't think you'll be scarred for life.'

'Here's Mrs Hale,' said the welfare assistant, getting to her feet. 'I'll go and put the first aid box away. Are you all right now, Tamsin?'

The child nodded, and gave her a rather watery grin. Then Jane Hale entered, escorting the two culprits. They both came from old Moxham families, and Kate had known them since toddler group. She was pleased to see that they looked extremely chastened, and had obviously been crying.

'Now,' said the head severely, folding her arms. 'You have something to say to Tamsin, don't you?'

'Sorry,' the two girls said in unison, and plainly meant it.

Tamsin stared up at them with more than a trace of her usual belligerence. 'O.K.,' she said at last. 'But you'd better not do it again.'

'Tamsin!'

'I don't think they will, Mrs Williams,' said Jane. 'Things just got a little out of hand, didn't they, Shelley and Claire? But as you know, we have a very strict anti-bullying policy at this school, and be assured that I will come down very hard indeed on anyone else who behaves as these two girls have done today. A letter will go home to their parents informing them of what has happened, of course.'

'My mum'll kill me,' Shelley muttered.

'I doubt she'll go that far, but she might be tempted,' said the head drily. 'Right, girls, you two are on help duties during every playtime for the next week, understand? Mrs Hall is clearing out the PE cupboard, so you can go and give her a hand now.'

The girls filed meekly out. Jane turned to Kate. 'I'm so sorry about this, Mrs Williams. They trapped her in a corner of the playground, out of my line of sight. Her friend Charlotte came running to tell me what was going on, and I caught them red-handed. As you know, I refuse to tolerate that sort of behaviour, and both girls have been warned that if it happens again, they'll be suspended. They're not usually trouble, so I don't anticipate any repetition. I'll speak to the whole school at assembly tomorrow, just to reinforce the rules.'

'Thank you,' Kate said. She grinned rather wryly. 'If I'd known what was going to happen, I think I would have kept my

139

mouth shut at the meeting last night.'

'*Don't* say that, Mum! You shouldn't take any notice of what those stupid people were saying!'

'Disagreeing with someone doesn't make them stupid,' Kate reminded her. 'We can't all think the same. But no one's threatened to beat me up, have they? It's you who's paid the price.'

'Worth it,' said Tamsin. She turned to Jane. 'Can I go back outside now, Mrs Hale?'

'Yes, of course, if you're sure—'

'I want to see Charlotte,' said Tamsin, getting rather stiffly to her feet. 'Ow, it hurts!'

'You can come back to the Court with me if you like,' said Kate. To her surprise, her daughter shook her head emphatically. 'No, thanks, Mum. I'm all right. Thanks for coming, though. See you later!'

'I think she wants to play the wounded soldier,' Kate said, smiling. 'I do hope there isn't any more trouble, though. I feel bad enough about speaking out as it is, and everyone seems to have got completely the wrong idea about why I did it.'

'That's the trouble with gossip,' said Jane Hale, who, sensibly, lived in Corsham, where her private life could stay private. 'Prejudice and rumour are usually much more attractive and interesting than the truth.'

'I wish I could disagree with you,' Kate said. 'Thanks, Jane. I know you'll deal with anything else that comes up. Anyway, it's quite a relief to find that Tamsin's the innocent party for once.'

'She's actually turning into a very nice, sensible, reliable girl,' said the head. 'She has her moments, of course, but don't we all?'

'Are we talking about the same Tamsin?' Kate demanded incredulously.

'Of course we are,' said Jane. 'And if she harnesses all that passion to something worthwhile, she'll go a long way. Wait and see!'

It had been a curiously uplifting interlude, Kate reflected as she cycled back to the Court. And she'd been greatly heartened by a glimpse of her daughter in the playground, showing off her injuries to an impressed and excited crowd of children while Charlotte stood protectively in attendance. Tamsin was tough and resilient. She could cope.

By five o'clock, the walled space between the swimming pool in the old orangery and the main wing of the house was beginning to resemble the Mediterranean courtyard of Tanya's fevered imagination. Camellias, yuccas and young citrus trees had been potted up and now stood carefully grouped in every corner. Kate swept up the spilt compost, put it back in a half-finished sack, and surveyed the fruits of her labours with a critical eye. It needed climbers: old rambling roses, or a summer jasmine, perhaps one with variegated leaves, planted in each of the small beds in front of the orangery's pillars. Plumbago and bougainvilia already grew in pots inside, thriving in the warm atmosphere around the pool. On a hot sunny day, with the tall arched french windows open all along the wall, she could imagine the bees softly humming as they bumbled between the flowers, while the heady scent of jasmine filled the air.

Tanya had gone shopping in Bath, so she couldn't ask for her opinion, and Charlie, of course, was still in New York and likely to be there for some time. She wanted the benefit of another eye, someone who could look at it critically and give her an honest opinion, and, right on cue, Jem walked in from the walled garden. 'Hi, Kate. How's tricks?'

'What do you think of it?' She gestured at the courtyard. The old stone flags bounced the warmth of the afternoon sun back into the air, and the small pool in the centre, newly stocked with plants and fish, gazed reflectively up at the sapphire sky. 'It's not finished, there's another batch of pots and plants due next week, but I'd like to know if it looks completely wrong.'

'It looks completely amazing,' said Jem, staring round. 'As if we'd suddenly been transported to Spain or Italy.'

'That's the effect Tanya wants. She's not here, though, so I need someone to point out the obvious.'

'The pots look much too new.'

'I know, but the poor things can't help that, they *are* new. Anyway, there's a neat little trick involving watered-down yoghurt and a large paintbrush, and they'll soon look suitably weathered. The ones coming next week are real secondhand Grecian urns – and *don't* ask me whether they get a drachma a day, I've already had that from Tanya. They'll be all mossy and lichened. And it'll look very different once the plants have had a chance to get established.'

'Who's going to have the job of watering them all?'

'Darren. I've already told him, morning and evening. There's no point in doing it any other time in hot weather, it'll just evaporate. But does it look *right*? Does it go with the house? That's what I'm worried about – I can arrange and rearrange pots until the cows come home.'

Jem gave the courtyard a long, considering inspection. Finally, he said, 'Yes. Yes, it does. I had my doubts too. I thought it was one of Tanya's lunatic fancies and bound to look wrong. Like the crimson wallpaper she insisted on having in the drawing room, you think it'll be awful and it isn't.'

'Thanks. I know it isn't up to me, I'm just the minion and I do what I'm told, but I had awful visions of having to send everything back.' She gave a long stretch, and grinned at him. 'Well, that's me finished for the day. What about you?'

'I came to tell you that I've got a lot more to do, unfortunately. There's a glitch in the wiring and it needs sorting out. I'll grab something to eat at the pub on the way past. I promised the sparks a couple of beers if he'd stay late and give me a hand. So expect me when you see me.'

'I will,' said Kate, and went to find her bike.

She stopped at Megan's house to pick up Tamsin, and was persuaded to have a cup of tea and a post mortem on the meeting. 'Simon said you spoke really well,' Megan told her.

'I said what I thought – and if it's led to trouble for poor Tamsin, then I really wish I hadn't bothered.'

'Tamsin can look after herself,' said Megan. 'She's a tough cookie. She said on the way home that if anyone tried it again, she'd *really* fight back. If those girls had done that to Charlotte, she'd be a weeping jelly.'

'Charlotte doesn't have a mother who makes a habit of shooting her mouth off. Tamsin may be tough, but I don't want her to have to be. And I don't like the way people have twisted my motives and assumed that I'm a toffee-nosed git who doesn't want the lower orders sharing my village. I'm not, am I?'

'Hardly.'

'But not for my mother's want of trying.' Kate grinned ruefully. 'Funny, isn't it? All I ever wanted was to be liked, but somehow I've managed to make all these people *dis*like me. First my mother, then Justin, and now half of Moxham.'

'It'll blow over,' said Megan, with infectious confidence. 'There's the flower show soon, and people will be so busy arguing about the results they'll forget all about Mermaid's Ground. Come on, have some more cake.'

It was nearly six when she finally got home with Tamsin. Luke wouldn't be back yet: he'd gone swimming with some friends after school. But the gate was open. *The postman must have forgotten to shut it*, Kate thought, wheeling her bike through the

142

gap, and then stopped so abruptly that Tamsin almost rammed her from behind. 'Watch it, Mum!'

'Wait.' Kate held out an arm to detain her. 'Look. Is that glass?'

Scattered liberally over the gravel between the gate and the front door were the remains of what looked like half-a-dozen milk bottles, broken into jagged pieces. The sunlight glinted wickedly on the sharp edges. Feeling suddenly sick, Kate said, 'This has been done deliberately.'

'Who? Who would do such a horrible thing to us?' Tamsin demanded, and then answered her own question. 'People who didn't like what you said at the meeting.'

'Oh, come on, this is *Moxham*, not some inner-city hellhole.' Kate leaned her bike against the hedge. 'Well, we can't stand here looking at it. We've got to clear it up before we let Smith out, it'd cut his paws to shreds. There are a couple of buckets and some gardening gloves in the garage.'

It took nearly half an hour of concentrated searching before Kate was sure that all the glass had been removed. To make certain, she went over the gravel with a rake, to turn up any pieces that might have been missed. Inside the house, the dog was hurling himself against the door in maddened frustration. At last, when she was positive that it was safe, she told Tamsin to take him down the lane for a run. She put the buckets of glass in the garage, and went indoors to start supper.

She was just slicing some onions when the doorbell rang. With some apprehension, Kate rinsed her hands quickly and, wiping them on her jeans, went to answer it.

An enormous bunch of red roses filled the porch. It was a moment before she realised that Justin was standing behind them. 'These are for you,' he said, rather unnecessarily. 'To give you some idea of how very, very sorry I am, darling Kate.'

Her first reaction was astonishment, that he seemed to think that such an offering would erase all memory of what had happened the night before. Obviously, he expected her to fall straight into his arms, cooing forgiveness. *Well*, Kate thought sternly, *he's got another think coming*.

'Thank you,' she said. 'But I'm not sure I should accept them.'

'What?' Justin stared at her in horrified amazement.

'You behaved abominably last night,' said Kate, warming to her theme with enthusiasm. 'You were rude, and drunk, and thoroughly unpleasant. And I don't think a lorry-load of red roses would be enough apology.'

'But, Kate . . .' Justin was evidently struggling for words. *He was so sure I'd be won over*, she thought, *that he doesn't know what to do*. 'Kate, darling Kate, I *am* sorry. I *am*. I got drunk because I was angry, and worried about us, and I didn't mean to be so horrible.' He looked at her appealingly. Washed, and shaved, and dressed in open-neck shirt and clean trousers, he might have been a different person entirely from the man who had shouted at her so abusively less than twenty-four hours before.

Kate hardened her heart. 'You frightened me,' she said. 'You really frightened me. And I find it very difficult to forgive that. It's hard enough trying to deal with all the rest of the fall-out from last night, without feeling you're going to do me over.'

'Kate! Oh, darling, you didn't really think that I would, did you?'

'Yes, I did.' She decided against telling him about the knife-block. 'So – so I think we'd better cool it for a bit, Justin. Until I've sorted out how I feel about things. That doesn't necessarily mean that we're finished or anything, it just means that I want a bit of space.'

'Oh, darling! Please—'

'Sorry,' said Kate firmly. 'But I've got a lot on my plate at the moment, and I can do without having to face any more of your drunken rages. You ought to get yourself sorted out, you know.'

'It's not a problem,' said Justin defensively. 'It's you, you know, Kate, you're driving me to distraction—'

'So it's my fault now, is it? *I* don't unscrew the top of the whisky bottle and pour it out; *you* do. And I think you ought to stop.'

She folded her arms and glared at him sternly. Justin said, 'I told you. There isn't a problem. I can stop just like that.' He snapped his fingers emphatically. 'And if that's what it takes to get you back, darling, then I will.'

'Good. I'm glad to hear it.' She smiled at him, enjoying the sensation of having the upper hand for once. 'But it isn't just that, it's several other things as well. So I want to step back from it, and get everything in perspective, and I can't do that if you're on the doorstep every five minutes. So I'd be grateful if you'd back off for a while.'

'You mean, a separation?'

'If that's what you want to call it,' said Kate, thinking that they had never really been together.

'Very well, if that's what you really want, darling,' said Justin at last, rather grudgingly. 'But what about the roses?'

'Oh, I'll have those,' said Kate, sweeping them out of his arms before he could object. 'Never turn away flowers, that's my motto. Thank you very much, Justin, they're lovely. Just don't think you can bribe your way back into my good books with them, that's all. I've got to get back to the kitchen, the onions are burning. Bye!'

She shut the door on his astonished face, and stuffed her hand into her mouth because it was her only chance of stopping the wild laughter leaping up inside her. She had won. The tables were turned: for the first time in their affair, she was calling the tune. And she found the prospect of a few days of freedom from the anxiety and uncertainty that had recently tarnished the relationship very alluring indeed.

Tamsin came back with the dog just as she was cooking the sausages. 'Hey, that smells good, Mum! I love bangers and mash. When's it ready?'

'About twenty minutes or so, and Luke should be back soon. Oh, there's the phone, could you get it for me?'

Tamsin ran out to the hall, and the ringing stopped. There was a long pause, during which Kate took the opportunity to slip a few dried herbs into the gravy without her daughter's knowledge. She called, 'Who is it?'

The girl came back into the kitchen, a puzzled expression on her face. 'I don't know. They didn't say anything.'

'What, do you mean they just hung up?'

'No, not straight away. Mum, it was really weird.' Tamsin was looking worried. 'I said hallo, and there was no answer, so I said hallo again, and then I could hear a sort of snuffling noise, so then I said hallo *again*, and then someone started laughing, quite softly, and it wasn't a very nice sort of laugh, so I put the phone down.' She stared at Kate. 'Do you think it was the same person who put the glass on the drive?'

Anger washed over Kate. 'It could well be. And if I find out who did it, I'll kill them!'

'I bet it's someone in the village,' said Tamsin. She shivered suddenly. 'Oh, Mum, I don't like this.'

'Neither do I, not one bit. Listen, let me answer the phone from now on.' She gave her daughter a reassuring smile, trying not to let her see how disturbed she was. 'You never know, it might be Granny Bennett next time.'

'Yuck,' said Tamsin at once. She came up to Kate and put her arms round her, something she very rarely did now. 'It's a good thing we've got Jem living in the house with us, isn't it?'

'Yes,' said Kate, with absolute truth. 'The best thing that's happened to us for a long while, isn't it?'

'You bet.' Tamsin paused, and went suddenly red. 'Mum, did Jem give you all those red roses in the hall?'

'No, of course he didn't! No, sweetheart, it was Justin, as a peace offering after last night.'

'You should have told him where to put them.'

'I nearly did, believe me! But just because I let him give them to me, doesn't mean I've forgiven him. He'll have to do a lot better than that before I let him back into my good books.'

'I hope you never do,' said Tamsin fiercely. 'He was horrible to you, and I hate him!'

'Oh, sweetheart, don't say that.'

'Why not? It's the truth.'

The phone in the hall began to ring again, demanding attention. Kate's blue eyes met Tamsin's hazel ones. 'I'll get it,' she said. 'After I've found the Williams patent nuisance-caller deterrent.'

She picked up the receiver at last, with the dog whistle ready in her hand. 'Hallo?'

There was a brief pause, during which she put it to her lips. Then a very well-bred English voice said, 'Can I speak to Jem Forrester, please?'

Kate gave Tamsin a cheering grin, and said, 'Sorry, he's not finished work, and he said he'd probably be a while yet. Can I take a message?'

'Just tell him Caroline called. I'll try again later. Thanks.'

'It's O.K.,' Kate said, putting the receiver down. 'That was Jem's ex-wife, from New York, I think. But still let me answer the phone, anyway, until we've cleared this business up.'

'His ex-wife? What does she want?' Tamsin asked suspiciously.

'Haven't a clue, and it's absolutely none of our business anyway,' Kate pointed out. 'Come on, let's get the supper cooking, or there'll be nothing to eat tonight.'

Jem arrived back at the cottage just after half past nine. The table lamp in the sitting-room window was lit, and the ginger cat, Sevvy, was sitting hopefully on the doorstep. When Jem opened the gate, he ran over, tail flagging a welcome, and began to weave in and out of his legs.

I could get used to this, Jem thought, as a thrush, perched on the topmost twig of Robin Hood's oak, began to pour out the beauty of the evening in song. *I really could*. He let himself in through the front door, and saw the extravagant bunch of roses in a tall blue vase on the hall table.

146

It was obvious who had been the donor, and why. Jem felt a pang of sadness, and disappointment. *After all that, she's still willing to take him back.*

'Jem? Hi.' Kate came out of the sitting-room door, a glass in her hand. 'Have you eaten? I've kept some supper for you.'

'Thanks, but I had something down at the pub. Sorry.'

'It doesn't matter. I'll put it in the freezer, Luke's got to learn how to defrost things some time. Would you like a drink? I've splashed out on another bottle of Pimms.'

'That'd be great, thanks.' Jem followed her into the sitting room. The lamp on the table cast a rich golden glow amidst the soft deep shadows, and the other cat, Greyling, lay sprawled luxuriously on the sofa, watching the two humans with her clear chartreuse eyes.

'Ice? I haven't got the full fruit salad, but I can manage some lemon.'

'Ice and a slice would be great, thanks.'

'I don't normally drink on my own,' Kate said, pouring a generous measure of Pimms into a long glass. 'The top of the rather slippery slope, in my view. But it hasn't been a very nice evening, and I felt I needed it.'

Jem looked at her, seeing the signs of strain in her face, emphasised by the strength of the shadows. 'What's happened?'

She told him about the glass, and about the sinister phone call. 'The logical conclusion is that it's someone who didn't like what I said last night. But I can't really believe anyone would do something so nasty, just because I spoke against the development. The phone call was bad enough, but that glass could have really hurt Smith, or damaged our bikes or the car.' She smiled at him bleakly. 'I just hope that's it, and they stop now.'

'Have you told the police?'

'What could they do about it? Short of catching whoever it is in the act, absolutely bugger all.'

'You can dial 1471.'

'I tried that, but the caller had withheld their number. Then the phone went again, and I was all ready to blast their eardrums with the dog whistle, but it turned out to be your ex-wife.'

'*Caroline?*'

'So she said, and all the way from New York. Perhaps she's met up with Charlie and they're having a passionate affair.'

Jem began to laugh. 'There goes a flock of flying pigs. She probably wants to find out when the money from the sale of the flat will come through. I know she's after some really flash place in Manhattan.'

'Well, she didn't say what she wanted, she just said she'd ring later. And to cap it all, Justin came round with a fortune in red roses, to say he was sorry.'

'I saw them. So you've made it up?'

Kate snorted into her Pimms. 'No, we have not. I told him exactly what I thought of him, and that I wanted a bit of space for a while, a sort of separation. I also said I'd take the roses, thank you very much, but that didn't mean he was forgiven. He was flabbergasted. I honestly think he expected me to fall into his arms as if nothing had happened. I sent him away with a whole flea circus in his ear.' She looked at him. 'Well, a small one, anyway. Did you know that there's a museum in Hertfordshire that has on display a flea dressed in Mexican national costume?'

'Nah,' said Jem, entertained. 'Pull the other one.'

'Honestly. Megan told me. She said she didn't believe it either, until Simon showed her. Tring, that's where it is. Apparently, there's some nunnery in Yucatan or somewhere like that, where the nuns have nothing better to do than dress up fleas.'

'You're having me on, Kate Williams!'

'No, I'm not, and Megan has the postcard to prove it. Shall we sit outside and look at the sunset? I'm saving the rest of the Pimms, but there's a nice Californian grenache in the fridge.'

Outside, the slabs on the patio were still giving back the stored warmth of the day. Kate kicked off her sandals and walked to the low wall which separated them from the lawn between house and orchard. In the trees behind Mermaid's Ground, an owl hooted thoughtfully, and was answered by another further away. The westward sky was flushed with pink and crimson, yellow and scarlet, and a single star, bright and triumphant, gleamed in the deep ultramarine above them. She said quietly, 'It's so lovely, it hurts. Why did he have to go and spoil it all?'

Jem didn't need to ask whom she meant. She went on, 'It was like that at the beginning. Wonderful, brilliant, too good to be true, really.'

'I know what you mean,' he said. 'It was the same with me and Caroline.'

'So it hurts much worse now than if it had never meant anything to start with. He said dreadful things to me last night – well, you know, you heard most of them. But this afternoon he was all smiles and apologies: he was drunk, he was angry, he didn't mean it. But in my experience, it's when you're drunk or angry, or both, that you *do* mean it. You say all the things that have been festering inside you and you've been too chicken or too polite to mention. And if he honestly does think deep down that I'm a lying bitch and he wants to make me regret it, then there's no hope left for us, is there? I thought he was going to thump me, I really did. And it's lucky for him that he didn't, because I'm like Tamsin, when I'm cornered I hit back, and hard.' She paused. 'And that was the other bad thing that happened today. Some girls laid into her at school because of what I said. It's all sorted now, but I feel it's so unfair on her. I can cope with it, but she shouldn't have to.'

'Nor should you.'

'Worse things happen at sea. It's not the end of the world. You've got to laugh, or else you'd cry. There I go, talking in clichés. I'm tired and fed up and I've had more Pimms than I should and it's bad for me. I'll feel better in the morning. But thanks for listening, anyway.'

'I wish I could do something to help,' he said.

'You *are* helping. Just by being here and listening and letting me tell you stupid things and telling me stupid jokes, you're helping. Tamsin said this afternoon that she was really glad you're here, and so am I. Very much.' She laughed again, more cheerfully. 'More welcome than a tax demand, you are.'

'And that really *is* damning with faint praise,' said Jem. He stood beside her, inhaling the soft evening air. 'What's that scent?'

'The nicotiana, probably. Tobacco plants. They smell absolutely wonderful, especially in the evening. I love scented plants – pinks, carnations, lavender, old roses, sweet peas. I'm going to plant a fragrance garden round the Folly, where all those shrubs have run riot. Charlie's mother is blind, so he was really keen on the idea.'

'I didn't know she was still alive. She must be pretty long in the tooth.'

'She's eighty-eight, and apart from her sight she's still got all her faculties, or so he said with great pride a few weeks ago, when I sounded him out. It's funny, isn't it? You'd think he was the type to sell his own mother, but instead he adores her.'

'The old East End moral code,' said Jem. 'Look at the Krays – the original hard men, but devoted to their mum.'

'Well, I'm not an Eastender,' Kate told him drily. 'I'm a Bristolian.' His presence was so relaxing, so normal and pleasant and genuine, that she found herself wishing that she could have a

149

relationship with someone like him. It would be a positive rest cure after all her present difficulties with Justin.

But Justin was still unfinished business, and she could do without any more complications in her life. In any case, Jem was just passing through, like those mysterious men in fantasy tales, or Westerns, who would solve everyone else's problems with a wave of a magic wand or six-shooter and move on, ignoring the pleas of grateful survivors, urging him to stay.

Smiling at the image of him in Clint Eastwood guise, she strolled back to the table where the bottle of wine stood, still half full. And into the peace of the night, the sudden shrill blast of the telephone intruded.

'I'll get it,' she said, and went into the house. The phone stood on the hall table, beside Justin's red roses. Smith's whistle, bought years ago in a vain attempt to control his wilder impulses, lay on the smooth pale beechwood. With her hand on it, Kate picked up the phone. 'Hallo?'

'I'm sorry to bother you again, but is Jem back yet? It's Caroline.'

'For you,' she said, holding it out to him as he came into the hall. 'From New York.'

No chance, she told herself, as she went back out to the garden. *Beautiful and sophisticated women like Caroline are more his style. Denim shorts and dirty fingernails can't possibly compete.*

But she knew it wouldn't stop her wondering, in the darkness, what it might be like if the situation could be different.

Chapter Twelve

'So, how does it feel to be famous?'

Kate glanced up from her encyclopaedia with a smile. 'Hi, Tanya. Not nearly as good as it's cracked up to be.'

'Whaddya mean? I thought that photo was great.'

'No, it wasn't. I had my mouth open like a dying fish and my hair was a total mess. Having it splashed all over the front page of the *Star* was the final straw.'

'All publicity's good publicity, innit,' said Tanya, with the wisdom of experience. She leaned over the table next to Kate, and peered with interest at the book. Outside, the rain battered relentlessly at the windows. Flaming June had given way to a wet and windy July, as precisely as if the weather was aware of a new page in the calendar, and gardening was out of the question in a thunderstorm. After a damp morning doing the necessary measuring and surveying, Kate had taken the opportunity to plan the next stage in the Court's transformation, the scented garden around the Folly.

'I like that one,' said Tanya, pointing to a particularly luscious plant with deep green leaves and waxy white flowers. 'How about that?'

'It's a stephanotis – used to tropical rainforests. It wouldn't survive a frost. It might do well in the pool, though.'

'I ain't swimming with that in there,' said Tanya, mischievously misunderstanding her. 'Grab you by the ankles and pull you under, from the look of it. Anyway, talking of swimming, I'm going in, and I'd like a bit of company. Fancy a dip?'

'I'd love to, but I haven't got a costume or a towel with me.'

'No problem, you can borrow one of mine, I've got hundreds. Come on, let's go up and I'll find you something nice.'

Without even a show of reluctance, Kate deserted her work and left the breakfast room. Although she was moderately familiar with the ground floor of Moxham Court, she had never been upstairs, and she was dying to see what the master bedroom was like, having heard graphic accounts from Tamsin. 'It's got wallpaper with pink roses as big as *footballs*, and her *wardrobe*'s bigger than our *bathroom*!'

She followed Tanya up the stairs, which were made of polished dark oak, the newels fantastically carved and the treads worn by four hundred years of feet. A succession of sentimental Victorian watercolours of idyllic rural scenes, the sort often reproduced on birthday cards, hung on the walls, which had been painted a colour known in the trade as Germolene pink and which was apparently genuinely antique. At the first floor, a corridor ran through the main part of the house, while a door on their right led into the master suite which occupied the whole of the south wing.

Tamsin's breathless description hadn't really done it justice, Kate decided, gazing round. The bedroom was huge, with mullioned windows on one side, looking down over the front entrance, and an oriel at the end, embellished with beautiful stone fan-vaulting, like a miniature cathedral roof. Personally, she wouldn't have chosen the wallpaper, which did indeed feature vast, overblown cabbage roses in several more or less delicate shades of pink, nor would she have gone for the matching curtains, fussily swagged and frilled and flounced. But the carpet was as thick and soft and warm as living fur under her bare feet, and the bed, occupying the blank space between the two side windows, was a giant four-poster that looked seductively comfortable.

'Good, innit?' said Tanya. 'I love pink, and I've always wanted a bed like that. Big enough for three, ha ha! Here, come and look at the bathroom.'

This was restrained compared to the bedroom. It had been tiled in cream, with pink flowers at strategic intervals. The bath was also a jacuzzi, and all the taps were gold. With pride, Tanya pointed out the bidet ('Charlie uses it to wash his feet, ha ha!'), the state-of-the-art power shower, and the his 'n' hers washbasins. A few dusty bottles of aftershave stood beside Charlie's: an impressive array of shampoos, lotions, hair preparations, talcs, perfumes and deodorants, most with expensive Parisian names, were ranked around Tanya's.

'Nice, eh? I could spend all day in here, laying in a steaming hot bath full of bubbles. Or have a bit more than just a soak, if you get my meaning.' Tanya giggled salaciously. 'This room has seen some action, I can tell you! Come on, let's find you that cossie.'

The walk-in wardrobe would have qualified as a double bedroom in most estate agents' details, and it was packed full of clothes, hanging shrouded in tissue or plastic on a rail that ran the length of the room, or stacked neatly in the floor-to-ceiling cubbyholes and drawers at the end. Tanya carried out a huge armful of swimwear and threw it on the bed. 'Here you are. You're a bit larger than me, but not much, and they'll stretch. What's your fancy?'

Kate's dubious eye ranged over costumes with frills, costumes with legholes almost up to the armpit, costumes with diamanté trims, costumes in leopardskin prints, costumes with plunging necklines, costumes with no backs, costumes with no bottoms. 'I don't know,' she said at last.

'How about this one, then? You've got a bit less boob than I have, it'll look great on you.' Tanya held up a tiny piece of turquoise lycra, splashed with orange flowers. 'No? Come on, have this one, you can lace up the front a bit in case Darren walks past.'

The costume's sober black was entirely eclipsed by the V-shaped neckline descending to the navel region and beyond. 'I'll give it a whirl,' Kate said, taking it doubtfully.

They went back down to the pool. Kate, more modest than the other woman, changed in one of the cubicles next to the sauna. Tanya just stripped off in full view of anyone who might be in the courtyard, leaving her clothes in a heap by the steps, and wriggled into the turquoise number. It left absolutely nothing to the imagination, and Kate was glad that she hadn't chosen it. Her own costume was at least two sizes too small, and seemed to squeeze her figure into a shape that nature had never intended. Feeling rather embarrassed, she dived hastily into the warm blue water, and swam two brisk lengths while Tanya settled herself luxuriously in an inflatable chair at the shallow end.

'This is the life, innit,' said Charlie's wife. 'Shame it ain't sunny, but you can't have everything. Not that it stops me trying, ha ha! That cossie suits you; would you like it?'

'It's O.K., thanks, I've got two or three at home,' said Kate, thinking of them, worn, comfortable and completely unsexy.

'Nah, go on, take it, I don't want it! You can keep it here if you like, save you having to remember to bring one. Unless you want Justin to see it, of course.' Tanya gave her a sly look. 'How are things in that department?'

'Non-existent at the moment. We had a row after the meeting, over a week ago, and I said I wanted to cool it.'

'And do you?'

'Yes. I saw a side of him I'd never seen before, and I didn't like it in the least. So I want some time to sort my feelings out, one way or the other.'

'Good on yer. Keep him dangling and he'll come round to your way of thinking sooner or later.'

'I doubt it,' said Kate. Their differences over Mermaid's Ground appeared to be an insurmountable barrier, and Justin obviously still thought that her objections were not only unreasonable, but a betrayal of their relationship. And his remarks about her children had hurt her deeply. One gift of red roses, however huge and expensive, was not enough to obtain her forgiveness, or make her forget the things he had said. And even after only a few days without him, she was already starting to look back on their affair as something that belonged in the past, not the future.

'You don't sound very keen,' said Tanya, obviously startled. 'So what's brought this on, then?'

'Lots of things.' Kate was wondering if confiding in her employer's wife was entirely wise. 'I think I'm beginning to discover the real Justin, and it seems as if everything I thought we shared was superficial window-dressing, ignoring little differences that weren't so little. The business over Mermaid's Ground just brought it to a head. I think he'd have been quite happy to let everything drift on for ever, popping round for a bit of nookie three times a week and no strings attached.'

'And you weren't?'

'No. I wanted at least *some* commitment, and I wasn't getting it. And every time I tried to pin him down, he sort of wriggled out of it with fine words and flattery.'

'Shame,' said Tanya. 'You done all right with him – rich, handsome, charming, and bang on your doorstep!'

'I know,' said Kate drily. 'But after the novelty had worn off, I found I was after something more than just a bit of fun.'

'Yeah, well, nothing wrong with fun.' Tanya grinned at her cheerfully. 'I'm going to do me twenty lengths and then I fancy a sauna. Join me?'

After the swim, the sauna and then another swim, Kate felt pleasantly exhausted. Fortunately, neither Darren nor any other male had appeared, and she changed back into her working jeans and T-shirt with considerable relief. She didn't want anyone else seeing her bulging out of Tanya's costume, particularly Jem. She

154

was his landlady, and his friend, and that was as far as it went. And she had no intention of doing, or wearing, anything that might possibly lead to embarrassing misunderstandings.

The trouble is, she thought, as she walked through the wet grass to the Folly to get her bike, *that just admitting the possibility is pretty significant. But I really do like him so much. I like his voice, and his quirky smile, and the way he gestures when he's talking, and his laughter, and the fact that he's so laid-back, such good easy company. I shall really miss him when he goes.*

At Mermaid's Cottage, the gate was closed, but she paused warily before opening it. There had been no other untoward incidents since the glass episode, and no more silent phone calls either, but she was still inclined to be cautious. And having her picture and her opinions all over the front of the *Wiltshire Star* might have incited her enemy, whoever he or she was, to further action.

All seemed well. She put her bike away in the garage, beside the elderly blue Astra estate which a combination of prayer and Andy Jessop, the village's mobile mechanic, had kept going for many years against all the odds. Then she went round to the porch.

There was something brown smeared across the red paint, and an unpleasantly familiar smell. With a sudden feeling of alarm, Kate put the key in the lock and pushed the door cautiously open.

It scraped disgustingly through a heap of dog poo on the other side. It couldn't be Smith, who had been shut in the kitchen, and a glance confirmed that someone must have pushed it through the letter box.

Kate felt sick. Swallowing her nausea, she stepped over it and found newspaper, an old cloth and some disinfectant. She had just cleared up the worst of the mess when the phone rang.

'Hallo?' she said.

Silence. Then a horrible, soft, sniggering laugh that seemed to go on and on. In sudden fury, Kate picked up the dog whistle, still lying on the table, and blew as hard as she could down the phone. Then she banged the receiver back on the hook.

By the time Luke came back from his friend Mark's house, she had scrubbed her hands until they were red, and splashed half a bottle of disinfectant over the hall floor. Then, in considerable need of fresh air, she had taken Smith out, leaving all the doors locked behind her. When she got back, despite her fears, everything was just as she had left it. She opened all the downstairs windows to get rid of the smell, and started a fry-up for supper.

The aroma of caramelising onions, however, could not mask the disinfectant, and Luke was not deceived. 'What's that awful pong?'

Calmly and dispassionately, Kate carried on turning the sausages while she told him about the dog mess. Luke's reaction was uncharacteristically swift and decisive. 'Mum, you really ought to tell the police.'

'What could they do about it?'

'Probably not a lot, but if whoever it is sees that you're taking it seriously, they might back off,' her son pointed out. 'And perhaps they could put a trace on the phone calls.'

'If they have anything to do with it.'

'They must do! The first one came just after you found the glass, didn't it? And the second one when you were clearing up the dog mess.'

'Yes.' Kate paused, reluctant to voice the obvious and unpleasant conclusion. 'So whoever it is must be watching us.'

'Which is why you should ring the police. Now.' Luke went into the hall and came back leafing through the telephone directory. 'Here's the number. Chippenham nick. Go on, Mum, please. It could be something worse next time.'

Like petrol, and a lighted match. *No, this is* Moxham, thought Kate fiercely. But she picked up the phone, and dialled.

The policeman was pleasant and helpful, and promised to send someone round that evening. In the meantime, she was advised to make sure that all the doors and windows were shut and locked if she went out, and to keep an eye open for anything unusual. Feeling much better now that she had done something about it, Kate carried on with the cooking, and tried to concentrate her mind on planting plans.

She had not really expected the police to turn up at all, but it was only half an hour after her call when the car drew up outside in the lane, and Tamsin, just arriving back from Charlotte's, shouted from the porch in ringing tones, 'Mum, the filth are here!'

'Ssh, they'll hear you,' Kate said, and went to the front door.

Thinking that policemen were getting younger was supposed to be a sign of imminent old age, so she was relieved to see that the man in the porch was obviously well into his thirties. 'Mrs Williams? PC Harris, Chippenham police. I understand you have a complaint.'

Sitting on her shabby, comfortable sofa, with a cup of tea at his elbow and Luke and Tamsin in eager attendance, he scribbled in his notebook as Kate described the various incidents. 'What kind of glass?'

'Clear, so it wasn't easy to see. I only noticed it because the sun was gleaming on it. I think it came from broken milk bottles.'

'And what did you do with it?'

'Cleared it all up, wrapped it in newspaper and put it in the bin. The dustmen took it away a couple of days later. I'm sorry – perhaps with hindsight I should have kept it.'

'It probably wouldn't have been much help, Mrs Williams. And the phone calls?'

'My daughter took the first one. Tell PC Harris about it, Tamsin.'

Carefully and precisely, the girl described what she had heard. 'The laughter – would you say it was a man's, or a woman's?'

'I don't know,' Tamsin said, after a long pause for thought. 'It sounded so horrible that I put the phone down straight away.'

'Why did it sound horrible?'

'It was sort of *sneering*,' Tamsin told him. 'Like saying, "I'm frightening you and I'm really enjoying it." '

'And you received a similar call, Mrs Williams?'

'Yes. I'd say the laughter was a man's, though. Yes, definitely a man. And, as Tamsin said, not at all a nice laugh.'

'Have you noticed any strangers hanging around, any cars parked in odd places?'

'No,' Kate said, thinking back. 'And this lane doesn't go anywhere, it just ends in a bridleway. So there's not a lot of traffic, and I'm sure I'd have noticed any strangers.'

'I saw a car the other day, a big dark blue Audi,' said Luke. 'But I assumed it was going down to Justin's.'

'That's our neighbour – he lives in the farm down the road,' Kate said. 'He runs a classic car business, so he often has potential customers driving up here, and they're usually in expensive cars. Anyway, it's possible that whoever is doing this is someone we already know.'

'Presumably you have a reason for that?'

'I do,' said Kate, and explained about the plans for Mermaid's Ground. 'It *could* be someone who doesn't like what I said at the meeting. The first incident was the following day. I find it really hard to believe that anyone could take it so seriously, but I can't think of any other motive. Up until now, we've never had any sort of trouble at all, and we've certainly never given anyone reason to dislike us so much.'

'And you haven't seen anyone you know hanging around? Groups of lads, perhaps?'

'No, but in any case this was done during the day, and it's term-time.' She paused, hearing the throaty roar of Jem's bike, and trying to ignore the sudden spark his arrival had ignited within her. 'Here's my lodger.'

'Will he have anything to add?'

'Hi.' Jem stood in the doorway, dressed in jeans and leather jacket, with his crash helmet under his arm. 'Problems, Kate?'

'You could say that.' Briefly, she told him about the dog mess and the phone call. 'You haven't seen anyone around who shouldn't be, have you?'

'No, and since the glass episode I've been keeping my eyes open.' Jem took off his jacket and sat down beside her. 'Are you O.K.?'

Resolutely, her eyes met his. 'Yes, I'm fine,' Kate said staunchly. 'Smithy was completely unhousetrained when we got him, so I'm quite used to clearing up dog poo.'

'You're not O.K., are you?' said Jem, very quietly.

'Sir?' The policeman cleared his throat. 'I'm sorry to have to broach this, but have you or Mrs Williams considered that these acts of vandalism might have something to do with your presence in the house?'

'You mean, because I'm black?' Jem stared at him, frowning. 'I suppose it might be, but I'd think it was unlikely. I've been here for six weeks, so why wait until now?'

'Have you encountered any prejudice in the village?'

'One or two people have made snide remarks,' said Jem. 'But they've been elderly ladies, and I doubt that broken glass and dog mess are quite in their line.'

'May I know their names?'

'I don't want to get them into trouble,' Jem said firmly. 'I know Kate might not agree, but I think hauling them in for questioning would be slightly heavyhanded.'

'Bet one of them was Mrs Starling,' said Tamsin. 'It could have been the awful Benjy's poo that was shoved through the letterbox!'

'Short of DNA testing, I doubt we'll ever find out,' Kate said drily. 'And this isn't exactly a murder enquiry, is it?' She turned to PC Harris. 'Look, I don't really want to go overboard about all this. If it's someone in the village trying to make a point, then the very fact we've called you in will hopefully put a stop to it.

There's enough bad feeling around as it is, and I don't want to make things worse.'

'It's all right, Mrs Williams. I know Moxham pretty well. My uncle lives here. A discreet word here and there, about how upset you are, emphasise the fact that it's frightening your children – that should sort things out. And if it doesn't, well, then I think a more high-profile level of police involvement is called for. But let's hope it doesn't come to that.'

'I don't suppose it will.' Kate went with him to the front door. 'Thank you very much for coming. I'm sure it's all a storm in a teacup really. I feel a bit of an idiot for making so much fuss.'

'But it's not very nice for you, is it?' said PC Harris. 'And it's not the sort of thing we want to encourage. Left unchecked, it could escalate. No, make 'em see we take it seriously, that should nip it in the bud. But if there's any more trouble, any more nasty phone calls, get in touch immediately. Here's the number, that gets straight through to my desk. I'll be back tomorrow, cruise around the village, take a look down here, and generally make my presence felt. And don't forget – if you see anything out of the ordinary, anything suspicious at all, make a note of it and ring me.'

She watched him drive back up the lane, and then went inside. Jem was hanging his jacket up on the hooks in the hall. He said softly, 'So it's happened again.'

'Yes. But I'm not too worried. Dog poo isn't as nasty as broken glass, is it? Not exactly life-threatening.'

'No, but it's not very nice to think that someone must be watching the house, or keeping track of your movements.' Jem was studying her thoughtfully. 'How about if I come back with you every evening? Then if there's anything else unpleasant, at least you'll have me with you.'

'That's very kind of you, but honestly, it won't be necessary—'

'Stop trying to kid me,' said Jem. 'It shook you, I can see it did. And I don't like the thought of you finding something else nasty when you're on your own. So let me. Please, Kate?'

In the face of his obvious concern, she relented. 'If you're sure it won't be a hassle. I mean, what if you have to work late?'

'Then I'll see you're O.K., then go back to the Court. It's no big deal. And I'd feel a lot happier knowing everything was all right. Especially if I'm the cause of it.'

'I'm certain you're not. Neo-fascist groups probably haven't got much of a toehold in Moxham, and I don't think Mrs Starling is running a secret cell of Combat 18.' Kate took a deep breath and smiled at him. 'Oh, Jem, thanks. I do try to be brave and not to make too much of it, because of the kids, but I can't stop thinking about it, thinking that it could be someone we know. That's the worst thing of all – that someone I know could be so spiteful.'

'And if I ever catch them in the act,' said Jem, 'I won't answer for the consequences.'

She hadn't wanted anyone's help, but his calm offer of support was enormously welcome. Instinctively, she knew she could trust him, absolutely and without reservations, as she had never, in her heart of hearts, been able to trust Justin. And with Jem's friendly kindness to guard her against the unknown assailant, she felt she could face almost anything: even a visit, a few days later, to that cauldron of gossip, rumour and speculation commonly known as Moxham post office.

She had gone in to pay the paper bill on her way home from work, so Jem was with her. It was a warm, muggy afternoon, with more thunder building up in the dark clouds in the south, and the door was open. Sal was leaning against the shop counter, talking to several women. She looked up, saw Kate, and their voices stopped instantly as everyone turned round.

It was obvious that she had been the subject of the conversation. Determined to behave as normal, she took a loaf of bread off the rack and walked up to the counter to wait her turn, while Jem chose a couple of bars of chocolate.

'I'm surprised to see you in here, *Mrs Williams*,' said Sal, with a cold stare that would have frozen the rivers of hell. 'Not being horrible, but I'd thought you were too good for the likes of us.'

'Oh, come on, Sal,' said Kate cheerfully. 'Apart from anything else, I owe you three weeks' paper money, and I don't like being in debt.'

'There's a lot of things you don't like, from what I've heard,' said one of the other women, who was a cleaner at the school.

'Yes.' Kate was hoping that she could preserve her deceptively jaunty façade. 'False rumours, for a start.'

'We had a cop car parked outside our house today,' said the woman. 'My Kev has kept out of trouble for three years, but that don't wash with some people as ought to mind their own business.'

'I don't think you'd mind your own business if you got nasty phone calls and dog dirt through your door and glass all over your front garden,' Kate pointed out, privately amazed at how calm she sounded. 'I think you'd call the police. I think you'd want whoever was doing it to stop, before they did something that hurt somebody. How much, Sal?'

'Sixty pence for the bread, and twelve pounds ninety for the papers, please.'

Kate counted the money out of her purse. 'And while I'm here, Sal, could you do something for me, please?'

'Depends what it is,' said the postmistress suspiciously.

'It's quite simple really. I'd be very grateful if you'd spread it around how upset I am about all this business over the planning application. People seem to have got it into their heads that I'm a raving snob who can't bear the sight of the lower orders. That's my mother, true, but it isn't me. I've lived in this village for ten years, and you all *know* it isn't me. I called the police because my daughter and I were frightened by what had happened, and not because I wanted to make more trouble. I haven't named any names because I haven't the faintest idea who it is, and I don't *want* to know, just so long as it stops, here and now.' She swallowed and went on, 'Do you think you could do that, Sal?'

'If you don't, I will,' said one of the other women unexpectedly. She was considerably older than her two companions, and Kate only knew her vaguely by sight. 'We all have our differences, but live and let live is my motto, and I don't agree with that sort of mindless vandalism under any circumstances. *I'd* be just as upset in your shoes, dear, never mind the fact that you deserve better.'

'I agree,' said the third woman, who was an assistant at the playgroup. 'I'm glad you took a stand, Kate. Somebody has to stick up for those who can't speak for themselves. That field needs to be protected. Of course we'd all like cheap houses, but the thought of all those rare plants being destroyed makes me feel quite sick. And the poor badgers driven out, too. So I'm with you all the way, and so are a lot of people I've been speaking to. In fact, I'm thinking of getting up a petition to save Mermaid's Ground.'

The cleaner gave a contemptuous snort. 'Didn't know you wanted to be pushed out of your own village, Jackie.'

'Don't be silly, Annette, of course it won't come to that. Some people have got themselves worked up into a lather for nothing, and made poor Kate here the scapegoat.'

'I know *I* wouldn't want all those houses blocking my view, even if they didn't cost more than a tenner each,' said the elderly woman firmly. 'And I'm sad to think that there might be someone here in Moxham as can't let anyone disagree with them without coming over all nasty and spiteful about it. That's no way to carry on.'

'Thank you both,' said Kate, giving her supporters a dazzling smile. 'You've no idea how wonderful it is to hear something nice. I was beginning to think everyone had turned against me.'

The other woman muttered under her breath and went out. 'Don't mind Annette,' the woman called Jackie said. 'She's upset because her eldest has been in trouble before, so of course she gets paranoid. But Doreen here's right – differences of opinion are one thing, but spiteful gossip and vandalism is another matter. You stick to your guns, Kate, and don't let them get you down. There's a lot more on your side than you might think.' She gave Kate a friendly touch on the arm, and followed her friend out of the shop.

'*Illegitimi non carborundum*,' said Jem, once they had also emerged into daylight. 'Don't let the bastards grind you down.'

'I thought carborundum was a sort of sandpaper.'

'It is. It's also very bad Latin.' He smiled at her. 'At least you've still got plenty of friends.'

'Kate!' The Colonel was limping across the green, waving his walking stick. 'How are you? Sorry to hear about your trouble. Terrible business, terrible, I don't know what the village is coming to, which rather proves our point, doesn't it, eh?' Without waiting for an answer, he turned to Jem. 'Are you free next Saturday? Big away match, you know, must field our best side.'

'I'm sorry, I have to go up to London to sort a few things out.'

'Oh, dear.' The Colonel looked extremely downcast. 'That's a shame, I was counting on you. Still, another time, eh? Goodbye!'

'You're too good for your own good, you know,' said Kate as they walked towards Silver Street. '*Are* you going to London on Saturday?'

'I hadn't planned to make it then, but I have to sometime soon, to finalise selling the flat, so I might as well use the excuse. Are you worried?'

'Of course I'm not! With any luck, all this will have persuaded Mr Nasty to stop. Anyway, I blew the whistle so hard down the phone the other day that I probably perforated his eardrum. I've got Luke, and Smith, not to mention Tamsin, who can be far more frightening than both of them put together, and that cricket bat you borrowed off the Colonel should make a very effective blunt instrument in case of need. Please don't worry about me,' Kate said firmly. 'I'm not worried about myself, so why should you be?'

'I'm a natural worrier.'

'No, you're not! You strike me as one of life's optimists.'

'Little do you know,' said Jem, in a portentous voice, 'of the hours I lie awake at dead of night, anxious about the state of the world and the desecration of the environment and whether a spoonful of sugar in my tea will make me fat.'

'Cobblers!'

'You are, of course, absolutely right. Have some chocolate, everything will immediately look much rosier. I'll go another time, if you like.'

'No, please, Saturday's fine. I promised the kids we'd do some shopping in Bath, and perhaps go and see a film afterwards, so we're not going to be around for most of the day anyway.'

'O.K., you've twisted my arm.'

'I said I was a good persuader, didn't I?' Kate grinned at him. It was extraordinary how these silly, teasing conversations had the power to lift her spirits, but she welcomed the effect they had on her. She'd always tried not to look too far ahead, and to take each day as it came. And now, walking with Jem down Silver Street through the heavy stillness, hearing the thunder grumbling ominously in the distance, she was very grateful for his ability to put all her problems into their proper and diminished perspective.

Chapter Thirteen

Kate had always loved shopping in Bath. Even on a Saturday in July, hot, sticky and crowded with gaping tourists and packs of foreign schoolchildren on language courses, the city had a vibrant, magical air that enchanted her. Usually she came in to buy essentials, and to window-shop. Today, with Jem's rent money, or what was left of it after the purchase of the new washing machine, burning a hole in her purse, she was exhilarated by the prospect of actually being able to spend something on treats.

Instead of leaving the car at Batheaston and taking the bus for the rest of the journey, she drove all the way in to one of the central car parks, and splashed out on a six-hour ticket. Then, with anticipation fizzing inside them, she and her children set out to enjoy themselves.

Luke needed a new pair of trainers, the ostensible reason for their visit. As he had cogently pointed out, he could hardly represent his school in the 800 metres with holes in his running shoes. They wandered through the overflowing streets, browsing, laughing, talking, with the specialist shop in Walcot Street their distant aim, and no need for hurry. Although Luke was still working for Justin, he had arranged to have the day off in exchange for an eight-hour session tomorrow.

Kate didn't know whether to be glad or sorry that the difficulties in her relationship hadn't seemed to put Luke off his job, or make Justin inclined to give him the push. Presumably, he thought that having her son still working for him would keep a line of communication open. But at least he had respected her desire for a breathing space: she'd heard nothing from him since the roses, and she was grateful for the opportunity to make some sense of her confused feelings.

'Mum! Look, Mum!'

Tamsin was dragging her towards the nearest shop. 'Look at that, Mum!'

There was a single mannequin in the window. She was wearing a long, slinky dress of stunning simplicity and subtle sexiness. Deep blue-green shot silk poured from slender shoulder straps and slithered over the model's contours to the floor.

'I'm not letting you wear that,' said Kate, laughing.

'It's not for me, Mum – it's for you!'

Kate gave the dress a startled glance. 'Oh, come off it, Tamsin, I'd never get into it. Tanya, yes, me, no.'

'But it's your colour, Mum, *exactly* your colour!' Tamsin was pulling at her arm. 'Come on, Mum, go in and try it on!'

'Don't be silly, I can't possibly. Apart from anything else, it must cost a fortune.'

'It hasn't got a price on it.'

'There you are, then. If you have to ask, you can't afford it. And I *definitely* can't afford it.'

'What's the hold-up?' asked Luke, coming back.

'Don't you think Mum would look great in that dress?' Tamsin appealed.

Luke, typically male, gave the mannequin a cursory glance. 'Possibly, but you couldn't wear it for gardening, could you?'

'Of *course* she wouldn't wear it for gardening, *idiot*! At a party or something.'

'I don't get invited to parties. The last one I went to was Simon Mortimer's fortieth, and that was over a year ago.'

'But Charlie's having a party, isn't he?' Tamsin gave her a sly look. 'To celebrate the studios being finished. Jayde told me about it in her last letter. It's going to be *very* posh, and you're bound to be invited. You could wear it then.'

'No, I won't. I've got that little black number, I can jazz it up with my gold necklace and a nice wrap.'

'*That* old thing?' Tamsin cried. 'Oh, Mum, you *can't*! You've had it for centuries.'

'Four years, actually, and it's the sort of thing that doesn't date. That dress there will be out of style before Christmas. And you know we can't afford to throw away hundreds of pounds just on a dress, however gorgeous. What about the Walkman I promised you?'

'And my CD player,' said Luke. 'Mum's right, little 'un. Nice thought, but out of our league. Come on, let's move on, we're blocking the pavement.'

Reluctantly, Tamsin followed them down the street. She could see the sense of what they had said, but still her impulsive instincts hungered after that dress. It was just what her mother needed, to lift her spirits and make her happy, and Charlie's party would be the perfect opportunity to wear it. But she was old enough now to accept that if they couldn't afford it, no amount of longing would make any difference.

Luke bought his trainers, and they had lunch in a delightful restaurant off Milsom Street. It was wonderful to be able to choose anything they wanted off the menu, rather than make do with the cheapest, and Tamsin had a prawn salad and an extremely rich chocolate gateau, smothered in fudge sauce and cream. Although it was her very favourite food, she ate almost mechanically, her mind on the party, although it was a couple of months away. She wanted her mother to enjoy herself, and she knew the Dobsons well enough to be certain that they, and their guests, would be tricked out in fabulous designer clothes. Kate's old black dress, secondhand and unflattering, would undoubtedly mark her out as the Cinderella of the ball.

And she deserves a lot better than that, Tamsin thought, absently spooning cream and cake into her mouth. *She's beautiful, she deserves to shine. I want everyone to notice her – and one person in particular.*

But of those hopes, she would say absolutely nothing.

After lunch, and the purchase of the promised Walkman and CD player, they went to the cinema. A considerable amount of wrangling had preceded their choice of a lighthearted and preposterous American comedy thriller, with plenty of action and even a few laughs. Kate bought Cokes and a huge bucket of popcorn, and enjoyed the film much more than she'd thought she would. They emerged blinking into the bright sunlight of late afternoon, and she walked with her children back to the car, listening to Luke's fake American accent and Tamsin's demands for a detailed explanation of the implausible plot, which contained so many loose ends and gaping holes that even Kate couldn't make sense of it. The conversation continued all the way home, with a break for a mock gunfight that startled the occupants of the car sitting beside them at the London Road traffic lights, and by the time they arrived back at Mermaid's Cottage, everyone was breathless with laughter.

It was nearly six o'clock, but Jem wasn't home yet. Kate left the car in front of the garage, and opened the front door with care. There had been no more incidents since the dog mess, but she was taking no chances.

There was nothing on the hall floor but a pile of post, mostly bills. Tamsin went into the sitting room to turn the TV on, and

Luke got Smith's lead and set off down the lane, saying he needed to do some running. In the kitchen, Kate sorted through her ranks of dog-eared recipe books, and decided on a chicken couscous for supper.

Just as she became aware that Luke had been out for considerably longer than usual, he came running round to the back door, his face flushed and anxious. 'Mum! Mum, has Smith come back?'

'No, he hasn't,' said Kate. 'Why, has he gone off, then?'

'I don't know.' Luke was frowning. 'It was really strange – one minute he was ambling along ahead of me, sniffing at the hedge, and then I stopped to do up my shoelace and when I got round the corner, there was no sign of him.'

'Where was this?'

'About half a mile along Weaving Lane, where the double bends are, before it goes down the hill. I was going to cut across the fields by the river. I looked and looked, and I called until I was hoarse, but he didn't come.' He stared at her, chewing his lip. 'I'm sorry, Mum. He must just have taken off after a rabbit or something.'

'We'll have to go and look for him,' Kate said. She took the saucepan off the stove, and went into the hall. 'Tamsin? Tamsin, Smith's gone AWOL. Come on, it's important.'

'I know it is,' Tamsin grumbled, emerging reluctantly from the sitting room. 'But I wanted to watch that programme.'

'Record it, then, and watch it later.' Kate picked up the whistle and a handful of doggie chocs, and followed her children out to the car.

Weaving Lane led out of the north-west part of the village, winding between the old grey houses, past Minty's Farm, where Tamsin, Charlotte and Jayde went riding, and on through fields and woods towards the steep, hidden valley of the By Brook, a couple of miles away. Kate drove slowly along it, while Tamsin and Luke hung out of the open windows on either side, their eyes searching amongst the cows and trees and grass for the familiar rangy black shape of their dog. They passed a jogger, and one of John Minty's farmworkers going home on his bike, but no one else: at this time of day, most of Moxham was at home having tea and watching *Gladiators*.

'It was here,' Luke said. 'I stopped just by that gate to tie my shoelace, and Smithy was about fifty yards ahead, you know what he's like, just ambling along. But when I got round the corner, nothing. Zilch. He'd vanished into thin air.'

Kate parked the car in the gateway and they all got out. Apart from the birds in the hedgerow, and the high, distant roar of an aeroplane flying towards Heathrow, there was silence, so still and perfect that she felt you ought to be able to touch it.

Luke put his hands to his mouth and bellowed at the top of his voice. 'Smith! Smi-ith!'

All the sparrows flew out of the hawthorn with an indignant chatter, and across the field beyond the gate, a rabbit sat up, listening intently.

'I bet he went off after one of them,' Luke said, pointing at it. 'Use the whistle, Mum.'

Kate put it to her lips, thinking of Humphrey Bogart and Lauren Bacall, and blew hard. The rabbit bolted towards the other side of the field, but there was no canine response. 'Let's leave the car and walk on a bit,' she suggested. 'You know what he's like when he's in full cry, he can't think of anything but what he's chasing. He's probably two fields away and wondering where the rabbit went.'

'Oh, I do hope he is, Mum,' cried Tamsin, who loved Smith dearly. 'I couldn't bear it if he was lost for ever.'

'Of course he won't be, sweetheart. We'll find him, you'll see, and if we don't someone else will and bring him back to us. He's got his name and address on his collar, and he'll go up to anyone, he's not timid.'

'As long as he hasn't caused an accident or something,' said Luke unhappily. 'He's got the road sense of a suicidal hedgehog.'

Kate, thinking of Tamsin, gave him a meaningful glare. Her daughter began to run down the road, calling frantically. 'Smithy! Here, Smith! Smithy, Smithy, Smithy!' With a look of guilty anguish, Luke took off after her.

They disappeared together round the bend, and Kate was suddenly and forcibly reminded of a ghost story she'd read once, about someone who'd walked round a corner in the road and out of the world. She was considerably relieved to see, when she rounded it herself, her two children standing on the verge as a car came past.

'I've thought of something,' said Luke, as she panted up. 'While I was tying my shoe, a car passed me, going in the same direction. I remember hoping that Smith wouldn't run in front of it. Yes, I do know I should have had him on the lead, but you can't keep up a steady pace with him stopping to sniff things all the time, and there's hardly any traffic along here.'

'What sort of car?'

'I didn't take much notice. Quite big, I think, and definitely old. It was dark blue.' Luke stared at her. 'You don't think he was *stolen*, do you? I mean, who on earth would want to dognap *Smith*?'

'Well, they'd have to be completely mad. Unless they wanted him to star in *The Hound of the Baskervilles*.'

Tamsin giggled. 'He'd upset all the lights.'

'Lick the camera lens.'

'And poo all over the set,' said Luke. 'Come on, let's look for clues.'

It was a welcome distraction for a few moments. Tamsin did find some pawmarks, but they were much too small to be Smith's, and probably belonged to a fox. Kate blew the whistle until her ears rang, and shouted with the children until they were all hoarse, but to no avail. Wherever Smith was, it was not here.

'I'll go back across the fields,' said Luke at last. He obviously considered himself to blame, and looked very upset. 'He might be heading for home. Can I take the whistle, Mum?'

'I want to come too!' Tamsin cried, almost in tears. Kate consented, and watched them climb over the gate and begin the long, semi-circular walk that would eventually bring them back to Silver Street. Then she went back to the car and drove home, telling herself that Smith would surely be waiting for her on the doorstep.

He was not, but a bright red Mark 2 Jaguar was parked in the drive. Kate put the Astra beside it and got out, just as Jem appeared at the front door. 'Hi,' he said. 'Do you like the new motor?'

'It's quite something.' Kate leaned forward to peer inside at the impressive row of dials and switches across the walnut dashboard. 'Wow, original leather seats, no less.'

'No dogs allowed in this one.' Jem came across the gravel to stand beside her. 'I got back a couple of hours ago and you weren't around, so I thought I'd go and pick it up. It's from that bloke Justin recommended, remember? First car I've owned for more than ten years, so that's why I wanted something special. It's not very practical, but it looks wonderful.'

'My uncle had one of them. I used to wriggle my bottom into the back seat and pretend I was a princess.' Kate ran a light hand across the gleaming paint. 'His was dark blue, though. I love this red.'

'So do I. It says, Notice me! I'm planning to call it the Tomato.'

'It'll refuse to go if you call it that,' Kate pointed out. 'Cars like this demand a regal name – Adelaide, or Dorothea, or Victoria. The Tomato isn't nearly posh enough.'

'Tough. The Tomato it is, unless Luke or Tamsin can come up with anything better.' He looked up. 'Come to mention it, where *are* Luke and Tamsin?'

'Looking for Smith,' said Kate, and explained what had happened. 'I was so sure he'd have come back here. You haven't seen him, have you?'

'No, I'm afraid not.'

'I know it's most likely he's just gone off after a rabbit – it's happened before, several times. But . . . I don't know, some awful instinct tells me otherwise. There was a car, in the right place at the right time.' She stared at him unhappily. 'He *could* have been taken. It is possible. And after everything else, I can't help thinking that's what's happened to him.'

'I know.' Jem made a movement towards her, and then stopped. Kate went on, trying to stop her voice wobbling. 'And the worst thing is that if he *has* been taken, we'll never be able to prove it. We may never know what's happened to him, and the kids will be distraught. He's a pain and a nuisance but he's still very dear to us.' She sniffed valiantly. 'Sorry. All this is starting to get to me. Do you think I'm being paranoid?'

'I don't know, but what I do know is that probably in half an hour he'll come scratching at the front door and you'll kick yourself for being an idiot.' Jem took her arm, and the place tingled under his hand, as if it had caught fire. 'Come on. Doctor Jem's orders. Prescription is a sit-down, a cup of tea and a very gooey slice of chocolate cake.'

'We haven't got any chocolate cake.'

'Well, one seems to have miraculously appeared in a carton marked Sainsbury's.' He grinned at her. 'I stopped there on my way home. It's small, but it's perfectly formed. Want some?'

'You bet. I love chocolate cake almost as much as Tamsin does, but I don't usually get a look in before she and Luke scoff the lot.'

'Well, now's your chance.' He led her inside, escorted her to the sofa and handed her into it as if she was a lady of great elegance. 'The pot's already brewing. Back in a moment.'

By herself, Kate rubbed a handkerchief across her prickling eyes. Practical kindness always undid her good intentions: the first time she'd really cried after Col's death had been when Megan had insisted on doing the washing up after the funeral.

She had more or less composed herself by the time Jem returned, carrying a tray on which stood a steaming mug of tea, and a plate bearing a thick slice of rich dark cake and a fork. 'Here you are. A sure-fire remedy for all ailments, especially sadness, tiredness and paranoia.'

'Just because you're paranoid,' Kate pointed out, 'doesn't mean they're not out to get you.'

'I know, but who'd want to nick *Smith*, for God's sake?'

'Perhaps they're recruiting disobedient dogs for one of those before-and-after TV shows.'

Jem grinned. 'I saw one of them a few years ago. The dogs had to retrieve an old sock, an egg, and a piece of steak. One of them managed the sock and the egg O.K., but, surprise surprise, he couldn't resist the steak.'

'Did *any* of them resist it?'

'Amazingly, yes. I don't know how they did it.'

'You'd have to put a muzzle on Smith to have any hope of success, and then he'd probably find a way to suck it in through the straps.' Kate grinned at him, feeling much more cheerful. 'I'll put his dinner in the bowl. He can hear the biscuits rattling from about three miles away.'

But there was still no sign of him by the time Luke and Tamsin returned, filthy and exhausted, an hour later. 'And we looked everywhere,' Luke said. 'We called and called, and we asked everyone we met, and no one had seen him.'

'We only met two people anyway,' Tamsin added. 'Old Mr Edwards walking his dog, and Derek.'

'I'm going to do some notices and put them up round the village,' said Luke. 'Someone must have seen him.'

Unless he has been stolen. The thought was still in Kate's mind, as it must have been in Jem's because she saw him looking at her. She gave him a deceptively cheerful grin and stood up. 'I've just remembered – I'd started a couscous.'

'Sit down again – I've finished it. Ready when we are.' Jem cast a glance at Luke and Tamsin. 'I think a change of clothes might be called for, guys. Did you both fall in the stream, or was it just Tamsin?'

'I slipped on the stepping stones by the ford, but I only sat in it,' said the girl. She looked at Kate, her eyes watering. 'Oh, Mum, I don't think we're ever going to see him again. How can I possibly eat anything when he's wandering about out there without his dinner?'

'I don't suppose it would put Smith off his if it was you that

172

was missing,' Kate pointed out. 'Come on, try to have something. And if you manage to eat your first course, there's chocolate cake for afters, courtesy of Jem.'

As she had expected, these words had a magical effect upon Tamsin, and she announced that she might just be able to force something down. But the meal was a quiet, subdued affair, and every time anyone heard the slightest sound from outside, there was a concerted rush to the door.

In vain: Smith did not come home. But just as they were finishing their supper, the phone rang, and Kate ran to answer it.

'Hallo?' It was a woman's voice. 'Have you lost your dog?'

'Yes,' said Kate, her heart leaping wildly with hope. 'Have you found him?'

'Well, yes, but I'm afraid it's not good news.' The woman paused. 'He was brought into our vet's surgery a few minutes ago. He's been involved in a car accident.'

'Is – is he all right?'

'The vet's examining him now, but it doesn't look very good, I'm afraid.'

'We'll be right over,' said Kate, aware that Tamsin, Luke and Jem were crowding round. 'Where are you?'

The woman told her.

Oh, God, Kate thought, horrified, *our worst fears were right. He was taken.*

'He's in Swindon,' she said, putting the receiver back. 'Pen, quick, I've got to write down the vet's address before I forget it.'

Before she had finished speaking, Jem was holding a biro and an old envelope in front of her. As she scribbled, Tamsin said, '*Swindon!* How on earth could he have got to *Swindon?*'

'Someone did steal him,' said Luke, stricken. 'Oh, God, Mum, I'm so sorry – it's all my fault.'

'No, of course it wasn't, you couldn't have known,' Kate told him. 'Come on, we have to go. He's hurt, he was hit by a car.'

She swept her keys off the hook, and was confronted by Jem. 'No, you don't. I'll drive.'

'I thought you said no dogs—'

'This is an emergency. I'll drive. The Jag will get there faster, anyway. Come on, I thought we were in a hurry?'

She ran back to lock the kitchen door, and by the time she had emerged at the front, the children were already in Jem's car, and he was revving the engine. She scrambled into the front seat, and with a throaty roar it reversed out of the drive, and shot off up Silver Street, towards Chippenham and the M4.

The vet's was in a sidestreet in Swindon's old town. Fortunately, Luke had remembered the booklet of Wiltshire town plans, and with its help navigation was easy. Within half an hour of the phone call, they were hurrying in through the door.

A woman in a green overall came out to greet them. 'Are you Smith's owners?'

'Yes,' Kate said breathlessly, her heart thumping so much that it hurt. 'How is he?'

The woman shook her head. 'I'm very sorry. I couldn't save him, his injuries were just too bad. He died a few minutes ago.'

Tamsin gave an anguished sob and buried her face in her hands. With one arm round her and the other round Luke, who looked as if he wanted to burst into tears too, Kate said, 'Can we see him?'

It was like a scene from *Casualty*, she thought, as they filed in to say goodbye to the exasperating, disobedient, loving and lovable dog who had ruled their lives for five years. Smith lay on the table, unnaturally still, most of his black hairy body covered by a green cloth. There was blood around his mouth, but no other sign of damage. Kate reached out and stroked his head, gently. 'Goodbye, Smithy,' she said, her voice breaking, and turned away, overwhelmed.

Warm arms enfolded her, and she wept against someone's shoulder. 'It's O.K.,' Jem said. 'Go ahead, cry all you want.'

'I can't,' Kate muttered. She didn't want to leave his embrace, she wanted to stay there for ever, but she knew that she must regain her composure, for the children's sakes if nothing else. She drew several long, deep breaths and then lifted her head. 'Sorry. It's just all been too much. I'll be all right now.' She gave him a valiant smile. 'Thanks. Your shoulder's just right for crying on.'

'Any time,' said Jem. 'It's there if you need it.'

There were forms to fill in, and a bill to pay. She asked for details of what had happened, and the vet shook her head. 'I don't know exactly. A man brought him in, saying that he'd run out in front of him on the main road. He didn't give his name, and he left before we could ask him. But at least the poor animal had a name-tag, so we could phone you.' She looked at Kate. 'Moxham is the other side of Chippenham, isn't it? So how did your dog find his way here?'

'He can't have managed it by himself. He only went missing a couple of hours ago,' said Kate. She glanced at Jem. 'I think we'll have to get in touch with the police, won't we?'

It was a sad and silent journey home. Jem, his eyes on the road, drove fast and accurately along the motorway. Tamsin, still distraught, sat and wept in the back, with Luke holding her hand and trying to comfort her. In happier circumstances, Kate would have loved the old-fashioned luxury of her surroundings, appreciated the comfort and the smell of leather and the beauty of the wooden dashboard, but the knowledge that Smith, decently shrouded, was lying in the boot, completely overpowered any other feelings.

It was almost dark when they arrived back at the cottage. Luke leaned forward as Jem switched the engine off, and said, 'Can we bury him tonight, Mum? I don't want to – to leave it until tomorrow.'

So a sombre little procession made its way down the garden a few minutes later. Luke led the way, torch in hand, followed by Kate and Tamsin, each carrying a spade. Jem brought up the rear, with the dog's body in his arms.

'Here,' said Kate, opening the gate into the orchard. 'Just by the hedge. There are some stone slabs left over from the patio, stacked behind the shed. We can lay those over the grave.'

They took turns to dig the hole, and when it was large enough, Luke laid Smith at the bottom of it. Tamsin, tears pouring down her face, shovelled the earth back on top. 'I can't believe it,' she said at last, laying down the spade. 'I keep thinking he's going to run up behind us, wagging his tail and asking for a walk.'

'I know, sweetheart. I do too.' Kate took her daughter in her arms as Luke and Jem put the slabs on top of the freshly dug soil. 'But at least the vet said it all happened very quickly. He wouldn't have known much about it, and he wasn't in pain for very long.'

'I wish we could have got there in time to say goodbye.'

'I wish it too, but these things happen, lovey. There's nothing we could have done about it.'

'But he was *stolen*, Mum,' Tamsin said, sobbing. 'Someone did it deliberately. Someone killed him!'

'The man who ran him over probably wasn't the same person who took him,' Kate pointed out. 'Whoever took him must have just dumped him in Swindon. They probably didn't even mean him to come to harm. They left his collar on, remember? So I expect they thought he'd be found and returned to us. But Smith is a country dog, he's not streetwise, he doesn't know much about cars. It was just his bad luck to be run over before someone could find him.'

'It wasn't his bad luck to be *stolen*!' Tamsin cried bitterly. 'Whoever it is must really *hate* us, to do that! Well, they're horrible, and I hate *them*!'

They walked slowly back to the house. As they went in through the kitchen door, the phone began to ring. *I bet it's Caroline, she always rings at this time*, Kate thought, going to answer it.

But it wasn't. A man's voice, very quiet, very menacing, said, 'Found your dog yet?'

'Yes,' Kate said. 'And he got run over and he's dead. Did you take him?'

'What a shame. How sad.' The laughter came, sneering and callous. 'Well, it's just a dog this time. Next time, it might be one of the kids. Think about that, Mrs Williams.'

'Why?' Kate cried. 'Why are you doing this to us? What have we done to you? I don't understand—'

'I should ask lover boy. Goodbye, Mrs Williams. *So* sorry to hear about your dog. Until the next time.'

The man rang off. Kate was left holding the receiver, seething with impotent anger. Then she punched 1471.

'The caller withheld their number.'

Of course they had. Aware of Jem's steady presence beside her, she found PC Harris's card and dialled again.

The policewoman at the other end was sympathetic but unhelpful. PC Harris was at present off duty, and wouldn't be back until the next day. She would try to send someone round that evening, but there had been a major incident and all the available officers were busy.

'Write down what he said,' Jem suggested. 'You might forget.'

'No, I won't.' Kate shuddered. 'I don't understand, I don't know what we've done to deserve this – this surely can't *just* be about Mermaid's Ground, can it? And when I asked why, he told me to ask lover boy. Does he mean Justin?'

'Who else can he mean?' said Tamsin. 'But what has Justin got to do with all this?'

'Search me.' Kate shook her head in bewilderment. 'Come on, it's very late. You ought to be in bed, Tamsin.'

'I don't want to. I don't want to be on my own.'

'It's O.K.,' said Kate. 'I'll sit with you for as long as you want.'

It was nearly midnight when she finally came downstairs, certain at last that her daughter was asleep. The kitchen was clear, the dining-room table tidy, the dishwasher sloshing through its cycle. She went into the sitting room and found Jem watching something raucous and in extremely bad taste on Channel 4. 'Thank you,' she said.

He glanced up, and smiled. 'What for?'

'Clearing up, of course.'

'It wasn't just me. Luke helped. Come and sit down, you look all in.'

'I feel as if someone had thumped me over the head with a sledgehammer.' She collapsed onto the other end of the sofa. 'I can't quite believe that all this has happened today – I feel that I ought to be waking up quite soon. I'm in such a mess, I'm furious and grieving and confused all at once, and I don't know what to do. And I can't understand *why*. If whoever-it-is didn't like what I said at the meeting, then why did he mention Justin? Justin *wants* the houses. Or perhaps . . .' She paused, her face intent, thinking. 'Perhaps this isn't to do with Mermaid's Ground at all. Perhaps they're trying to get at Justin through me because of something else.'

'Unlikely. Why not just do it all to Justin instead of you?'

'I don't know. I'm too tired to think straight.' She smiled at him gratefully. 'Thanks for everything, Jem. I don't know what I would have done without you.'

'Coped, I expect,' he said. 'You're a very strong person, Kate.'

'No, I'm not. I'm feak and weeble.' She managed a laugh. 'More stupid jokes. I cope because I have to, because there's no one else around. I was so dependent on Col, it was ridiculous. He did everything, the finances, the DIY, he made all the choices, he booked the holidays . . . my whole life was wrapped up in his. And don't get me wrong, I loved him. I loved it all – but I don't think it was very good for me. And – and it's awful to say it, but I think his death *was*. It forced me to face reality, it forced me to be strong and do things that I'd never dreamed I'd be capable of. I had to rely on myself, not on him, and I had two children relying on *me*. Luke was ten, and Tamsin was five. I had to get myself up every day and get them off to school, I had to pay the bills and sort out the money and mend their toys and put the rubbish out. I didn't want to, I wanted to curl up in a ball and tell the world to bugger off, but I *had* to cope. Not heroism, but necessity.'

'That's what I mean. You're strong. This is awful, but you'll survive it. So will the children.'

'Oh, I know. That's why I wanted to bring poor Smithy home, to say goodbye to him properly, and then we can try to put it behind us, as the agony aunts would say. I've dealt with grief before – been there, at the bottom of the black hole. And when all's said and done, he was only a dog. A lovely dog, but only a dog. And there'll be other dogs, other pets, just as nice and probably much better behaved.' She smiled. 'They could hardly be worse. But I'll keep Greyling and Sevvy in tonight. It'd be awful if something happened to them too.'

Jem stood with her at the back door as she rattled the box of Munchies. To their considerable relief, the two cats came running in almost immediately, and she gave them some of the biscuits and put the lock on the cat-flap. 'They're probably the only members of the household who won't miss him. Armed neutrality is the best description of their relationship, though they weren't above cuddling up to him on cold winter nights.'

'Will you get another dog?'

'Oh, yes, and fairly soon, I think. I expect the children will want to go over to the RSPCA first thing tomorrow, but I think we'll leave it for a week or so.' She bent to stroke Sevvy, who was leaning against her legs, and came up smiling. 'I must go to bed, or I'll be asleep on my feet. Thank you, Jem, from the bottom of my heart, for all your help.'

'I was glad to,' he said, and meant it as sincerely as she did.

Chapter Fourteen

'Mum! Jayde says, can I sleep over tonight?'

The summer holidays, every child's delight, every parent's nightmare, were in full swing. It was over a month since Smith's death, and the flowers that Tamsin had put on his grave had long ago shrivelled and turned brown. But, as Kate had promised, the family now had another dog.

Emma was six months old, as far as the vet could tell, and had been found abandoned in Bath. They had spent many entertaining moments trying to guess her precise ancestry (the most convincing so far being a mix of Afghan and Lassie), and wondering why she had been given that name (Jem had suggested that her immediate neighbours in the kennels had been called Ida, Jay, Kay and Elsie). Like many rescued dogs, she was pathetically grateful for her new home, and even the occasional accident had not dented Tamsin's adoration. After an hour of howling, on the first night, she had sneaked Emma up to her room, and Kate had been so relieved at the ensuing blissful silence that she had, so far, turned a blind eye to the fact that the dog now slept, neatly curled, on Tamsin's bed. One morning, there had even been two heads on the girl's pillow, one dark and curly, one long and whiskery, with one ear up and one ear down. There would never be another Smith, but already Emma was taking her own place in the household, and Kate was secretly delighted at the undeniable fact that their new dog was, even at this early stage, far less trouble than the old one.

There had been no more attacks: as if, Kate thought with tentative relief, the shock of Smith's end had brought their unknown assailant to his senses. The police had taken the incident very seriously, especially the implied threat to the children, but their enquiries had been fruitless. No one had seen Smith's abduction, nor had anyone witnessed him being dumped in Swindon. The sinister call had come from a phone box in Chippenham, and the man whose car had hit the dog had later reported the accident to the Swindon police, who had exonerated him completely. They had even questioned Justin, who had expressed complete bewilderment as to why he might be involved. In PC Harris's last conversation with Kate, he had suggested that the incidents had indeed been racially motivated: 'lover boy' might have meant Jem, because the attacker had assumed that she was having an affair with him.

'Well, if that's the case, he's barking up completely the wrong tree,' she had said to Harris. 'And if whoever it is really does think that, then why have the attacks stopped? After all, Jem's still living here.'

So there were no answers, and now, halfway through August, those episodes had taken on the quality of an unpleasant dream, that no longer had the power to hurt or frighten them. Even the furore over Mermaid's Ground had died away, replaced as a subject for village gossip by the imminent Moxham flower show, just as Megan had predicted. Several respected conservation bodies had tabled objections to the plans, and Kate had received a number of heartening messages of support from friends and neighbours. The council was due to meet shortly, but their decision was certainly not the foregone conclusion that it had seemed a month ago. And even though Tamsin was still passionate about the fate of the field and her beloved oak tree, Kate was so busy that she had no time to think about what might happen. She had spoken first, and now others, better qualified, had taken up the fight. And despite everything that had happened, she didn't regret making a stand.

But Justin, it seemed, had not forgiven her. After his peace offering of roses, when she had asked him to give her space to think, she had realised with relief that she had done the right thing. The memory of those delightful first months still coloured her emotions, but she knew that there could never be a return to them. He had shown her a glimpse of what lay beneath the affable, charming exterior, and she didn't like it at all. The thought of resuming a relationship in which she would be forever creeping on tiptoes to avoid an explosion of capricious and unreasonable rage, fuelled by whisky, did not in the least appeal. She was enjoying life again, and apart from some wistful moments of nostalgia for the distant days of ignorant bliss, Justin's absence caused her no distress. And since he made no effort to contact her, Kate presumed that he felt the same.

She finished the planting plans for the Folly garden, and showed them to Charlie, who had returned from his extended

180

visit to the States, and was now arranging his next trip, to Japan. He had been delighted, and told her to go ahead. 'And start thinking about the party, darlin'. It's set for the first Saturday in September, so you ain't got long.'

'Will the studios be ready by then?' Kate had asked doubtfully. Jem had regaled her with a series of amusing but alarming stories about the botched job that the other contractors were making of the guest suites, and he had been working twelve hours a day, six or seven days a week, for more than a fortnight. As a consequence, she had hardly seen him, and she missed his comforting, invigorating presence far more acutely, if she was honest with herself, than she missed Justin.

'Of course they'll be ready,' Charlie had said cheerfully. 'I've promised everyone a bonus if they are. Anyway, they gotta be, Captain Haddock's booked in for the fourteenth. So, got any ideas for this party then, darlin'? Tarn fancies lots of lights everywhere, and dancing in the courtyard.'

'Fine by me,' Kate had said, imagining it with a smile. 'What sort of lights? Twinkling and fairy? Bright and coloured? Lasers? Candles? Lanterns?'

'That ain't my department. You have a chin-wag with the missis, darlin', sort out what you want between the two of you. I'm off to Tokyo next week, megabucks involved, and I'll probably be there till the end of the month, so I don't want to be doing with a lot of fancy fiddles. Make it look good, Kate darlin', and don't mind what it costs, I'll pick up the tab.'

So a great deal of her time over the past few weeks had been spent in consultation with Tanya, sometimes over long cool cocktails in the pool, or, less luxuriously, in the big office suite on the second floor of the Court. Charlie's wife wanted the courtyard walls covered in tiny white lights, 'like at Christmas only better', and illuminated walks round the other gardens. At her suggestion, Charlie's old band Serious Money – in the process of re-forming and attempting to resuscitate their long-dead careers – had been booked to play. Invitations had gone out to five hundred people: friends, business associates and an impressive clutch of celebrities, and Tanya had already had two fittings for her party frock, which was being made by a top designer in London. Kate privately thought that five thousand pounds was a bit steep for something which, from Tanya's description, seemed to consist entirely of two strips of stretchy black lace held together with gold chains, but kept her counsel. She also refused to be drawn on the garment that she herself planned to wear, saying only that she had something in mind. She hadn't forgotten that lovely silk dress, but even if it proved to be beyond her reach, she'd find something just as good, if she had to search every charity shop and dress agency in Wiltshire and Bath.

'It's a real shame you're not coming,' she had said to Megan, over the inevitable pot of tea and cake. 'We could gossip and rubberneck at all the celebrities together.'

'I don't mind,' said her friend. 'After all, we hardly know Charlie, so it's not as if we were expecting an invite. Anyway, it's the weekend before term starts, and we've arranged to stay in my cousin's flat in London while she's away. I've promised to take Charlotte to a show, and Simon's taking the twins to the zoo and the Science Museum.'

'All that, *and* three weeks in a Tuscan villa,' said Kate, grinning. 'I'll just settle for the party – it's much less hectic.'

Megan and her family were in Italy now, and Kate couldn't really envy her. Simon loathed organised holidays, so instead his wife, stuck in the villa, would have to organise the three children, all day, every day, while he toured the vineyards and the cultural high spots in the hired Fiat, *Fodor* in hand. If she managed to prevent one or both of the twins drowning themselves in the swimming pool that their father had insisted on, it would be a miracle.

Very generously, they had invited Tamsin, and offered to pay for her ticket, but Kate had declined. She didn't want to feel indebted to Simon's vastly superior purchasing power, and besides, her daughter, asked for her honest opinion, had decided that she didn't want to go. Kate suspected that she was looking forward to having Jayde, and the wonders of Moxham Court, all to herself.

'A sleep-over?' she said now. 'Of course you can.'

'Oh, *great*!' Tamsin did an exuberant dance round the sitting room. 'And can I go with her tomorrow to choose her new pony?'

'I don't see why not.' *Poor Jayde*, Kate thought. Tanya's daughter was living proof that money couldn't necessarily buy happiness, and that having a beautiful mother didn't inevitably bestow beauty on the child.

Tamsin skipped off to ring her friend back: Jayde had her own phone, and her own number, and a suite of rooms that was bigger than her parents'. Kate sat down with her plans of the gardens at the Court, and tried to concentrate on lights location.

It was Saturday, and Luke was round at Justin's. Fortunately for him, it seemed that the end of his employer's affair with his mother had not affected his job, and this morning he had been looking forward to valeting the latest addition to Justin's stock, an immaculate E-type. If Tamsin was going off to see Jayde, and Jem was up to his eyeballs in soundproofing materials, then Kate would be guaranteed a peaceful afternoon in which to sort out exactly how many yards, or more likely miles, of lighting would need to be ordered.

But her mind kept wandering, distracted by the thumps from upstairs as Tamsin packed her bag. She couldn't stop thinking about Jem. Now that she and Justin were no longer together, she could indulge in the luxury of fancying the lodger with a clear conscience, and fancy him she certainly did. Over the past few weeks, she had frequently found herself looking at him with a lascivious interest that would have done credit to Tanya. When he took off his shirt to mow the lawn, one hot Sunday afternoon, she had gazed at his lithe, muscular dark body and wanted him so much it had hurt. *Honestly*, she had scolded herself. *Get a grip on yourself, woman, or he'll see you with your tongue hanging out.*

But it had made no difference. She tried to tell herself that it was only because she didn't have Justin any more: that it was just the sex she was missing, and nothing to do with Jem himself. The first halfway personable apparition in trousers would have been just as good. But in her heart, she knew that it wasn't true.

She wanted to tell him about her feelings, but she couldn't. If he was going back to London in a few weeks, there wasn't much point in embarking on a new relationship. And although she was certain now that she had never loved Justin in the way that she had loved Col, the memory of his arrogant selfishness was still raw. Even though she was utterly certain that Jem would never behave like that, she was still reluctant to commit her emotions again so soon.

Her thoughts were rudely interrupted by Tamsin, who came galloping in, bag in hand and her coat on. 'I'm ready, Mum, can we go?'

'Now?'

'Of course now, I told Jayde I'd come straight away. And it's raining again, so can we go in the car?'

The Astra had been used yesterday, for the weekly Sainsbury's trip, so it started first time. Kate eased it out of the garage, taking special care to avoid the Tomato, crouching beside it like a slumbering predator, and drove round to Moxham Court.

Jayde was waiting in the porch. In a fairy-tale world, she would have been even lovelier than her mother, but this was reality, and Tanya's daughter had a small, pale face with a slightly receding chin, overlarge brown eyes and prominent teeth. To compensate, she was clever and artistic, and, miraculously, apparently entirely unspoilt by the riches heaped on her mousey head. A lot of people made the mistake of underestimating Jayde, including her mother: but she was the apple of Charlie's indulgent eye, and his obvious adoration went some way towards cancelling out Tanya's apparent indifference.

Tamsin leapt out of the car and ran to meet her friend, leaving Kate to ferry her bag to the house. By the time she arrived in the hall, the two girls had already disappeared upstairs. Feeling like a hotel porter, Kate followed them.

Jayde's suite occupied the first floor of the north-east wing. She had a sitting room, a huge bedroom dominated by a four-poster dripping with flounces and veils, and her own bathroom, including a jacuzzi. The door to this was open, and Kate peeked in as she passed, marvelling at the contrast between the immaculate, gleaming interior and the untidy squalor that Tamsin invariably left in her wake. Of course, three or four cleaners were employed at the Court, whereas Kate only did the housework in odd pockets of spare time, but Jayde was a neat child who liked to have a place for everything, and everything in its place.

Shrieks and giggles came from the sitting room. Kate looked round the door. Jayde had a computer, with more processing power than the average office PC, and it was loaded with a very sophisticated graphics program. 'This is what I was doing for the school magazine,' Charlie's daughter was saying, as she came in. 'There's Spider, that's what we call our headmistress, Mrs Webb. That's our history teacher, in the toga, because she's got a thing about ancient Rome, and the bald one is the science master, Mr Plunkett.'

'They're very good, Jayde,' Kate said, with genuine admiration. The cartoons were beautifully drawn, and she suspected that they were wickedly accurate too.

'I want to be a journalist,' said Jayde, looking up at her. 'Or a cartoonist. I'm working on a strip about a pop group. Dad helps me with all the background stuff, but I make the story up and do all the drawing.'

'It's really cool, Mum,' Tamsin said. 'I wanted her to put

Captain Haddock in with lots of rude bits about how awful they are, but she said there was a law against it. *Is* there?'

'I think there is.'

'It's called libel,' said Jayde. 'And if you're found guilty you have to pay *thousands* of pounds to the person you've libelled. It happened to Mummy once, some newspaper said *terrible* things about her that weren't true and she sued them and won.'

'And you still want to be a journalist?'

'Oh, yes,' said Jayde. 'But I'll be the sort who only writes the truth.'

Oh, dear, Kate thought wryly. *You* have *got a lot to learn.*

Leaving the girls giggling over the comic strip, she went into Jayde's bedroom. Despite the heaps of soft toys, the flowery wallpaper and the pretty pictures, it was a curiously unwelcoming place, as if it had been designed purely with the object of a feature in *Hello*. As well as the four-poster, there was a single bed in the corner, between the mullioned window and the Elizabethan stone fireplace. Kate put Tamsin's shabby bag down amongst the cushions, and smiled to herself. Probably the huge wardrobe concealed hundreds of pretty, frilly dresses with vast price tags. And Jayde was wearing a baggy black T-shirt with an air-brushed picture of a wolf on it, and bright pink leggings that had very obviously seen better days.

She went back into the sitting room, and found her daughter applying her usual fierce concentration to the production of her own cartoon. 'O.K., Tamsin? I'd better get back, I've got lots of things to do. Where's your mum, Jayde?'

'Somewhere around,' said the girl, glancing up. 'It's O.K., Kate, she never minds what I do. Hey, Tam, that's brilliant!'

Feeling distinctly superfluous to requirements, Kate left them to it and went home.

It was a very pleasant, peaceful afternoon, despite the rain rattling incessantly on the conservatory roof. She did some essential housework, cleaning and tidying and washing up, and then, feeling that she'd earned a break, put some Vivaldi on, for soothing background music, and began to read the novel she'd got out of the library two weeks ago, and which she hadn't yet had the chance to open.

By six o'clock, the peace, initially so welcome, was beginning to become oppressive. She swapped the classical music for the Strangers' *Greatest Hits*, and went into the kitchen to make herself a cup of tea. She was leaning against the worksurface, ironically humming 'Always the Sun' while looking through her

Balti cookbook and waiting for the kettle to boil, when Jem appeared at the back door, dripping wet and accompanied by an even wetter Sevvy, looking round nervously in case Emma was about, although, unlike Smith, she would never have dreamed of chasing him.

'You must be psychic,' Kate said, as Jem stood on the step, shaking the water out of his dreadlocks with the same carefree vigour as a dog. 'Would you like some tea?'

'Is the Pope Catholic?' He came in, holding his trainers and leaving a trail of water. 'It's coming down in stair-rods out there, and there's thunder grumbling in the distance. At this rate I'll be glad to get back to London.'

'You should have taken the car.'

'It wasn't raining this morning,' Jem pointed out. 'In fact, it was bright sunshine.' He grinned at her. 'Still, the rain's warm. Where shall I put these?'

'Bottom of the Aga, they'll soon dry off.' She made two big, steaming mugs of tea, trying to ignore the feelings that his presence was arousing. 'Fancy a curry for supper? Tamsin's spending the night at Jayde's, so there's only you and me and Luke.'

'Doesn't she like curry?'

'Can't stand it, so she says, but then she's never even tried it. Luke does though, but not too hot, so I thought I'd do a Balti.'

'How about you take the evening off and let me cook it?'

Kate stared at him in surprise. 'Don't be silly, you've been working all day.'

'I'd like to. I enjoy cooking, and I seem to remember saying before I came that I'd do some. I think it's about time I pulled my weight, don't you?' He grinned at her. 'So you go and put your feet up.'

'I've been putting them up all afternoon. Hey, let's compromise. How about if we *both* do the cooking? You chop and I'll stir.'

They made a good team, she thought later, as the rich, aromatic smell of Indian food permeated the house. Jem was quick and efficient with the knife, and added a few suggestions of his own to the spice mix. In the rather confined spaces of her kitchen, it was quite difficult to avoid bumping into each other, but her sharpened awareness of him had the paradoxical effect of increasing her agility.

'It's like a dance,' Jem said, as she squeezed against the sink to let him past with a bowl of chopped peppers and tomatoes. 'The

Balti waltz. *One*, two, three, chop, *one*, two, three, hurl, *one*, two, three, mix.'

'Or *Macbeth* – beg its pardon, the Scottish play. "Hubble, bubble, toil and trouble, Aga burn and saucepan bubble." '

'How about a rap?' He began to beat out a rhythm with the wooden spoon on the side of the stove. 'I was cookin' with ma lady, the other day, I suggested a korma, she said, "No way!" A whole ton of chillies went in the pot, because ma little lady, she's hot, hot, hot!'

'That's brilliant,' said Kate, laughing. 'Go on, encore!'

'My brain's run out of steam. Oh, all right, if my adoring public insists.' He held the spoon like a microphone, and began a complicated series of dance steps. 'So she gave me a spoonful, set ma mouth on fire, I said, "You's killin' me," an' she said, "Liar! Chillies is good for you, so you eat the whole lot, and then, like me, you'll be hot, hot, HOT!" '

He bowed, and Kate clapped, delighted. 'I don't know when I last laughed so much.'

'Dear me, you are easy to please.' He grinned at her. 'Think I've got a future as a rap artist?'

'Probably not, and if you let the Balti burn you won't have a future as a cook either.'

By the time the meal was ready, without any more musical interludes, it was nearly eight o'clock, and there was still no sign of Luke. Kate dialled Justin's number, and got only the answering machine. 'I'm sorry,' said her former lover's recorded voice, sounding echoey and far plummier than usual. 'There's no one available to answer your call at present. Please leave a message after the tone, and I will get back to you as soon as possible.'

Kate left a message, urging Luke to come home for supper, and rang off. Jem appeared at her elbow, proffering a glass of wine. 'I thought we deserved cooks' nips. Is he coming?'

'Mind-reader! Thanks.' She took it gratefully. 'I only got the answerphone. He's probably deep in car chat with Justin in his garage. If he hasn't shown up in half an hour, could you go round and get him?'

Jem didn't ask why she didn't want to do it. He smiled. 'Sure thing, lady.'

The wonderful smell of the Balti, gently festering on the stove, was making her stomach clench with hunger. They went into the sitting room, and Kate turned on the TV and flicked through the channels, to no avail.

'How about some music while we chill out?' Jem suggested. 'Requests?'

'Anything, as long as it's something relaxing,' said Kate.

She sank into the sofa, her eyes closed, and listened with burgeoning delight as the first notes of *Summertime*, one of her favourite songs filled the air around her. Her father had always loved *Porgy and Bess*, and she had grown up with the music. Surrounded by the anguished wail of a saxophone, the instrument that lay at the heart of soul, she felt a deep and glorious happiness. This was it. This was right. This was perfection.

As the last notes faded, she said, 'How did you know I love that song?'

'Masculine intuition,' said Jem, smiling lazily, 'I love it too. Which doesn't stop me trying to do it a serious injustice by playing it.'

'On the sax?'

'When no one's around to hear. Maia always says it sounds like a dying cat, and she's probably right.'

'You don't want to believe everything people tell you,' said Kate. 'Just because I always do.' She finished the wine and looked at her watch. 'Where the hell has Luke got to? I'll give him another ring.'

'Isn't there a phone in the garage?'

'Yes, but if Justin's left the answering machine on, then he probably won't bother to pick it up.' She hauled herself out of the sofa and went into the hall.

Once again, the machine answered. Annoyed, and also a little worried, Kate put the receiver down and turned to Jem. '*Could* you go and find him? I know it's still raining, but once he gets stuck into something, he's quite capable of carrying on all night unless someone goes and hikes him out.'

'No problem,' said Jem, and went to find his trainers.

They were still a little damp, but their warmth more than made up for the discomfort. Outside, the rain had faded to a dreary drizzle, and it was fast growing dark, the summer sky shrouded by the thick grey clouds. Jem opened the front gate, closed it behind him, and jogged down the lane towards Silver Street Farm.

He had passed it several times, usually on walks with Smith, and more recently Emma, but had never yet gone in. The windows of the elegant Georgian house, set well back from the road with trees and a gravelled drive in front, were quite dark, but light and sound blazed from the long outbuilding at the side

188

of the yard behind it. Jem ran over and opened the door.

A workbench, piled with tools and bits of car, ran down the left-hand side, under the windows. Lined up at the back, as if ready for a race, stood half-a-dozen sleek, immaculate examples of British car manufacturers' excellence. A radio was playing something completely tuneless, so loudly that the thump of the bass rattled the windows and squeezed the heart. Jem looked round, and eventually located Luke in the far corner, kneeling down and polishing the wire wheels of a white E-type. He had to go right up to him and shout before the boy noticed him, and leapt to his feet, knocking over the can of polish.

'Turn it down!' Jem yelled. His face hot and flustered, Luke hurried to obey. The silence was breathtakingly welcome.

'Sorry,' Luke said. 'I like music when I'm working, and Justin isn't here, so I thought I'd have it loud. What's the time, Mr Wolf?'

'Supper time. Your mum thought you'd forgotten, so I came round to fetch you home.'

Luke grimaced. 'I haven't forgotten. I'm ravenous. But Justin told me to finish the E-type, and the way he's been recently, I thought I'd better do it, however long it took, or I'd probably be out of a job.'

'Like that, is it?' Jem said, probing gently and sympathetically.

'Yeah.' Luke fiddled with the soft yellow duster in his hands. 'I used to really enjoy working here, it was great doing all the cars and everything, but Justin's got so grumpy recently, he's always biting my head off for no reason. He found a tiny scratch on the E-type this morning and said it hadn't been there when it came in, so I must have done it. But I *know* I didn't! I tried to tell him, but he just shouted at me and told me to finish it today or else. So I thought I'd better get it done.'

Another boy would probably have informed Justin where he could stuff his E-type, and gone home. Jem said, 'I don't think anyone could reasonably expect you to carry on working as late as this.'

'Perhaps.' Luke shuffled his feet and looked down at the floor. 'But I do want this job, I really do. I mean, look at them all!'

He waved his hand at Justin's stock. 'How often do you get to *see* cars like that, let alone sit in them and look after them? Two Astons, and the E-Type, *and* an AC Cobra.'

'I thought he just dealt in British cars.'

'He said he'd make an exception for the Cobra. It's worth two hundred thousand. Carter Henderson, you know, the singer, he came to look at it a few weeks ago, but he didn't bite.'

Jem wondered where Justin had obtained the money to buy it. 'If he's having trouble selling it, no wonder he's a bit pissed off.'

'Or he could be missing Mum,' said Luke. 'But he's only got himself to blame there, hasn't he?' He gave Jem a narrow glance. 'I really thought they were going to get married, but he blew it. He shouldn't have been so nasty to her over Mermaid's Ground.'

'I think that's only one reason, out of several.'

'Yeah, well, it would have been nice, but perhaps she's well out of it.' Luke sighed. 'Anyway, thanks for coming over, but tell Mum I'll have to wait until Justin gets back. I don't want to leave this lot unattended.'

'Don't you ever get bothered about being on your own in here?'

'This is the first time after dark, actually,' said Luke. 'He went out after lunch, and he said he might be late.'

'And what if he doesn't show?'

'He will.' But the boy didn't sound very confident. Jem looked at his tired, dispirited face and came to a sudden conclusion. 'You're done in. Go home, have a bath and something to eat, and come back later. I'll stay here and hold the fort. I might even do some polishing.'

Luke hesitated, duty obviously battling with temptation. 'Are you *sure*?'

'Of course I'm sure. Go on, bugger off before I change my mind. Just as long as you come back and rescue me. I don't fancy being here all night, the Cobra might decide I'm edible.'

Luke gave him a grateful smile. 'O.K. There's a kettle over there, and some teabags and instant and some milk. Biscuits in the tin with the Lotus on it. You know where the radio is. See you later.'

He paused at the door, and turned. 'Thanks, Jem. Thanks a lot.'

'Don't mention it. Go!'

Once the boy had gone, it seemed very quiet. The rain had almost stopped, to judge from the gentle hiss on the roof above him, and outside, surprisingly close, he heard the hoot of an owl. He made himself a cup of tea, took three digestives out of the biscuit tin, and retuned the radio. Then he sat down on the battered, oily old chair and began to leaf through a pile of car magazines.

He had nearly finished the tea when he heard a car pull up in the lane. He got up, rehearsing what he would say to Justin to

190

explain his presence here, and hoping that he wouldn't succumb to temptation and lose his cool.

Outside, it was very dark. He narrowed his eyes and walked forward, trying to see. Several people were coming through the gateway. He said courteously, 'Can I help you?', and for answer, the first of them punched him in the face.

It was so sudden, so unexpected, that he staggered back and fell. One of them had started kicking him before his playground instincts took charge. He rolled over, grabbed a leg, and pulled it, hard. Its owner fell heavily, right on top of him. Jem's formative years had been spent in an inner-city comprehensive, and he knew how to hit where it would hurt most. There was a yell of pain and the man scrambled clear. Jem leapt to his feet and swung a punch at the nearest of his assailants. It connected with a force that jarred his arm right up to the shoulder, but before he could follow it up, someone grabbed him from behind, and the man he'd just hit delivered a heavy blow just below his ribcage. As he doubled up, winded and gasping, something crashed into the side of his head.

Chapter Fifteen

A bright light was shining blindingly into his face. 'Jesus Christ,' said a voice, loud with fury, 'it's a fucking coon!'

'How very observant of you to notice,' Jem said sarcastically. His head felt as if it was coming apart, and his whole body ached fiercely every time he breathed. 'Did you get the wrong guy then, dickhead?'

'Come on,' said another voice. 'Better get out of here quick.'

'He hurt me. I'd like to teach him a lesson.' The biggest of the dark shapes crowding round him stepped forward and kicked Jem spitefully in the ribs.

'Christ, you fucking gorilla, leave it and let's get going, come *on*, mate!'

The light whipped round, and went out, but not before Jem had caught a sharp, brief glimpse of three men, clad in dark clothes and balaclavas. *Like a* Crimewatch *reconstruction*, he thought, trying to fix the details in his memory. *Except I'm in such sodding agony, it must be for real*.

It hurt to breathe, and to move, but somehow he struggled to his feet. Doors slammed, an engine started, and before he had reached the gate, the car was out of sight down the lane.

Jem leaned on the dark smooth wood, wondering with curious detachment if he was going to be sick. Nausea was coming over him in waves, and he felt as dizzy as if he'd just sunk fifteen pints.

But he couldn't stay here. With grim determination, he heaved the gate open and set off up the middle of the lane towards Mermaid's Cottage, hoping that Justin wouldn't come back, because he didn't think he'd be able to get out of the way in time.

The lights of Mermaid's Cottage were like a beacon of hope in a naughty world. *Christ, my mind's wandering*, Jem thought, with distant surprise. He threw up the biscuits on the verge outside the gate, and the tea on Kate's lawn. Then he aimed for the light in the porch, and much to his astonishment, managed to reach it successfully. His keys were already in his hand, and he remembered that he'd used them to jab one of his attackers in the face. He found the lock at the fourth attempt, and pushed the door open.

'Jem, is that you?' Kate's voice came from the kitchen. He must have said something, because she appeared in the hall, wiping her hands on a tea-towel.

He saw the horror flood into her face, and she dropped the cloth. 'Oh, God, Jem, what's happened?'

'Some goons jumped me,' he said painfully. 'I'm sure it looks worse than it is.'

'Someone *jumped* you? You mean, they *attacked* you?' Kate ran to him. 'Oh, your face – Luke? *Luke!*' Her words tumbled over one another in her concern. 'Get a cold cloth or a flannel or something and an ice-pack – no, a bag of frozen peas, and the first aid kit, you know where it is—'

Luke's face, the blue eyes wide with shock, appeared over her shoulder. 'What's happened – was it a car?'

'No, it was three gorillas too thick to tell black from white in the dark,' said Jem. 'Kate, sorry, but I've got to sit down before I fall down.'

Somehow he made it to the sofa and dropped into the bottomless cushions. The room oscillated alarmingly, and he closed his eyes. Kate said, her voice cracking suddenly, 'Stay there. I'll call an ambulance.'

'It's all right,' he said as she ran for the phone. 'I don't think I could move if I tried.'

After that, he had a confused impression of activity, and Luke kept asking him questions, but nothing seemed to make sense. He felt a deep, exquisite cold, probably the frozen peas, pressed suddenly against his face. Gradually, to his intense relief, the pain and the turmoil inside his head began to diminish, and his thoughts started to resemble something approaching normality. Then, distant but unmistakeable, he heard the wail of a siren.

'It's O.K., the ambulance is coming,' Kate said. 'Come on, Jem, wake up!'

He heard the alarm in her voice, and smiled at her reassuringly. 'It's all right, I wasn't asleep. Just examining the insides of my eyelids, that's all.'

'I don't know how you can make a joke of it,' said Kate, but she managed a smile in response. 'Luke's gone to make sure the ambulance finds us. How are you feeling?'

'A bit better, but still pretty rough. They really laid into me.'

194

He touched his face gingerly. 'What does that look like?'

'Do you want the truth? Bloody awful.'

'Good thing I'm black, then. Bruises always look much worse on white skin.'

'Did they hurt you anywhere else?'

'I got kicked and punched in the ribs, and bashed on the side of the head, but that's all.'

'*All!*' Kate stared at him in horrified dismay. 'Oh, God, Jem, they could have killed you!'

'I don't think that was on the agenda. They just wanted to give me a good going-over. Trouble is, I don't think I was their intended victim.'

'The police are coming too,' Kate said. 'Is that O.K.? After all that's happened, I thought they'd better know.'

'I'd tell 'em what I had for breakfast six weeks ago, if it meant they could catch the bastards.' Jem fingered the wound on the side of his head. 'That feels even worse than the other one.'

'They're here.' Luke entered the room, followed by a man and a woman in green paramedic uniforms. 'And the police have just arrived, too. Shall I put the kettle on?'

'The English answer to everything,' said Kate ruefully. 'All the ills of the world, to be cured with a cup of tea.'

The next few moments were somewhat painful for Jem, as the paramedics poked, prodded and investigated his various injuries, shone lights in his eyes, tested his reflexes and asked detailed questions about what had happened.

'I think we'd better take you in,' said the woman, at last. 'That head needs further investigation. I *think* there's no major damage, but you can't be too careful with injuries like that. And I don't like the look of those ribs. At least one of them could be broken.' She turned to the WPC, who was hovering with a mug of tea in one hand and her notebook in the other. 'If you don't mind, we'll get him to the RUH now, and you can take a statement there.'

It was painfully reminiscent of what had happened to Smith, Kate thought, as she got the Astra out of the garage and waited for Luke to lock up. But with the vital difference that Jem was alive, and apparently not too seriously hurt. He had looked so ghastly, though, standing in the hall with blood pouring down his face, that she had thought for a moment that he was dying. And the shock had burnt away all her uncertainties and focused her mind like a laser on the shining, unavoidable truth.

But it was no use knowing what she wanted if she was sure that she couldn't have it.

Arrival in an ambulance meant that Jem was seen straight away. With Kate and Luke beside him in the cubicle, the cut on his cheekbone was bathed and stitched, and the head wound examined, by a cheerful young doctor from Nigeria who told him, with considerable amusement, that his dreadlocks had probably absorbed some of the impact of the blow.

'First time they've ever been any use,' said Jem. 'Perhaps I won't go for the shaven look after all.'

Before he was taken off to X-ray ('Just a precaution,' the doctor had said. 'You've got a very hard head, Mr Forrester'), the WPC came in to take his statement. Kate listened, appalled, to his brief account of the attack.

'Three of them,' said the WPC, who looked very little older than Luke. 'And did you get any details of their appearance at all?'

'Not a lot. Like I said, it was very dark. There are no street lights down there, and the garage door is on a spring and it shut behind me.' He stopped. 'Oh, Christ. I didn't lock it. Half a million quids' worth of car inside it, and anyone could walk in and pinch the lot.'

'Don't worry, Mr Forrester, two of my colleagues are down there at the moment, looking for evidence. So, you can't give me any kind of description of these men?'

'Not much,' said Jem. 'One of them was much bigger than the others, and nastier too. He was the one who kicked me last of all. Even his mate called him a gorilla.'

'No names mentioned?'

'None. I can tell you one things for certain, though. They weren't after me. They'd intended to attack someone else.'

The WPC stared at him in surprised disbelief. 'Really? But it wouldn't be very easy to mistake your identity, surely.'

'I keep telling you,' Jem said patiently, 'it was very dark. I came out of the garage and the door shut behind me, so no one could see a lot. I couldn't see what they looked like, and they didn't realise I was black until they had me on the ground and shone a torch in my face.' He grinned ruefully. 'Then one of them said, and I quote *almost* exactly, "Christ, it's an effing coon".'

The WPC was writing it all down. 'Are you sure about this, Mr Forrester?'

'Absolutely. I pointed out their cleverness in noticing this important fact, and then they decided to leave, but not before the chief gorilla had buried his toecap in my ribs. By the time I'd managed to get up and stagger to the gate, they were gone.'

'So – no description of the car?'

'Sorry. It was dark-coloured, probably a saloon, and it ran on petrol. That's all I can tell you.'

'Well, there isn't much to go on,' said the WPC. 'Perhaps my colleagues have found something at the scene. I understand you've already been the subject of harassment, Mr Forrester?'

'Us, more than him,' Kate said. 'Jem's my lodger. The house was vandalised a couple of times; not seriously, though it wasn't very nice. Then our dog was stolen, and dumped in Swindon, where he got knocked down and killed by a car. There were threatening phone calls, too. This was around the end of June, beginning of July, and there hasn't been anything since. I thought – hoped – that it had all gone away.'

'Perhaps this isn't connected,' Jem said. 'Harris thought the vandalism might have been directed at me, for racist reasons. But if the goons tonight didn't realise I was black when they jumped me, then racism couldn't have been a motive, could it?'

The WPC was still looking extremely sceptical. 'But if they hadn't meant to attack you personally, Mr Forrester, then who was their intended victim?'

'Justin,' said Kate. 'It has to be Justin.' She turned to the WPC. 'He owns the place where Jem was attacked. The cars are worth a fortune, so perhaps it was a robbery that went wrong.'

'And,' said Luke, his voice aghast, 'if Jem hadn't stayed to watch the place while I went home for supper, then they would have taken the lot – or attacked me!'

It was well after midnight before Jem was finally allowed to go home. The X-rays had revealed no broken bones, only extensive bruising, and everyone seemed to think that he had been very lucky. 'You'd be surprised how easy it is to damage someone with your foot,' the Nigerian doctor had commented. 'You've got off very lightly, Mr Forrester.'

'If that's supposed to be lightly,' Jem said, wincing as he explored his ribs, 'then I hope I never get the full treatment.'

He fell asleep in the back of the car, and Kate stopped so that she and Luke could cover him with the rug, and make him comfortable. Then she drove on through the dark, her mind still working busily while her driving skills were functioning on autopilot. There had to be a connection between the attacks on Mermaid's Cottage and the attack on Jem, but she could not think what it might be. On second thoughts, the idea that a robbery had been planned seemed unlikely. Why not just make sure that Jem was out of action, and then take the cars? No one else had been around to stop them. And although the WPC was obviously unconvinced, Kate suspected that the assault had indeed been planned for Justin. She knew how utter and absolute the darkness could be at the further end of Silver Street, well away from the comforting orange glow of the lights in the village.

There was still police activity down at Justin's when they reached Mermaid's Cottage. Jem woke up, briefly, and she and Luke helped him out of the car and into the house. The doctor had told her not to worry if he became drowsy, as long as he did not feel dizzy, nauseous or have pains in his head. But Kate could not help being anxious as they escorted him to his room, and helped him to undress, because his ribs were too painful to allow him to bend. Looking at the truly spectacular bruises, she could not believe that nothing was broken.

'I'll be O.K.,' Jem said, yawning cavernously. 'Nothing a good night's sleep won't put right.'

'I'm going to bed too,' said Luke. 'Hey, Mum, I hope Tamsin hasn't been trying to ring us. She'll be worried.'

'I can't imagine why she'd want to,' Kate pointed out. 'She's probably even now having a cosy midnight snack with Jayde. Don't worry about her, Luke, we've got enough to think about.'

She waited until she was sure that her son was in bed, and then got the torch and slipped outside. There were still lights blazing at the farm, silhouetting the trees in Mermaid's Ground, so she walked down the lane.

A policeman stopped her at the gate. 'I'm sorry, you can't go in. It's the scene of a crime.'

'I know that,' said Kate. 'The victim is my lodger. I just wanted to find out if you'd got any clues or anything.'

'I'm afraid that if we had I wouldn't be allowed to tell you,' said the policeman. 'I suggest you go home, madam, and go to bed. We'll be here a while yet, and if we want any more statements from you or Mr Forrester someone will be round in the morning.'

'O.K.,' said Kate. 'Is Mr Spencer back yet?'

'He arrived about half an hour ago, and he's being interviewed at the moment, that's all I can tell you.'

She thanked him, and went back to her own bed. It was only when she had attained the horizontal that she realised how desperately tired she was: and not very long after that until she slept.

She woke to the phone ringing beside her bed. Cursing sleepily, she sat up and answered it, noting at the same time that it was half past eight. 'Hallo?'

'Kate?' said Justin. 'Sorry to call you so early, but I was ringing to enquire how Jem is.'

His voice was as formal as if they were distant acquaintances. 'He's fine, as far as I know,' she said, matching his cool manner. 'A bit bruised and shaken up, that's all.'

'Good. I'm very glad to hear it. Look, is Luke planning to come over today? Because he hasn't finished the E-type yet, and I need it done by tomorrow.'

'I'll ask him, but I think he's made other arrangements.'

'Well, tell him that I'll give him a bonus if he does it today,' said Justin. 'And you can tell him, too, that I'll be around, so he's no need to worry. Anyway, they won't be back. I've had the police here half the night, and the general consensus seems to be that they were planning to steal at least one of the cars, but panicked and fled. That's the basis they're working on, anyway. I've called a security firm and they'll be fitting new alarms as soon as possible. Anyway, what was Jem doing on his own here? Where was Luke?'

'At home having his tea. He hadn't had anything except biscuits since breakfast, and he was starving. And I'm very glad he did go, because otherwise it would have been him pulverised by that gang, not Jem. Jem got off lightly because he's fit and strong, and he fought back. Luke might have been killed.'

'Well, I'm very glad he wasn't.' Justin was sounding more affable now. 'And I'm very grateful to Jem. He probably saved me a packet. Don't forget to tell Luke, will you? Thanks. Goodbye, Kate.'

'Goodbye,' she said, and put the receiver down. She'd been so sure that he would ask her out that she'd been mentally rehearsing her refusal. But at least they now seemed to be back on friendly terms, which was a relief. They were neighbours, after all, and festering bad feelings would make life extremely awkward.

Kate got dressed and went downstairs, wondering how Jem was. She found him in the kitchen, wearing shorts and a T-shirt, making himself some breakfast. The aroma of frying bacon filled the air, and she inhaled luxuriously. 'God, that smells wonderful!'

'Want some? There are a couple of rashers left.' Jem lifted the pan and shook it with brisk expertise. 'Egg? Eggs?'

'Look, you shouldn't be doing that. You should be in bed, waited on hand and foot.'

'That's never been my style,' Jem said, grinning. 'How's the face looking, then?'

'A bit less swollen than it was, I think,' Kate said. 'But I'm serious, Jem – please, *please* go and sit down.'

'No,' said her lodger. He adopted a belligerent pose with the bacon tongs. 'You gonna make me?'

'O.K.,' said Kate, smiling reluctantly. 'But I think you're quite, quite insane. If that had been me, I'd have taken the opportunity to put my feet up.'

'Well, it wasn't you,' said Jem. He cracked two eggs into the second pan and then turned, his face suddenly serious. 'Listen, Kate, be careful. They might come back. And until we know for certain who they are and what they're after, I don't want you taking any chances. No more lonely walks down the lane, even with Emma.'

'She'd be useless,' said Kate. 'She'd turn tail and run for home at the first sniff of trouble. But don't worry about me. When Col died, one of the first things I did when I was getting my act together again was to go on a women's self-defence course. I can look after myself.'

'You probably can. I wouldn't want to meet you on a dark night. But there are three of them, and they aren't nice people. Just don't do anything silly.'

'You mean, like women in TV thrillers? The ones who *always* end up being chased in a tight skirt and four-inch stilettos? The ones who get notes saying "meet me at midnight in the deserted alleyway" and keep the appointment without telling anyone about it, let alone arranging full police surveillance? Credit me with a little more intelligence than that, *please*.'

'O.K.,' Jem said. 'Over easy or sunny-side up?'

'Do you know, I've never understood what that means. Bog standard fried egg, please. Has Luke appeared yet?'

'No. He's probably even more knackered than me.'

'I doubt it.' Kate watched as he deftly turned the eggs. Behind her, the coffee machine puffed valiantly through its cycle, filling the kitchen with yet more wonderful smells. She added, 'I think it's really worried him. He knows it could easily have been him, not you, and he's probably feeling frightened and guilty, even though he's got no reason to. Luke doesn't say a lot, but he's a deep thinker, and I've learned what the signs mean. I don't think I ought to let him work there on his own again.'

'He won't buy that. He'll want to prove he's got bottle.' Jem flipped the eggs onto the waiting plates, added the bacon and presented one to her with a flourish. 'Breakfast is served, madame. Coffee?'

'Without it, I'm not human,' said Kate. 'Don't worry, I'll see to it. You go and sit down.'

They ate at opposite ends of the dining table, with the usual heap of pending post, newspapers and magazines in between. As he finished, Jem said, grinning, 'It's a shame some of the guys I knew at school couldn't have seen me last night. I didn't quite give as good as I got, but that wasn't for want of trying. And it might have put paid to the vicious rumour that my real name was Jemima.'

Kate choked over the last of her bacon. 'Is that what they used to call you?'

'Some of them, yes. When they weren't hurling racist abuse, that is. You have to learn to fight back, or you go under. Being a comedian helps, too. By the time I left, I'd earned *respect*, man!'

'It can't have been easy.'

'It wasn't, but it was no nightmare, either. I got by. And once I was in the sixth form, it was a lot better. At that stage, you're there because you want to be, not because you have to be. I got called a Bounty bar, of course – black outside, white inside – because I worked hard and stayed out of trouble. But I reckoned if they wanted to spend their time hanging round the streets and drawing the dole, that was their lookout. I had different ideas, and I didn't fancy wasting the rest of my life getting perfectly balanced chips like treetrunks on both shoulders.' He glanced at her, smiling. 'It wasn't easy for you, either, was it?'

'No, in some ways it wasn't.' Kate thought back to the misery of her own adolescence. 'And the pupils at a private girls' school can be just as nasty as those at a rough comprehensive, though they tend to use different methods. I hated it. And as you can imagine – well, you've met her – my mother didn't want me to get a sheaf of academic qualifications. All she thought I'd need were a few typing certificates and my sights set on marrying the boss. Dad insisted I did A levels instead of going on a secretarial course, and when I decided I wanted to go to university, he backed me up. So I did an English degree, and met Col. He was the older brother of one of my friends. I planned on doing a teaching course once I'd got my degree, but I got pregnant with Luke before I'd finished my finals, so we got married and moved to Bath.'

'You were young to have a baby.'

'Twenty-two. Very wet behind the ears. I hardly knew which way up he was, and Mother wasn't a lot of help, though she was delighted to have a grandson. Anyway, Luke survived, amazingly, and so did I. And talking of Luke, I'd better give him his wake-up call in a moment. He's supposed to be going off to his friend Mark's this morning.' She paused in the middle of stacking the plates. 'What are you going to do? It looks as if it'll be a nice day, I should take it easy if I were you.'

'No such luck. I'm going over to the Court now.'

Kate stared at him. 'You can't!'

'Watch me. I'll take the Tomato rather than jog, but that's the only concession I'm going to make. If I don't show, work gets put back a day.'

'Rubbish. No one's indispensable.'

'Perhaps not, but I have delusions of grandeur.' He grinned at her. 'Anyway, I've got all this fancy bruising to show off.'

'Don't let Tanya kiss it better,' Kate warned him.

'Ow – don't make me laugh! No, I won't. Anyway, I think she's got a new interest.'

'Funny you should say that, I got that impression too, but she's been keeping him very dark.'

'Well, I'm very grateful to him, whoever he is, he's got me off a rather awkward hook.'

'It's probably her personal fitness trainer, giving her a thorough workout.' Kate giggled, and then slapped herself reprovingly on the wrist. 'Sorry. Sometimes I can't help being an incorrigible gossip.'

'You don't seem to need much incorriging to me,' said Jem. As Kate groaned, he added, 'Puns are the only jokes that aren't at someone else's expense. So don't mock.'

'And Shakespeare was very fond of them, after all. Some of his would have gone down well in a *Carry On* film. And Chaucer is full of them too. Puns have a long and honourable history.'

'So that's all right then. I could stay here talking all morning, but I'd better go. See you later. Do you want me to bring Tamsin back, by the way?'

'Yes, please, if you can drag her away from the new pony.'

'Consider her dragged. And remember, take care, Kate, won't you?'

'The four-inch stilettos stay in my wardrobe,' she told him, and made him laugh again.

★ ★ ★

Sundays in Moxham, especially Sundays in August, were peaceful, leisurely hours, to be spent in the house or in the garden, at church or, at lunchtime, in the pub. Justin Spencer ate at the Unicorn between one and three, and told everyone who was listening about how he had so nearly been robbed, and the details of the significantly enhanced security system he would shortly be installing. Bob Wiltshire, propping up the bar, pointed out to his own cronies that someone had also nearly been killed, and to his way of thinking that was worse. He also noted, and commented freely on it later, that Mr Spencer couldn't half put away the whisky these days.

That afternoon, a police car cruised slowly down Silver Street, pausing first at Mermaid's Cottage. There, they were redirected by the owner, hard at work in her garden, to the Court, where Mr Forrester could be found, very foolishly also hard at work despite bruised ribs and a head injury. The car went on to the farm, only to find that Mr Spencer was out. There was no one around to tell them where he was, and the barn was securely chained and padlocked. The car turned round in the drive and went off to the Court, to ask the victim of the assault further questions. Mr Spencer would have to wait until Monday for advice about security at his premises.

Justin did not return to Silver Street Farm until after midnight, when all the houses along the lane, including Mermaid's Cottage, were shrouded in darkness, and only the moon gave light. And, his mind clouded by too much whisky, he did not notice that there was someone waiting for him, in the shadows under the trees by the gate.

Chapter Sixteen

The sirens wrenched Kate from a confused dream about being pursued by a traffic warden in Bristol. It took her a few moments to realise that she could still hear them, even though she was wide awake. And as she sat up, they shot past the house, shrieking alarm, and stopped almost immediately.

They've gone to the farm, she thought. *Oh, God, not more trouble.* Her heart thudding, she leapt out of bed, pulled on leggings, a T-shirt and a pair of canvas shoes, and ran downstairs.

The clock in the hall said half past five. As she went to the front door, Luke appeared above, clad only in a pair of pants. 'Mum! What's happening?'

'That's what I'm going to find out,' said Kate.

'Wait for me!' Her son disappeared and she heard sounds of drawers being opened. Tamsin's voice said sleepily, 'What is it? What's going on?'

Another siren was approaching. Kate opened the door, and saw an ambulance going past, blue lights flashing.

'What is it?' Luke cried, running up with his arms still struggling into a sweatshirt and his fair hair sticking out all round his head, as if he'd been plugged into the mains. 'Is it the farm?'

'Must be,' said Kate. She looked round for Tamsin, just as her daughter came panting out of the front door, still wearing her nightshirt with a palomino rearing across the chest. Behind her was Jem, barefoot. He hopped across the gravel and joined them at the gate. 'Trouble?'

'We'd better go and see,' said Kate, and led them all at a run down the lane.

The entrance to Silver Street Farm was jammed with emergency vehicles: two police cars, and the ambulance. As they squeezed through, Kate glanced at the barn where the cars were kept. The big doors had been propped open with bricks, and there was nothing inside except heaps of rubbish and debris.

'It *was* a robbery!' Luke cried. 'Look, they've taken all the cars!'

'I don't care about the cars,' said Kate, her heart full of foreboding at the presence of the ambulance. 'What about Justin?'

There was a policeman in the barn, and when he saw them he shouted something and hurried out to intercept them. 'Excuse me, madam, but you can't come in here.'

'We're friends of Mr Spencer's. We live next door,' Kate said breathlessly. 'Is he all right?'

'I can't say, madam. All I know is that there's been a burglary, and an ambulance was called. Now if you'd get back and wait by the gate, madam, they'll be out in a moment. In fact, here they come now.'

They watched as the two paramedics, the pair who had tended Jem two nights previously, carried the stretcher carefully down the two steps from the front door. Justin lay on it, wrapped in a red blanket. There was blood on his head, and as they bore him past to the waiting ambulance, Kate saw the marks of a rope, bruised deep and purple into the skin of his wrists. But to her considerable relief, he didn't seem too badly hurt, for he was talking to one of his bearers.

PC Harris was following, and stopped when he saw her. 'Mrs Williams! What are you doing here?'

'We heard the sirens, and we've come to see if Mr Spencer is all right,' Kate said. 'Is he O.K.?'

'I don't know,' said Harris. 'He's been tied up and beaten. They'll take him off to hospital in a moment. But he doesn't seem too seriously hurt, fortunately.' He drew them to one side, and added quietly, 'You heard the sirens. Did any of you hear anything else last night?'

'I didn't,' Kate said. 'But then my room is at the back of the house. Luke? Tamsin?'

'I *think* I heard a lorry or something go down the lane, very late,' said her son, after a pause for thought. 'But I was just dropping off to sleep, and I may have imagined it.'

'What sort of time would that have been?'

'After one o'clock,' said the boy, with certainty. 'Because I stayed up to watch a late movie, and it didn't finish till quarter to.'

'What about you, Tamsin?' the policeman asked.

She shook her head. 'No. Mum says I sleep like a log.'

'Logs don't snore,' muttered Luke, and earned a glare from his sister.

'And I took a couple of painkillers,' Jem added. 'Out like a light before ten.'

'Well, I'll probably be round later to take some statements,' said Harris. 'In the meantime, try and remember anything suspicious that you might have seen over the past few days.'

'Like being done over by the gang of three?' Jem enquired.

'We can't say at present whether the two incidents are connected,' Harris told him. 'I must admit it does seem too much of a coincidence, but of course it's early days yet, and there's a lot of evidence to sift through. You do casual work for Mr Spencer, don't you, Luke? Can you give me any idea of what has been taken?'

As he began to list the missing cars, the ambulance drove off down the lane, its lights flashing. Jem glanced at Kate. 'O.K.? You don't want to follow it, do you?'

'No, I don't. Actually, what I could really do with at this precise moment is some breakfast,' said Kate, and a hungry growl from the region of her stomach gave point to her words.

'So could I,' said Tamsin. 'I'm *starving*. Can we have bacon and eggs? Please?'

'I'm beginning to feel like a chef in a greasy spoon,' Kate said, grinning. 'All our food seems to come out of a frying pan these days.'

'Oh, Mum, *please*!'

'But I think we could all do with a hearty filling calorific cholesterol-laden breakfast experience. Come along when you've finished, Luke.'

'Don't forget the coffee,' said Jem, as they began to walk back to Mermaid's Cottage. 'I thought you said you weren't human until the first cup of the day.'

'Correct.' She smiled at him. 'I'll put on a couple of gallons. God, I haven't even brushed my hair! Does it look a complete mess?'

'It's tidier than a haystack,' said Jem, with a sly sideways glance.

'You weren't meant to say that! I thought you were supposed to be tactful and diplomatic.'

'If you can't insult your friends, who can you insult?' said Jem cheerfully.

'How are you feeling? Did you sleep O.K.?'

'Like I told the cop, out like a light until I heard all hell breaking loose. Those painkillers are pretty strong. No, I'm all right. It hurts if I bend or twist, but as long as I pretend there's a broomhandle stuffed up my back, I'm O.K.' He yawned. 'I could have done with a couple of hours more kip, though. I'm not an early morning person.'

'It's lovely, though,' said Kate. She waved a hand at the lush verges, the blackbird singing in the hedge bordering Mermaid's Ground, the pale, rain-washed blue of the sky and the sunlight glittering silver on the dew-soaked grass of Ford Meadow, on their right. 'So peaceful, so quiet – and yet *that* has happened, while we slept. I mean, this is *Moxham*. Robberies and violence belong somewhere else, not here.' She glanced at him, her pale, beautiful face full of distress. 'I know we shouldn't think we're immune from it. I know we aren't, the Brimley post office was robbed last year. But it's so easy to forget what the real world can be like, until it forces you to realise that you can't build walls and shut it out. This may seem like paradise but it isn't, it isn't at all, and it's horrible to be reminded of it so brutally . . .' She paused for breath. 'I'm sorry. I have this awful tendency to get all emotional and carried away.'

'It's hardly surprising, after everything that's happened,' Jem pointed out, as he opened the gate into the cottage. 'And it's amazing how good a strong cup of coffee is, at putting things back into perspective.'

By the time Luke returned from the farm, a dozen rashers of bacon were sizzling on the Aga, and the coffee machine was wheezing and puffing like a steam train. Throughout breakfast, which lasted some time, he and Tamsin, who was still in her nightshirt, talked incessantly about the robbery. Kate found, to her surprise, that the incident had not affected her as deeply as she had expected. It was shocking, certainly, but at least Justin seemed to have escaped serious injury. Compared to what might have happened to him, the loss of his cars, while unfortunate, was hardly the end of the world. And she knew that he would be extremely well insured.

Once Jem had gone off to the Court, taking with him Tamsin, who was dying to give Jayde all the gory details, she rang the hospital to enquire about Justin. After a long wait while they tracked him down, she was eventually put through to his ward.

'Mr Spencer is asleep at the moment,' the nurse said. 'I don't think he'll be awake for some hours. I told the police to come back after lunch, so if you want to visit, I'd make it after three. He's in a private room, so there are no restrictions.'

'Is he going to be all right?' Kate asked.

'He's comfortable,' said the nurse, and would not give her any more information, as she was not family.

'The only family he's got is his sister in Los Angeles,' Kate said to Luke as she put the phone down. 'Oh, and his ex-wife, of course. She and the children live in London somewhere, with her new bloke, and he hardly ever mentions them. If he wants them to know, he can get in touch himself.' She glanced at Luke, who was doodling down the margins of the *Western Daily Press*. 'If I go and see him this afternoon, do you want to come?'

She had expected him to jump at the chance, but he shook his head. 'No thanks, Mum, if you don't mind. I'd rather stay here, I ought to do some homework.'

'O.K.,' said Kate, though she didn't really want to go alone. It might give Justin ideas, and now that she had finally decided to end their relationship, she knew that she shouldn't put off telling him any longer. She was almost certain that he had arrived at the same conclusion. But if he hadn't, a hospital room, even a private one, was hardly the venue for the kind of violent fury he had exhibited after the meeting on Mermaid's Ground.

She would have to take at least the afternoon off, so she rang Tanya. After drawing a blank at the Court, she finally reached her on the mobile. Her voice sounded giggly and breathless. 'Hallo, Kate! Make it quick, Max is giving me a massage.'

Gotcha, thought Kate, grinning. Briefly, she explained what had happened to Justin, and that she had decided not to come over to the Court that day, but to work on the plans at home.

'Gawd almighty, is he all right?' demanded Tanya.

'I think so, though they'd only say he was "comfortable", you know what hospitals are like.'

'Don't I just, been through it all with me dad. Comfortable in your coffin, he used to say. Well, well, poor old Justin. And all his motors gone?'

'It certainly looks like it.'

'Bloody hell. Hope he's insured, then.'

'I'm sure he is. He's always very careful about that sort of thing.'

'Oh well then, he'll be O.K.,' said Tanya. 'He's the kind what always falls on his feet. Which ward's he in? I'll get him some flowers.'

Kate told her. 'He's in a private room, of course. You won't catch Justin in an NHS ward with all the hernias and hip replacements.'

'Can't say I blame him, ha ha! Cheers, Kate, ta-ra, gotta go, there's a nice warm pair of hands waiting for me.'

She rang off. Kate looked at the receiver, grinning, and then replaced it. Tanya's cheerfulness was so infectious that she'd make people laugh on her deathbed.

Tamsin rang a while later, to ask if she could bring Jayde over, as they planned to do a nature survey of Mermaid's Ground for the benefit of any conservation organisations who might be interested. Just after their arrival, PC Harris called round, with a female colleague in attendance, to interview them about the events of the previous night. Once he had confirmed that neither Kate nor Tamsin had seen or heard anything suspicious, he concentrated his questions on Luke's vague memory of the small-hours lorry.

'I'm sorry,' the boy said, after a fruitless pause for thought, 'but I still can't even be sure I did hear it. I just have a sort of feeling that I did.'

'That's all right,' said WPC Glenn, who was a brisk, dark-haired young woman with an air of decisive ambition. 'We'll leave the lorry for the moment. Have a think now about Mr Spencer. We know about the three men who attacked Mr Forrester. Have you seen anyone else acting suspiciously? Hanging around?'

'Well . . . no, not really,' Luke said. 'When I'm working I'm in the barn most of the time, because the polishing's always done under cover. Justin doesn't want birds' mess all over the cars,' he added in explanation. 'So I don't see much.'

'Do you know if Mr Spencer has had any visitors at all in the last couple of weeks?'

'Someone came to look at the Cobra,' said Luke. 'Carter Henderson, have you heard of him? He's a big rock star.'

'Or used to be,' said the WPC. 'He was in one of my favourite bands, then they split up. He lives in Surrey now, and races classic cars. When did he come?'

'Last week. Tuesday, I think, but I wasn't there. Mum doesn't like me working all the time in the holidays,' Luke added, with an apologetic glance at Kate. 'So I only do three or four days a week.'

'Carter Henderson.' Harris wrote the name down. 'That should be easy enough to check. Who else?'

'There's a bloke from London, he's a friend of Justin's I think, he's been down quite a lot recently.'

'Do you know his name?'

'Ian – something Scottish, I think it's McPherson.'

'And when did he last visit the farm?'

'Wednesday. He and Justin had a bit of an argument, I heard some of it. It was something to do with the Cobra, I think.'

'A serious argument?'

'There was a bit of shouting,' said Luke. 'Justin was telling him not to worry, of course he could sell it, and the other guy, Ian, he said he hoped he bloody well could, or there'd be trouble, only he said it a bit more strongly than that.' He glanced at Kate again.

'And this was all you heard?'

'Yeah, more or less.'

'Is this Ian often on bad terms with Mr Spencer, would you say?'

'I haven't seen him often enough,' said Luke. 'Usually, as soon as he arrives Justin takes him into the house. Sometimes he has a look round the cars, but he doesn't know a lot about them. He thought Justin's Aston was a Vantage and it isn't, it's a DB5, like James Bond's.' His voice revealed his scorn for someone who could make such an elementary mistake. 'But last week was the first time I've seen him angry. He and Justin came out of the house arguing, and they had a barney just outside, so I couldn't help hearing some of it, once they started shouting at each other.'

'So this man is called Ian, you think his second name may be McPherson, and he comes from London. Can you give me a description?'

'He's quite a bit older than Justin, he's tall and thin with thick grey hair, and he's always very smart – he's into posh suits and silk ties. Drives a Merc.'

'What type?'

'Brand-new silver-grey convertible,' said Luke promptly. 'Must have cost a bomb.'

'Registration number?'

'The letters are CPW, I remembered them because they were Dad's initials, but I don't know the rest.' He looked at the two police officers. 'Do you think he might have had something to do with the robbery?'

'We have to follow up all lines of enquiry,' said WPC Glenn.

'It's a shame about those cars,' said Luke sadly. 'They were so beautiful – and I hadn't finished the E-type, either. Where do you think they've been taken?'

'If we knew that, we wouldn't be here,' Harris told him. 'But they'll be most likely sent abroad. There's a big market in the Far East for good quality classic cars, no questions asked. And the

211

thieves took all the documentation as well, so it seems. If we don't find them, they'll probably be shipped out to Malaysia or Saudi or somewhere like that. At the moment, there isn't much to go on, but once Mr Spencer is well enough to give a statement, we should have a better idea of who we're looking for.'

'God, I hope he is insured,' said Kate, once the police had gone. 'If he isn't . . . *How* much did you say they were worth, Luke?'

'Nearly half a million, I reckon. The Cobra is about two hundred thousand just on its own, then the Astons are over eighty grand apiece; the E-type's a V12 so that's about thirty-five, there was a big Healey about the same, and the cheap ones were the TVR, which was around ten thousand, and the little Frog-eye Sprite, that was in pretty good nick, so it was about eight or nine.'

'*I* don't think nine thousand pounds is cheap,' said Tamsin. 'And Justin actually let you *polish* them when they were worth that much?'

'Of course he did,' said Luke. 'I'm a good worker, he trusted me.'

'Well, that's your job gone,' Tamsin said, not without a certain regrettable *Schadenfreude*. 'You can't polish Justin's cars if he hasn't got cars to polish.'

'I suppose not, but I don't mind very much,' said Luke, sounding only mildly regretful. 'I was getting a bit fed up with it anyway. Justin's been really off recently, bawling me out for no reason at all. Honestly, I'm not bothered. What's for lunch? I'm starving.'

Kate hoped that he was telling the truth, and that he wasn't nursing secret grief about the end of his job, not to mention the end of Justin's relationship with his mother.

After lunch, Luke went up to his room to work on his holiday project. Tamsin and Jayde collected an impressive assortment of jars, nets, magnifying glasses, notebooks and Kate's much-loved wildflower guide, and went into Mermaid's Ground, which was fortunately at present free of cows, with Emma frisking joyfully round them. Happy that her offspring were gainfully occupied for the afternoon, Kate picked a bunch of roses from the garden and set off to see Justin.

The rich scent of the flowers, hot and heavy with sunshine, filled the Astra as she drove over to Bath. She parked in one of the city centre streets and spent a pleasant half hour in Waterstone's, choosing books. A brief visit to an expensive and delightful little shop in Shire's Yard yielded a box of handmade Belgian liqueur chocolates, gift-wrapped and tied with gold ribbon. Her conscience assuaged, she drove up to the hospital.

'Mr Spencer is much better this afternoon,' said the nurse on duty. 'In fact, I think he'll be discharged tomorrow. Goodness me, *more* flowers! We've run out of vases. I've already had to scrounge a couple from the next ward.'

More flowers? wondered Kate, carrying her offerings along the corridor. *But apart from Tanya, who would have sent him flowers?*

The room was filled with them. Huge bouquets of carnations, irises, lilies, crowded every available surface. Kate stood in the doorway, clutching her wilting roses and the books and chocolate, and stared in amazement. 'My God, Justin! Is there room to move?'

'Kate. Hallo.' He was sitting in an armchair, watching cricket on television. There was a spectacular white bandage round his head, but he appeared extremely well.

'How are you?' she asked, coming in and shutting the door behind her. 'You don't look too bad, I must say.'

'I've had dreadful pains in my head. They're sending me for a scan later.' He touched the bandage with tentative fingers.

'Oh, poor Justin,' Kate exclaimed sympathetically. 'Do they think it might be serious?'

'I don't know. Just a precaution, they *said*. You know what they're like, they won't tell you anything straight.' He looked at the roses, still clutched in her hand, and dripping petals. 'More flowers. How nice. There might be room in one of those vases, if you squash them in.'

'So who sent you all these?' Kate asked. She pushed her once-beautiful roses in amongst carnations as red as strawberries, which completely overpowered them and would certainly kill them if they shared the water for too long.

'Tanya,' said Justin. 'She came to see me a couple of hours ago. She said you'd told her what had happened, and she brought them over to cheer me up.'

'*All* of them? Good grief,' Kate said, staring round at the massed vases. 'There must be half a florist's shop here – a bit OTT, surely.'

'Well, you know Tanya, no half measures,' Justin pointed out. 'She brought those, as well.'

Kate saw the pile of best-sellers beside his bed, and decided not to offer her two cheap paperbacks. She produced the chocolates instead. 'They're the sort you like best, I got them at Marie's.'

'Thanks,' said Justin, putting them down on the floor by the side of his chair. 'I might have one later, if I'm feeling up to it. Have the police been to see you yet?'

'Yes, but we couldn't tell them very much. Luke was the most helpful, I think, because they wanted to know what visitors you'd had recently. In case one of them was sniffing round, I suppose.'

'So what did he say?'

'Well, he told them about that rock star, the one who was going to buy the Cobra.'

'And didn't. I was badly let down there.'

'And of course there was that friend of yours – Ian somebody.'

'McPherson. Yes, he's my partner.'

'I didn't realise you had a partner,' said Kate, thinking that there seemed to be a great deal she didn't know about him.

'Didn't you? Ian and I go back a long way. I sold him a very nice Lotus once, and we kept in touch. When I started up the business, he came in with me. He's often down. Haven't I mentioned him before?'

'You never talked very much about that sort of thing,' Kate reminded him. She paused, wondering what to say. Despite her earlier intentions, this was hardly the time, or the place, to tell him that she didn't want to go back to him. And he was so off-hand, and so evidently found her presence unwelcome, that it wasn't necessary to put it into words.

Still, she thought charitably, *he must be feeling ghastly, and he's been through a terrible experience, so it's not surprising if he doesn't feel up to visitors, especially after Tanya; he could probably do with a rest.*

She added sympathetically, 'Was it really awful?'

'I don't want to talk about it,' said Justin, with annoyance. 'I've been over it all once with the police, and I don't feel like doing it again with you.' Pointedly, he turned his eyes back to the screen, where England were putting up a good defence against the Australian bowling.

Kate stood irresolutely by his chair. Part of her wanted to be really rude in return, but her better, more generous half reminded her once again that he was in pain, and shock, and probably still adjusting to the loss of his cars. In the end, she said quietly, 'I'll be off now. I hope you feel better soon. The nurse said you'd be home tomorrow.'

'Did she? I doubt it. Oh, well hit!' An England batsman had just scored a spectacular four.

'Bye, Justin. See you soon.' Kate turned and crept out of the room. Behind her, the bandaged figure in the chair gave no sign that he had even noticed her departure.

'Are you *sure* he'll be well enough to go home tomorrow?' she said to the nurse, on her way out. 'He doesn't seem very good to me.'

'Oh, dear, I'd better take a look then. He's probably tired, poor man,' said the nurse, sympathetically. 'The visitor he had earlier must have worn him out. I could hear them laughing all the way down the corridor.'

'Well, she is rather the life and soul of any party,' said Kate waspishly, and left the ward before she could succumb to the temptation to go back to Justin's room and tell him exactly what she thought of him.

She marched back to the Astra, wishing that she hadn't bothered to come, and thinking of all the other things she could have been doing with her time.

'Ungrateful bloody man!' she said aloud, as she opened the door. 'Well, that's it, mate, you've had your chance, and you blew it, so tough, as Tamsin would say.'

The old lady just getting out of the car next to her gave her an astonished look. Kate grinned back at her, and waved cheerfully. Then she started the engine, revved it with a vigorous roar that would have done credit to Damon Hill, and drove back to Moxham with her window open and the wind whipping her hair, and her tape of favourite summer songs turned up loud. *That's it. Done and dusted. He's history*, she thought, as Stevie Winwood sang, 'If you see a chance, take it.' *And now I'm going to forget all about him, and enjoy Jem's company while I still can.*

Chapter Seventeen

For a week now, there had been only one topic of conversation in the Unicorn. Even the impending flower show had wilted into the background, overwhelmed by the events at Silver Street Farm. The theft of Justin's cars had been the top story on the regional TV news, and had even made the national press. All the following week, the village had been crawling with reporters, cameramen and interviewers, every single one of them gleefully contrasting the picturesque buildings and tranquil (or previously tranquil) atmosphere with the brutal armed robbery which had taken place only yards, as the man from the *Telegraph* pointed out, from the typically English village green, with its duckpond, pub and row of quaint thatched cottages.

The journalists had concentrated on Justin, whose public-school good looks and wealthy background made him an ideal subject for their sympathy (though the *Mirror* described him as 'plummy-voiced playboy toff Justin Spencer, first cousin of Lord Berbidge', and seriously overestimated the value of the stolen cars). The attack on Jem, the previous night, rated a small paragraph in the *Guardian*, a line in the *Independent*, and not a single word in any other paper. Characteristically, he accepted his apparent invisibility with cheerful good humour.

In contrast, Justin seemed positively disgruntled by his brief period of fame. He snapped at the more intrusive reporters, and after a few days the entrance to Silver Street Farm was kept shut and locked. After his churlish ingratitude at the hospital, Kate felt no inclination to see him again, especially as she strongly suspected that he had exaggerated the effect of his injuries. And she couldn't help comparing his behaviour with Jem's, to her ex-lover's disadvantage.

Anyway, she was much too busy to spare any thought for Justin. The designs for the party decorations – if that was the right word for the splendid and incredibly expensive display which she had planned – had entranced Tanya, who had immediately given the go-ahead. Georgia, Charlie's put-upon but extremely efficient PA, had spent most of her time on the phone, ordering table linen, lights, flowers, and checking the catering arrangements. She and Kate had a hard job to persuade Tanya that her latest idea, a marquee-style pink canvas roof over the courtyard garden, was absolutely out of the question.

'But what if it rains?' demanded Charlie's wife.

'Then we'll just have to hold the party indoors,' Kate had said cheerfully. 'It's not as if you haven't got room for five hundred people, after all.'

'Oh, all right, then,' Tanya had said, grinning. 'But if it does rain, I'm holding you personally responsible.'

'It won't,' Kate assured her. 'I've got a personal hotline to the weather department. Rain will not be permitted.'

She hadn't been losing sleep over the possibility: it was pointless to get all worked up about the weather, especially English weather. But she had been increasingly anxious, all this week, about the fate of Mermaid's Ground. Today, the planning committee was due to meet. Today, with luck, or not, everything would be decided. And she hoped very much indeed that the development would be turned down.

With considerable apprehension, she cycled down to the Unicorn at half past five. She had arranged to meet Luke and Tamsin for an early evening meal there, and she was also acutely aware that if there was any news, she'd be bound to hear it in the pub. She parked her bike against the front fence and went in, her heart thumping. Marcia was behind the bar, chatting to the usual knot of villagers: Keith Parker, who ran the football club, Arthur Parrot, secretary of the Allotment Association and chairman of the flower show committee, and Bob Wiltshire, who was wearing his summer uniform of cap, stained vest, and ancient trousers tied round his waist with binder twine. 'All right then, Kate?'

'Surviving,' she said, with a smile. 'Any news?'

'None yet,' said Arthur, who had been one of those who had unexpectedly supported her. 'But it won't be long before we hear. Your garden ready for the competition, then? The judging's on Sunday, remember.'

'It's as ready as it'll ever be,' said Kate. 'But it's not looking its best, I've had too much else to do this year.'

'I wonder if Mr Spencer will be in here later to celebrate, if things go his way,' Marcia said, pencil poised over her notebook

to take Kate's order. 'I've hardly seen him since it all happened –
he's come in once, I think.'

'Good grief,' said Kate, in genuine astonishment. 'I thought he
was part of the furniture.'

'Given he a shock, see,' said Bob, from further along. 'Shook
he up something powerful, I d'reckon, and twas enough to put
he on the wagon.'

'And pigs will fly,' Arthur Parrot commented darkly. 'I hope
you've got plenty of fizz stashed away, Marcia, he'll be back afore
long, even if he don't win it.'

Marcia, surprisingly, didn't seem to be especially keen on the
idea, and Kate remembered Bob saying that Justin hadn't paid
his slate at the Unicorn for some time. 'Are the kids here yet?'
she asked the landlady.

'Out in the garden,' Marcia told her. 'Which reminds me, one
of the clematis has died, in the far corner.'

'Probably clematis wilt. It sometimes happens, and there's
nothing you can do about it, unfortunately. Two Cokes with ice,
a St Clement's, ham, egg and chips twice, and the honey and
mustard chicken with rice and a salad, please, Marcia.'

'Add a pint of best and the sea bream to that,' said a familiar
voice from behind her. 'Hi, Kate. Don't worry, I'll pick up the tab.'

'You can't keep doing this,' she said, turning to face her
lodger. 'I'm perfectly capable of paying my way, you know.'

'I do know, but I'm feeling in a generous mood. The computer
system's connected up and running, and so far, touch wood, we
haven't found anything wrong with it.'

'Give it a few days, and you will,' Kate told him. 'So does that
mean we'll be seeing a bit more of you from now on?'

'Doubt it – I'm still up to my eyeballs. But after working
fourteen hours a day for about three weeks, I felt I deserved a
night off. So no arguments: my treat.'

Luke and Tamsin were sitting at their usual table, by the well.
Kate put the drinks down in front of them. 'Hallo, guys. Food's
on its way.'

'About time too,' Tamsin grumbled. 'I'm *starving*!'

'And thank Jem for it, ungrateful infant,' Kate added.

'Thanks, Jem,' said her offspring, in unison.

As the two adults sat down, Tamsin turned vehemently to her
mother. 'Mum, did you know that Justin owes Luke lots of
money?'

'No, I didn't,' said Kate, sipping her orange juice and lemonade. 'How much, Luke?'

'Forty-five quid,' said the boy, looking distinctly embarrassed. 'I totted it all up. He hadn't paid me for two weeks before the robbery, and of course I haven't been round there since.'

'Well, he's probably forgotten,' said Jem. 'He has had other things on his mind, you know.'

'I think Luke ought to go and ask him for it,' said Tamsin.

'I know, but I want to wait for the right moment. He was in a really foul mood the last time I saw him, and of course the robbery's happened since then. I don't want him to bite my head off.'

'Would it help if I rang him and put in a word?' Kate asked.

'No, Mum.' Luke shook his head vigorously. 'I mean, thanks, but no thanks. I've got to do it soon, anyway. It's Granny Bennett's birthday next week, and I'll need the money for her present.'

'I don't see why you should have to give her anything,' said Tamsin. 'She's so horrible, she doesn't deserve it!'

'She always gives me something really nice for my birthday,' Luke pointed out. 'So I ought to give her something nice back.'

'You see?' Jem said to Tamsin. 'Good rule for life. Give and take. Do as you would be done by. And even if it doesn't get you anywhere, you've still got the comfort of the moral high ground.'

'Huh?'

'Moral philosophy for ten-year-olds,' said Kate. 'A very slim volume, with a few basic and extremely obvious statements, endlessly repeated.'

Fortunately, at this moment Kelly appeared with the ham, egg and chips, so they were spared any further comments. Jem watched her flirtatious glances and saucy walk with amusement. 'I haven't had a come-on like that since you-know-who turned her attentions elsewhere.'

Kate glanced at her children, but they were busy eating. She said softly, 'Any idea who it is? My money's on Max – you know, the trainer from her health club.'

'Absolutely none, and I don't want to know either. Anyway, Charlie's due back next week, so that'll cramp her style more than a little.'

'*Nothing* cramps her style. Have you heard about the courtyard garden roof idea?'

'Indeed I have, in considerable detail. I tried to tell her that the span was probably too great, that if anything went wrong her celebrity guests would be suffocated under several tons of pink canvas, and that in any case it would cost a fortune. I think she took me seriously in the end. But anyway, it shouldn't need a gimmick like that. Everything will look wonderful.' He grinned at her. 'With you in charge of the designs, it couldn't look anything else.'

'Don't be silly,' said Kate, failing dismally to hide her pleasure. 'It'll be complete chaos. I shall probably be so knackered and sick of it all when the day comes, that I'll go home and lie in a boiling hot bath instead of dancing the night away to old Serious Money hits I'd hoped I'd forgotten.'

'I tried to persuade Charlie to have someone more up-to-date, but the old reprobate insisted. He's relaunching them, *big* mistake in my view, but who am I to offer an opinion? I'm only the button-pusher. And at least you can dance to them without needing chemical stimulants to keep going.'

'Which probably won't stop most of the people at the party indulging in them anyway,' Kate commented. 'The children are desperate to go, so I suppose I'll have to let them, even though it'll be way past Tamsin's bedtime before things start to happen. But Jayde's invited her over for the night, so hopefully they'll soon get bored and go upstairs to play computer games until they fall asleep.'

'Are Captain Haddock coming?' Luke enquired, through a mouthful of chips.

'The lead singer is. The rest of the band can't stand the sight of him, so they've all suddenly discovered previous engagements,' said Jem, grinning. 'It's a standing joke; the more they all loathe each other, the more it's reflected in their music. When they started out, they were all speaking to each other, and it was quite pleasant to listen to.'

'Melody,' Luke announced, 'is the enemy of aural purity.'

'As Mozart always used to say,' Kate commented drily. 'Oh, good, here's ours. I was beginning to think they'd had to catch the chicken and the bream first.'

Rather later, and fuller, than Kate had intended, they all set off back to Mermaid's Cottage, she and the children on their bikes, and Jem jogging briskly alongside. 'I don't know how you can do that on a full stomach,' she said, secretly admiring his long, easy stride. 'I'd be doubled up after a few yards.'

'I'm not sure I can do it either, but we're nearly there now. Who's that waiting by the gate?'

'It's Justin,' said Tamsin, who was further ahead. 'Now you can ask him for your money, Luke.'

As they cycled up to him, Kate could see from the set of

Justin's face that something had made him very angry indeed. Ignoring the unmistakeable signals, she smiled at him in friendly fashion. 'Hi, Justin. What's up?'

Jem had obviously read the situation in one glance, for she was gratefully aware of him ushering the children firmly towards the house.

'I want a word with you,' said her ex-lover. 'Now.'

'O.K.,' said Kate calmly, although her mouth had gone dry with apprehension. 'What's the matter? What's it about?'

'I'll tell you what the matter is,' said Justin, and his voice was shaking with rage. 'Thanks to you, you fucking interfering bitch, they've turned the plans down.'

So Mermaid's Ground was safe after all. Joy leapt up inside Kate, but she knew better than to reveal her delight. 'I don't understand,' she said in honest bewilderment. 'Why do you think it's my fault?'

'Of course it's your fault, you were the one who told everyone about all those fucking so-called rare plants and that stupid tree, and now they've decided not to allow it "because of the valuable wild-life on the site".' His voice was full of contempt. 'You should have kept your mouth shut – you were my partner, remember? You should have been loyal, you should have backed me up. And instead you went behind my back and interfered, and you've cost me one-and-a-half million fucking quid, and it's all your fault.'

He was looming over her in the evening shadows, and Kate suddenly felt really frightened. Determined to keep calm, she said reasonably, 'I don't think it's very fair to put all the blame on me. I wasn't the only objector. And the conservation groups would have been involved anyway.'

'You shouldn't have said anything! You betrayed me, you lying little bitch!'

'You knew what I thought about it, you knew I didn't agree,' Kate said. 'Anyway, the planning committee doesn't have the final say, does it? You can always go to appeal.'

'The developers have pulled out. They reckon it'd have no chance. *One-and-a-half million pounds* down the drain!' Justin cried, his voice cracking with fury. 'God, I wish I'd never set eyes on you! And it's not as if you were worth it anyway, you're just a flabby middle-aged housewife!'

The complete injustice of his attack had incensed Kate. She flung caution aside and launched her own offensive. 'That's pretty rich coming from you, when you're five years older than I am! And if you really think that it was me that saved Mermaid's Ground, then I'm glad, because it was a completely unsuitable site for all those houses anyway, and you were too greedy to realise it!'

His face distorted with rage, Justin grabbed her shoulders. Kate tried to twist out of his grasp, but he was too strong for her. She saw the savage hatred in his eyes, and smelt the blast of whisky on his breath, and shouted, 'Let me *go*!'

'Not until I've taught you a lesson you won't forget in a hurry, you fucking bitch.' With every word, he shook her until her head swam dizzily, and his grip was agonising. She struggled frantically. 'Justin, for God's sake, let go, let *go*!'

The small voice in the back of her head spoke the words of her instructor on the self-defence course, years ago. '*Forget his balls, go for his shins. Easier to reach, and almost as painful.*'

But she was wearing canvas shoes, with soft rubber soles. That hadn't been the only piece of good advice, though. With a strength born of utter desperation, she brought up her right hand, the first two fingers extended, and jabbed him as hard as she could at the base of his throat.

It was even more effective than she had expected. Justin gave a harsh, strangled cry, and staggered back, clutching his neck. Kate pushed him away and ran towards the house.

She bumped into someone so hard that she overbalanced. Strong hands caught and held her before she could fall. 'Christ, Kate,' said Jem's voice. 'What's happened?'

'Justin,' she said, and gave a wild squawk of laughter. 'They've thrown out the plans for Mermaid's Ground, and he was *furious*. He's lost out on all that money, and he thinks it's my fault.'

'Are you all right? Kate, what did he do to you? Are you hurt?' His arms were round her, holding her close. She shook her head, and managed a rather wobbly grin. 'He thought he'd try to shake some sense into me, that's all. And then I remembered my self-defence class.'

'Is he still alive?'

'I think so. He was certainly making some very interesting noises just now.'

'What did you do to him?'

'I jabbed him in the throat. I never dreamed it would work, but it did.' Gently, she slipped out of his arms. 'And serve him right.'

'Do you want me to make sure he's O.K.? Wait here and I'll take a look.'

He was back in a few moments. 'No sign of him, so you can't have done him that much damage. Are you *sure* you're O.K., though?'

She nodded firmly. 'Quite sure. It was really horrible, just for a bit, but somehow it doesn't seem so awful now. Probably that's because I hit back. Winning makes you feel so much better. The only thing I regret is not going for his balls afterwards.'

Jem chuckled. 'If you'd like *me* to oblige—'

'God, no, you don't want to get involved. Anyway, it's over, done, finished. Even if I've fractured his larynx, I honestly couldn't give a toss. I marvel at myself, really. Whatever did I see in him?'

'Well, they do say love is blind.'

'I don't think love had a lot to do with it, actually. I have this inconvenient tendency to believe people, you see. And when someone tells you you're gorgeous and wonderful and desirable, it's very easy to fall into their arms. Especially if you're feeling lonely and a bit vulnerable. I couldn't believe my luck. And it took me a while to realise what he was really like. Until Mermaid's Ground, in fact.'

'You don't regret speaking out, do you?'

'Of course not,' she said, smiling. 'Worth all the trouble, every bit, to save it. And it *is* saved. The developers have backed out, that's why he's so furious. They'll probably try to find another site in the village now, and Justin's million-and-a-half quid will go to some other lucky blighter.'

It was almost dark now, but she could see him smiling back at her, and her resolve almost melted. For a brief, mad moment, she wondered what would happen if she said, 'Stay'. She imagined his arms around her again, and the feel of his lips on hers, and the sensations that his closeness was already beginning to arouse.

Flabby middle-aged housewife. With those few words, Justin had dealt a fatal blow to her hard-won self-esteem. All that wonderful flattery had been false, lying words to get her into bed. And when she'd stood up to him, and refused to be the blindly loyal doormat he evidently wanted, he'd dumped her.

'Come in,' said Jem. 'Have a cup of tea, or, better still, something stronger – you can't tell me you don't need it.'

'Do I look O.K.? Not too battered? I really don't want the kids to know about this. Tamsin would be round there setting fire to the place before I'd finished speaking.'

'Too right. Anyway, don't worry, you look absolutely fine to me.'

'Good. And if I tell them that Mermaid's Ground is safe, they'll be so delighted they won't notice anything else. Over the moon. Life must go on. Don't cry over spilt milk. Why do I always want to talk in clichés in a crisis?'

'You're not the only one afflicted. Look at politicians. And tabloid editors. "Attractive thirty-something Merry Widow Kate Williams told our reporter she was as sick as a parrot." '

'Daft as a brush, you are. Anyway, why are parrots sick, and why is it always the moon you're over? And why can you always make me laugh even when I'm feeling, well, as sick as a parrot?'

'It's this special talent I have. I'm not one to hide my light under a bushel.'

'*Now* who's talking in clichés?' said Kate, and marched resolutely up to her front door.

As she had predicted, the news about Mermaid's Ground was enough to drive all other thoughts from Tamsin's head. She did a victory dance all round the room, singing 'We are the champions!' very loudly, and even Luke smiled. With a mug of hot, comforting tea on the table beside the sofa, Kate gave Luke and Tamsin a brief and highly expurgated account of her talk with Justin, trying successfully to convey the impression that it had been a civilised discussion rather than a bad-tempered and finally violent encounter.

'We ought to celebrate properly,' Tamsin said, her face glowing with joy, 'now that Mermaid's Ground is safe.'

'Indeed we ought,' said Kate, smiling back. Already the memory of Justin's rage was receding with merciful rapidity, to be replaced with a share of her daughter's happiness. 'I still can't quite believe it's true, but it is, and it's wonderful. Trouble is, there's no champagne.'

'There's a bottle of dry Lambrusco in the wine rack,' said Jem from the hall.

'Not *quite* the same cachet, but it'll do for now,' said Kate, jumping up to find some glasses. 'And tomorrow evening we'll all go to that nice bistro in Corsham, and really celebrate in style!'

Chapter Eighteen

Conscientiousness is not a common characteristic of teenage boys, but Luke Williams possessed it in spades. It would, probably, bring him a handsome clutch of exam results next year. And it had made him an excellent polisher, happy to rub Justin's cars with wax and soft cloths until they shone like glass.

But, being conscientious himself, Luke expected it in other people, and was disappointed when he found them lacking. He knew that this reaction was a little unreasonable when applied to his employer, for Justin had recently had a great many other more important things to think about, and as he usually dealt with very much larger sums of money, quite possibly he had forgotten all about the comparatively trifling amount which he owed to Luke.

However, as both his mother and his sister had pointed out, forty-five quid might be small change to Justin, but to Luke it was a very substantial sum. And he needed it to buy his grandmother's birthday present. True, Diana was still not on speaking terms with Kate, but this had made no difference to her feelings for Luke, whom she adored. She had rung a few days previously, ostensibly for a chat with her grandson, but she had taken care to slip a couple of pointed references to the imminent day into the conversation. She had even let him know that she wanted a boxed set of classic arias and, when Luke innocently said that he would try to get it for her, immediately gave him the label and reference number, which were evidently waiting conveniently to hand.

So he'd ordered it from a shop in Corsham. The four CDs came to forty-four pounds ninety-nine. And he'd spent so much on discs for his new player that he hadn't any of his previous wages left. Being Luke, he had kept all of this quite dark while he wrestled with his conscience. He couldn't tell Kate, because if she knew that Granny had asked him for such an expensive present, she would tell him to get something cheaper, and then

227

Granny would ring her up to complain. Luke hated anger and argument, unless it was with his sister, and the rift between Kate and Diana disturbed him deeply. He wanted to mend it, not make it worse.

So, in the end, he had to grit his teeth, gird his loins and go to see Justin, because, little though he relished the prospect, it was better than what would happen if he didn't.

The morning after the news that Mermaid's Ground was safe was sunny and warm, although thunder was threatened for later. Luke slipped out of the cottage after breakfast, in shorts and trainers, saying he was going for a run. Jem was already round at the Court, so he wouldn't have company. It took a complete circuit of the village, however, before he had gathered enough courage to pass his own house and jog the further hundred yards or so to Silver Street Farm.

The gates were padlocked, and there were no cars in the drive. Left without any wheels at all, Justin had hired a big Rover saloon while the insurance claim was sorted out, but it was always left in the empty barn overnight. Luke climbed over the gate and, his heart thumping apprehensively, went up to the front door.

The sound as he banged the handsome brass dolphin knocker echoed through the house behind. Luke waited. At this hour, Justin was probably having breakfast, the one meal which he usually organised for himself. He noted the interesting patch of lichen on the stones to the right of the door, and the fact that the white paintwork was badly in need of refurbishment.

Just as he was nerving himself to knock again, he heard footsteps approaching down the hall, and the door swung open. 'Oh, it's you, is it?' said Justin, with rather less than his former affability. 'What do you want?'

He was wearing a navy-blue towelling bathrobe, with his initials on the breast in red scrolled embroidery, and he had, obviously, just emerged from bath or shower. Luke, committed, took a deep breath. 'Sorry to disturb you, Justin, but I – I've come for the money you owe me.'

Faced with silence, he added in a rush, 'I've worked it out and it's forty-five quid, and I need it to buy my grandmother's birthday present, so if it's all right with you, can I have it now, please?'

Justin glowered at him. He said, 'You could have picked a more convenient time.'

'Yeah, well, sorry,' said Luke apologetically. 'I didn't think—'

'Oh, all right,' Justin said, with distinct lack of grace. 'Wait here, and I'll get it.'

He went back inside, leaving the door only slightly ajar. Luke felt a rising tide of annoyance. *He doesn't have to be so rude about it*, he thought resentfully. *I've earned that money, fair and square, and it's mine by right. And it's not as though he's skint, either.*

A car came up the lane and stopped outside the gate. Luke glanced round, and saw Justin's partner, Ian McPherson, get out. He wondered if he would have to climb over the gate too, and watched with interest to see what he would do.

'Here!' McPherson was noticeably Scottish. 'Would you do me a favour, lad, and let me in?'

'I can't, I haven't got the key!' Luke called back. 'But here's Justin.'

His former employer emerged from the house with two twenties and a tenner in his hand. When he saw the immaculately dressed man on the other side of the gate, his face stiffened. 'Ian! I wasn't expecting you.'

'So I see,' said McPherson. 'Are you going to let me in?'

Furtively, Justin thrust the notes into Luke's hand. 'Keep the change, and don't let him see it,' he hissed, and then, at greater volume, 'Luke will open the gate for you.'

The boy stuffed the money into the pocket of his shorts and took the keys. With Justin watching from the doorway, and Ian McPherson from his car, he unlocked the padlock, pulled the chain free, and dragged the gates back to let the big grey Mercedes past. Then he went back to the house.

McPherson had already gone in, and Justin was waiting on the step with his hand outstretched. 'Thanks,' he said shortly, taking the keys. And he shut the door on Luke before the boy could ask permission to go into the barn to get the belongings he'd kept there before the robbery.

Feeling distinctly peeved, Luke paused irresolutely on the doorstep. The overalls and mug weren't important, but his collection of tools had belonged to his father, and he cherished them. Besides, Jem wanted to tinker under the Tomato's bonnet when he had some spare time, and he'd asked Luke to help him.

'Oh, sod it, why shouldn't I?' Luke said aloud, and marched round to the barn.

He had already noted that although the main doors were shut and locked, the small side entrance was half open. Hoping that Justin wasn't looking, he slipped inside.

He didn't dare turn any lights on, and the two long, narrow

windows gave surprisingly little illumination. His overalls were still hanging where he had left them, but his mug, with a picture of Garfield on it, was lying broken on the floor by the kettle. He put the overalls on the workbench, and began the hunt for his tools.

It took much longer than he had thought. The robbers had evidently ransacked the place, and equally evidently, no one had bothered to put anything back. The oil-stained concrete floor was littered with spanners, sockets, blackened rags, cans of paint and scattered bits of paper, mixed with assorted pieces of car, some of it swept into heaps to make room for the hired Rover, parked by the doors. Eventually, he located the box, with his father's initials painted on the top, and began the painstaking task of sorting through the debris for everything else.

There were only a couple of spanners and a ratchet handle still missing when he heard raised voices outside. Curious, he crept over to the side door and peered cautiously round it.

Justin, now dressed in cream trousers and a blue-and-cream-striped polo shirt, was standing nose to nose with McPherson. 'Of course I haven't lost my nerve! Everything's all right, they don't suspect a thing, so what are you worried about? You'll have your money just as soon as the insurance company pays us! So just get off my back, will you?'

McPherson's voice was quieter, but far more menacing. 'Not until you pay me what's owed. We had an agreement, remember? You said I'd have my money back with interest, inside six months. Well, it's been well over a year, laddie, and I've lost my patience. And if I don't get it by the end of the month, that's it.'

'Well, what do you propose to do? Have me beaten up like you did the chap next door?'

'That was a mistake. I'd told them to teach you a lesson, but unfortunately they picked the wrong guy. And your girlfriend was lucky you saw sense and paid me enough to persuade me to call my men off – temporarily. Dogshit doesn't burn too well, but petrol does. And I don't think you'll manage to cheat the insurance company twice.'

'Are you threatening to burn my house down? Because if you do, you won't get your cash, will you?'

'No, so I'll hold them off – for the moment. But if your house burns down, and it's obviously arson, then someone's going to smell a rat, aren't they? And judges don't like fraud. You could be looking at five years, even longer, and it won't be a picnic for someone like you.'

'You wouldn't do it,' Justin said. 'You wouldn't dare.'

'Oh, wouldn't I? Let me tell you, laddie, I'm sick and tired of your excuses. I want my investment back, and I want it soon. And if you won't play ball, I'm quite happy to see you go down, even if it means I lose my money. You're not the only one who owes me, and if I'm soft on you, the others will take note.'

'I don't know when the insurance money will come,' Justin said. 'But it will, believe me. Everyone's convinced the robbery was genuine.'

'So you hope. But you're getting two lots of money for those cars, remember, and I want what you owe me the moment it lands in your lap, or what happened to your girlfriend will seem like a vicarage tea-party compared to what I'll have them do to you. Understand?'

Justin's response was inaudible. Luke, pressed to the inside wall of the barn, heard the Mercedes door slam, and the roar as the car drove fast out of the gate and down the road.

He was shaking, and his palms were damp with sweat. He didn't think he could move, even if he wanted to. If Justin decided to come into the barn, he'd see him straight away. And he would know that Luke had been listening to that damning, incriminating argument.

But he didn't come in. Luke heard him swearing savagely, and then the front door slammed. The boy stayed where he was, thinking hard. If he tried to walk across the drive to the gate, Justin would almost certainly notice him. But if he crept out of this side door, and round the back of the barn, there was a gate into Mermaid's Ground. He could slip along the hedge, and be home in a few minutes. Only two of the farmhouse's windows overlooked the field, so there was a good chance he wouldn't be spotted.

He picked up the overalls and the toolbox, and tried to calm his pounding heart. He could only think of the next few minutes, of the absolute necessity of getting home without being seen.

What he would do with his dangerous knowledge, he had absolutely no idea.

Even before he reached the safety of Mermaid's Cottage, Luke had begun to wonder whether that argument was all a wild figment of his imagination. Had Justin really admitted to faking the theft of his precious cars in order to pay off his business partner?

If he had, and the fraud was discovered, McPherson had indicated that he would certainly go to prison. Alone in his

231

bedroom, Luke wrestled with moral dilemmas that he had never expected to encounter. Once upon a time he had liked Justin, very much. And if he had learned all this a few months ago, his loyalty to his former employer would have overridden every other consideration.

But in those months there had been the deception over Mermaid's Ground, Justin's increasing reliance on alcohol, and the end of his relationship with Kate. He had revealed a rather less pleasant side to him than the generous, charming man who had captured her heart, and Luke didn't like it. And he had his own disagreeable memories as well.

At primary school, he had once done a project on Ancient Egypt. He could remember very little of it, but one wall painting had stuck in his memory: the jackal-headed god of the dead, Anubis, weighing the heart of a man against the feather of truth. Now, fatally, Justin's side of the scale had grown heavy with lies and deceit.

But Luke, ignorant of Justin's attack on his mother, still could not bring himself to do anything, or to tell anyone. It would set in motion things that he didn't, in his heart, actually want to happen, despite the evidence of his own ears. And what if he'd misunderstood?

He also possessed what Kate called the Hamlet flaw – the ability to see all sides of the question as well as his own. If McPherson really was behind the vandalism at Mermaid's Cottage, the abduction of Smith and the attack on Jem, then Luke could well understand Justin's desperate need for money. He didn't know how much was owed, but it must run well into six figures; the sort of sum that only the sale of Mermaid's Ground, now fallen through, or the insurance payment on seven stolen cars, could provide. And Justin wouldn't want to give up his extravagant lifestyle, or sell the house that had been in his family for generations.

So I can't blame him really, Luke thought miserably. *In his place I'd have been tempted to do the same, even if I didn't actually have the courage to fake a robbery*. He wondered who had taken the cars, and whether Justin would indeed get twice their value, once from their illicit sale, and once from the insurance company. He couldn't help admiring, either, the sheer nerve of the man. Arranging the theft must have needed a certain amount of resolve and ingenuity, but to have also submitted willingly to being hit over the head and tied up for hours, in the interests of authenticity – *that*, Luke decided, *takes real guts. And defrauding*

232

the insurance company isn't really stealing – lots of people do it, in one way or another. Besides, McPherson's obviously a major villain, with heavies to do his dirty work for him. It explains everything, even Justin's bad temper.

So he did nothing. He threw himself into his holiday tasks, and tried to think about the new school term, now less than two weeks away. The only people he might possibly have confided in were Jem and Tamsin. But Jem was still frantically busy at the Court, so their lives hardly coincided at all. He saw him in passing at the breakfast table, but that was neither the place nor the time for such devastating revelations. And Tamsin, who viewed everything in deepest black or purest white, wouldn't understand her brother's doubts and scruples. She would be delighted that the despised Justin was nothing more than a common criminal, and insist on informing the police. She obviously suspected that something was wrong, but Luke ignored her pointed probings. And daily, the weight of guilt and worry and uncertainty grew greater.

Until the following Saturday afternoon, when Bob Wiltshire made a surprising discovery in the hothouse at the Court.

It was a story that lost nothing in the telling, and gained a great deal. By five o'clock, Sal knew, and was busy spreading the word to the last-minute rush of customers coming in to buy lottery tickets. By seven, Marcia at the Unicorn had been regaled with the lurid details, transmitted in Bob's own inimitable style. 'And I seed en there, humping away for dear life in amongst all the pots – twas a sight for sore eyes, I can tell ee! Mind you,' with a sly wink for his riveted audience, 'that Tanya's bit off more than she can chew this time around, if you get my drift!'

Simon Mortimer, just arrived back from holiday in Tuscany, dropped in for a quick early evening pint to escape from the chaos at home, and listened with astonishment, and considerable amusement, as old Bob recounted, for the umpteenth time, how he had found Tanya Dobson *in flagrante* in the hothouse with her latest lover. Then he went home and told his wife.

In Mermaid's Cottage, it was teatime. Luke and Tamsin were watching a very tacky game show, and Kate was making a grown-up sauce, with sun-dried tomato paste, pesto and wine, to go with the lamp chops she was defrosting. It had been a trying day. She had rung her mother to wish her a happy birthday, and had received a distinctly frosty reply. 'Thank you for the book token, Katherine. I suppose you have been so busy recently that you haven't had time to look for a *proper* present.'

Tamsin would have informed Diana that she was a selfish, malicious, ungrateful, manipulative old bat who didn't deserve any present at all. Kate, summoning every ounce of self-control that she possessed, said sweetly, 'I'm so sorry you feel like that, Mother. It must really have spoilt your day.' And had put the phone down before the querulous, complaining voice at the other end could start again.

Then Caroline had rung, wanting Jem. This was becoming an increasingly regular occurrence, and Kate had begun to suspect that she might be trying to get back into Jem's life. She had to remind herself, very firmly, that he was her friend, and that in a few weeks he'd be back in London, without ever knowing how significant he had been to her. And she couldn't summon the courage to tell him, because the inevitable gentle rebuff would be too humiliating even to contemplate.

In the hall, the phone began to ring again. Wooden spoon in hand, Kate went to answer it.

'Hallo, Kate,' said Megan's voice, sounding rather breathless.

'Hi! You're back! Did you have a good holiday?'

'God, no, it was an absolute nightmare. The plane was delayed, the hire car broke down, the filtration unit in the swimming pool didn't work, and we all had the runs,' said Megan. 'But I'll tell you about it another time – that isn't why I called.' She paused, and then continued, in unusually serious tones. 'Listen, Kate, I've just heard something fairly awful, and I think you ought to know about it.'

'Oh.' Kate took a deep breath, aware of some apprehension. 'Come on, then, I suppose you'd better spit it out. What is it?'

'It's all over the village, so I thought I'd better tell you now, before you find out from Sal or Mrs Starling or one of those,' said Megan. 'And they'd gloat, it would be horrible . . .'

'Oh, *please* tell me,' Kate cried. 'I'm imagining all sorts of terrible things, and they're probably far worse than the reality.'

'I doubt it.' Megan paused again, and Kate could tell that passing on this particular piece of gossip gave her absolutely no pleasure at all. 'It's about Tanya. Bob Wiltshire found her in the hothouse at the Court this afternoon, with her latest lover. Bonking.'

'In the *hothouse*? Isn't that a bit uncomfortable? Not to say public?'

'I don't know about that. I just know that he found them, at it like rabbits up against the geraniums. But . . . Oh, God, Kate, that's not the worst of it. It was Justin. She was bonking Justin.'

Justin. A little voice in the back of Kate's head whispered, *I knew it. I knew it!*

No wonder he'd dumped the flabby middle-aged housewife; something very much more attractive had come along. But she didn't care about that now: she was glad it was all over. In fact, the main sensation currently filling her mind was the urgent desire to laugh.

But Megan was obviously expecting that she'd be upset. Kate struggled vainly for a moment, and then finally gave in.

'Kate! Kate, are you all right?'

'Y-yes,' she spluttered, while a wonderful vision of Justin and Tanya rose to her mind, shagging away obliviously amid a shower of cascading geranium pots, and Bob Wiltshire's gleefully salacious face peering through the murky green glass of the hothouse windows like a bucolic satyr . . .

'I'm sorry,' she said at last, still giggling. 'The thought of it's just so funny, that's all.'

'*Funny?* But – but I thought you'd be really upset,' said Megan doubtfully.

'Why should I be? Justin and I were as good as finished months ago. The only person I feel sorry for in all this is Charlie, and as he's in Japan, with any luck he won't know what's happened.'

'I doubt it, if Bob Wiltshire saw them. The entire county has probably heard about it by now,' said Megan, sounding much more like her normal self. 'I suppose it *is* rather amusing, isn't it, really? I'm surprised it took them so long to get off together. I mean, they're two of a kind, aren't they?'

'Oh, no, they're not. The only trouble with Tanya is that her powers of discrimination are a little inadequate, that's all. Justin, on the other hand, is a selfish, arrogant, lying bastard, and, worst of all, when he's dressing he puts his socks on first.'

'God, he doesn't!'

''Fraid so. Awful, isn't it? And to think it took me close on a year to realise it. About him being a selfish bastard, I mean, not about the socks.'

Megan giggled. 'Well, you weren't the only one who was fooled.' There was a pause, filled with distant childish demands, and then she said, evidently to Simon, 'What? Can't they wait? Oh, all right then, I'm coming. Sorry, Kate, got to go, the twins want me to read them a story. Look, I'll phone you tomorrow. Are you *sure* you're O.K.?'

'Couldn't be better,' said Kate, and put the receiver down.

Rather belatedly, she became aware that both her children, and Jem, were standing in the hall watching her. 'What's up, Mum?' Luke asked, with a very worried expression. 'What's Justin done now?'

'Him and Tanya,' said Tamsin, arriving effortlessly at the correct conclusion. 'Have they been bonking? *Ugh*, how *could* she?'

'Pretty easily, I expect,' said Luke, still looking extremely anxious.

'I don't really think it's the sort of thing we want to talk about,' Kate said firmly. She was no prude, but she didn't fancy discussing this incident with her children. 'It's nothing whatsoever to do with us any more, anyway.'

'No, it isn't,' said Luke suddenly, and turned and went upstairs. After a pause, Tamsin ran up after him.

'Her sense of timing is superb,' said Jem drily, when Luke's door was safely shut. 'Charlie phoned this morning to say he'd be back tomorrow, three days early. Christ knows what will happen if he finds out.'

'Will he? Who on earth is going to tell him?'

'Not me, that's for sure. Trouble is, the success, if you can call it that, of Charlie's marriage is entirely based on him being able to turn a blind eye to what Tanya gets up to. But if some do-gooding busybody lets him know what's been happening, he won't be able to ignore it.'

'And bang goes her meal ticket for life,' Kate commented, as she went back into the kitchen to stir the sauce.

'Perhaps. And perhaps not. He'd be more likely to find some way of getting back at Justin. Charlie's a devious old sod, and he likes his revenge served cold. When he was starting out in management, a certain well-known record label ratted on a deal. Ten years later, he bought the company and sacked the man who'd made the decision. If I were Justin,' Jem said thoughtfully, 'I'd watch my back very carefully indeed.'

Chapter Nineteen

As Jem and Kate were discussing the transgressions of Tanya and Justin, Tamsin stood in the middle of her brother's room with the beady glint of curiosity in her eye. 'What's up, Luke?'

'Go away. Go on, piss off, this is my room and you're banned.'

'Who's gonna make me? You and whose army?' said Tamsin challengingly. 'Come on, *something's* wrong, I know it is.'

'Nothing. I'm fine. Now go away.' Luke flung himself down on the bed and glared miserably at her.

Tamsin stood her ground. Her eagle eye spotted something sticking out from under the duvet. She dived forward and before Luke could stop her, whisked a couple of magazines through his clutching fingers and brandished them triumphantly. 'If you don't tell me, *I'll* tell Mum about these!'

'No, don't,' said Luke, his normally placid, fair-skinned face suffused with embarrassment. 'Tam, please, let me have them back.'

His sister glanced down at them. She'd been expecting the sort of thing stocked on a newsagent's highest shelf, but these seemed fairly innocuous. A longer look, however, gave her ammunition. 'Ooh, have you read this one? "Twelve Pages of the Best Babe Beaches"; "Does Size Really Matter? The Naked Truth"; "Six Flash Cars to Pull the Birds".'

'Tamsin!' Luke cried despairingly. '*Please* give them back!'

'Yeah. When you've told me what's up. It's something to do with Justin, isn't it?'

Cornered without hope of escape, Luke surrendered to her superior tactics. 'Yes,' he muttered at last. 'Yes, it is.'

'Right. Then tell me, or I go downstairs and wave these under her nose.'

'That's blackmail,' said Luke. He sighed, and patted the bed. 'Come on, little 'un. You win. I've been wanting to tell someone, anyway. But promise you won't fly off the handle? And promise you won't tell anyone else?'

'I promise, I promise,' Tamsin assured him, sitting down eagerly beside him. 'Come on, what is it?'

'I've found out something awful, about Justin,' said Luke, and told her what he had overheard at Silver Street Farm.

True to her word, she sat still without interruption, her eyes growing wider and wider as the true extent of Justin's villainy was revealed. 'You mean, all those phone calls and the glass and Smith and everything were meant to persuade him to cough up? So he *knew* who was doing it and why and he never said anything? The rat!'

'Apparently he did pay up, some of it,' Luke pointed out, under the influence of some residual desire to be fair. 'Which is why the attacks stopped.'

'But they started again, didn't they,' Tamsin said, after a pause for thought. 'Those men who beat up poor Jem – they *were* after Justin!'

'So he must have decided to arrange the fake robbery, to get enough money to pay McPherson off once and for all,' said Luke.

'There's something I still don't understand,' Tamsin went on. 'Why didn't he just go to the police and tell them what this Mac-somebody was doing?'

'I've thought about that. McPherson is obviously a villain, but he's also Justin's partner – that means he'd put money into the car business, the money which he wanted back. But what if it was a dodgy deal to start with? I mean, the money could have come from a bank robbery or fraud or something, and Justin knew about it.'

'I bet that's it,' said Tamsin exultantly. 'I *knew* he was a crook, I *knew* it!'

'Well, there's no need to go on about it. The question is, what do I do now?'

'Go to the police, of course,' his sister said.

'But what if I didn't hear it right? I mean, I *could* have got hold of the wrong end of the stick. They could have been talking about something else.'

'Oh, don't be silly, of course they weren't.'

'I don't know,' Luke said unhappily. He had thought that unburdening himself to Tamsin might help to clarify his dilemma, but it seemed to have made everything even muddier. He added, 'But it'll be my word against theirs, and the police are bound to believe them, not me. And then I'll have made everything much worse for everyone.'

'You're not *still* worried about Justin, after all he's done!'

'I can't help it,' Luke said miserably. 'McPherson's a really nasty piece of work. Justin must have been desperate.'

'Honestly, I give up!' said Tamsin. 'You *know* what he's like and you're *still* feeling sorry for him!'

'One day you'll grow up and then you'll realise life isn't as simple as you think it is,' Luke told her. 'You're just a kid, you don't know what reality's like. People aren't pure good or pure evil, they're all shades of grey.'

'Oh?' said Tamsin. 'Then Justin's a very very *very* dark grey, and if you can't see that, big brother, then you're as blind as a bat!'

Quivering with righteous indignation, she flounced out, slamming the door. Downstairs, she could hear Jem, obviously on the phone. 'Yes, Charlie's coming back tomorrow, apparently, so I can ask him if it's O.K. for you to come . . . after all, it's his party, not mine . . . no, I shouldn't imagine there'll be a problem. Although I needn't ask you to play it cool . . . you know what I mean, don't hassle people . . . yes, you do.'

It sounded as though Caroline was inviting herself to the party. At any other time, the news would have caused Tamsin considerable disquiet, but at this particular moment she had a more pressing problem to solve. She walked down the stairs, thinking hard. She might be only a kid, but she watched enough television to know that Luke's information could be devastating if revealed to the right people – the police, for instance. But she also knew that they were unlikely to take her seriously. And then Justin would know that Luke had eavesdropped, with possibly awful consequences.

Torn, she paused at the foot of the stairs. Jem grinned at her, and Tamsin grinned back. She wanted to tell him, but she had promised Luke that she would keep his secret.

Someone else ought to know, though, she thought. *If Justin suspects . . .*

'I'm just going out for a bit,' she hissed to Jem. 'I'll be back before supper, promise!' And she nipped out of the front door before he could protest.

Her bike was still leaning up against the tree by the gate. She scrambled on and set off up the lane, pedalling as frantically as if a host of McPherson's heavies were pursuing her.

But as she approached the Court, some of her resolve faltered. While Charlotte was in Tuscany, Tamsin and Jayde had shared many confidences in the overdecorated bedroom, or around the computer, or while riding the new pony. But she didn't know her opinion of Tanya's latest indiscretion: indeed, she didn't even know if Jayde was aware of it.

But she had to tell someone about Justin, someone who wouldn't think she was a silly kid. Involuntarily, she glanced behind her. It was always at this moment that the baddies turned up with guns, ready to stop the heroine from spilling the beans . . .

The road behind her was empty. Defiantly, Tamsin stuck out her left hand, and whizzed into the driveway of Moxham Court.

Jayde would probably be upstairs, watching television. She and her mother seemed to lead almost separate lives, cocooned in their luxurious suites at opposite ends of the house. At first this had worried Tamsin, but now she accepted it. The Dobsons were fabulously rich, and this fact alone entitled them to be quite different from ordinary people.

She leaned her bike against the side of the porch, and rang the bell, hoping that Tanya wouldn't answer it, and then, as she waited and waited, praying that someone would.

At last she heard running feet, and then the door was opened by Jayde, wrapped in a towel with her hair in wet spikes. She stared at Tamsin in astonishment. 'What are you doing here?'

'I'm on a mission of great importance,' Tamsin said dramatically. 'Is there somewhere we can talk?'

'Alone?' Jayde was blessedly quick on the uptake. 'Come upstairs. Mum's in the pool, but I was getting out anyway. You go on up and I'll tell her where I am, or she might come looking for us.'

Tamsin trotted up the stairs to her friend's suite. It seemed obvious that Jayde hadn't got a clue about what her mother had been up to that afternoon, and she really didn't want to tell her, especially since she knew only the vaguest details herself. But she could certainly give her the news about Justin's other, more criminal activities. Jayde was clever and streetwise. She would know what to do.

'So, what's up, Doc?' Jayde asked, when the two girls were settled side by side on the sofa, in front of a video that Kate probably wouldn't even let Luke watch, never mind his little sister. 'It must be important, or you wouldn't have come.'

'It is.' Tamsin took a deep breath, and said, 'It's about Justin. You know, Justin Spencer.'

'Heard it,' said Jayde, with nonchalant aplomb. 'Mum's gone and made a fool of herself again. I mean, honestly, the *hothouse*!

Why couldn't she have picked somewhere more private? And I thought Justin was *your* mum's bloke, not mine.'

'Not any more, he isn't,' said Tamsin, not without a certain relish. 'They had a big bust-up over Mermaid's Ground, and I'm really glad. Justin's a rat, a slimy horrible rat, and he deserves everything he gets.'

'Couldn't agree more,' said Jayde. 'If my dad finds out he'll have his guts for garters.'

'What about your mum?'

'What about her? She's an embarrassment,' said Jayde, carelessly. 'She dresses like she's fourteen or something, and she's always running after blokes, and I wish she wouldn't. I wish she was like other people's mothers – like yours, for instance. Your mum's nice, she's a *proper* mum, she makes you do things and clear your room up and tell her where you're going. My mum couldn't care less what I did.'

'Oh, I'm sure that isn't true.'

'Oh, it is,' said Jayde bitterly. 'Dad cares, when he's around, he's great, but *she* doesn't. Oh, she's a lot of fun sometimes, it's more like having a big sister than a mum, but I'd swap places with you any day.'

Tamsin was staring at her in disbelief. 'With *me*? Oh, come on!'

'Yes, I would. Pony, computer, posh school, all this—' She waved a hand at the luxury surrounding them. 'I don't want any of it, not really. You know what I'd *really* like? If my dad could marry your mum. That'd be perfect.'

Tamsin said hastily, 'I don't think Mum would want to. I mean, your dad's really nice and everything, but he's a bit old for her.'

'If he's too old for Kate, then he's way too old for my mum. Perhaps that's why she collects toyboys.'

'Anyway, *I'd* like her to get together with Jem,' said Tamsin, with enthusiasm. 'He's lovely and I'm sure he likes her, but the trouble is, he'll be going back to London soon.'

'He might not,' said Jayde. 'Dad wants him to stay, and I know he was thinking about it. He hasn't actually said no yet.'

'Oh.' Tamsin fell silent as she considered the sudden wonderful possibilities that her friend's words had conjured up. 'Are you sure?'

'No, but anyway Dad's coming back tomorrow, so if you like I can find out.'

'O.K. Thanks.' Tamsin grinned at her. 'That would be great. If

Jem's staying, then that makes *everything* different.'

'You really like him, don't you? I do, too,' said Jayde. 'He's a much better bet for your mum than that horrible smarmy Justin.'

'He's not just smarmy, either. He's a criminal!'

'A *criminal*? You mean, like a robber or something? What's he done?'

Acutely aware of Jayde's gratifyingly eager interest, Tamsin gave her the gist of what her brother had overheard.

'If the police find out, he'll go to prison for a long long time,' said Jayde, with satisfaction. 'And serve him jolly well right!'

'That's what I think. But Luke won't do anything about it. He's *hopeless*! He just whinges on about what if he heard wrong, and he told me to grow up. And meanwhile Justin gets away with it scot free.'

'Well, he won't,' said Jayde decisively. 'Not if I have anything to do with it, anyway. You're right, though, if we told the police they'd just pat us on the heads and tell us to run away and play like good little girls. It needs a grown-up. And as soon as possible, too, before Justin gets rid of the evidence.'

'What evidence?'

'Oh, there's bound to be evidence,' said Jayde, with the confidence born of watching a hundred TV cop shows. 'Listen, what if I told my dad when he comes back tomorrow? He'd know what to do. He knows *everything*.'

'I don't know,' said Tamsin, all her certainty suddenly evaporating at the thought of taking such an irrevocable step. 'Are you sure?'

'Course I'm sure, idiot! And he won't like Justin after what he's done with Mum, so he'll want to get his own back too. Trust Dad,' said Jayde, with a smile disturbingly like her father's at his most ruthless. 'He'll get it sorted.'

Aware that she'd been out for a while, and just before supper too, Tamsin took her leave of Jayde soon afterwards, and cycled at breakneck speed back to Mermaid's Cottage, expecting to be told off for her disappearance. She put her bike away in the garage and went round to the back door, ready prepared with what she hoped would be a convincing explanation for her absence, and found the new dog, Emma, sitting disconsolately outside with her nose pressed to the cat-flap.

'What are you doing out here?' Tamsin cried. She opened the door, and Emma slunk in with both ears down and her tail clamped between her legs. She crept into her basket and curled up very small, watching the humans with an extremely anxious expression.

'She's in disgrace,' said Kate, with a glare at the unfortunate animal. 'I turned my back for two seconds and she pinched the chops.'

'Oh no,' said Tamsin, aware of the large hungry hole in the pit of her stomach. 'Did she eat them all?'

'Afraid so. Your dinner really is in the dog,' said Jem, who was standing by the Aga. 'But I don't think she'll be doing it again.'

'You didn't hit her, did you?' Tamsin asked her mother, in alarm.

'Of course I didn't. She's got a much thinner skin than Smith, in every sense of the word. Angry shouts and eviction is more than enough to let her know she's done wrong. There's still the sauce, but it's got a load of things you don't like in it. Shall I do something else for you that's quick? It's getting quite late.'

'I've got a better idea,' said Jem. 'Is there a take-away in Corsham?'

'A couple of Chinese, an Indian, a chippie and a kebab house – take your pick.'

'Chinese,' said Tamsin. '*Please* can we have a Chinese? I want chow mein and Luke likes cashew chicken.'

Over her head, Kate grinned at Jem. 'Looks like you're lumbered.'

'My pleasure,' he said. 'I'll be half an hour.'

'Don't you want to know what I want?'

'Trust me,' he said, grinning, and went out of the door.

When Jem returned with the take-away, Tamsin was in the back garden, hitting tennis balls for Emma to retrieve. He took the two carrier bags through into the sitting room, and found Kate lying with her eyes closed on the sofa. Her head was pillowed by a cushion on one of its arms, and her bare feet rested on the other. He stood in the doorway, watching her, a curious smile on his face. She seemed so vulnerable and defenceless, with her face scraped clear of make-up and her straight pale hair falling back from her forehead. And yet she possessed more strength and courage than anyone he had ever known.

'I'm not asleep,' she said, still with her eyes closed. 'I'm just examining the insides of my eyelids.'

Jem laughed and came in. 'How did you know I was there?'

'The delicious aroma wafting past my nose. The plates are warming up in the bottom oven, and there's wine in the fridge.' Kate sat up, pushing her loose hair away from her face and swinging her legs down to the floor. 'I'd better give the kids a shout.'

'No, you don't,' Jem told her. 'Stay there, I'll sort it.'

Before she could protest, he had dumped the bags on the coffee table, cleared of its usual burden of magazines and papers, and disappeared in the direction of the kitchen. The CD player clicked softly as it changed discs, and the delicate notes of an acoustic guitar, full of grace and passion and gentleness, crept into the air.

'That's nice. Who is it?' asked Jem, coming back in with the plates in his hand and the bottle of wine tucked under his arm.

'Mark Knopfler. Call me old-fashioned, call me hopelessly untrendy, but I could listen to that man playing all night.'

'Don't worry, I'm not a music fashion victim either. I like anything that's good – soul, Tamla, the blues, rock, even a bit of folk when I'm in the mood. And I'll still be listening to them when the likes of Captain Haddock have long since been forgotten.' As Luke and Tamsin arrived, breathless and hungry, he laid out the silver cartons with a flourish. 'Here you are – food of the gods. Chow mein, chicken and cashew nuts, sweet-and-sour pork, stir-fried prawns, mixed veg and special flied lice. Enjoy!'

It was hardly a gourmet meal, and the surroundings were less than splendid, but the music and the company more than made up for it. Afterwards, Kate could not remember what they had all talked about, but they had laughed a lot, and swapped silly stories, and happiness had surrounded her like an antique shawl, beautiful and rare, and all the more precious for the knowledge, at once sweet and bitter, that soon it would be gone.

Chapter Twenty

'And how's my princess, then?' Charlie Dobson swept his daughter up into his arms and planted a smacking kiss on her forehead. 'Hallo, darlin'. Have you missed me?'

'Like a hole in the head,' said Jayde, kissing him back.

It was an old joke between them. 'Better than a slap in the face with a wet fish,' Charlie informed her, putting her down. 'I know you get sick of people telling you you've grown, darlin', but you have, you know.'

'I know. My jeans are too short – look.' Jayde displayed her ankles for inspection. 'Mum says she'll take me into Bath before term starts, and buy me a whole new wardrobe.'

'You had a lotta clothes last Easter, darlin',' said Charlie. 'Don't tell me you need more.'

'Well actually, Dad, I don't,' Jayde said conspiratorially. 'But you know what Mum's like.'

'Don't I just!' said Charlie cheerfully. 'And talk of the devil, here she is!'

His wife came into the hall. She had spent a lot of time choosing what she would wear that morning, and rather less flesh was on display than usual, despite the bright sunshine outside. Charlie surveyed the sleek, understated and extremely expensive lines of her long, dark blue linen dress with fond approval. 'And don't she look lovely,' he said. 'What a sight for sore eyes!'

If this particular choice of words struck any unfortunate chords with Tanya, she did not reveal it. She kissed her husband with considerable enthusiasm, and fluttered her eyelashes flirtatiously. Charlie, who knew the signs, gave his daughter a wink. 'Here, she's up to something!'

'Course I ain't,' said Tanya, slipping an arm round what had once been his waist. 'Just pleased you're back, that's all.'

This was not strictly true. She had lain awake for much of last night, too unhappy and apprehensive to sleep, wondering what to do when Charlie came home. The strings of brainless, handsome boys had been easy to dismiss, in her mind and her husband's, if not theirs, as passing flings, transient and unimportant. Justin was different. Justin was class. And Justin was, all too evidently, not going to melt discreetly into the background at the contemptuous push of a finger.

But she had only discovered that inconvenient fact when it was too late: when the identity of her latest lover had been made extremely and embarrassingly public. Indeed Tanya had wondered, in particularly anxious moments, if Justin had actually engineered their discovery in the hothouse. It had been his idea, and his ardour had overwhelmed her doubts. She had been so lost in passion that she hadn't noticed the discomfort or the danger, until Bob's salacious chuckle had brought her back to reality with an extremely painful thump.

She had carried it off well at the time, cheekily flaunting her bare boobs for the old man's delectation, and acting as though she couldn't care less. Inside, though, she felt as cold as stone. Everyone knew that Bob Wiltshire was the biggest gossip in the village. And sooner or later, inevitably, Charlie would come to hear of it.

She could have explained away the flowers, the chocolates, the absent afternoons, allegedly in the company of her fitness trainer (who, being in Charlie's phrase 'as bent as a nine-bob note', was ideal cover for her activities), but not this. And so she had, reluctantly, come to the conclusion that it would be better to give him her side of the story before anything else reached his ears. Because he knew her extremely well, he would also know that Justin didn't fit the usual pattern of her lovers. And for that reason, Justin presented a danger that all the other himbos had not.

It was a shame, because Justin was flatteringly attentive, generous with gifts, and very accomplished in the sack. The fact that in a sense she had stolen him from Kate didn't trouble Tanya. It was obvious that Justin was entirely wrong for her, and that she'd be better off without him. In her heart, Kate wanted someone permanent, whereas Justin and Tanya were both just after uncomplicated, mutually pleasurable sex.

Or so it had seemed. But Justin didn't appear to understand that the affair had to be kept a secret from Charlie. He couldn't see how Tanya's husband could know, and yet not know, about her lovers. In vain, Tanya had tried to explain that Charlie was quite happy to turn a blind eye, as long as it wasn't obvious. But what could be more obvious, she had thought miserably during that long dark night, than being found humping in the hothouse by Bob Wiltshire?

She was beginning to think that giving in to Justin's temptation (not that she had needed much inducement) had been one of the biggest mistakes of her life. For she was only playing, and it was becoming alarmingly evident that he was not. He was actually serious. He wanted her all to himself, and he couldn't understand that it wasn't possible. Which was probably why he had persuaded her to make love in the hothouse, knowing the risks. Discovery would force her hand.

As indeed it had, but not in the way he wanted. Tanya liked sex, and plenty of it, but not as much as she liked the luxurious, carefree lifestyle which was guaranteed by continued marriage to Charlie. In addition, she had to admit that she was genuinely very fond of the old sod. And so she had arrived at the conclusion that if it came down to a choice between her husband or her lover, then her husband must win.

And because she knew that Charlie loved her, it was, in the end, easy to procure his forgiveness. In the vast, rose-patterned four-poster bed, she made love to him with passion and tenderness, and thoroughly enjoyed herself. And in the rosy afterglow of mutual pleasure, she confessed her sin, with tears and remorse, and, as she had hoped and prayed, received absolution.

So, when Jayde approached Charlie in the courtyard garden that afternoon, and asked for a serious talk, he was able to grin at her cheerfully and say, 'Gawd, darlin', not you as well! It's all right, Princess, I know what your mum's done and she's said she's sorry and what a silly girl she's been, and it's all sorted, so don't worry about it, eh?'

'But it's not that,' said Jayde, her brown eyes vast and anxious. 'It's something else that Justin's done.'

'Blimey, not more!' Charlie said. 'Well, you'd better tell me, angel, get it off your chest.'

It was a curious conversation: on a superficial level, conducted between concerned parent and troubled child, but on a deeper one, informant to secret agent. Jayde knew precisely the value of the intelligence she was passing on, and the use that her father would make of it: and Charlie, too, was well aware of how much she understood.

'He shouldn't be allowed to get away with it, should he?' she said, when she had finished. 'He's been really horrible to poor Kate over Mermaid's Ground. Don't let him get away with it, Dad.'

'Don't worry, darlin',' Charlie said, his eyes narrowed and calculating. 'He won't. Not if I have anything to do with it.'

Confiding in Tamsin, despite his secret doubts as to the wisdom of it, had made Luke feel a great deal better. He had been certain that she had gone off to tell Jayde straight away, but as the days went by, and his former employer remained at large, swanning around in his hired car and running up large bills in the Unicorn, he decided that his sister must have kept the secret after all. And he still couldn't make up his mind whether he was glad, or sorry.

But, of course, Tamsin could choose to reveal it at any time. Luke loved his little sister dearly, but he recognised that she was a much stronger character than he was, and that her childish certainties would carry her much further than he would ever want to go himself. Tamsin dealt in clear lines and boundaries and absolutes. The inner landscape of his own head was blurred and fuzzy by comparison. And the conspiratorial grins which she frequently sent in his direction did nothing for his peace of mind.

Term was looming, and he threw himself into his English project. It involved reading a great many books in which cars did not feature very prominently, and which consequently bored him to tears. He tried not to think about his former employer at all, but even the delights of exploration under the Tomato's elegant bonnet could not entirely distract him from unpleasantly vivid images of suave, luxury-loving Justin, banged up in some dank Victorian nick with a cell full of thugs for company.

Kate worried about him, but she knew better than to ask what was disturbing her son; one whiff of her concern and he'd clam up for ever. In any case, most of her waking hours were so busy – when she wasn't working at the Court, she was keeping Mermaid's Cottage running smoothly, or walking Emma, or planning the scented garden – that she hardly had time to blink, let alone think about what would happen on the other side of Charlie's party, when Jem was gone.

There was an old song by Bruce Springsteen, which she loved, called 'All that Heaven Will Allow'. She wasn't sure how much Heaven would allow her, but she knew that in these hectic days, whatever happened thereafter, she was truly and absolutely happy. She was determined, too, that even the prospect of Caroline, blonde and beautiful and terrifyingly sophisticated, gracing Charlie's party with her elegant presence, would not spoil her mood. For she was damn sure that she was going to take whatever Heaven offered her, and forget about the future.

Then the lights for the party arrived at last, with only a few days to go, and half a dozen workmen to help arrange them. It was a long and tedious job, especially as the full effect could only be seen when they were switched on after dark, and there was consequently a great deal of guesswork involved. The fact that the workmen didn't seem able to tell left from right, or to have any sense of symmetry or proportion, didn't help either, and Kate, stopping at the Unicorn for a reviving drink after a particularly exasperating afternoon, told Jem that if her minions didn't watch it, she'd hang them all by the flex from the mulberry in the sunken garden.

'I don't think it's advisable,' Jem said. 'You wouldn't be able to go to the party if you were on remand.'

'At this rate, I shall be too knackered,' Kate told him.

'Oh, come on, how else are you going to see all the fruits of your labours?'

'I see Luke and Tamsin quite often enough as it is. Oh, *those* labours!'

'As you know very well, Mrs Williams.' Jem grinned at her and at Marcia, who was standing poised for instructions. 'I'm having a pint of best, how about you?'

'You've twisted my arm, very slightly. Long cool Pimms with the full salad, please.'

'There's bound to be some at the party.'

'There is indeed, and champagne by the crate. I shall probably fall asleep halfway through, and everyone will assume it's the Pimms. I don't think I've felt this tired since Tamsin was a baby. And there's another problem. I haven't got a *thing* to wear!'

'Then buy something, dear Liza.'

An image of that lovely dress, seven weeks ago in Bath, rose instantly to her mind, along with the words, *Go on, treat yourself, you deserve it after all that hard work*.

'Fairy godmother required,' she said. 'But I'll think about it.'

'Make sure you do. It's about time you had some fun in your life.'

'Is that another of Doctor Jem's prescriptions?'

'Of course, along with this.' He handed her a pint glass of the true amber nectar, chinking with ice, and garnished with slices of lemon, orange, cucumber and a pert green sprig of mint.

'If I know nothing else,' said Marcia, with justifiable satisfaction, 'I know how to make a good Pimms. Is that to your liking, Kate?'

'You bet. It looks wonderful. It *is* wonderful.' She sipped it gratefully, wryly amused by the fact that since the village had learned of Justin's perfidy, everyone (except Mrs Starling) had fallen over backwards to be nice to her. 'The only trouble with a Pimms is that it sort of sneaks up on you from behind. After this, I won't be able to ride my bike straight.'

'Don't worry,' Jem assured her. 'I'll help you steer. If I can muster the strength, that is. It's been a long, hard day.'

'Ditto. Are the studios on schedule?'

'If Charlie can be persuaded that red carpet will do instead of the blue he wanted, then yes. Otherwise, there'll just be bare boards. Fortunately, he's not picky on details. Anyway, he's in a good mood. The Japan trip went very well.' He glanced round, but there was no one within earshot, and Marcia had gone to serve a couple in the back bar. 'And I think he's made it up with Tanya. She looks like the cat who's got the cream, and she's being frighteningly . . . what's the word I want? Uxorious.'

'It sounds like a character in an Asterix book.'

'Well, that's what she's being.'

Behind them, someone came in. Jem glanced round, and put his hand lightly on hers. 'Don't look now, but guess who's arrived . . .'

Kate sat on her bar stool, her fingers clamped round the Pimms and her heart thumping. She wanted to run away, she wanted to be somewhere else, but the drink was beginning to fizz recklessly inside her. She took a heartening gulp of it and turned her head.

Justin was standing at the bar, a few feet away. He looked cool and elegant, in pale immaculate trousers and striped, open-neck shirt, with a red silk cravat loosely knotted at the throat, probably to hide a very large and painful bruise. Marcia came bustling in from the other bar with her 'welcome customer' smile on her face. It faded rapidly when she saw who it was. 'Good evening, Mr Spencer. Your usual, is it?'

'Of course, and make it a double.' Justin put a twenty-pound note down on the counter. 'Have one for yourself, Marcia, while you're about it.'

'Not this evening, thank you, Mr Spencer,' said the landlady, with chilly politeness. She reached up for a bottle of his favourite malt, and poured two measures into a glass. Justin must have known that his ex-lover was sitting almost within touching distance, but he gave no sign of acknowledgement.

'Do you want to go?' Jem whispered to Kate.

'No,' she said, shaking her head vehemently. 'I wouldn't give him the pleasure. And besides, I want to finish my drink.'

The pub was beginning to fill up. Simon Mortimer came in for his after-work pint, and spent some time describing, in tortured detail, everything that had gone wrong on the disastrous Tuscan holiday. Grateful for the distraction, she commiserated with him, aware all the time of Justin's presence, spoiling the pleasure of the evening. She noticed when he had another double, and another.

'I hope he's not driving,' Jem said softly.

Simon Mortimer frowned. 'I'm afraid he is. His car's outside. He comes in here almost every evening, gets himself tanked up and then drives home for more. One of these days he'll find himself done for drunk driving, and I for one won't be sorry. You were well shot of him, Kate.'

'I know. Don't worry, I've got no sympathy.' She swallowed the last of the Pimms and set the glass back on the counter. 'I suppose I'd better get home before I take root. You coming, Jem?'

'Wait.' He tipped his head back to finish the beer. She looked at the long line of his throat, and the breadth of his shoulders, and wanted him so much that it hurt. *No*, she told herself sternly. *Forbidden territory, signposted Heartbreak and Farewell. I'm not even going to think about it.*

Three men had come into the pub. They paused, eyes searching in the gloom. Jem put his glass down and nudged her significantly. 'Old Bill.'

'How can you tell?'

'Apart from the regulation issue hobnail boots? I'm a Londoner and I'm black, I can spot 'em a mile off.'

The tallest of the men walked up to the bar. Marcia, her face rather wary, went along to serve him. 'Yes, sir?'

'I understand a Mr Justin Spencer may be in here.'

Justin glanced up from contemplation of his third glass of whisky. 'I am indeed. What can I do for you?'

'Justinian Henry Blount Spencer, I am arresting you on suspicion of attempting to defraud the Royal Lion Insurance Company of a sum in excess of four hundred thousand pounds. You do not have to say anything, but it may harm your defence if you do not mention, when questioned, something which you later rely on in court. Anything you do say may be given in evidence.'

'What?' Justin's face was suddenly suffused with rage. 'What the hell do you mean by this?'

'Exactly what I said. Now, sir, if you will come with us, you'll be given full opportunity to explain everything.'

'Like buggery I will! I've told you all I know. There's been some mistake, you've got no right—'

'I really would advise you, sir, to come with us quietly. If there has been a mistake, we'll soon get it sorted. Now, sir.'

There was clear menace in his voice. Justin ignored it. 'Well, you can at least let me finish my sodding drink.'

'I hope you weren't planning to drive home, sir.'

'Of course not. Leave my car here and walk, always do.' Justin poured several fluid ounces of best malt down his throat with criminal speed. 'Very well, *gentlemen*, since you insist.'

As one of the policemen took his arm, he stared with bleary arrogance round at the eager spectators. For an instant, his eyes met Kate's, and then moved on. The other customers watched with avid interest as he was steered, rather erratically, towards the door. Furiously he shook the policeman off, and found himself pinioned with painful force. Then the officers towed him out, shutting the door behind them. There was a brief, stunned silence, before the whole pub burst into loud and astonished comment.

'Good God,' said Simon, his glass still poised halfway to his mouth. 'If he's been accused of defrauding the insurance company—'

'Then that robbery must have been a fake!' Kate finished. 'I don't believe it – he was hit over the head and tied up for hours, I saw him!'

'So did I,' said Jem. 'And if it was a set-up, it was a very convincing one. It definitely had me fooled.'

'But not the police, it seems, though they certainly took it seriously to start with.' The Pimms was making Kate's head a little fuzzy, and she giggled suddenly. 'I never knew his name was really Justinian. He kept that really dark.'

'So would you, if you were saddled with it,' Jem pointed out. 'And this isn't the moment to confess that my name is actually Jeremiah.'

'It isn't! Is it?'

'What do you think? No, it's James. James Garfield Forrester. Called after Gary Sobers, by the way, not the cat.'

'That's your excuse. What was Justin's?' Kate slid off the stool and grinned at him. 'Come on, Jem, you'd better take me home, before I get *really* silly. See you, Simon. Don't forget to give Megan the full unexpurgated story.'

'I'll try not to,' said her friend's husband, with his tight-lipped, dry smile.

Most of the pub had gone outside to see Justin driven off, and Kate had to struggle through a considerable crowd to find her bike. By the time she had put her helmet on, the show was over, and the two police cars had disappeared round the corner towards Chippenham.

'I'm trying to feel sorry for him,' she said to Jem. 'But I'm finding it rather difficult to summon up much sympathy. Now I suppose we'd better go home and tell the kids.'

Luke had spent a long and tedious day immersed in *Lord of the Flies*, and trying to make enough sense of his chaotic thoughts to commit them to paper. It was hard work for a boy who infinitely preferred working with the concrete rather than the abstract, and even harder to concentrate when all the distractions of a lovely August day were pulling his mind out of doors and away from books. The knowledge that Tamsin was round at the riding stables with Charlotte didn't help either. By half past six he was tired, fed up and so hungry that he had actually gone to the trouble of frying a couple of eggs for himself.

When Kate and Jem walked in, he was in the sitting room with his half-eaten snack on his knees, watching the local news. There was no hope of hiding the evidence, with the whole house smelling of frying oil, but fortunately his mother didn't seem in the mood to make much of his culinary efforts. 'Oh, good, you've got yourself something. Where's Tamsin?'

'Out in the garden with Charlotte, I think. They came back about half an hour ago.'

'I'll give her a call,' said Jem, and went off to the back door. Luke saw Kate's face and said curiously, 'What's happened? You look like you've won the lottery.'

'Chance would be a fine thing. No, it's nothing like that. It's . . . well, wait until Tamsin comes in and I'll tell you both.'

Her daughter trailed into the house a few minutes later, grubby and hot in jeans and T-shirt. Charlotte, just behind her, was wearing beige jodhpurs that still looked immaculate despite a day of riding and mucking out. 'What's up, Mum?' Tamsin asked. 'Jem said it was important.'

'It is.' Kate paused, and then said, in a voice as neutral as she could manage, 'Justin's been arrested.'

Her daughter gave a wild whoop of delight and punched the air. '*Yes!*'

In contrast Luke, Kate saw, looked absolutely stricken. 'What for?' he asked anxiously.

'Insurance scam,' Jem told him. 'The robbery was a set-up. Or so the police obviously think, though I've no idea why.'

'I have,' Tamsin said exultantly. 'Go on, Luke, tell them.'

'Do you two know something about this?' Kate asked, looking at her children suspiciously.

'*He* does,' said Tamsin, pointing at her brother. 'Go on, you can't keep it under wraps any more, tell them what you heard.'

'I think you'd better,' Jem said. 'It could be vitally important.'

Luke glanced round at the four other people in the room. 'It's all your fault,' he said to his sister. 'You *promised* not to tell anyone else, and you went off and blabbed it all to Jayde, didn't you?'

Kate was looking more and more bewildered. 'Luke, please tell me, what's all this about? You – you haven't got involved in this scam, have you?'

'It's all right, Mum,' said Luke. 'I haven't done anything wrong, really I haven't. I just didn't want to tell anyone, that's all.'

'I think it would be a good idea', Jem said quietly, 'if you told us all now, everything that you know.'

The two girls perched together in the armchair opposite Luke's, while Kate and Jem occupied the sofa. Acutely uncomfortable with so much attention focused on him, the boy related the damning details of the conversation he had overheard a few days previously.

'And he actually admitted all this?' said Kate incredulously.

'Well, if I hadn't been around who else was there to hear? It's pretty private down there, they obviously felt quite safe. Anyway, the attack on Jem must have really worried Justin, he knew he had to come up with the rest of the money quickly. So he must have thought up the fake robbery.'

'But he couldn't have done that on his own! He must have had accomplices. And how on earth would he know where to find the sort of people who'd do something like that?'

'I think there's quite a lot we don't know about Justin,' said Jem. 'And I suspect that it might not be very pleasant.'

Kate shivered suddenly. 'I never thought – I never dreamed it wasn't for real! He was hit on the head and tied up – how could he have planned that?'

'He had to, to make it seem convincing,' Jem pointed out. 'I'm sure they were careful not to do him serious damage.'

254

'Yes, come to think of it, I did get the feeling he was making rather a lot of his injuries,' Kate said. 'But I thought that was . . . well, being a typical male wimp. Present company excluded,' she added, with a smile for Jem.

'Thank you for those few kind words. What else did you hear, Luke?'

'McPherson knew the robbery was a scam, and Justin didn't deny it. And he'd get the money twice over, once from the insurance company and once from the people who'd taken the cars. He had to, because McPherson said he'd set fire to the farm if he didn't.'

There was a small silence. Luke went on, his voice cracking with distress. 'So that's why I couldn't tell anyone! I mean, McPherson's a real villain, like the Krays or something. He meant what he said. Justin must have been absolutely desperate, I didn't want to grass him up. I knew I ought to, but I couldn't decide what to do.'

'So he told me,' said Tamsin. 'And I told Jayde. And Jayde said her dad would get it sorted, and I think he has.'

'*Charlie?* You mean *Charlie* told the police about it?'

'I don't suppose they're aware it was Charlie,' Jem pointed out. 'Knowing him, he probably rang Chippenham nick from a phone box somewhere, and gave them an anonymous tip-off.'

'But I told Jayde last Saturday,' Tamsin said. 'I thought nothing was going to happen.'

'They wouldn't arrest Justin in the pub just on the strength of a tip-off,' Kate pointed out. 'They must have spent some time investigating it, and found enough evidence to take it further.' She gave her son a long, serious look. 'You're going to have to go to the police yourself, you know, and tell them.'

'I don't want to,' Luke said, his expression haunted. 'I really, *really* don't want to.'

'You probably won't have to give evidence against him if they've got actual proof,' Jem told him. 'But what about McPherson? If they haven't got anything against him yet, what you heard could be vital. And you can't tell me you're squeamish about shopping him after what happened to Smith, can you?'

'Or the attack on Jem,' said Tamsin. 'You've *got* to do it, Luke. He's the real villain, even more than Justin, you *can't* let him get away with it!'

There was a long silence. Luke's face was very red, and Kate hoped that he was not going to cry. In the end, though, he nodded slowly, deliberately. 'Yes. O.K., I will. But can you come with me, Mum?'

'Of course I will, sweetheart, of course I will.' Kate slipped off the sofa and went to hug him. 'I'm proud of you, Luke. It must have been really horrible for you, having it all weighing on your conscience. I'd have felt the same, you know. Loyalty's a great quality to have, but sometimes it can get you into a real tangle.'

'Thanks, Mum,' said Luke, brushing a quick hand surreptitiously across his eyes. 'Look, can we go now? I don't want to leave it till tomorrow and lie awake all night thinking about it.'

'You've been doing quite a lot of that, haven't you?' said Kate sympathetically. 'Yes, of course we can go now. All of us.'

'Before he gets cold feet,' muttered Tamsin, in a voice that her brother was meant to hear.

'No, I won't,' he said fiercely. 'I've made up my mind now, and nothing's going to stop me – nothing!'

But as they all went outside, he knew this would be the most difficult thing he had yet faced, in all his life.

Chapter Twenty-One

It was dark when they at last emerged from Chippenham police station. Luke's throat ached with the effort of talking so much, and he was still ravenously hungry, despite the tea and biscuits which he and Kate had consumed in the interview room, while Jem and Tamsin waited outside. But he felt at ease with his conscience, for the first time in weeks. As Kate had suspected, the police were very interested in McPherson, and Detective Inspector Murdoch had asked Luke a great many questions about Justin's partner and all his visits to Silver Street Farm.

'And what will happen now?' Kate had enquired, when Luke had signed his statement. 'Will he be asked to give evidence in court?'

'We've a long way to go with the McPherson enquiry,' said Murdoch. 'And of course we'll have to liaise with our London colleagues. There is a chance of it, but if we can put together a strong enough case without Luke, then we will. As for Mr Spencer, well, there shouldn't be any need. He has already been charged.'

'Oh, God,' Luke had said, in sudden panic. 'I'm not going to meet him in the corridor, am I?'

'No chance,' Murdoch told him, smiling. 'He's safely banged up for the night. His brief's going to make application for bail tomorrow. Anyway, you've got nothing to be worried about. You did the right thing, Luke, and we're very grateful to you. Well done.'

And with those words echoing gratifyingly in his memory, and a vast burden lifted from his shoulders, Luke was able to fall asleep instantly that night, for the first time for over a week.

'What really makes me livid,' Kate said to Jem, very late, over another long strong glass of Pimms, 'is that Justin must have known who was making those phone calls and all the rest of it, and yet he did nothing about it, for ages.'

'He did eventually. He paid McPherson some of the money.'

'Yes, but not soon enough. Not soon enough to save Smith. If he'd only gone to the police and told them that he was being threatened—'

'Perhaps he couldn't, for reasons we don't know about. You never know, maybe the money he put into the business was dodgy to start with. Anyway, it'll all come out in the wash – or at the trial.'

'I just can't imagine Justin – *Justin*, for heaven's sake – being locked up in a prison cell. It just doesn't seem possible.'

'He wouldn't be the first public schoolboy to go to jail,' Jem observed. 'And I doubt he'll be the last.'

'If it comes to that. He'll probably just flash his posh accent and county credentials at the magistrate, and get off with a fine.'

'It's not like you to be bitter and twisted!'

'Oh, I am. The past few weeks have taught me to be deeply cynical where Justin is concerned.' Kate sipped her Pimms thoughtfully. 'Anyway, whatever happens to him, I can safely say that I have no sympathy. I don't care how desperate he was, he caused us a lot of grief and he deserves all he gets.'

'And there speaks your daughter's mother!'

'Tamsin would hang, draw and quarter him if she had her way. And as for Luke – well, I honestly think that if he was given the key to Justin's cell, he'd be tempted to turn it in the lock and let him go. Poor Luke. He really admired Justin to start with. And I think in his heart of hearts, he still can't quite believe it.' She gave a wry laugh. 'God, it's just as well I never ended up marrying him, isn't it?'

'Would you really have done it, if it came to the crunch?'

'I don't know.' Kate, curled up in the saggiest armchair, gave him a quick glance. 'Probably not, if I'm honest with myself. Even before all of this happened, I was having serious doubts. The trouble was, he didn't measure up to Col – but then I knew that *no one* could do that, so I was prepared to settle for less. I'd never have pinned him down, though. He made eels look sticky.'

Jem laughed. 'You're mixing your metaphors.'

'Never mind the metaphor – what's a hammaphor?'

'Knocking nails in, of course. I'm not the idiot I look, you know.'

'I do know,' Kate said, smiling at him. He was sitting in the chair opposite her, on the other side of the fireplace, with a beer in his hand, perfectly relaxed. She loved the humorous quirk of his smile, and the way his eyebrows peaked slightly in the middle, and the mischievous glint in his eyes, and the lithe, hidden strength of his body under the T-shirt and Levis. *But I was wrong,* she thought, with a strange mixture of sorrow and joy. *You measure up to Col, in every possible way. I love you, and want you, and need you. And in a couple of weeks you'll be gone, and I'll never see you again.*

Get a grip on yourself, said her realistic, sensible side, sternly. *Stop being so bloody maudlin. You're only just getting over Justin, for Christ's sake, you need a break before you start jumping into bed with someone else.* And then, inevitably, the real reason why she must keep her feelings secret. *Anyway, what makes you think he'll look at you? You're just a flabby middle-aged housewife.*

She could have forgiven her ex-lover many things, but the callous cruelty of those words had destroyed any affection she had ever felt for him.

'You look sad,' Jem said softly. 'Are you O.K., Kate?'

'Of course I am,' she lied. 'I was just thinking, that's all. About Mermaid's Ground. I suppose it really is safe now, if Justin's going to prison.'

'I should think so. One less thing to worry about, anyway.'

'Oh, things have been so manic recently that I haven't had the time to think about anything except lights and lights and, just for a change, lights. God, what a week it's been! I still can't quite believe that it's all happened. Moxham will be talking about this for years and years. It'll pass into legend, like the woman murdered in the churchyard in 1764. You wait, in a hundred years' time the Silver Street Farm Robbery will be re-created in some holographic pageant beamed to every home from the parish TV studios, with computer-generated actors and virtual reality terminals so that you can alter the ending if you don't like it.'

'Is that what you'd like to do? Alter the ending?'

'I want to see justice,' Kate said firmly. 'I want to see McPherson brought to book, and I want Justin to understand that being wealthy and well educated and related to the aristocracy doesn't entitle him to get away with fraud and deceit. Do you think that's too much to ask?'

'I don't, but I shouldn't hold your breath.'

'*Now* who's being cynical? But I'll bet you anything you like,' said Kate forcefully, 'that this is the only night he ever spends in a police cell.'

Tanya spent the morning after Justin's dramatic arrest at her health club in Bath, feeling that after all the unpleasant shocks of the past week she deserved a bit of pampering. She had had an hour of massage and a reflexology session, followed by a manicure and a full facial. Mindful of the extremely skimpy dress she planned to wear at the party the day after tomorrow, she had also gritted her teeth and endured a full leg and bikini wax. Now she was relaxing by the pool, her hair swathed in a towel and her sleek, voluptuous body almost enclosed within one of the club's luxuriously soft, thick robes. A long, cool cocktail stood on the table by her lounger, and she had been skimming idly through the latest copy of *Vogue*.

The discreet chirrup of her mobile phone disturbed the peace. 'Oh, Gawd, now what?' she muttered, stretching out a languid, elegant hand, the talons freshly painted red, as if they'd been dipped in blood. 'Hallo?'

'Darling! At last!'

'Oh, it's you, Justin. What do you want?'

If her lover was disconcerted by this decidedly cool greeting, he gave no sign of it. 'Listen, darling, can you meet me for lunch? It's vitally important.'

'You out, then?'

'Yes, yes, of course I'm out – I got bail this morning. The police didn't like it, of course, but the magistrate was an old friend of my mother's. Look, I don't want to talk now. I'll meet you at Beau's – you know, the French place near the Theatre Royal – at one o'clock. Be there, darling. I must speak to you.'

He rang off, leaving Tanya staring with puzzled annoyance at the phone. What was he on about? Why all the rush?

She glanced at her diamond-set Rolex. A quarter past twelve. It would be tight, but she could just make it. And although she had made up her mind to give Justin the elbow at the first opportunity, her lively curiosity was aroused.

With a feeling of pleasurable anticipation, she finished the cocktail and went off to find her clothes.

At ten past one (it never did any harm to keep them waiting), she sauntered into the restaurant. Charlie had taken her in here a couple of times, and she knew that it was one of Justin's favourite places. Tucked away in a sidestreet, it was small, discreet and frighteningly expensive. Despite the gold card nestling in her handbag, Tanya resolved to let Justin pay.

He was sitting at a table in a secluded corner, well away from the bustle of overpaid businessmen having lunch on expenses. Tanya noted gleefully that he was looking round nervously and fiddling with his cutlery. When he saw her, relief flooded into his face. 'Thank God, darling! I was beginning to think you weren't coming.'

'Sorry 'bout that, couldn't find nowhere to park,' said Tanya, who had left her convertible two streets away and spent the last twenty minutes trying on evening sandals in her favourite shoe shop. 'How you doing? Sleep well?'

'Not a wink,' said Justin. He beckoned to the waiter and ordered a bottle of vintage champagne. Tanya perused the menu briefly and handed it back. 'I'll have a green salad and grilled Dover sole. Gotta watch the pounds, eh, Justin?' She reached forward and, to his evident embarrassment, patted the definite bulge above his waist. 'You could do with going on a diet an' all.'

'Don't be ridiculous!' said Justin sharply. But his own order, Tanya observed with secret satisfaction, was almost as spartan as hers.

'So what's all this cloak-and-dagger stuff about, then, eh?' she enquired as the waiter glided off. 'What's so important it can't wait?'

Justin cast a quick look round the restaurant before leaning towards her and saying very softly, 'My flight leaves Heathrow at eight o'clock this evening.'

'Your *flight*? But ain't you on bail?'

'Yes, of course I am,' said Justin irritably. 'I haven't been asked to hand in my passport, though.'

'Gordon Bennett.' Genuinely stunned, Tanya stared at him. 'So you're gonna to skip the country, then?'

'Well I'm not going to all this trouble just to go to Glasgow, am I?'

'S'pose not,' said Tanya. She gave him a sly glance from under the thick lashes. 'So go on – give us a clue. Where *are* you going, then?'

'California. My sister lives in LA.'

'Lovely and warm there, innit,' said Tanya. 'Bin there a few times, doing modelling and that. Palm trees, hot tubs, all that sunshine – you lucky bleeder.'

'I know. So, are you coming with me?'

Astonished for the second time in a few minutes, Tanya squawked, 'You want me to come with you? Just like that? Pack up and leave?'

'Of course I do, darling. I want you with me.' He picked up her hand, lying lax on the table, and caressed her palm with erotic intent. 'Come on, darling. There's nothing for you here. California is the place to be. And I couldn't bear to leave you behind. You're so beautiful, so . . . so desirable.'

'Ooh,' said Tanya, as frissons of lust ran through her. 'Ooh, you make me go all weak at the knees, you do.'

'Then you'll say yes. Oh, darling, please say yes. I want you so much.'

'But what'll we do for money? I ain't got none of my own left, you know, it all comes from Charlie. And what about the bail?'

'Fifty grand?' Justin waved it a nonchalant farewell. 'That doesn't matter. I've signed the farm over to my sister this morning, and she's going to sell it for me. It should fetch a couple of million, easily. You'll live like a princess, darling, don't worry about that.'

'And Jayde? What about her?'

'Oh, she'll be all right. She's away at school most of the time, and anyway she'll still have Charlie. After all, darling, it's not as if you take much notice of her. Hardly surprising, she's a plain little thing.'

If he had been less sure of himself, he might have noticed a change come over Tanya. Her blue eyes narrowed, and her mouth hardened. But her voice was still soft and seductive as she said, 'You've got it all worked out, haven't you?'

'Of course I have. You didn't imagine I'd just sit back and let them walk all over me, did you? Prison is for losers, darling Tanya, and I'm not a loser. I'm a winner. I've won all my life, and I don't intend to stop now. So come with me, let me show you what life's all about. You deserve more than marriage to that moth-eaten superannuated old gangster.'

'You mean Charlie?'

'Of course I mean Charlie.'

'You know he's the one what shopped you to the old Bill, don't you?'

'*What?*' For the first time in their conversation, Justin's arrogantly confident demeanour was disturbed. 'How the hell did he know?'

'Haven't a clue,' said Tanya cheerfully, though she had already wangled the full story out of her adoring husband.

'God, I'll – I'll kill him!'

'That's what he said when he found out about you and me,' she said, watching him closely from under those remarkable eyelashes. 'But he changed his mind; he reckoned grassing you up would hurt you more. He quite liked the thought of you sharing a prison cell with half-a-dozen murderers and druggies.'

'Dear God,' said Justin. 'Well, we'll have the last laugh, won't we, darling?'

'Will we?'

'Of course we will. He won't be able to touch us once we're in the States. And we don't have to stay in California. Hawaii, Australia, South Africa – I've got friends everywhere.'

'You're forgetting one thing, ain't you?'

'What's that?'

'I ain't said I'm going with you yet, have I?'

The waiter was approaching with their food. Tanya unfolded her damask napkin and placed it daintily in her lap. Justin stared at her in horror, unable to say anything until the man had gone away again. Then he leaned over his grilled chicken with Mediterranean vegetables, and hissed, 'But you *must* come with me, darling, you must!'

'Why?'

'Because I love you, of course!'

'Do me a favour,' said Tanya, with rich contempt. 'You've never loved anyone but yourself, you lying selfish greedy bastard. D'you really think I'd give Charlie the elbow – and he may be an old sod but at least he loves me – and throw away all I've got for a few months in the sun with a podgy, toffee-nosed has-been who thinks with his dick? Sorry, Justin, it was fun for a while but that's all it ever was – a bit of fun. I know which side me bread's buttered, and it ain't yours.'

Justin was staring at her, transfixed. Quite unabashed, Tanya took a generous sip of champagne. 'Nice, this, innit?'

'Christ, you've got a fucking nerve,' Justin said viciously. 'You're not so young yourself, are you? If you don't come with me, *darling*, you'll regret it. Tied to that old man, getting more and more desperate while your tits and bum sag lower and lower. You won't find it so easy to hook all those pretty boys then, will you?'

'You seen yourself in a mirror lately, Justin?' Tanya enquired, rising gracefully to her feet with a toss of her head that disguised how much his words had hurt her. 'About five months gone with that beer belly, you are, and the face ain't looking so good either. You'll have a real boozer's nose soon if you keep on at the whisky, and a liver transplant too, I shouldn't wonder. Enjoy yourself in LA, won't yer. Ta-ra!'

With her famous walk, she flounced out of the restaurant, pausing at the door to blow him a cheery kiss. She knew he wouldn't be able to run after her: they'd make him pay the bill first.

So, she reflected, as she drove home along the A4, much too fast, she'd had the last word. She'd given twice as good as she got. And if she stopped at the next phone box and rang Chippenham nick with the time of his flight, then her revenge would be absolute. She really wanted him to suffer, for what he had done to her, and also to Kate.

She had a guilty conscience about Kate. And when she got back to the Court, after a brief pause in a certain lay-by on the outskirts of Corsham, she went in search of her husband's head gardener.

With only two days left till the party, Kate was afraid that she'd still be seeing lights in her sleep. But least the courtyard was finished, and although it was difficult, in daylight, to gauge the effect when they were switched on, she was moderately satisfied with the result. Out in the sunken garden, however, cables still trailed everywhere, and the mulberry tree had been done no less than five times and still looked lopsided. The flares which were supposed to keep midges at bay smelt, as Charlie had pointed out, worse than cat's piss and would have to be replaced. There were supposed to be fifty of them, but Kate had only found forty-six, because Darren, in an excess of enthusiasm, had already put them out all round the garden, in some very peculiar and out-of-the-way places.

To her surprise, she saw Tanya strolling over the grass towards her. She had gained the distinct impression that her employer's wife had been avoiding her since the revelation of her fling with Justin. Tanya's uncharacteristic discretion, however, was misplaced: far from being furious with her, Kate suspected that the other woman had in fact done her a considerable favour. However, Tanya had the purposeful air of a woman with a mission, so perhaps she had come to offer her apologies.

'You'll never guess who I had lunch with,' was Tanya's opening salvo. 'That well-known jailbird.'

'God, did he get bail after all?'

'Certainly did. The beak was an old friend of his mum's, or something. Fifty grand it cost him, so he ain't that strapped for cash after all, your Justin.'

'He hasn't been mine for months,' Kate said, acutely conscious of the contrast between her frayed T-shirt and filthy shorts, and Tanya's smart jacket and filmy white blouse. 'And anyway, I don't think he ever was.'

'You're right there,' Tanya said. She looked round at the

264

untidy lawn, the heaps of rejected candles and the reels of cable. 'Selfish bastard, ain't he?'

'You can say that again.' Kate wiped her hands on the side of her shorts. 'God, what a mess. I just hope it'll be ready in time.'

'Don't worry, course it will.' Tanya paused, and then looked Kate straight in the eye. 'I've come to say I'm sorry. About Justin and all that. I didn't want to hurt you or nothing, but you know what I'm like – and what he's like, come to that.'

'It's O.K.,' said Kate, and smiled suddenly. 'It really is. I wasn't upset at all, honestly. Nothing to do with me any more.'

'Good,' Tanya said, with an answering grin. 'I felt bad about that. I knew you'd said you wanted to cool it for a while, but I thought you might still be wanting to get back with him.'

'It didn't take me that long to decide I was better off without him. He really couldn't take the fact that I was prepared to speak out about Mermaid's Ground. He said a lot of very unpleasant things, and I knew I'd been wrong about him. And when he lost the planning application and blamed me for it, I knew I'd done the right thing.'

'We'd been screwing for quite a while before that,' said Tanya. 'Just after your poor dog got killed, we started. Nearly two months ago.'

'I suspected you had someone,' Kate told her. 'But I'd no idea it was Justin. I thought it might be Max.'

Tanya went off into one of her raucous peals of laughter. '*Max?* He wouldn't know how to show a girl a good time if she laid flat on her back with her legs apart and no knickers on! Blokes, though, that's different.'

'Oh,' Kate said ruefully. 'I didn't realise. I've led a rather sheltered life, I'm afraid.'

'So what? Takes all sorts,' Tanya said. ''S funny, you know, since all this happened with Justin, I've got even fonder of old Dobbin than I was when we got hitched. So it's done me some good. And you.'

'Yeah – you could say you've washed that man right out of my hair.' Kate grinned at her. 'It's O.K., honest. I don't mind, I really don't. Simon Mortimer said the other day that I was well shot of him, and I am.'

'Did you really love him? You don't sound as though you did.'

Kate shook her head. 'No. And in my heart of hearts I know I didn't. I know what it should be like, and whatever I felt for Justin, it certainly wasn't the same as what I felt for Col. But I thought that was a once-in-a-lifetime thing. Does that make sense to you?'

'Nah,' said Tanya cheerfully. 'I don't believe in love. Lust, yeah, can't get enough of it. Love, that's something else. Leads you up the garden path and dumps you in the shit.'

'It doesn't have to be like that,' Kate said, slightly on the defensive. 'It wasn't with Col.'

'Your husband? Yeah, well, you was lucky there. But you never know,' Tanya said, with a wink. 'You might get lucky again one day.'

'I doubt it. Who'd look at me twice?'

Tanya gave her a hard stare. 'He got at you an' all, didn't he? The bastard!'

'Who? Justin?'

'Of course Justin! He can't take being dumped, can he? He said some horrible things to me this afternoon. Talk about the pot calling the kettle black, I told him to look in a mirror before he slagged anyone else off. So he did it to you too, did he?'

'He called me a flabby middle-aged housewife,' Kate said, and flushed.

'Well, that ain't true,' said Tanya. She looked at the other woman more narrowly. 'But you've half a mind to believe it, ain't you. Gordon Bennett! *You* oughta look in a mirror sometimes. You're lovely, you are.' She paused, as if weighing something up, and then spoke rapidly. 'Listen, how about if you come along to my club on Saturday? I'll sign you in, that won't be a problem, and you can have the works – massage, facial, manicure—'

'On these nails? They'd be lucky to find them under the dirt.'

'Bollocks,' said Tanya. 'Go on, treat yourself. I bet you haven't had a good pampering like that for donkey's years. We can spend the whole day there if you like. There's a pool, sauna, sunbeds, gym . . .'

'It sounds absolutely wonderful,' Kate said fervently. 'Oh, Tanya, it's a lovely idea, and thank you so much, I'd love to come, but I can't. I've got too much to do for the party. I can't just run away and leave everything.'

'Cobblers, you deserve a treat. We can have a girls' day out, and sod the bleeding party.'

'If only I could! But I couldn't let Charlie down, he's counting on me to come up with the goods. And I'd be letting myself down, too, if I didn't get it finished in time.' She grinned suddenly. 'But if a miracle happens and I *do* have the time, then yes, great, you're on.'

'That's more like it,' Tanya said briskly. 'So, what are you going to wear?'

'For the party? I've got one or two nice things. I'll think of something.'

'And don't worry about Tamsin, Jayde's going to lend her one of her outfits, did she tell you?'

'No, she didn't. It's awfully kind of you, Tanya, I hope Tamsin doesn't spill something down it.'

'It won't matter if she does, plenty more where they came from and Jayde never wears them anyway. She's a good kid, but she ain't into clothes at all. Takes after her dad, I suppose,' said Tanya, with a grin. 'Well, think about what I said. *I'm* going, anyway, so if you change your mind, let me know. It's still on the table, O.K.?'

'O.K.,' said Kate. 'And thanks.'

'Don't mention it. I owe you one – and lots more. Ta-ra, then, see yer later!'

It was an extremely tempting offer, and Kate, watching her walk back to the house, wished that she could take it up. She began a mental review of schedules. *If* they could get the sunken garden sorted out, and *if* nothing went wrong, and *if* she could manage to work late tonight and tomorrow, she might be able to squeeze it in. There wouldn't be much point, though, in spending too much time and money tarting herself up, because Caroline was coming, and Kate knew that it would be pointless to compete with her.

And the prospect of sitting on the sidelines all night watching Jem slip back into a passionate relationship with his glamorous ex-wife was not an alluring one. She knew that it would hurt more than anything Justin had ever said or done to her, because she cared for Jem far more than she had ever cared for Justin.

Tomorrow do thy worst, for I have had today. A line of seventeenth-century poetry, forgotten for years, crept cheeringly into her head. She had today. She had her children, and her job, and a good friend who, whatever he felt for her or for his ex-wife, surely wouldn't vanish from her life forever. And she couldn't help a sudden frisson of excitement at the thought of the party, when all her hard work and ideas would finally come together.

Whatever happened, she'd cope. She'd coped before, with much worse, and she would again. And she was beginning to think quite seriously once more about her plant nursery. Perhaps she'd use the rest of Jem's rent money to buy a big greenhouse. It would have to be a secondhand one, or a poly-tunnel, but that didn't matter. She didn't need five acres to grow old pinks and auriculas. She could do it in a corner of her orchard. And the idea was so attractive and absorbing that within a few moments she was too busy working out the details to worry about what would happen on Saturday night, and afterwards.

Chapter Twenty-Two

The BA check-in desk at Terminal Four was very busy when Justin Spencer arrived at Heathrow. He had made excellent time along the M4, and arrived nearly two hours before his flight was due to leave. He parked the hired Rover in the short-stay car park, and left it without a qualm. They'd find it eventually, long after he was out of reach of them and their bills.

He glanced disdainfully at his fellow passengers, waiting ahead of him with fretful children and bulging luggage. At least he was flying first class, with plenty of leg room, unctuous service, and the chance of getting some sleep. And he could do with several stiff drinks. It had been a difficult day, but despite Tanya's defection, he was feeling very pleased with himself. It would have been nice to have her with him, but there were plenty more fish in the sea. Justin was supremely confident of his powers of attraction. He was still comparatively young, good-looking, and above all, wealthy. In Los Angeles they'd love his English accent, and they'd be queuing up to climb into his bed.

No, he had few regrets about Tanya. She was stunningly beautiful, but also stunningly common. He'd been well and truly hooked at the time, but now he was free of her he could look back on their brief but intense affair with some relief. She'd soon have become a liability in the States. And he wouldn't have been able to trust her, either, with any pretty boy within her grasp. Justin liked his women to be exclusively loyal and faithful to him, until he discarded them.

Oddly enough, he felt much more nostalgic affection for Kate. He hadn't loved her – it was doubtful whether he had ever loved anyone outside his immediate family – but he had liked her, very much. She wasn't as obviously gorgeous as Tanya, true, and she didn't make nearly enough of her looks: he liked other men to envy him the woman on his arm. But she possessed indefinable, undeniable class. Unfortunately, she had also had scruples, and a well-developed sense of independence. He had thought he had her nicely placed under his thumb, kept there by flattery and sex and romance. But he'd been wrong. And now, when it was much, much too late, a part of him wished that it could have been different.

Still, no use crying over spilt milk. He smiled at the delightful blonde behind the desk, and handed over his ticket and passport.

'Mr Spencer?' It wasn't the girl speaking, but some jobsworth official standing beside her. 'Would you like to accompany me, sir?'

An awful presentiment of doom filled Justin. He fought the primal urge to strike and run, and forced himself to say calmly, 'Is there a problem?'

'If you would just come with me, sir, I'm sure we can sort it out.'

'Well, don't forget I have a plane to catch,' said Justin, with rather forced joviality. 'What about my luggage?'

'My colleague will look after that, sir,' said the official, glancing at the three immaculate matching suitcases. 'Now, sir . . .'

He went with him, because he didn't have any choice. But inside, he was seething with fury. Someone had shopped him. Once more, he had been betrayed. And only one person had known that he was planning to leave the country.

Tanya. Tanya was responsible. And as he was ushered into the bare little room, and saw the grim face of the Chippenham detective who had charged him with fraud only yesterday, he knew that the years of prison to come would be her parting gift.

Friday the second of September was cool and cloudy, but warm sunshine was forecast for the following day. Tamsin was looking forward eagerly to the party, and absolutely delighted with the news of Justin's arrest, which was already the talk of the village. But she was concerned about Kate.

Tamsin was a perceptive and observant child, and she knew her mother well. She had seen the way that she looked at her lodger when he was unaware of it, and the light in her face and the smile in her voice when they were in the middle of one of their silly conversations. *He makes her laugh; he makes her so happy*, Tamsin thought. *And he likes her, I know he does. Perhaps he's hanging back because he thinks she still loves Justin.* Or, more likely, because he was due to go back to London very soon.

She wanted desperately to bring them together, and the party at the Court was the obvious opportunity, but she didn't see how she could do it. She didn't want to say anything to either of them, because that would probably mess everything up. And if she was wrong . . .

The expected arrival of Caroline was another complication. Tamsin was sure that Jem's ex-wife, beautiful and powerful and ambitious, was trying to get back into his life. And she hoped very much that Jem didn't want her there.

Sometimes, in her more realistic moments, she scolded herself for being so stupid. Her mother might be pretty and funny and above all *nice*, but against the likes of Caroline she stood no chance, especially when clad in some out-of-date secondhand creation with half the Court's garden under her fingernails. Kate needed a make-over, and she needed a new dress. And Tamsin had already thought of a way to achieve the first of these goals.

A few words to Jayde had sufficed, and she had been delighted to learn, a few days later, that Tanya had offered to take Kate to her health club on the morning of the party.

'And you're going, of course,' she had said eagerly.

'I'd love to, but I've just got so much to do,' Kate had said. 'Still, you never know; if I get it all finished in time, I might.'

It was better than nothing, but it didn't satisfy her daughter. When she thought about the wasted opportunity, she could have cried. But she wasn't going to give up on her plans, not now. She was made of stern stuff. And what Tamsin Rebecca Williams wanted, she generally got.

But now Friday was here, and there were less than thirty-six hours left until the party, and she was no nearer a solution. Charlotte and her family had gone to stay with some cousins in London, and Jayde's mother had whisked her off to Bath to buy clothes. Luke was upstairs, working hard on his English project because school started on Monday. Normally, the imminent end of the summer holidays would have had a very depressing effect on Tamsin, but this year she had much more important things to worry about.

She was reading in the conservatory when the phone rang. With both Justin and McPherson now safely behind bars, there was no risk involved in answering it, so Tamsin dropped her book and ran into the hall to pick up the receiver. 'Hallo?'

'This is Caroline, calling from New York. Is Jem there, please?'

Oh, God, it's his wife. Tamsin had never spoken to her before, and found her cut-glass voice unpleasantly reminiscent of her grandmother's. 'No, he isn't, I'm afraid,' she said, with uncharacteristic politeness. 'Can I take a message?'

'Yes, please, if you would.' Caroline, at a distance of several thousand miles, seemed unaware that she was speaking to a child. 'Can you tell him that I've changed my flight? I'll be on the 10.30 from New York tomorrow morning.'

A wonderful, dangerous, wicked idea woke fully armed inside Tamsin's head. Even before she had thought of the possible complications, she had uttered the lie. 'I'm afraid the party's been cancelled.'

'Cancelled? But that's the main reason I'm coming over.'

'Yes.' Thinking hard, Tamsin improvised. 'Charlie was rushed to hospital this morning. Suspected heart attack. So of course his wife doesn't want to hold it until he's better.'

'Oh, dear.' Jem's ex-wife sounded annoyed rather than concerned. 'How terrible. Is it serious?'

'We – we don't know. We're waiting to hear. I'll get Jem to give you a ring when he gets in, but it won't be until this evening.'

'No, don't bother. Before I decided to come over for the do at the Court, someone I work with invited me to his house at Martha's Vineyard this weekend. If the party's off, I think I'll go there after all, so there's no point in him trying to get in touch before Monday. O.K.? I hope poor Charlie gets better soon. Thank you, Kate. Goodbye.'

'Goodbye,' said Tamsin, and put the phone down with shaking, sweaty hands. She could hardly believe what she had just done. She had uttered barefaced lies, and successfully deceived a high-powered grown-up.

But it's all in a good cause, she thought, with blossoming delight. *The best cause of all. And with Caroline safely out of the way, I can surely persuade Mum to go with Tanya tomorrow – and to buy that wonderful dress.*

As she turned to go back to her book, though she was far too excited to concentrate on reading, the phone rang again. *Oh, no,* Tamsin thought with alarm. *It's probably Caroline calling back to say she's coming after all.*

It wasn't. A man's voice said, 'Andrew Rossiter here, of Cavendish and Rossiter, estate agents. Can I speak to Mr Forrester, please?'

'I'm sorry, he's not here,' Tamsin informed him, unsteady with relief. 'Can I take a message?'

'If you would, please. Ask him to ring me at the Chippenham office as soon as possible. I'll be here until six. We've just taken instructions on a property which may interest him.'

'I'll tell him,' Tamsin promised. 'Goodbye.'

She put the receiver back and took a deep breath. It didn't seem possible. With two phone calls, all her problems had been solved. She still had some work to do, of course, but those apparently insurmountable obstacles had vanished, and her path lay clear and shining before her.

'Yes!' she cried aloud, with jubilation. 'Yes, yes, *yes*!'

'Tam?' Luke was hanging over the banisters on the landing, a biro in his hand. 'Who was that on the phone?'

'Caroline. You know, Jem's wife.'

'Ex-wife. What did she want?'

'She's changed her mind. She's not coming to the party, she's spending the weekend with some bloke instead.' It was astonishing how easy it was to lie, and how convincing it sounded. *And it's almost the truth, anyway*, Tamsin told herself. *By the time anyone discovers different, it'll all be sorted, one way or another, and no one will mind too much.*

'So I've got to go and tell Jem,' she added. 'She asked me to let him know at once.'

'O.K. If you see Mum, can you ask her what time she's coming home? I'm ravenous.'

'What did your last slave die of?' Tamsin demanded rudely. 'If I can make toast and open a tin of beans, then so can you, lazybones.' And she skipped jubilantly out of the front door, ignoring his protests.

The sensation of triumphant glee stayed with her all the way to the Court. As she pedalled madly up the gravelled drive, she saw Tanya's little red sports car parked outside the front door, which meant that Jayde must be back. This time, however, she had a different quarry. Tamsin shot round the side of the house, past the walled garden, and braked to a halt in front of the stables.

The lorries and cement mixers and piles of bricks and breeze blocks that had cluttered the yard for months had all gone now. The cobbles had been swept clean, and the round water trough in the centre was filled with compost and planted up with geraniums from the hothouse. Tamsin leaned her bike against the freshly-painted gates, and walked in, with rather more confidence than she actually felt. Fooling Luke and Caroline had been easy. Jem would be much more difficult to deceive.

She couldn't resist having a nose before she went in search of him. The door on her left was open, and she slipped inside, remembering to wipe her feet on the mat. A corridor ran round the outside edge of this wing, lit by small high windows that would look out onto the walled garden. Off it were half a dozen

273

rooms for band members, A&R men and the like. In less than a fortnight, the argumentative components of Captain Haddock would be staying here. Tamsin contemplated putting pondweed in their beds, and decided against it: she had grown out of that sort of childish prank. She peeked into one room, and couldn't help feeling deeply envious of the thick soft carpet, the luxurious king-size bed, the gold-trimmed bathroom and the TV, video, fridge and every other possible legal convenience that a spoilt rock star's jaded heart could desire.

There was no one about. At the end of the corridor, a lobby led into a sitting room, equipped with the full range of audio equipment as well as a huge wall TV, and a kitchen chock full of gadgets and so new and clean that it made her eyes ache. She opened the third door and found the rehearsal room, in what had once been the coach-house. There was nothing in it yet but a huge black grand piano in the corner. Tamsin couldn't resist it. She scurried over, lifted the lid from the keyboard, and touched middle C.

It sounded wonderful. Tentatively, she played Chopsticks, and then, with more confidence, Au Clair de la Lune. She was just starting on Tallis's Canon when a door opened and a voice said forbiddingly, 'Can I help you?'

She jumped up, with the last note still ringing softly inside the instrument, and put her hands behind her back. 'Sorry,' she said. 'I'm looking for Jem Forrester. I've got a message for him.'

'And you are?' The man was wearing overalls, and had paint on his face. 'You're not Charlie's kid, are you?'

'No, but I'm one of Jayde's friends – Tamsin Williams. Jem's our lodger.'

'Ah, why didn't you say so? Come on, Tamsin, I'll show you where he is. He's down in studio two. Having a look round, were you?'

'Yes – I hope you don't mind.'

'As long as you haven't messed anything up, that's O.K. The opening's tomorrow, you know. Play the piano, do you?'

'Not really, but my friend Charlotte has lessons and she taught me a bit.' Tamsin made up her mind to ask her mother if she could have lessons too.

Her new friend led her out of the rehearsal room and along another corridor, the twin of the one in the opposite wing. Instead of bedrooms, though, she saw bare soundproofed studios and mixing rooms, with unlit signs above each door that said RECORDING in red letters. There was a crimson carpet underfoot, and about half a dozen lengths of electric cable running along the floor by the skirting. 'Not quite finished yet,' said the man, seeing her look around. 'But as near as makes no difference.'

Suddenly, the mournful wailing notes of an alto saxophone burst into the air. Tamsin stopped dead. 'What's *that*?'

'That's Jem, trying out the microphone system. He's pretty good, isn't he?'

She had heard the haunting tune before: it was one of Kate's favourites. 'He's brilliant. What's he playing?'

' "Summertime". It's Gershwin – from *Porgy and Bess*.' They stopped outside a door that had Studio Two written on it in elegant red script, and the man stood aside to let her go through. 'He's in there. Use the microphone on the desk to speak to him, there's a button you press just beside it. Mind how you go!'

She thanked him and walked in through two sets of doors, both wedged open. The first room contained a huge mixing desk, with hundreds of levers and switches, and speaker grilles all round the walls. Beyond the desk was a glass wall, and in the room on the other side stood Jem, his eyes closed and a look of intense concentration on his face, while the wonderful music poured through the speakers.

Tamsin stared at him, and an overwhelming sensation of terror flooded over her. What if she blew it by doing something stupid? He was so good, so *right* for her mother, she couldn't bear it if something went wrong now, when she was so close to success.

But she had to, for Kate's sake. She leaned forward and rapped gently on the glass.

He was so absorbed in his playing that he didn't hear her. She saw the microphone, pressed the button and spoke into it. 'Jem? Jem, can you hear me?'

The glorious sound broke off suddenly, and his eyes flew open. On the other side of the glass, she waved, and he grinned at her. His disembodied voice came down from the speakers. 'Hi, Tamsin, what are you doing here?'

'I've got a message for you. From Caroline.'

'From *Caro*? Hang on a minute, I'm coming out.'

He put the sax down and opened a door by the side of the desk. Tamsin, her eyes shining, said, 'You play really well. Why don't you play at home?'

'I've too much respect for your eardrums,' said Jem cheerfully. 'Well, what does my dear distant ex-wife want?'

'She rang to say she's changed her mind and she isn't coming to the party,' Tamsin told him, watching his reaction closely.

He didn't look in the least disappointed: in fact, the expression on his face was obvious relief. 'Thank God for that. I'm almost fond of her when she's three thousand miles away, but she's a bit overpowering in the same room. Did she say why she's not coming?'

'Someone she works with has a house in Martha's Vineyard,' Tamsin said. 'I think that's where it was, anyway. And he invited her there for the weekend.'

'Well, I can't say I'm sorry.' Jem stretched luxuriously. 'I might almost enjoy the party now.'

'There was another message, too. From an estate agent in Chippenham.' Tamsin screwed up her face with the effort of remembering. 'His name was Rossiter, I think. Anyway, he wanted you to ring him urgently.' She paused, and then, emboldened by the success of her cunning, added innocently, 'Are you looking for a house here, then? I thought you were going back to London.'

'So did I,' said Jem. He looked down at her, and smiled suddenly. 'But I changed my mind a while ago.'

'Why?'

'I like it here. I like the Court, and Moxham, and even all of you lot, amazingly enough. When I first came down to Wiltshire, I thought I couldn't wait to get back to the city. Then after a couple of months I realised that I was dreading the prospect. My old flat's sold now, so I thought, why not? Charlie's made me a very good offer, better than I'd get anywhere else, so I've accepted it.'

'Mum will be pleased,' said Tamsin daringly.

Jem looked sceptical. 'I doubt it. She'll be glad to see the back of me. Well, Tamsin, can you do me a favour? Keep it under wraps for a bit. I'd like to choose the right moment to tell her. So not a word about the househunting. That's our secret, O.K.?'

'Trust me,' she said, and zipped her mouth tight shut with her fingers. 'Not a word.'

Bursting with delight, she said goodbye to him, skipped joyfully out of the studios, and went to find her mother.

Kate was in the sunken garden, distributing the new batch of flares, scented rather more pleasantly than the last, around the beds and terraces. She looked up as her daughter approached, and said in surprise, 'Hallo, sweetheart. What are you doing here? Nothing wrong, I hope?'

'No, of course not. I came to give Jem a message from

Caroline, so I thought I'd find out what time you were coming home.' By now, Tamsin was so intoxicated with the triumph of all her scheming that she felt nothing could possibly go wrong. 'Luke's ravenous, he said.'

'Well, you can tell him to open a tin or fry some eggs, I'll be an hour or so yet.' Kate paused, and glanced at her daughter's face. 'What did Caroline want, or is that a trade secret?'

'Oh, no, she rang to say she's spending the weekend with some bloke, so she won't be flying over for the party.' It was hard pretending indifference, and Tamsin didn't want to spoil things at the last minute, but she couldn't resist a quick peep to see how Kate had taken this momentous news.

She looked as if a vast burden had been lifted off her shoulders. '*Really?* Are you sure?'

'Course I'm sure, she told me herself.' Tamsin risked a gentle prod. 'Are you pleased, Mum?'

'Um, no, not especially,' said Kate, with a nonchalant shrug which was so patently false that her daughter almost laughed.

'You know,' she said cautiously, 'you really ought to get a new dress for tomorrow.'

'Like that lovely turquoise one, you mean?'

'Yes, you'd look really great in that. And you like nice clothes. Go on, Mum, you've lived in jeans for weeks and weeks, you deserve something really special.'

She watched Kate hover on the brink of the vital decision. 'And I'm sure you can afford it, with Jem's rent and everything.'

'And the bonus Charlie's going to give me for all my work for the party,' Kate said. She straightened her shoulders and smiled suddenly and brilliantly at her daughter. 'You're right, sweetheart. And I'll take Tanya up on her offer of a session at her club tomorrow, as well. There's hardly anything left to do here, and if there is then Darren can see to it.' She swept Tamsin into a swift, joyful hug. 'Thank you, fairy godmother. Cinderella *shall* go to the ball!'

'Can I help you, madam?'

Before her descent into comparative poverty, Kate had often bought clothes at shops like these, and the assistant's rather intimidating stare held no terrors for her. Besides, she had scrubbed her hands and nails, washed her hair, and put on make-up and her best dress, the one with the scattered daisies, for this trip to Bath, and for the first time since her final row with Justin she felt satisfied with her appearance.

'I saw a dress in your window, about six weeks ago,' she said. 'An evening gown, in turquoise silk. Do you have it in a size twelve?'

'No, madam, I'm afraid we have quite sold out in all sizes of that particular colour. We do still have an example of the same style in gold, however, which is the favourite shade this season, and another in midnight blue. Would you care to try one on?'

'I'd like to see them both, please,' Kate said.

She was shown to a spacious fitting cubicle, with cunningly angled mirrors and a vase of pink carnations on a low table in the corner. The assistant brought her the two garments, and withdrew. Outside, the shop was quiet, and she could hear the noise of traffic in Orchard Gardens, and the irritating commentary from one of the open-topped tourist buses.

She hadn't asked the price, but there was a label on the gold dress. She turned it over, and gulped. It was a great deal of money, far more than she could possibly, justifiably spend on herself. And that vivid, insolent yellow was definitely not her colour.

The blue was though. It was deepest indigo, shot with purple, and the silk slithered softly, seductively through her fingers. Her heart thumping, she undressed and slipped it over her head.

It fitted. It was lower at the front than she'd expected, and it had no back at all, but that didn't matter. It clung to all the right places before falling in sleek folds to the floor, and she knew that, despite the cost, she had to have it. And as she looked at herself in the mirror, Justin's cruel words finally faded impotently out of her mind, vanquished by the truth.

She handed over her credit card without a qualm, and watched as the lovely gown was folded reverently up inside sheets and sheets of tissue paper. Then, with joy springing in her step and the tune of one of her favourite songs humming on her lips, she splashed out on a taxi and told the driver to take her to Tanya's club, close to Victoria Park.

It was called Body Talk, and the reception area was so crowded with greenery that at first Kate couldn't locate the desk. The young woman behind it was charming and helpful. 'Yes, Mrs Williams, Mrs Dobson has signed you in. She's in the solarium at the moment, would you care to join her?'

'No I'm not, I'm here,' said Tanya, strolling in. She was wearing a creamy white towelling robe, and even with her face bare of make-up she looked stunningly beautiful. 'Hallo, Kate. Did you get it, then?'

'The dress? Yes, I did.'

'Let's have a butcher's,' said Tanya eagerly.

Kate shook her head, smiling. 'No, you can't. Wait till this evening.'

'Oh all right.' Tanya grinned at her. 'Well, what you gonna have? Waxing? Facial? Manicure? There's a hairdresser an' all. You can have as many as you want, and top it all off with a workout and a swim, that's what I usually do. The food's good, too. So, what's your fancy?'

She chose a massage first, followed by an aromatherapy session, both so wonderfully soothing that she almost fell asleep. The waxing was a necessary evil, as was the manicure. Her strong, slender hands looked sleek and alien afterwards: she couldn't remember when she'd last worn nail polish. After a splendid lunch, she had a facial, with make-up advice, followed by a brief spell in the gym. Max was there, 'Maxi Muscles' as Tanya insisted on calling him, in his presence, and he was so vain and so camp that Kate could hardly keep a straight face. But he knew what he was doing, and under his expert tuition she managed to try out several machines without either rupturing herself or breaking into helpless laughter.

By the time they reached the pool, it was half past three, and she felt deliciously relaxed. She swam a few lengths, showered and washed her hair, and joined Tanya on the sun terrace for a drink.

'I could get used to this, you know,' she confessed, sipping her Pimms (not as good as Marcia's, but within striking distance). 'How much does membership cost?'

'You don't need to worry about that, I'll always sign you in.'

'No. I don't want to keep sponging off you.'

'You ain't. Like I said, I owe you several. Anyway, it won't be often, you'll still be working, won't you? But it's nice to have a bit of company once in a while. Just give me the nod, O.K.?'

'Thanks,' said Kate, with genuine gratitude. 'It's really kind of you.'

'Glad to know I'm appreciated,' Tanya said, grinning. 'So, what made you change your mind?'

'About coming here? I just thought, why not?'

'Nah, there's more to it than that, ain't there? Something to do with a certain New York editor deciding not to turn up?'

'Who told you?'

'Never you mind,' said Tanya, grinning slyly. 'But I don't know why you was ever worried about her. A right bitch she is, one of them control freaks, you know, real Miss Bossy-boots. She couldn't hold a candle to you.'

'I don't believe you,' Kate said. 'Charlie said she was gorgeous.'

'Yeah, well, there's gorgeous and gorgeous, ain't there,' said Tanya, with heavy significance. 'Don't worry, your secret's safe with me. I won't say nothing.'

'Thank you. I think I'd die of mortification if you did.'

'But don't forget,' Tanya went on, her voice suddenly serious, 'there's a lot of people rooting for you, one way or another. Don't go and waste it all, will you?'

Kate knew exactly what she meant. She smiled. 'I won't, promise. I'll go to the party and let my hair down and have a ball. And who knows? I might even get lucky after all.'

Chapter Twenty-Three

It was half past four when Kate and Tanya returned to the Court. Three white vans from the catering firm were parked outside, and teams of minions were ferrying goodies into the kitchen, where Mrs Wallis was doubtless organising everything with an iron hand. Tanya took one look and cast her eyes to heaven. 'Gawd almighty, I didn't order any strawberries! Just the sight of 'em brings Charlie out in a rash! Sorry, Kate, but I'd better go and sort it pronto. Here, d'you want one of the bedrooms to change in later? You won't want to be poncing through the village in your glad rags. The Floral one's free, second floor, just at the top of the stairs, know where it is? And if you don't fancy going home tonight,' she added, with a sly wink, 'well, what's another face at the breakfast table, eh? Tamsin'll be staying here anyway, an' your Luke's big enough to look after himself. Gotta go, see you later!'

Kate watched with some bemusement as Tanya, exchanging her 'vain flighty blonde' persona for a 'give 'em hell and kick ass' model, disappeared in search of someone to berate. Then she nipped upstairs to inspect the room so generously offered, wondering, in view of her hostess's taste, whether it was possible to be more floral than the examples she had already seen.

It was. The Floral Bedroom, looking down from a gable window in the west wing onto the bright red bonnet and black soft-top of Tanya's little MG parked below, had blue pansies on the wallpaper, blue and pink pansies on the curtains, a huge bunch of blue and pink paper flowers on the chest of drawers, and, the crowning touch, huge vibrantly patterned blooms on the carpet. The only relief was the ceiling, which was mercifully plain. Kate carefully extracted the dress from the tissue paper. With luck, hanging it up for a few hours would get rid of most of the creases. She held it in front of herself, and looked in the mirror. The soft fine silk, so deep and rich a blue that it was almost black, drooped lifelessly from her hands. Hoping she had made the right choice, she hung it in the empty wardrobe. She would come back later with the rest of her things. Before that, however, she must inspect the gardens and make sure that everything was ready.

As she walked into the sunken garden, it was immediately apparent that there was a problem. Darren, Bob Wiltshire and Pete, the other under-gardener, were standing in a circle looking up at the mulberry tree. Kate strode up to them purposefully. 'Now what's happened?'

'They don't work, see,' Bob informed her, not without some malicious glee. 'I said they wouldn't work, didn't I?'

'Oh dear,' Kate said, staring up at the recalcitrant lights. 'Have they not worked at all, or did they go pop suddenly?'

'They worked when we had 'em on the ground,' said Pete, who was a gloomy young man with a hundred reasons for things going wrong. 'But not once we'd put 'em up. And there are seventy-five bulbs on that string, it could be any one of 'em.'

'Well, isn't it just like Christmas-tree lights?' Kate demanded. 'There are several spare bulbs, aren't there? Why don't you get up a ladder and start testing them?'

The three men looked at each other in surprise. Rather sheepishly, Darren volunteered. Trying in vain to hide her amusement, Kate went off to check the lights in the courtyard.

Fortunately they were still functioning, although they looked pallid and completely overpowered by the afternoon sun. Tables and chairs had been set along the high wall which separated it from the walled garden, and each table was draped in white, with a glass vase of flowers, artistically arranged, in the centre. All the pots and tubs had been pulled to the sides to make room for dancing, and Kate hoped that no one would fall into the pond. She peeked through the door into the drawing room, where the band was to play. The carpet had been taken up, most of the furniture removed, and the wide stone windowsills filled with lilies and delphiniums and roses. Probably the Court hadn't seen an occasion like this since before the war; and then, Kate thought, smiling, the guests had danced decorous waltzes and foxtrots. Tonight would be entirely different: the poor old building wouldn't know what had happened to it.

The guest list, of course, would be full of celebrities: musicians managed by Charlie, models and actresses who were friends with his wife, record company moguls and top producers, all eager to check out the new studios and partake of Charlie's generous hospitality in the process. It would be an opportunity to have fun and do business at the same time. With Caroline now out of the way, Kate felt much happier. Even if she knew hardly anyone there, apart from a brief acquaintance in the pages of the gossip columns or *Hello!*, the chance to rub shoulders with an assortment of more-or-less notorious household names was undeniably an exciting and intriguing prospect. And she had already resolved to take it all with a hefty sack of salt. That world seemed so artificial, its concerns so trivial, compared to her own life. But it would be fun to dress up for the night, to enjoy a little glamour.

And also it was a chance, perhaps her first and last chance, to snare Jem. Tanya hadn't thought that she would be wasting her time, and Tanya was an expert in her field.

Go for it, girl, Kate thought, and with a sudden sense of joyful anticipation, ran from the room.

She met Tamsin and Jayde in the entrance hall. They'd evidently been spending the afternoon with the pony: a definite equine aroma hung around them, and her daughter had suspicious stains all down the legs of her jeans. 'Hi, Mum,' she said, beaming. 'Did you get it?'

'Did I get what?' Kate enquired, feigning ignorance.

'Oh, *Mum*! The dress, I mean, the *dress*! Did you buy it?'

'Oh, that dress. No, I didn't. They didn't have any left.'

Tamsin looked so crestfallen that Kate took pity on her. 'But they did have one exactly the same, in a very dark blue, and I bought that.'

'You did? Oh, supercool! Can I see it?'

'Sorry. You'll have to wait until the party. Meanwhile, what are you going to do until it starts? You've got nearly four hours.'

'We're going to have a swim, and then we're going to watch telly for a bit, or have a go on the computer,' Jayde said. 'Don't worry, Kate. We're fine. You go home and put your feet up for a bit.'

She sounded comically adult and serious, but Kate could not laugh. 'I've spent most of the day doing that, at your mum's club,' she said. 'I've got lots of things to check on here, and then I'm going home to get everything I need, and come back to change.'

'What about Luke?' Tamsin asked.

'I don't know if he's back from Mark's yet. He'll probably come on later.'

'*Please* tell him not to bring his Captain Haddock CDs to be signed. I'll *die* of embarrassment if he does,' said Tamsin, rolling

283

her eyes up to heaven. '*And* Jayde says Annabelle Andrews is coming, you know, the model, and he's keen on her, he's got a stack of pictures of her hidden under his bed, and he'll probably spend the whole evening following her around.'

'I doubt it,' said Kate. 'He's going to be helping Darren and Pete to direct all the cars, and from what Charlie said, I don't think he's going to have much spare time. Anyway, you know what Luke's like – he'd probably curl up and die if this Annabelle woman even looked in his direction.'

'And she certainly wouldn't do that,' said Tamsin, who had a very low opinion of her brother's ability to attract the opposite sex. 'C'mon, Jayde, I'm boiling, let's go and get our cossies!'

They disappeared like the proverbial herd of elephants up the stairs, and Kate went to see how Darren was getting on with the lights.

He had, he assured her, replaced every single bulb and still it wouldn't work. 'And what he d'need,' said Bob Wiltshire, whose capacity to stand around and watch lesser mortals make complete fools of themselves was legendary, 'be someone who know what he be doing. An electrician.'

'I'll see if there's one lying about somewhere,' Kate told him, and went off to the stables.

As Tamsin had done the previous day, she found the quadrangle deserted. Some comedian had stretched several yards of very wide, bright pink ribbon across the entrance, and tied an enormous bow in the middle. Presumably, Charlie would be expected to perform a ceremonial opening. Kate grinned, suspecting the hand of Jem. She ducked underneath, and went into the door on the right.

This was evidently the reception area, with a large desk, a switchboard, and low comfortable chairs. Disconcertingly, there was a strong smell of tomatoes, which Kate eventually traced to the brand-new carpet. She walked to the door beside the desk, which was propped open, and peered through. Down the long corridor, she could hear masculine voices.

Jem and three other men were standing in the third studio along, in earnest discussion. Kate, pausing at the door, realised with some amusement that the topic of conversation was not the building work, or even the party, but the disastrous performance of the England batsmen in the last test match. She raised her hand in a parody of a schoolgirl. 'Excuse me?'

'Hi, Kate,' said her lodger, turning with a smile. 'Come to inspect?'

'No, actually, I'm after an electrician.'

'I'm sure there's a book or a play or a film where a wizard summons an electrician and gets a rather bewildered Benjamin Franklin. Why do you want a sparks?'

Kate explained about the lights. Jem frowned. 'Have you tried the fuses? It could be something as simple as that.'

'I shouldn't think it's occurred to them. It certainly didn't occur to me.'

'I'll come,' Jem said, with a glance at his colleagues. 'We've almost finished here, anyway. Do you like the pink ribbon? Charlie doesn't know about it yet.'

'I've got a pair of big gold-coloured scissors at home you could borrow.'

'That should look suitably pretentious – I mean impressive. Well, thanks, guys, and I'll see you later, O.K.? Time for all good men to come to the aid of the party!'

'*Is* it done?' Kate asked, as they went round to the garden. 'I saw quite a few wires trailing about.'

'Ssh, don't tell anyone! No, there are still one or two things to be sorted, but that can wait. The important thing is that it *looks* finished.'

'And very impressive, too. Once you get rid of the wires, of course.'

'You perfectionists are all the same! What's it like in the house and the garden? Everything ready there too?'

'More or less, I think. Apart from the lack of lights in the mulberry tree. Oh, and Darren's got to go round lighting all the garden candles at dusk. If he can manage it without setting fire to himself or anything else, it'll be a miracle.'

'It'll look wonderful,' Jem said. 'You wouldn't guess it, Charlie's so laid back, but there's a lot riding on this evening. The more people go away impressed, the better his bank balance is going to look, eventually. And he may be a millionaire several times over, but he's invested a great deal of money in this project, so he really does need it to be a success. I thought you said the lights didn't work.'

'Oh,' Kate said, staring at the mulberry tree. 'They're working now.'

'One bulb he hadn't tried,' Bob grumbled, coming over. 'Till I says to him, I says, "Have ee changed the one at the top?" And of course the silly uckle haden done it. Afeard of heights, I d'reckon, I had to do he for en.' He gave her a shrewd stare. 'Going to the party, gal?'

'Try and stop me,' said Kate, grinning.

'Well, don't ee do anything I woulden,' said Bob, with an extremely dubious chuckle, and stomped back to the tree.

'Sorry to drag you away under false pretences,' Kate said to her lodger.

'That's O.K. As I said, we'd virtually finished anyway, but I've still got one or two things to sort out. Getting rid of those cables, for a start.' He grinned at her. 'See you later. I'll be back at the cottage at some stage, to put my glad rags on.'

Kate waved goodbye, and watched as he walked away across the lawn towards the house. Her whole body seemed to ache with longing. She folded her arms and shivered suddenly. If that dress and the excitement of the occasion failed to work their enchantment, then she knew that nothing would. It was not just Charlie who was gambling the future on the coming evening.

She arrived back at the cottage after seven, to find Luke occupying the bathroom and a black suit she didn't recognise hanging over the banisters. She announced her arrival through the door, and then went into her own room.

In five minutes she had packed a small bag with her best silk underwear, her evening sandals, a tiny bottle of very expensive perfume that had been her birthday present to herself last year, her favourite make-up, and a toothbrush and clothes for tomorrow, in case she stayed the night at the Court. Defiantly, tempting fate, she tucked a packet of condoms into the inner pocket of her evening bag. Choosing jewellery from her small collection took rather longer. Finally, she settled on the gold necklace that Col had given her, the last Christmas before his death. It was very simple but unusual, being made up of slender curved rods joined by rings, and it would go with her gold hoop earrings and her best watch. She couldn't help feeling that wearing her dead husband's gift would compensate, a little, for the fact that she had removed her wedding ring.

You don't mind, do you? she said to his shade, though any sense that he was still with her had vanished long ago. *But you were always a generous man. And I've fallen in love with someone else, so much in love that I can hardly think straight, or concentrate on anything, and if I can't have him then I honestly don't know if I can bear it. You'd have liked him, Col. You'd have gone down the pub and talked sport and music over a pint of beer, and I could never see you doing that with Justin, however hard I tried. So wish me luck, Col, because I want to be happy again, and I know that I can be with Jem.*

286

'Mum?' Luke's head appeared round the door, making her jump. 'Hallo.'

'And about time too,' said Kate, grinning at him. 'What were you doing in there, growing webbed feet?'

Luke blushed. 'Just having a good scrub,' he said. She noticed a small cut on his chin, and realised that he must have been trying to shave, but wisely decided not to mention it. 'Whose is the suit?'

'Mark's older brother's. He's grown out of it, and it fitted me, so he said I could borrow it. Is that O.K., Mum? I haven't really got anything else to wear that's smart enough.'

'I'm sorry,' Kate said, with sudden remorse. 'I've been so selfish, just thinking about me, and I'd completely forgotten that you'd need things too.'

'That's O.K., Mum, I don't mind. Anyway, Mark's sorted it. He's lent me some aftershave, too,' Luke added, with a rather shy grin. 'Can you smell it?'

'I can, and it's really nice.' Kate sniffed appreciatively. 'Go on, put the suit on and let's see how you look.'

It hardly seemed any time at all since her son had been an angelic toddler with chubby knees and round soft cheeks and flaxen, silky hair. She gazed at the tall, smart, handsome young man standing in front of her in his borrowed clothes, and felt her eyes prickle. 'You want to watch it,' she said, unwilling to embarrass him by revealing how much the sight had affected her. 'You'll have all the girls chasing you.'

'Oh, don't be silly, Mum,' Luke said, but he had turned red with a mixture of pleasure and bashfulness. 'Are you going to get changed now?'

'I'm going to have a nice long scented bath, *if* you've left any hot water, and then I'm going to put some clean clothes on and go round to the Court to change. I bought a dress like the one we saw in Bath,' she added. 'And it's much too fragile and precious to traipse through the village wearing it. Are you going to come with me? I'll probably be leaving around half past eight.'

'That's O.K., there's something on telly I'd like to watch before that. When's Jem coming back?'

'I haven't a clue,' Kate told him cheerfully. 'Right, go on, scarper, I'm going to have that bath.'

By half past eight she was ready to go, and so was Luke. They were just getting into the car – if necessary she could always leave it at the Court and walk home – when Jem arrived, looking more than a little hot and bothered. 'Bloody last-minute hitches! I'm going to have a quick shower and get changed. I'll see you there. Save some canapés for me!'

She decanted Luke at the Court's front gate, and drove round to the parking area beyond the stables. There were several cars there already, almost all registered within the past two years. The old Astra looked very shabby beside all that gleaming paintwork and sparkling chrome, but Kate backed it defiantly into a space between a blue Mercedes and a silver-grey Bentley, and walked away with her head high.

She didn't want to use the main entrance, so she went through the shrubbery at the back of the stables, past the bare beds that would be transformed by next year into the scented garden around the folly, and so to the side door by the breakfast room. The passage to the kitchen was crowded with waiters and waitresses bearing trays of drinks and food. She dodged past them and hurried up the stairs to the Floral Bedroom.

She had half expected to find that someone else was occupying it, but the room only contained blue and pink flowers. She locked the door, drew the curtains, and took off the dress she had worn all day. Then, with careful elation, she began her transformation.

It took some time, because she was enjoying this. She exchanged her plain cotton underwear for her best silk and lace set, and anointed herself with small dabs of perfume. Her nails and hands were already immaculate after the manicure at Body Talk, and she had given her feet similar treatment after her bath. She had washed and dried and brushed her fine blond hair until it crackled with static, and now it swung loose to her shoulders in a sheet of pale, shining gold. She sat for a long time in front of the mirror on the marble-topped dressing table, applying make-up sparingly to enhance her best features, her large blue eyes and her wide, generous mouth. Finally, she put on her jewellery, and slipped the indigo dress over her head.

It had not been a mistake. She stared at the alluring, sexy stranger looking back at her in the mirror, a tall slender blonde in a gown that fitted her like a glove to the hip, and then swept to the carpet in subtly glimmering folds. The light caught the curve of her breasts under the silk, and the gleam of the gold around her throat echoed the sheen of her hair. She had ceased to be down-to-earth Kate Williams, with her mundane worries and her aching back and dirty fingernails and old jeans: she had become an enchantress from another age, mistress of a magic as old and as powerful as time.

Don't be absurd, she scolded herself. *Back to reality with a bang, come midnight*. But she smiled at the mirror, all the same, and silently thanked Tamsin for seeing what she herself had failed to notice. Then, with her eyes bright and her heart thudding painfully inside her ribs, she left the room and descended to the hall.

Her employer and his wife were standing by the door, welcoming their guests. Charlie was unusually smart in a very formal tuxedo suit, though the effect was rather spoilt by his grey ponytail, tied with a black satin ribbon. Beside him, his lovely wife, in her two small strips of stretch lace, was effortlessly hooking the eyes of every man in the room. Kate paused, gathering her courage, and then glided forward.

Tanya, who never let the decorum of any occasion spoil her sense of fun, let out a squawk of delight. 'Kate! Ooh, you look stunning!'

'Don't she just,' said Charlie. 'Go on, darlin', give us a twirl.'

Kate obliged with a neat pirouette, the indigo skirts swirling gracefully around her, and finished with a demure curtsey. Tanya clapped. 'That dress is gorgeous, where'd you get it? Oh, I know that place, real class it is.' She leaned forward and added *sotto voce*, 'If he ain't all over you in half an hour, he's been struck blind. And if you don't get lucky, I should ask for your money back. Go on, you go and enjoy yourself.'

'She deserves it, after all the hard work she's put in,' Charlie said to the man next to him, whom Kate was sure she had seen on the telly. 'All the lights, the gardens, she done 'em all with her own fair hands.'

'Not quite,' Kate said, laughing. 'I did have some help.'

'Ah, but you designed it all,' said Charlie. 'And you should see it now it's getting dark, like something out of a fairytale it is. Go and have a butcher's, Kate, you ain't never seen it at night, have you? There's food in the morning room, and gallons of bubbly going round, so don't hold back.'

'I won't,' she promised him. 'Thanks, Charlie.'

Deliberately, she didn't look out of the windows, averting her eyes until she reached the door into the courtyard. Then she paused, overcome with wonder. The lights sparkled everywhere, entwined along the windows and over the doors, and glittered amongst the branches of the wisteria which grew along the further wall. The air was warm and still and scented, and moths, dazzled and hopelessly confused, bumbled overhead. Behind her, a DJ, keeping the party spirit alive until the re-formed

289

Serious Money took the stage, put on a particularly tuneless and frenetic example of contemporary dance music when, Kate thought wistfully, it should have been something by Cole Porter or Gershwin.

In the shadows, a few couples were sipping drinks and talking quietly, and Kate felt suddenly thirsty. She wondered whether Jem had arrived yet: a glance at her watch showed that, amazingly, she had spent over an hour getting ready.

Which shows how much it matters to me, she thought with a smile. *Well, as Charlie's supplied all this vintage champagne, I'd better help him get rid of it.*

She went back into the drawing room. There was a middle-aged couple, he in the inevitable black, she in a fuchsia-pink frilly number that was far too young for her, gyrating happily around the floor. And, dancing together in a corner, her daughter and Tanya's.

'Mummy!' Tamsin cried, and ran over. 'Oh, Mum, you look *wonderful*!'

'It is rather special,' Kate admitted, doing a twirl for her benefit. 'Weren't you clever to have spotted it?'

'I *knew* it was right for you, I just *knew* it!' Tamsin said exultantly. 'Look, Jayde, isn't it a lovely dress?'

'It's beautiful,' said her friend, with enthusiasm. 'You look really nice, Kate.'

'Thank you. And so do you both. Let's have a good look.'

The girls turned obediently. Jayde had chosen a long satin skirt in navy and green tartan, not quite Black Watch, with an embroidered white blouse, as if she was about to dance a highland fling. Tamsin wore wide blue-and-white-striped trousers and a shiny blue stretch top that looked as if it might be a leotard in another life. They wouldn't win any prizes in a fashion contest, but they were obviously delighted with their outfits, and Kate had no intention of telling them any different.

'They've got wonderful food next door, and I'm *starving*!' said her down-to-earth daughter. 'Can we have some, Mum?'

'Let's go and see, shall we?'

Already there was a crowd round the tables. Waiting their turn, Kate saw a famous supermodel, wearing even less than Tanya, escorted by the lead guitarist of the band who'd won Best Group in last year's Brit Awards. Further back in the food queue there were a couple of footballers more notorious for their antics off the pitch than on, the rather seedy-looking presenter of a TV game show and his bleached-blond and facelifted wife, and an actress who had recently bared her all in a Channel Four drama heavily criticised by certain sections of the media for its poor taste. Hovering round the fringes like vultures round a corpse were a couple of photographers, waiting to pounce. The guitarist kissed the model, and lights flashed.

Jayde, of course, was quite blasé in the presence of all these famous, or infamous, people, and Tamsin, to Kate's amusement, was carefully imitating her friend's matter-of-fact demeanour. After a cursory look at the adults around them, she whispered to her mother, 'Is Jem here yet?'

'I don't know. I haven't been here very long myself,' said Kate, in what she assumed to be a properly casual manner. Within, of course, she was a seething cauldron of elation and terror, but only the subtle flush on her cheeks and the brightness of her eyes gave away the excitement she was feeling. 'My goodness, what a magnificent spread. Go on, girls, your turn now, help yourselves.'

With many pauses to ask what they were helping themselves to, the two children piled their plates high and retreated. Of course, the food was beautifully presented – no curling ham sandwiches here – and the twin centrepieces, two huge salmon, had overlapping scales of cucumber and lemon. Kate was not particularly hungry, but she took a few canapés, and a glass of champagne from a passing waitress. Then she joined the girls at the last free table, right by the door, from which they had an excellent view of the other guests, and of the room beyond. Charlie had just introduced Serious Money, who were now playing their greatest hits, and, amazingly, tempting more than a dozen couples onto the floor.

'Come on, Mum,' said Tamsin, leaping up with her food only half eaten. 'Come on, let's dance.'

'I didn't know you were a fan,' said Kate, as her daughter towed her into the drawing room, and earned a bewildered glance. The music might be seriously naff, but the beat was lively and infectious, and Tamsin was jigging around with unselfconscious energy and a complete lack of rhythm. Jayde joined them, and Kate noted that she was an excellent dancer. With much merriment, she began to teach them the steps she remembered doing with her friends at school discos twenty years ago, and in a few moments the three of them were moving more or less in unison, hands joined. A photographer popped out of the crowd and recorded the moment before Kate had even realised what was happening.

'Don't worry,' Jayde yelled at her above the music. 'That's Bernie, he's nice, he won't print it if you don't want him to.'

'Who does he work for?'

'*Hello!* and stuff like that,' said Jayde, as nonchalantly as if it had been the parish magazine. Before Kate had time to digest the implications of her moment of fame, the band finished the current number, to a surprisingly lively round of applause. In a brief interval while the lead guitarist re-tuned his instrument – though it was doubtful whether anyone would notice the difference – she became aware of a presence beside her, and a dearly familiar voice said, 'Hi, ladies. Mind if I join you?'

'Jem!' Tamsin cried, with such heartfelt relief that Kate blushed for her. She turned, and saw him tall and magnificent in a dark suit that had probably cost more than her dress. Beneath it, the antique embroidered waistcoat he had worn that first evening, long ago in May, gave him an air of exotic flamboyance, considerably enhanced by the crisp white shirt and the dreadlocks. *Oh, God*, thought Kate, in sudden panic. *He's superb, totally gorgeous, he could have any woman he wanted – how could I have imagined that he'd ever be attracted to me?*

But he was gazing at her with astonished delight, and his smile dispelled all her fears. 'Oh, Kate – you look amazing.'

'Thank you,' she said demurely. 'You're pretty splendid yourself.'

'Oh, this old rag? Picked it up from some Italian guy,' Jem said. Serious Money had started again, this time playing a rather leaden cover of 'Maybelline', and the girls were practising the movements she had shown them, hand in hand, Jayde rather more successfully than Tamsin. 'Dance?' he added, with a grin. 'Do you jive?'

'Only when nobody's looking,' said Kate, but before she could object he had seized her hand and pulled her into the centre of the floor. Breathless, laughing, she followed his lead, joyfully aware of his eyes on hers, the graceful movements of his body, the sureness of his touch. She twirled and stepped and spun to the music, and wished it could go on for ever.

On the last notes, Jem pulled her into his arms. His hands were warm on her exposed back, and his eyes were fixed on hers. 'Has anyone ever told you, Kate Williams, just how wonderful you are?'

'Only liars,' she said, laughing, and still trying to catch her breath.

'I'm not a liar,' Jem said. 'Or not to my friends, anyway. Do you want some champagne, before this crowd of greedy liggers drink it dry?'

She glanced round at Jayde and Tamsin, but they were still happily dancing with each other. Her daughter looked up, caught her eye, and grinned. It was a conspiratorial, encouraging grin, and Kate felt suddenly and totally carefree. 'Why not?' she said, with a smile. 'Lead on.'

His arm was still round her as they made their way to the edge of the room. She could feel his touch, light on the bare skin of her shoulder, and underneath his fingers she knew that she was trembling with anticipation and desire, like a guitar string that has caught the echo of another note. He whisked two tall glasses off a passing tray, and handed one to her with a bow and a smile. 'Here's to you, lovely lady, and may luck and happiness stay with you for ever.'

'A bit of a tall order,' she said, sipping it with appreciation. Justin's fondness for champagne had spoilt her own taste for the drink, but now she was remembering just how much she liked it.

'Not in the least,' said Jem. 'If you want something, go for it.'

He was looking at her very intently. Acutely conscious of his gaze, she smiled at him. 'Don't worry, I will. Have you seen the courtyard yet?'

'No, I was waylaid by a bloke I used to know, a long time ago. He's got his own record company now, and he's on a roll. Spent half an hour telling me about it, and short of flooring him with a sharp right uppercut, I couldn't get away.' He grinned. 'But if I'd seen you, I'd have left him stranded in the middle of the hall. Have I told you how gorgeous you look?'

'Yes, twice, but I'm not tired of hearing it yet.'

'Then I'll say it again. You're gorgeous. Utterly delightful. Don't laugh, I'm being entirely serious for once. That dress makes you look like something out of a fairytale.'

'The Wicked Witch of the West? An Ugly Sister? The Third Little Pig?'

Jem chuckled. 'No way. Cinderella, the Belle of the Ball.'

'So I change back into a pumpkin at midnight?' said Kate. The champagne, nearly finished, was already fizzing inside her, giving her a wonderful sense of wild and brilliant freedom, as if tonight she could do anything, say anything, and the magic would not abandon her.

'This conversation is getting *very* silly,' said Jem. 'More bubbly? Whatever else you can say about Charlie, he certainly knows how to spend his money. And then I want you to show me your courtyard.'

Kate told him to close his eyes. When he had obeyed her, she led him to the outside door, fortunately without bumping into anyone. On the threshold, she paused, and said softly, watching his face, 'You can look now.'

He stared at the myriad lights, like netted stars, and she saw the slow, appreciative curve of his smile. 'Oh, Kate. It's absolutely wonderful. How the hell could you set it up in daylight without knowing how it would look in the dark?'

'I'm not quite sure either,' she said, delighted by his obvious admiration. 'Pure fluke, really.'

'Liar. I bet you knew exactly what you were doing. There's a table free over there – you go and sit down, I'll be back in a minute.'

Before she could ask him why, he had vanished back inside the house. She drifted across the flagstones, aware of several interested glances from various male guests at the other tables, and feeling an extraordinary sensation of intoxicating power. The spells had been cast, the enchantment was working, and she held her future like precious water in the curve of her hands. And she had no intention of letting it trickle through her fingers, into the dust.

She sat down at the corner table. It was a mild night, but she shivered suddenly as she sipped her champagne. Above her, the stars of Cassiopeia glittered in the soft and infinite dark, and a pale shimmer beyond the roofs and chimneys of the Court betrayed the rising of the moon. All her senses abnormally acute, she could hear the murmur of voices around her, the more distant thump of the music, and far beyond them, in the oak trees of the park, the eerie hoot of a hunting owl. A breath of air stirred against her warm skin, and she closed her eyes, absorbing the essence of the night.

'Kate?'

Jem stood in front of her, a bottle of champagne in his hand. 'Are you O.K.?'

'I feel wonderful,' she said, with absolute truth. 'God, *more* bubbly? I warn you, I'll make a complete idiot of myself. But then, what's new?'

'You've got a serious problem with your self-esteem, you know,' said Jem, sitting down beside her. 'A little fun once in a while never did anyone any harm, and besides, we've got something to celebrate.'

He was fiddling with the cork as he spoke, and it exploded with a bang that momentarily stopped all conversation in the courtyard. There were several cheers. Champagne bubbled up over the neck of the bottle and streamed down over Jem's hand. Hastily, he poured it into the glasses and wiped his fingers on the hem of the tablecloth. 'Here you are, lovely lady. Let's drink a toast. To my new job.'

Kate sat quite still, all her elation trickling away. 'Your new job?' Her voice sounded very flat and thin. 'I didn't know you'd applied for any.' *That was why he was so long talking to his old mate who runs a record company*, she thought. *He was being made an offer he couldn't refuse.*

And so, the brief enchantment was over. It didn't matter what she said, what she wore, what she did, because whatever happened, he would soon be leaving her.

Chapter Twenty-Four

He would never know what it cost her, to smile as if it didn't matter, and to lift her glass and say casually, 'Congratulations. When do you start?'

'Monday,' Jem said.

Kate stared at him in horror. '*Monday?* That doesn't give you a lot of time to move out.'

'Who said anything about moving out? Unless Tamsin's been saying what she shouldn't, anyway.'

Totally bewildered, Kate put down her glass. 'What's Tamsin got to do with all this? You're surely not planning on commuting to London, are you?'

'Read my lips,' said Jem, slowly and distinctly. 'I am not moving out. Not until I find a place of my own, anyway. The job is Charlie's. Managing the studios.'

Stupidly, she was struggling to make sense of it. 'The studios?'

'Yes,' said Jem patiently. 'You know. The ones I've been working on. In the stables. Here.'

'You mean, you're *staying*?'

'Well, I'd hardly want to move back to London just for the dubious pleasure of driving down the M4 to junction 17 every day,' Jem pointed out. 'Of course I'm staying. Are you all right, Kate?'

Suddenly, she felt like laughing and crying simultaneously. 'Yes, I'm all right. Much, much *more* than all right. I was so sure that you were going to leave, that's all – and now you're not, and it's wonderful!' And, moved by champagne, and joy, and the overwhelming sense that at last the right moment had come, she flung her arms round him and kissed him on the mouth.

At once, his lips opened under hers, and he was kissing her back, with a strength and passion that astonished and delighted her. Then he pulled her close, and she knew that he wanted her as much as she wanted him.

'I think we'd better come up for air,' he murmured, as at last their mouths separated. 'Oh, God, Kate, I've been wanting to do that for so long—'

'Have you really?' She drew back a little, her arms resting on his shoulders. 'I didn't know – I thought you just wanted to be friends.'

'Wasn't that what you wanted?' His eyes were very intent: she recognised the look in them now, and the strength of his desire melted her bones. She shook her head, the pale fall of hair swinging vehemently across her face. 'No. Much, much more than just friends.'

'Looks like there's been a pretty serious misunderstanding here,' said Jem. 'There was I, hanging back because I didn't want to muscle in on you and Justin, and thinking you just needed a friendly shoulder to cry on. And *you* thought . . .'

'That there was no point in telling you how I felt because you'd be going back to London in a few weeks, and anyway I didn't want to muscle in on you and Caroline.'

'*Caroline?* Whatever gave you the idea I wanted to get back with her? I'd rather shack up with Margaret Thatcher, she's much less bossy.'

Kate giggled with euphoric relief. 'But she was always ringing you, and you invited her to the party—'

'Correction, she invited herself. She wanted to schmooze a few people for exclusive interviews. She's not interested in me any more, if indeed she ever was. Anyway, that's past history. Right now, all I care about is you.' He bent his head to kiss her again, and his hands caressed her bare back, her shoulders, her hair. And Kate, lost in rapturous sensation, forgot everything except the feelings which he was arousing in her, and the rising passion which both of them were struggling to control.

A sudden brilliant flash of light wrenched her back to reality. She jerked out of his embrace, and saw one of the photographers, unfortunately not Bernie, standing a few feet away with his camera poised for a second attempt.

'Oh, piss off and leave us in peace,' said Jem, with amiable exasperation. 'God, it comes to something when you can't even kiss your lady at a party without some jerk sticking a lens up your nose.'

'So I'm your lady, then,' said Kate, as the photographer retreated with grovelling false apologies.

'Oh, yes, you're my lady. Beautiful, gorgeous, sexy Kate, shall we slip into somewhere more comfortable? Not to say private?'

'I know just the place,' she told him softly. 'Come with me?'

'To infinity, and beyond,' he said, and took the hand she stretched out to him.

Laughing, she led him out of the courtyard and through the drawing room, now packed with dancers attempting to recover their long-lost youth. Astonishingly, they all looked as if they were having fun, but Kate felt not the slightest wish to join them. To her relief, Jayde and Tamsin were nowhere to be seen, but she spotted Tanya dancing energetically with a man so much older and uglier than her usual escorts that he must be either extremely rich or extremely important. She caught sight of them, and gave Kate a knowing, salacious wink.

The entrance hall was empty, and they reached the stairs without meeting anyone, except a waitress hurrying back to the kitchen with a tray of empty glasses. Above them, the shadows reached down from the top of the house, soft and silent. With the anticipation of desire bubbling inside her, Kate slipped her hand out of his, kicked off her sandals, and ran up the thickly carpeted steps.

He caught up with her at the first turn, where they could not be seen from below, and she fell, laughing, into his arms. He kissed her again, long and slow, his lean body hard and taut against hers, his hands exploring the soft high roundness of her breasts under the thin silk.

'Come on,' she whispered at last, dizzy with longing, knowing that he had only to ask and she would lie down here, halfway up the stairs where anyone passing would have to walk over them, and make love. Somehow, still locked in each other's arms, they stumbled up through the darkness, kissing, caressing as if they could not bear to stop touching, drunk with champagne and desire.

She found the Floral Bedroom, more by luck than judgement, and he followed her inside. Moonlight poured in through the open curtains, printing the pattern of the leaded windows across the flower-strewn floor. Behind her, Jem closed the door, and locked it. Then he turned to her, with that slow, seductive smile. 'Stand just there . . . let me look at you.'

She paused by the bed, the pale streams of light illuminating her hair and her face and gleaming on the curves of her body beneath the night-blue dress, and her eyes were wide as she returned his gaze. Then she smiled at him, and murmured, 'I hope looking isn't all you want to do.'

'It isn't.' He had taken off his jacket, and dropped it on the floor with complete disregard for its expense. 'I want to kiss you

299

again, and then I want to unwrap that wonderful dress and kiss you all over, and then I want to make love to you all night, and the next night, and the next . . . Is that what you want too, beautiful, wonderful, adorable Kate?'

'You know it is,' she whispered, shaken by the strength of emotion, raw in his voice. 'And you said yourself – if you want something, go for it.'

Then he was beside her, his mouth on hers. She searched for the buttons on his waistcoat, and undid them one by one, her fingers fumbling in her haste, then began on his shirt. Even the flimsy fabric of her dress was too great a barrier to be tolerated. He slid the silk down until her breasts were exposed; she felt his hand touch her nipple and shivered with desire. And his voice, ragged with the urgency of passion, murmured breathless against her hair. 'Oh, Kate, I love you so much – I've loved you for a long time. Do you love me?'

'You know I do,' she said simply, and turned his head so that she could kiss him.

Their clothes discarded at last, they lay together on the bed, their bodies tangled dark and pale in the moonlight, using mouths and hands and skin to explore each other with passion and urgency and also with loving gentleness. At last, when neither of them could wait any longer, he slid inside her, and she began to move with him, matching the rhythm to his so easily and instinctively that it seemed that her body had been waiting for this all her life. And when the devastating flood of pleasure began to engulf her, she knew that the same sensations were overwhelming him too.

The tide receded, and left her stranded, gasping, unable to believe what had happened to them. His dreadlocks were tickling her face, and his weight lay warm and heavy on top of her. Then he moved, slowly, as if the energy they had just expended had left him utterly spent, and raised his head to look down at her. 'Kate?'

'Mmm?'

'Do you feel like I feel?'

'I don't know. How do you feel?' Joyful laughter was beginning to sparkle inside her. 'This conversation could go on all night.'

'Which is more than I can. You've worn me out.'

'You've worn *me* out.' She reached up and brought his head down for a long, loving kiss. 'Absolutely exhausted. Even more than after keep-fit class.'

'Another example of damning with faint praise. Making love

300

with Jem Forrester is better than aerobics.'

Kate snorted with laughter. 'Idiot! Try, making love with Jem Forrester is better than anything I've ever done in my whole life.'

He became suddenly very still. In the moonlight, she could not read the expression in his shadowed eyes. Then he smiled. 'Do you really mean that?'

'I wouldn't say it if I didn't. I love you, every pore and cell and particle, and I feel as if I've known you for ever – as if our souls and our bodies were made for each other. Does that sound silly?'

He shook his head, the dreadlocks swinging. 'No. I feel the same. Like becoming whole suddenly, when I never knew before that there was a part of me missing.'

'Judging by your performance just now, I don't think any part of you is,' Kate murmured wickedly, making him laugh.

'Flattery will get you everywhere. Can you breathe with me lying on top of you like this?'

'Just about.'

'Better? A gentleman should *always* take his weight on his elbows.'

'My mother says that a gentleman always uses the butter knife, *even when alone*.'

Jem choked with sudden laughter. 'I won't ask what for! Funny, your mother didn't *look* the type to be into that sort of thing.'

'Watch it. I'm the only one who's allowed to be rude about her!' She paused, and then said softly, 'You said you'd loved me for a long time. How long?'

'The difficult ones now, eh? I don't know. It sort of crept up on me, to coin a phrase. But I think I realised it first when Smith died, and you were so upset. I would have given anything to make it better, and I couldn't.'

'You could have tried kissing me.'

'Believe me, I wanted to.' He set his lips on hers, briefly. 'Right there and then, in front of the kids and the vet. And you'd probably have thumped me.'

'No, I wouldn't. I'd have kissed you back.'

'What a lot of opportunities we've missed, over the last few months!'

'So let's make up for lost time,' said Kate.

A long while later, he lay in her arms, his head on her shoulder and his hand on her breast, and said, 'I don't think I'll ever be able to move again.'

'Nor me, but we'll have to eventually, I suppose.'

'So how long have you loved me, then?'

'I think I *fancied* you from the first moment I saw you. Love took a little longer, because I was trying to fight it.' She giggled. 'I didn't do very well, did I?'

'Oh, I wouldn't say that.' His fingers traced letters on her skin, an I and an L, a U and a V and another U. 'But in the end, it doesn't matter, because now we've found out the truth. Love conquers all, et cetera. Your daughter will be pleased. She's been trying to get us together for weeks.'

'*Tamsin?* Really?'

'She took a message for me yesterday. From an estate agent. I had to persuade her to keep it under her hat until I could tell you. I wanted to pick the right time.'

'I was totally convinced you were going to go back to London. And I couldn't bear the thought of being without you.'

'You were the reason I wanted to stay.'

'Well, you don't have to find a house now. You can live with me, if you like.'

Jem leaned up on one elbow and surveyed her. 'Are you sure about that? I don't want to rush you into things.'

'Of course I'm sure. We've got plenty of space. The kids like you. You live with us already, so it seems silly to chuck you out. And I'm dying to be able to drive the Tomato – if you'll let me, of course.'

'Of course I will. I don't have old-fashioned ideas about women drivers, you know.'

Kate giggled suddenly. 'My dad did. He always used to say that the only thing a woman could drive well, was a man barmy. Very politically incorrect.'

'I think I'd have liked your dad, politically incorrect or not. He sounds quite a laugh.'

'Well, he had to be a bit of a joker, really, considering his name was Gordon.'

Jem thought about it for a few seconds, and then began to laugh. 'Now you really are taking the mick.'

'No, I'm not. Gordon Arthur Bennett. He said that was why he had the gift of the gab.'

'Now I know where you get it from. Silly word games are obviously carved into your genes.'

''Fraid so. But at least you can't say you haven't been warned.' She smiled at him. 'Well? Are you going to become a permanent member of the household?'

'I *think* so,' said Jem, with exaggerated caution. 'But on one condition.'

'Which is?'

'That I no longer have to sleep in the annexe.'

Laughing, she kissed him. 'I'll let you into my bed, if you're *very* good. As good as you were just now. What's that?'

Something electronic was beeping on the floor. Jem rolled to the edge of the bed and leaned over. 'My watch, telling me that it's half-past eleven.'

'God, is that all? I feel as though a lifetime's gone by in the last couple of hours.'

'You too, huh? But I set it to the time when Charlie was going to open the studios. You know, pink ribbon cutting, speeches, thanks. And I'm supposed to be there, to show prospective punters round and answer questions.'

'Which you can hardly do in your present state of undress,' Kate pointed out. 'Come on, we'd better get our skates on.'

'And our clothes,' said Jem, beginning to retrieve them. 'One gloriously seductive dress, scanty and sexy. One bra and one pair of knickers, even scantier and sexier. Where did you leave your shoes?'

'At the bottom of the stairs, remember? I'll pick them up on the way down.'

'They should be made of glass,' Jem said, beginning to button up his shirt. She noticed with approval that he was evidently a socks-on-last man. 'Nearly midnight, after all.'

'But the dream won't end,' said Kate, and put her arms round him. 'No pumpkin, no rats, no rags. Just happy-ever-after.'

And she knew, as she walked with him down the stairs, that now all the ghosts from her past, whether good or bad, had finally been vanquished.

It was astonishingly quiet. She found her sandals, still lying where she had left them, and slipped them on, leaning on Jem for support. Even the kitchen was silent: no chink of glasses, no clatter of dishes. The hall was empty, and so, beyond it, was the morning room. Kate surveyed the half-eaten food on the plates, a cigarette still gently smoking in an ashtray, and laughed. 'God, it's like the *Marie Celeste*! Have they really all gone off to the stables?'

'I hope so,' Jem said. 'Or a giant green monster has come up out of someone's subconscious and eaten them all.'

'Like in *Forbidden Planet*.' Kate shivered suddenly in her flimsy dress, and Jem put his arm round her and drew her close.

The drawing room was also empty, and Serious Money's instruments stood propped on stands around their amplifiers and microphones. 'Perhaps they might sound better unplugged,' Jem suggested mischievously.

'Or you could play something. I've never heard you play, and Tamsin told me you were great on the saxophone yesterday.'

He glanced down at her with a smile. 'Believe me, the noise I make is nothing to write home about.'

'It doesn't matter,' said Kate. She turned to face him. 'Play "Summertime" for me, one day. I won't mind all the bum notes. I just want to hear your soul in the music.'

'It's a promise,' Jem said, and kissed her.

The quickest way to the stables from here was through the courtyard door into the walled garden. Once in Bob Wiltshire's domain, there were no lights except the big one hanging in the sky, but Kate knew her way past the strawberry patch and the rows of lettuces, and found the little gate in the far corner which led into the gravelled area where all the cars had been parked. They squeezed between a Rolls Royce and a very nice Jensen, which drew a passing glance of admiration from Jem, and joined the back of the crowd around the entrance to the stables.

Charlie must have climbed onto a table, because his head was clearly visible above all the others. He spotted Jem at once, and his voice came crackling clearly above the buzz of unamplified conversation all around. 'And there he is! Both of 'em, in fact. Can you fight your way through, you two? Come on, ladies and gentlemen, *mind* your backs, make way for 'em.'

Good-naturedly, the other guests let them past. To her amusement, Kate found herself in brief but extremely close proximity to the luscious Annabelle Andrews, whose chief assets had obviously been surgically enhanced. Then she and Jem were decanted breathlessly into a small space just in front of Charlie's table. Tanya was standing beside it, grinning broadly. 'So you did get lucky, then, eh?' she hissed to Kate. 'Good on yer!'

'Come on, don't stand there gassing to me missis, get on up here!' said Charlie. He stretched out a hand. Perhaps sensibly, Jem ignored it and vaulted lightly up onto the table beside his employer. Five hundred faces, illuminated by the security lighting, gazed at him expectantly. He spotted Luke, hovering at the back of the crowd, and, right at the front next to Tanya, Jayde and Tamsin. He grinned at Kate's daughter, and made a covert thumbs-up sign. In response, her delighted smile was almost as breathtaking as her mother's.

304

'For those of you what don't know him from Adam,' Charlie was saying, 'this is the bloke I'd like to thank for all his hard work over the past few months. He designed the studios, he helped build them, and from next week he's going to be managing them an' all, so it looks like he's a permanent fixture round here – which will probably make one person I know very happy.' He caught Kate's eye and winked at her: obviously, Tanya had been filling him in on the situation. 'So, thanks, Jem, it's all been down to you, mate, and I think you deserve a round of applause! Oh, and for those of you what might need a sax player, he's willing to fill in on the old reed – for a small consideration, of course. Ladies and gentlemen, Jem Forrester!'

Amid the explosion of flashguns, he could see Kate, clapping wildly. He smiled at her, his whole body still tingling with the memory of what they had been doing an hour ago, and the expectations of what they would do later. Then Charlie handed him the microphone. 'Come on, mate, let's have a few words.'

'Christ,' said Jem, grinning. 'I don't know what to say, really.'

'Blimey, that's never bothered you before!' Tanya called, and earned a burst of laughter.

'Well, I think I'd better make one thing quite clear,' Jem said, hearing his own voice bouncing disconcertingly round the walls. 'This is undoubtedly a flagrant breach of the planning conditions, and if we wake up the village, the studios will be closed down before they've even been opened. So I'll keep it short. Thanks to Charlie, for giving me the chance to do this, and also for being the perfect employer, willing to chuck his money about, and not throwing a wobbly when the carpet supplier sent the wrong colour. And thanks to all the blokes who did the actual work – I know a lot of you are here. I've never supervised a better bunch, and for those few kind words I'll expect a jar or two down the Unicorn next week, O.K.? Thanks, everyone.'

He jumped down, amidst a renewed torrent of applause, and Kate hugged him. 'Did I ever tell you how wonderful you are?' she whispered. 'And how much I love you?'

'Several times, but don't stop, it does wonders for my ego.'

'There's someone else I'd like to thank,' Charlie was saying above them. 'I've had so many people say to me tonight how great the gardens look, and that's all down to one very lovely lady – so, Kate Williams, get up here and take a bow!'

Laughing in disbelief, Kate found herself lifted in her new lover's capable hands and deposited gently on the table beside Charlie. It wobbled, and he hastily grabbed her arm. 'All right, darlin'? This is Kate. There ain't no one what can make plants grow like she can, and she's pretty good at deciding where lights go too – as well as being a real stunner, of course. You done well there, Jem, I should hang on to her if I were you. Let's put your hands together for Kate, gardener supreme!'

Laughing, she bobbed a quick curtsey as the lights flashed again, and found the microphone thrust firmly under her nose. 'You ain't gonna get away with saying nothing,' Charlie informed her. 'Go on, darlin', let's have a few words.'

'They'd better be just a few, I'm going to fall off this table any minute.' Dazed by her unaccustomed moment of fame, Kate took a deep breath and determined not to panic. 'Thanks to Charlie, for giving me the chance to muck up his gardens.'

'You done that all right, darlin'. You should have seen the heaps of manure what went on it last winter!'

Amid laughter, Kate went on. 'No, it's been great, I've really enjoyed myself, and thank you all very much for being apprecia-tive.'

As she was lifted down again by Jem, Tanya stepped forward. 'You got a spare minute after this is over, you two? Charlie's got something to tell you.'

Before Kate could ask her anything, Charlie's voice was ringing cheerfully out again. 'Well, you've all been standing here long enough, and there's still plenty of bubbly left, so I'm not going to keep you much longer. I'd now like to ask my gorgeous wife Tanya to perform the opening ceremony. Come on, Tarn, do your stuff.'

With a coy flutter of her impossibly long lashes, Tanya came forward, Kate's gold scissors in her hand. She set them against the pink ribbon, and spoke in a high, artificially regal voice. 'My husband and I would like to declare the Stable Studios – open! And may God bless 'em and all who wail in 'em!'

Amid cheers and groans, the ribbon fell to the ground. 'Feel free to have a wander round,' Charlie called. 'That's what you're all here for, innit? Nose about and ask what you like.'

Eagerly, the guests began to stream past into the courtyard. Kate found herself grabbed by Tanya. 'Come on, quick, before we get nobbled. You too, Jem. Back in the house for a bit, won't take long.'

Mystified, Kate allowed herself to be led against the tide, through the press of people and round the side of the house. Jayde and Tamsin came puffing up behind. 'What's going on? Can we come?'

'Why not?' said Tanya cheerfully. 'The more the merrier's what I say. Come on, in here, it's all ready.'

Increasingly bewildered, Kate and Jem followed her through the empty hall and into the little sitting room beside the staircase, which had been kept locked during the party. On the table by the window, looking out over the sparkling courtyard garden, stood a magnum of vintage champagne, and four glasses.

'Charlie reckoned this was as good a time as any,' said Tanya. 'If you want a sip, Jayde sweetheart, you can have a bit of mine quick, before your dad comes.' She gave her daughter a cheerful wink, and slipped her arm round her. 'God, where's he got to, then?'

'What's it all about?' Kate asked, feeling that her curiosity was soon going to suffocate her.

Tanya laid a coy finger to the side of her nose. 'Never you mind, just wait till Charlie gets here, he shouldn't be long. Ah, that's him now.'

'Sorry I'm late, had to do a bit of hand-squeezing.' Charlie bustled into the room, beaming. 'Hallo there, Princess, might have known you'd get in on the act. Must be long past your bedtime.'

'I'm not tired, Dad,' said Jayde, and spoilt the effect by yawning widely.

'Not tired, eh? I could see your tonsils then, and Tamsin's just as bad. Still, it's not as if this sort of thing happens every day, is it?'

'Just as well,' said Jem drily. 'O.K., Charlie, what's up?'

'It don't really concern you,' said his employer, with a sly grin, 'but since you seem to have got your act together with this lovely lady, you might as well be in on it. Kate? Kate, come over here, darlin', I've got something I'd like you to see.'

'Dirty bugger,' said Tanya to Jem, with a wink. 'Can't trust him anywhere.'

'Now then, none of that, not with the kids present.' Charlie drew Kate over to the table. Beside the champagne and the glasses lay a piece of the thick creamy paper used for legal documents, with the words 'lease' and 'agreement' prominent in red ink at the top.

'Go on,' Charlie said, handing it to her. 'Have a butcher's at that.'

Even in the clear light of day, Kate's brain would have found it hard to disentangle any meaning from the tortuous legal phrases. Now, her mind still bubbling with joy and excitement and champagne, she could not concentrate at all. She stared at Charlie with a puzzled smile. 'Sorry, but my mind's gone blank. What's it about?'

'It's a lease,' said Tanya. 'That's why it's got "lease" written at the top.'

'Don't be cheeky,' said Charlie, pinching her bottom and getting a loud squeal in response. 'She's right, though, it is a lease. For that little paddock next to the Home Farm, you know it?'

'The one Dave Castle used to keep his daughter's pony in a few years ago? Yes, I know it.'

'Well, it's mine, part of the park really, and it's sitting there doing nothing, so I thought, why not let Kate have it?'

Jem was reading over her shoulder, and Tamsin was hopping about trying to see. 'I don't understand,' Kate said, still completely bewildered. 'I mean, what would I want it for?'

'Gordon Bennett, darlin', you mean you can't guess? I know what you'd have liked to put on Mermaid's Ground, given the chance, but if the council won't let houses be built on it they ain't likely to let you put greenhouses on it neither, and it seems a shame after all you done to save it. Anyway, I thought of this little plot doing nothing, and it seemed just the ticket. I've put in an application to build on the bigger field next to it, the one you suggested, and they're all cheap houses like what the village wants, so that'll keep them happy. And my accountant's always on at me, telling me to invest a bit of spare, gets out of paying tax, so I reckoned I'd do just that, and do you a favour in the process. You want it for that nursery of yours, darlin', and it's yours for as long as you like.'

Kate stared at him in complete amazement. 'My *nursery*?'

'That's what I said, darlin'. You want the chance, I'll give it to you. You can lease the field for as long as you want, and I'll be your sleeping partner—'

'Not in the biblical sense, I hope, ha ha!' Tanya said.

'Don't take no notice of her, she's been at the bubbly. How much d'you reckon it'd take to get off the ground? Hundred grand enough?'

'God,' said Kate, staring at him. 'I don't know. I don't know what to say.'

'It's a serious offer, darlin'. You think about it if you like. We'll need to do a lot of planning, whatever. If you don't want to do it, well, fair enough – it'll be hard work. And I'm not going to do anything else with it, so it don't matter if you change your mind.

But it's there for you, on a plate, if you want it.'

'Oh, Charlie!' Kate found she was crying, with happiness and terror mixed. 'You know I want it. I've wanted it for years and I never thought I'd ever get it, it was just a dream.'

'Well, just once in a while dreams come true. I'm your fairy godfather.'

'A pink tutu wouldn't suit you,' said Kate, laughing amidst her tears. 'Oh, God, Charlie, this is wonderful. Are you *sure*?'

'Course I'm sure. You're good, you are. Ain't she, eh, Jem?'

'You don't have to tell me.' His arm tightened around her. 'What are you going to do, Kate?'

'What *do* I do, when I have all my dreams come true in the space of a couple of hours? And I really don't deserve it,' she added, trying not to sniff.

'Here's a hanky, Mum,' said Tamsin, handing her a small and rather grubby square. 'Go on, *please* say yes, it'll be brilliant!'

'I won't be able to work here if I'm starting up a nursery,' Kate said.

'That don't matter, I can give Darren the job!'

'You *dare*,' said Kate. 'If you do, you won't have any garden left inside a month.'

'O.K., O.K., just kidding. But seriously, darlin', that really don't matter. It's on its way, and you ain't gonna be on the other side of the world, are you? I can keep you on as a sort of expert adviser, if you like. Anyway, there it is. Home Farm Paddock. Don't sound quite as good as Mermaid's Ground, and it ain't so big, only a couple of acres, but Dave told me it's fertile land, and it's yours. Take it, or leave it?'

'If it's what you want, go for it,' said Kate, with a smile for Jem that took his breath away. 'Yes, yes, yes, Charlie, I'll take it. And thank you so much.'

She put her arms round him and kissed him. Tanya whistled. 'Here, put him down, you don't know where he's been! Right, now that's all sorted, can we have some of that bubbly?'

As she poured it out, with much laughter, Tamsin came up to Jem, her face sharp with anxiety. 'I've got something to tell you.'

'Tell away, then.'

'Um . . . you might not be very pleased,' said Kate's daughter, with a look of considerable apprehension. 'I told a lie, you see, and I shouldn't have done.'

'Come on then, angel, spit it out,' said Charlie, overhearing. 'Can't be that bad, can it?'

Tamsin took a deep breath and glanced at her mother. Kate's

309

face was shining with happiness, and her overwhelming joy informed every movement. *It was worth it*, she thought. *To get her and Jem together*, anything *would have been worth it*.

'I told Caroline that the party had been cancelled,' she said at last.

'You *what*?' Kate stared at her in amazement. 'Is *that* why she didn't come, then?'

'Uh-huh.' Tamsin nodded. 'She thought I was you, you see, so she believed me.'

Jem began to laugh. 'God, I wouldn't have had the nerve to do that. So what did you tell her? What reason did you give?'

'Um . . .' This was the really awful part. Tamsin looked at Charlie apologetically. 'I said that you'd been rushed to hospital with a heart attack.'

There was a startled silence. Then their host threw his grizzled head back and roared with laughter. 'You never! And she swallowed it!'

'Hook, line and sinker,' said Tamsin. She added, feeling suddenly much happier, 'And she didn't care about you being ill at all. She was cross because it had been cancelled.'

'Selfish cow,' Tanya commented, covertly refilling her glass.

'Do you mind very much?' Tamsin appealed to Jem. 'I'm sorry, but I couldn't think of any other way to stop her. I didn't think Mum would enjoy the party much if Caroline was coming.'

'I don't mind at all,' Jem assured her. 'I'd love to see her face when she finds out she's been tricked by a ten-year-old.'

'And I don't mind either,' said Kate, giving her daughter a hug. 'Not that lying's a good thing, mind you, but under the circumstances I'll let you off, just this once.'

''Cos I've done you a big big favour really, haven't I?' said Tamsin slyly, and made everyone laugh.

Much, much later, when the happiness of Kate and Jem, and the future success of the nursery, had been amply toasted, they went back to the stables. Charlie and Jem were soon besieged by guests asking questions, and Kate, spying Luke drifting past, took the opportunity to tell him the good news.

'Oh, that's great, Mum,' he said eagerly. 'Really good of Charlie.'

'I know. And I just hope I'll be up to the responsibility. It's going to be a lot of very hard work, starting something like that more or less from scratch, even if I have got a generous benefactor. I still can't quite believe it's happened.' She smiled at him apologetically. 'I'm afraid I'm going to be awfully busy for a long time.'

'I don't mind,' said Luke. 'And I'll help, if you want.' He paused, blushing, and then added, 'Tamsin's told me about you and Jem. I'm really, really pleased, Mum. He's a good bloke.'

'I know. And I know I can trust him, through and through. Which is more than I could ever say about Justin.'

'Well, he got what he deserved,' Luke said. 'And you've got what you've always wanted.'

'I know. And I still can't quite believe my luck.'

'Luck had nothing to do with it,' said Jem, coming up to them. 'Charlie doesn't throw his money away on lost causes, you know. He wouldn't have made you that offer if he didn't think he'd get a return on it. If I know him, he's done his homework. Now all you have to do is make a success of it.'

'Definitely easier said than done,' Kate pointed out. 'The thought terrifies me. And yet I can't wait to get started, my mind is buzzing with ideas and plans.'

'Well, try and put them on hold for the rest of the night,' said Jem, taking her arm. 'If you'll excuse me, Luke, I just want to borrow your mama for a bit. I've got a promise to keep.'

'Go ahead,' Luke said, with a cheerful wave, and watched as Kate and Jem, hand in hand, disappeared into the studios.

A while later Tamsin, in search of her mother, walked yawning into the reception area. By now, the party guests had almost all returned to the house and the rest of the champagne, but someone was still here, because she could hear music.

It was the same tune that Jem had played on the saxophone yesterday: yearning, beautiful, full of soul. She tiptoed down the long, carpeted corridor to studio two, and sneaked inside.

The rich sound poured through the speakers, warm as honey, smooth as silk. Beyond the glass, Jem was playing his heart out, his eyes fixed on the rapt, beautiful face of her mother, who sat watching him in her wonderful indigo gown, love and joy glowing all around her like a flame.

Smiling, Tamsin crept away, and left them lost in their own enchantment.

Perfect Timing

Jill Mansell

Poppy Dunbar is out on her hen night when she meets Tom Kennedy. With his dark eyes and quirky smile, he could lure any girl off the straight and narrow, but what really draws Poppy to him is the feeling that she's known him all her life. She can't go through with the meeting they arrange – but she can't go through with her wedding either.

Suddenly notorious as 'The Girl Who Jilted Rob McBride', Poppy moves to London. Soon she's installed in the bohemian household of Caspar French, a ravishingly good-looking young artist with a reputation for breaking hearts. But even in her colourful new home, Poppy can't get Tom off her mind. Until she's tracked him down, she'll never know if their meeting was destiny – or if the future holds something entirely different for her . . .

Praise for Jill Mansell:

'Fabulous fun . . . to read it is to devour it' *Company*

'A riotous romp' *Prime*

'A jaunty summer read' *Daily Mail*

'Sexy and mischievous' *Today*

'Frothy fun' *Bella*

0 7472 5444 3

HEADLINE

The Real Thing

Catherine Alliott

Everyone's got one – an old boyfriend they never fell out of love with, they simply parted because the time wasn't right. And for thirty-year-old Tessa, it's Patrick Cameron, the gorgeous, moody, rebellious boy she met at seventeen; the boy her vicar father thoroughly disapproved of; the boy who left her to go to Italy to paint.

And now he's back.

'You're in for a treat' *Express*

'Alliot's joie de vivre is irresistible' *Daily Mail*

'Compulsive and wildly romantic' *Bookseller*

'An addictive cocktail of wit, frivolity and madcap romance . . . move over Jilly, your heir is apparent' *Time Out*

0 7472 5235 1

HEADLINE